MADELIN...

Ravishing in Red

"Richly spiced with wicked wit and masterfully threaded with danger and desire, the superbly sexy first book in Hunter's Regency historical quartet is irresistible and wonderfully entertaining." —*Booklist* (starred review)

Provocative in Pearls

"Hunter gifts readers with a fantastic story that reaches into the heart of relationships and allows her to deliver a deep-sigh read." —*Romantic Times* (Top Pick)

Sinful in Satin WITHDRAWN

"Hunter deftly sifts intrigue and exquisite sensuality into the plot of the third book in her exceptionally entertaining quartet." —*Booklist*

Dangerous in Diamonds

"Hunter . . . masterfully weaves a sensual web . . . Fans will be delighted." —*Publishers Weekly*

The Surrender
of Miss Fairbourne

MADELINE HUNTER

JOVE BOOKS, NEW YORK

THE BERKLEY PUBLISHING GROUP
Published by the Penguin Group
Penguin Group (USA) Inc.
375 Hudson Street, New York, New York 10014, USA
Penguin Group (Canada), 90 Eglinton Avenue East, Suite 700, Toronto, Ontario M4P 2Y3, Canada
(a division of Pearson Penguin Canada Inc.)
Penguin Books Ltd., 80 Strand, London WC2R 0RL, England
Penguin Group Ireland, 25 St. Stephen's Green, Dublin 2, Ireland (a division of Penguin Books Ltd.)
Penguin Group (Australia), 250 Camberwell Road, Camberwell, Victoria 3124, Australia
(a division of Pearson Australia Group Pty. Ltd.)
Penguin Books India Pvt. Ltd., 11 Community Centre, Panchsheel Park, New Delhi—110 017, India
Penguin Group (NZ), 67 Apollo Drive, Rosedale, Auckland 0632, New Zealand
(a division of Pearson New Zealand Ltd.)
Penguin Books (South Africa) (Pty.) Ltd., 24 Sturdee Avenue, Rosebank, Johannesburg 2196,
South Africa

Penguin Books Ltd., Registered Offices: 80 Strand, London WC2R 0RL, England

THE SURRENDER OF MISS FAIRBOURNE

A Jove Book / published by arrangement with the author

PRINTING HISTORY
Jove mass-market edition / March 2012

ISBN: 978-0-515-15046-9

JOVE®
Jove Books are published by The Berkley Publishing Group,
a division of Penguin Group (USA) Inc.,
375 Hudson Street, New York, New York 10014.
JOVE® is a registered trademark of Penguin Group (USA) Inc.
The "J" design is a trademark of Penguin Group (USA) Inc.

PRINTED IN THE UNITED STATES OF AMERICA

10 9 8 7 6 5 4 3 2 1

This book is dedicated to the memory of my brother,
Nicholas Cirillo

Chapter 1

The final sale at Fairbourne's auction house proved to be a sad affair, and not only because the proprietor had recently fallen to his death while strolling along a cliff walk in Kent. It was also, from the viewpoint of collectors, comprised of very minor works, and hardly worthy of the reputation for selectivity that Maurice Fairbourne had built for his establishment.

Society came anyway, some of them out of sympathy and respect, some to distract themselves from the relentless worry about the expected French invasion for which the whole country had braced. A few flew in like crows, attracted to the carcass of what had once been a great business, hoping to peck a few morsels from the body now that Maurice did not stand guard.

The latter could be seen peering very closely at the paintings and prints, looking for the gem that had escaped the less experienced eyes of the staff. A bargain could be had if a work of art were incorrectly described to the seller's detriment. The victory would be all the more sweet because such oversights normally went the other way, with amazing consistency.

Darius Alfreton, Earl of Southwaite, peered closely too. Although a collector, he was not hoping to steal a Caravaggio that had been incorrectly called a Honthorst in the catalogue. Rather, he examined the art and the descriptions to see just how badly Fairbourne's reputation might be compromised by the staff's ineptitude.

He scanned the crowd that had gathered too, and watched the rostrum being prepared. A small raised platform holding a tall, narrow podium, it always reminded Darius of a preacher's pulpit. Auction houses like Fairbourne's often held a preview night to lure the bidders with a grand party, then conducted the actual sale a day or so later. The staff of Fairbourne's had decided to do it all at once today, and soon the auctioneer would take his place on the rostrum to call the auction of each lot, and literally knock down his hammer when the bidding stopped.

Considering the paltry offerings, and the cost of a grand preview, Darius concluded that it had been wise to skip the party. Less explicable had been the staff's failure to tell him of their plans. He learned about this auction only through the announcement in the newspapers.

The hub of the crowd was not near the paintings hung one above another on the high, gray walls. The bodies shifted and the true center of their attention became visible. Miss Emma Fairbourne, Maurice's daughter, stood near the left wall, greeting the patrons and accepting their condolences.

The black of her garments contrasted starkly with her very fair skin, and a black, simple hat sat cockily on her brown hair. Her most notable feature, blue eyes that could gaze with disconcerting directness, focused on each visitor so completely that one would think no other patron stood nearby.

"A bit odd that she is here," Yates Elliston, Viscount Ambury, said. He stood at Darius's side, impatient with the time they were spending here. They were both dressed for riding and were supposed to be on their way to the coast.

"She is the only Fairbourne left," Darius said. "She probably hopes to reassure the patrons with her presence. No one will be fooled, however. The size and quality of this auction is symbolic of what happens when the eyes and personality that define such an establishment are lost."

"You have met her, I expect, since you knew her father well. Not much of a future waiting for her, is there? She looks to be in her middle twenties already. Marriage is not likely to happen now if it didn't happen when her father lived and this business flourished."

"Yes, I have met her." The first time had been about a year ago. Odd that he had known Maurice Fairbourne for years, and in all that time he had never been introduced to the daughter. Maurice's son, Robert, might join them in their conversations, but never Robert's sister.

He and Emma Fairbourne had not spoken again since that introduction, until very recently. His memory of her had been of an ordinary-looking woman, a bit timid and retiring, a small shadow within the broad illumination cast by her expansive, flamboyant father.

"Then again . . ." Ambury gazed in Miss Fairbourne's direction with lowered eyelids. "Not a great beauty, but there is something about her . . . Hard to say what it is . . ."

Yes, there was something about her. Darius was impressed that Ambury had spotted it so quickly. But then, Ambury had a special sympathy with women, while Darius mostly found them necessary and often pleasurable, but ultimately bewildering.

"I recognize her," Ambury said while he turned to look at a landscape hanging above their heads on the wall. "I have seen her about town, in the company of Barrowmore's sister, Lady Cassandra. Perhaps Miss Fairbourne is unmarried because she prefers independence, like her friend."

With Lady Cassandra? How interesting. Darius considered that there might be much more to Emma Fairbourne than he had assumed.

He did not miss how she now managed to avoid having that penetrating gaze of hers connect with his. Unless he greeted her directly, she would pretend he was not here. She surely would not acknowledge that he had as much interest in the results of this auction as she did.

Ambury perused the sheets of the sale catalogue that he had obtained from the exhibition hall manager. "I do not claim to know about art the way that you do, Southwaite, but there is a lot of 'school of' and 'studio of' among these paintings. It reminds me of the art offered by those picture sellers in Italy during my grand tour."

"The staff does not have Maurice's expertise, and to their credit have been conservative in their attributions when the provenance that documents the history of ownership and supports the authenticity is not clean." Darius pointed to the landscape above Ambury's head. "If he were still alive, that might have been sold as van Ruisdael, not as follower of van Ruisdael, and the world would have accepted his judgment. Penthurst was examining it most closely a while ago, and will possibly bid high in the hopes the ambiguity goes in van Ruisdael's favor."

"If it was Penthurst, I hope it was daubed by a forger a fortnight ago and he wastes a bundle." Ambury returned his attention to Miss Fairbourne. "Not a bad memorial service, if you think about it. There are society luminaries here who probably did not attend the funeral."

Darius *had* attended the funeral held a month ago. He had been the only peer there, despite Maurice Fairbourne's role as advisor to many of them on their collections. Society did not attend the funeral of a tradesman, least of all at the start of the Season, so Ambury was correct. For the patrons of Fairbourne's, this would serve as the memorial service, such as it was.

"I assume everyone will bid high," Ambury said. Both his tone and small smile reflected his amiable manner, one that sometimes got him into trouble. "To help her out now that she is alone in the world."

"Sympathy will play its role in encouraging high bids, but the real reason is standing next to the rostrum right now."

"You mean that small white-haired fellow? He hardly looks to be the type to get me so excited I'd bid fifty when I had planned to pay twenty-five."

"He is astoundingly unimpressive, isn't he? Also unassuming, mild-mannered, and unfailingly polite," Darius said. "Unaccountably it all works to his advantage. Once Maurice Fairboune realized what he had in that little man, he never called an auction in this house again, but left it to Obediah Riggles."

"And here I thought that fellow over there was the auctioneer. The one who gave me this paper listing the things for sale."

Ambury referred to the young, handsome man now easing the guests toward the chairs.

"That is Mr. Nightingale. He manages the exhibition hall here. He greets visitors, seats them, ensures they are comfortable, and answers questions regarding the lots. You will see him stand near each work as it is auctioned as well, like a human signpost."

Dark, tall, and exceedingly meticulous in his elegant dress, Mr. Nightingale slithered more than walked as he moved around the chamber, ushering and encouraging, charming and flirting. All the while he filled the chairs and ensured the women had broad fans with which to signal a bid.

"He seems to do whatever he does quite well," Ambury observed.

"Yes."

"The ladies appear to like him. I expect a bit of flattery goes far in helping the bids flow."

"I expect so."

Ambury watched Nightingale for a minute longer. "Some gentlemen seem to favor him too."

"You *would* mention that."

Ambury laughed. "I expect it causes some awkwardness for him. He is supposed to keep them coming back, isn't he? How does one both encourage and discourage at the same time?"

Darius could not swear that the exhibition manager did discourage. Nightingale was nothing if not ambitious. "I will leave it to you to employ your renowned powers of observation and let me know how he manages it. It will give you something to do, and perhaps you will stop complaining that I dragged you here today."

"It was not the where of it, but the how. You deceived me. When you said an auction, I just assumed it was a horse auction, and you knew I would. It is more fun to watch you spend a small fortune on a stallion than on a painting."

Slowly the crowd found seats and the sounds dimmed. Riggles stepped up on a stool so he showed tall behind the rostrum's podium. Mr. Nightingale moved to where the first lot hung on the wall. His perfect features probably garnered more attention from some of the patrons than the obscure oil painting that he pointed to.

Emma Fairbourne remained discreetly away from the action but very visible to everyone. *Bid high and bid often,* her mere presence seemed to plead. *For his memory and my future, make it a better total than it has any right to be.*

Emma kept her gaze on Obediah, but she felt people looking at her. In particular she felt one person looking at her.

Southwaite was here. It had been too much to hope that he might be out of town. She had prayed for it, however. He went down to his property in Kent often, her friend Cassandra had reported. It would have been ideal had he done so this week.

He stood behind all the chairs, dressed for riding, as if he had been heading down to the country after all, but had seen the newspaper and diverted his path here. He towered back there and could not be missed. Out of the corner of her eye she saw him watching her. His harshly handsome face held a vague scowl at the doings here. His companion appeared much more friendly, with remarkable blue eyes that held a light of merriment in contrast with the earl's dark intensity.

He thought he should have been told, she guessed. He thought it was his business to know what Fairbourne's was doing. He was going to want to become a nuisance, it appeared. Well, she would be damned before she allowed that.

Obediah began the sale of the first lot. The bidding was not enthusiastic, but that did not worry her. Auctions always opened slowly, and she had given considerable thought to which consignment should be sacrificed like this, to give the patrons time to settle in and warm up.

Obediah called the bids in his smooth, quiet fashion. He smiled kindly at the older women who raised their fans, and added a "Quite good, sir" when a young lord pushed the bid up two increments. The impression was that of a tasteful conversation, not a raucous competition.

There were no histrionics at Fairbourne's auctions. No cajoling for more bids, and no sly implications of hidden values. Obediah was the least dramatic auctioneer in England, but the lots went for more than they should when he brought down his hammer. Bidders trusted him and forgot their natural caution. Emma's father had once remarked that Obediah reminded men of their first valet, and women of their dear uncle Bertie.

She did not leave her spot near the wall, not even when Mr. Nightingale directed the crowd's attention to the paintings and objets d'art near her. Some of the people in the room would remember that her father stood here during the sales. Right in this spot where she now was.

As the final lots approached, Mr. Nightingale retreated from his position to stand beside her. She thought that odd, but he had been most solicitous today in every way. One might think his own father had taken that fatal fall, from the way he accepted the condolences of the patrons during the preview, almost losing his composure several times.

As soon as the hammer came down on the last lot, Emma exhaled a sigh of relief. It had gone much better than she had dared hope. She had succeeded in buying some time.

Noise filled the high-ceilinged chamber as conversation broke out and chairs scraped the wooden floor. From his place beside her, Mr. Nightingale spoke farewells to the society matrons who favored him with flirtatious smiles and to a few gentlemen who condescended to show him familiarity.

"Miss Fairbourne," he said while he bestowed his charming smile on the people passing by. "If the day has not tired you too much, I would like a few words with you in private after they have all gone."

Her heart sank. He was going to leave his situation. Mr. Nightingale was an ambitious young man and he would see no future here now. He no doubt assumed they would just close the doors after today. Even if they did not, he would not want to remain at the auction house without the connections her father had provided him.

Her gaze shifted to the rostrum, where Obediah was stepping down. It would be a blow to lose Mr. Nightingale. If Obediah Riggles left, however, Fairbourne's would definitely cease to exist.

"Of course, Mr. Nightingale. Why don't we go to the storage now, if that will suffice."

She walked in that direction with Mr. Nightingale beside her. She paused to praise Obediah, who blushed in his self-effacing way.

"Perhaps you will be good enough to meet me here tomorrow, Obediah? I would like your advice on some matters of great importance," she added.

Obediah's face fell. He assumed she wanted advice on how to close Fairbourne's, she guessed. "Of course, Miss Fairbourne. Would eleven o'clock be a good time?"

"A perfect time. I will see you then." As she spoke she noticed that two men had not yet left the exhibition hall. Southwaite and his companion still stood back there, watching the staff remove the paintings from the walls in order to deliver them to the winning bidders.

Southwaite caught her eye. His expression commanded her to remain where she was. He began walking toward her. She pretended she had not noticed. She urged Mr. Nightingale forward, so she could escape to the storage chamber.

Chapter 2

"With your father's tragic passing, things are much changed, I think you will agree," Mr. Nightingale said. He stood before her in his impeccable frock coat and cravat. He always looked like this. Tall, slender, dark, and perfect. Emma imagined the hours it must take him each day to put himself together with such precision.

She had never liked him much. Mr. Nightingale was one of the many people who showed a false face to the world. Everything about him was calculated, and too smooth, too polished, and too practiced. While imitating his betters, he had assumed their worst characteristics.

They were in the large back chamber where items consigned for auction were stored for cataloguing and study. It held bins for paintings at one end, and shelves and large tables for other objects. There was also a desk where she now sat. Mr. Nightingale had positioned himself to her side, so she did not have the distance of the desktop between them, the way she would prefer.

Emma of course agreed with his assessment that things were much changed. It was one of those statements that was so true as to need no articulation. She disliked when people spoke this way, explaining the obvious to her. Men in particular had this habit, she had noticed.

She merely nodded and waited for the rest. She wished he would hurry up with it too. These preliminaries were all beside the main point, which was that he was leaving, and some plain speaking would be welcomed.

Worse, she was having difficulty even paying attention to him. Her mind was back in the exhibition hall, wondering what Southwaite was doing and whether he would still be there when she exited this room.

"You are alone now. Unprotected. Fairbourne's has lost its master, and while our patrons were kind today, they will quickly lose confidence in the sales if you think to continue them."

That got her attention. Mr. Nightingale had always struck her as a walking fashion plate. All surface and artifice. Not at all deep.

Now he had revealed unexpected capacities for insight, if he had surmised that she considered continuing the auctions at Fairbourne's.

"I am well-known to the patrons," he forged on. "Respected by them. My eye for art has been demonstrated time and again during the previews."

"It is not an eye such as my father possessed, however." Nor that she possessed, she wanted to add.

"No doubt. But it is good enough."

Good enough was not, in this situation, truly good enough, unfortunately.

"I have always admired you, Miss Fairbourne." He flashed that charming smile. He had never used it on her before. She did not find it nearly as winning when directed her way as she did when he cajoled a society matron to consider a painting that had been overlooked.

He was a very handsome man, however. Almost unnaturally so. He knew it, of course. A man could not look like this and not know just how perfect his face appeared. Too perfect, as if a portrait painter had taken a normally handsome face and prettied it up too much, to the point it lost human distinction and character.

"We have much in common," he went on. "Fairbourne's. Your father. Our births and stations are not dissimilar. I believe we would make a good match. I hope that you will look favorably on my proposal that we marry."

She just stared at him. This was not what she had expected. She found herself at a loss for how to respond.

He took a deep breath, as if fortifying himself for an unpleasant task. "You are surprised, I see. Did you think I had not noticed your beauty these last years? Perhaps I have been too subtle in communicating my interest. Credit that to my respect for both you and your father. You have quite stolen my heart, however, and I have dreamed for many months that one day you might be mine. I have always believed that you and I had a special sympathy, and under the circumstances I now am free to—"

"Mr. Nightingale, please, let us discuss this honestly if we are to discuss it at all. First, we both know that I am not beautiful. Second, you and I have held no secret sympathy. Indeed, we have rarely had informal conversation. Third, you have not been too subtle in communicating your feelings because you have entertained no such feelings to begin with. You almost choked on your words of love just now. You began making a practical proposal, and perhaps you should continue on that tack and not try to convince me of your long-secret love."

She put him off his game for a moment, no more. "You have always been a most direct female, Miss Fairbourne," he said tightly. "It is one of your more . . . *notable* qualities. If honest and practical suit you better, so be it. Your father left you a business here. It can continue, but only if it is known to be owned and managed by a man. No one will patronize Fairbourne's if a woman is the responsible authority. I propose that we marry, and that I take your father's place. You will still have the comfortable life that Fairbourne's has provided, along with continued security and protection."

She pretended to think it over, so as not to insult him too much. "How thoughtful of you to try to help me, Mr. Nightingale. Unfortunately, I do not think we will be a good match at all."

She attempted to stand. He refused to move. Mr. Nightingale no longer appeared charming as he gazed down at her. Not at all.

"Your decision is reckless, and not sensible. What is the good in inheriting Fairbourne's if you do not continue its affairs? Today's take will hardly keep you long. As for another match, one that you may consider better, I doubt such an offer will come now if it has not already."

"Perhaps one has indeed come already."

"As you demanded, let us be honest and practical. You are, by your own admission, not a great beauty. You have a manner that is hardly conducive to a man's romantic interests, what with all your plain speaking. You are headstrong and at times shrewish. In short, you are on the shelf for a reason; several, in fact. I am willing to overlook all of that. I have no great fortune but I have skills that can keep Fairbourne's a going concern. Fate throws us together, for better or for worse, Miss Fairbourne, even if love does not."

She felt her face warming. She might admit to headstrong, but, really, shrewish was going too far.

"I can hardly argue with your remarkably complete description of my lack of appeal, sir. I daresay I should be grateful that you would be willing to take me on at all. I fear, however, that your calculations are in error on one major point, and that your willingness to sacrifice yourself will be much compromised once I explain it, since it is the only point that you see in my favor. You assume that I am my father's heir. In fact I am not. My brother is, of course. If you marry me, you will not get Fairbourne's as you think. At least not for long."

He had the audacity to groan in exasperation. "A dead man cannot inherit."

"He is not dead."

"Zeus, your father harbored unrealistic hopes, but it is

inconceivable that you do as well. He drowned when his ship went down. He is most certainly dead."

"His body was never found."

"That is because the damned ship went down in the middle of the damned sea." He collected himself and lowered his voice. "I have consulted with a solicitor. In such cases there is no need to wait any length of time to have a person declared dead. You need only go to the courts and—"

This conceited man had dared to investigate how she could claim the fortune he wanted to marry. He expected her to deny her own heart's certainty that Robert still lived, in order to accommodate his avarice. "No. I will not do it. If Fairbourne's is preserved at all, it is preserved for Robert when he returns."

He drew himself up tall and straight. "Then you will starve," he intoned. "Because if I do not leave here with your acceptance of my offer, I will not return to preserve this business for you, let alone for him."

He glared at her, convinced she would not pick up that gauntlet. She glared back, while she quickly calculated how much trouble his removal would create. Potentially a good deal of trouble, she had to admit.

"Obediah will calculate what you are owed. Once today's payments are made, your wages will be sent to you. Good day, Mr. Nightingale."

Mr. Nightingale turned on his heel and marched out of the chamber. Emma rested her head in her hands. One door to her future plans had opened with the success of today's auction, but another had just closed with the loss of the exhibition hall manager.

Weariness wanted to overwhelm her. So did humiliation at the bold description Mr. Nightingale gave of her faults. He had spoken as if he had even worse ones on the list, and thought limiting it to these had been an example of discretion.

You are on the shelf for a reason. That was certainly true. Mostly she was on the shelf because all of the proposals had, to one degree or another, been similar to today's. Men might as well just say, "Marriage to you does not interest me at all, but inheriting Fairbourne's will make the match easier to swallow."

She was not even supposed to mind. She probably shouldn't. Yet she did.

A tap on the door requested attention. The door opened a crack, and Obediah's head stuck in. "A visitor, Miss Fairbourne."

Before she could ask whom the visitor might be, the door swung wide. The Earl of Southwaite strode in with an invisible storm cloud hovering over his dark head.

Exit one handsome, conceited man, and enter another. Southwaite had to know that she did not want to see him. It had been a tiring and trying day, and she was in no mood to match wits with him now.

She suppressed the impulse to groan in his face. She rose and made a small curtsy. She forced a smile. She urged her voice to sound melodic instead of dull.

"Good day, Lord Southwaite. We are honored that you chose to call at Fairbourne's today."

Emma Fairbourne did not appear the least embarrassed to be greeting him, finally. She sat behind the big desk in the storage chamber and smiled brightly. She acted as if he had just tied his horse outside a few minutes ago.

"Honored, are you? I am not accustomed to being cut by someone who is honored, Miss Fairbourne."

"Do you think I cut you, sir? I apologize. If you attended the auction, I did not see you. The good wishes and condolences of the patrons absorbed my time and attention." She angled herself closer to the desk. "Yet, isn't a cut a social matter? If I had neglected to acknowledge your presence, I do not see how it could be a cut when we have no social connection."

He held up one hand, to stop her. "Whether you saw me or not does not matter. You certainly see me now."

"Most definitely, since I am not blind."

"And when last we met, I specifically informed you that I would study the future of Fairbourne's, and meet with you within the month to explain my plans for its disposition."

"I believe you may have said something to that effect. I cannot swear by it. I was a little overcome at the time."

"That was understandable." She had been most overcome. She had appeared ready to kill him, she was so irate. Her emotional state was why he had put off the reckoning. That had clearly been a mistake.

"I doubt you do understand, sir, but pray, go on. I believe you were working your way up to a lecture. Or a scold. It is hard to know which just yet."

Damnation, but she was an irritating woman. She sat there, suspiciously composed. From the way Nightingale had stormed out of this chamber, one gathered she had already enjoyed one good row with a man today and now was spoiling for another.

"Neither a lecture nor a scold will be forthcoming. I seek only to clarify that which perhaps you did not hear that day in the solicitor's chambers."

"I heard the important parts. It was a shock to learn that my father had sold you a half interest in Fairbourne's three years ago, I will admit. I have accepted it, however, so no clarification is required."

He paced back and forth in front of that desk, trying to size up where she truly was in her emotions and thoughts. A stack of paintings against a wall interfered with his path in one direction, and a table of silver plate did so in the other, so it became a short and unsatisfactory circuit. The black of her costume kept pressing itself on his sight. She was still in mourning, of course. That checked his simmering anger more than anything else.

Well, not entirely more than anything else. Ambury had been correct that, while Emma Fairbourne was no great beauty, she had a certain something to her. It had been evident in the solicitor's chambers, and now was notable here too. Her directness had a lot to do with it, he supposed. The way she eschewed all artifice created a peculiar . . . intimacy.

"You did not inform me of today's auction," he said. "I do not think that was an oversight. Yet that day I told you that I expected to be informed about any activities here."

"My apologies. When we decided not to send out invitations, due to having no grand preview, I did not think to make special arrangements for you, as one of our most illustrious patrons."

"I am not merely one of the patrons. I am one of the *owners*."

"I assumed you would not want that well-known. It so smells of trade, when you get down to it. To have made an exception and brought attention to you in that way among the staff—well, I thought you would prefer I not do that."

He had to admit that made a certain amount of sense. Damnation, but she was a fast thinker.

"In the future, please do not worry about such extreme discretion, Miss Fairbourne. Of course, there will be no cause for it, now that the final auction has been held, albeit without my permission."

She blinked twice at the word *permission*, but she did not otherwise react.

"It went well, it appeared," he said, stopping his pacing and trying to sound less severe. "It should provide enough for you to live until the business is sold, I expect. The staff did a commendable job with the catalogue. I found no obvious errors in attribution. Mr. Nightingale's contribution, I assume?"

Her expression perceptibly altered. Softened. Saddened. Her voice did as well. "Obediah's contribution, not so much Mr. Nightingale's. Obediah often helped my father with the catalogue and much, much more, and has an excellent eye. Although, to be honest, most of the catalogue had been completed before Papa's death. This auction was just sitting here, almost all prepared and ready to go."

She looked up at him directly. So directly that her gaze seemed to touch his mind. For a moment that lasted longer than time would count, his thoughts scattered under that gaze.

He found himself noticing things in detail that his perceptions had absorbed in only a fleeting way before. How the light from the window made her skin appear like matte porcelain, and how very flawless that skin actually was. How there were layers to the color of her eyes, so many that one felt as if eventually one could see right into her soul. How that black dress, so simple in design, managed with its high waist and broad ribbon under her breasts to suggest a form that was womanly in the best ways and—

"I thought it made no sense to hand all those consignments back when it was only a matter of opening the doors and letting Obediah do what he does so well," she said.

"Of course," he heard himself muttering. "That is understandable."

"I am so relieved to hear you say that, Lord Southwaite. You appeared angry when you walked in here. I was afraid that you were most displeased by something."

"No, not so much. Not angry at all. Not really."

"Oh, that is so good to know."

He exerted some effort to piece together his normal self. As his thoughts collected, he took his leave of Miss Fairbourne. "I am going out of town," he said. "When I return, I will call on you to discuss . . . that other matter." He had some difficulty remembering still just what that other matter had been.

"Certainly, sir."

He returned to the exhibition hall. Ambury fell into step beside him.

"Are we finally ready to ride?" Ambury asked. "We will be at least an hour late meeting up with Kendale, and you know how he can be."

"Yes, let us go." Hell, yes.

"Did you come to a right understanding with the lady, the way you said you must?"

Darius vaguely remembered blustering something of the sort before he barged into that storage chamber. His mind, all his own again, sorted through what had actually happened after that.

"Of course I did, Ambury. If one is firm, right understandings can always be achieved, especially with women."

While he mounted his horse, however, Darius admitted the truth of it to himself. Somehow Miss Fairbourne had turned the tables on him in there. He had roared in like a lion and bleated out like a lamb.

He hated to say it, but that woman may have made a fool of him today.

Chapter 3

"We will not be lying, Obediah. We will merely allow people to assume that which they will be inclined to assume anyway. It isn't as if I can do it without you. You have an auctioneer's license, and the authorities will never give one to me."

Obediah appeared substantial and competent only when on the rostrum. Once that hammer left his hand he became a pale, small man possessing an unassuming manner and large eyes that made him look perpetually astonished. Right now those eyes also communicated discomfort about the small deception that Emma had just explained to him.

The silence stretched. While Obediah accommodated his shock at her unusual request, Emma lifted a small, framed oil painting from where it rested against the wall of the storage chamber.

"The owner claims this is a study by Angelica Kauffman," she mused, tipping the painting to get better light on its surface. "I am inclined to accept that, as was my father. It is good enough, and in her style. Do you agree with the attribution to her?"

"I've not the eye to agree or not, Miss Fairbourne. That is why your idea will not work. I could not tell the difference between a Titian and a Rembrandt if you held a pistol to my temple, let alone recognize a painting by that woman."

"But I can. As for these paintings already in storage, Papa documented them, so they are all secure."

Alarm now. Utter bewilderment. "Do you intend to put these in a new auction? I assumed you had only pulled out the better paintings so that the weaker ones would not bring down their value. I was preparing to return them to their owners."

"I pulled them because I intend to build a magnificent auction around them. If we must close, I want to do so brilliantly, not with third-rate works such as yesterday's sale contained."

Trailed by Obediah, Emma walked out to the exhibition hall. The walls were empty now. Those paintings were on their ways to their new owners.

"This will be most odd. Everyone thought yesterday was the final auction. Now there is to be another final auction," Obediah muttered.

"It will not be another. It will really be the second half of yesterday's, since so many works that it will include came in around the same time as those sold yesterday."

"So this will be the final part of the final auction?" Obediah was not a complicated man, and he puzzled hard over the knot of not-quite-final finalities.

Actually, if she could pull this off, there might be no final auction at all, for years to come. She had resolved that Fairbourne's would survive for her brother, and also for her father's memory. Considering Obediah's confusion, she decided not to burden him with those details now.

"Miss Fairbourne, I know how to call an auction, whether it be for paintings or pigs, but that is all. Your father brought in the consignments, and authenticated them. He also managed the finances and records. I cannot take his place in those things the way you request."

"I can, Obediah. I aided my father more than you know.

I learned at his side. I apprenticed as surely as Robert did."
She experienced a small panic, because Obediah was
sounding stubborn for the first time in her memory. "I can
see this through, but only if you let people think that you
lead the house now. A small ruse is all I propose, because
no one will trust a woman's management." She heard her
voice assume a pleading note. "I am sure that my father
would have wanted Fairbourne's to continue at least awhile
longer."

She gestured to the ceiling and walls, and to all that her
father had built. It would be horrible to have it end in a blink.
The very thought made her heart sick. She dreaded the idea
of her brother, Robert, returning home, only to find the most
important part of his legacy gone. She also could not bear
the thought of losing the business that had been Papa's great
achievement.

With the purchase of this property three years ago, her
father had announced that Fairbourne's had arrived. The
location right off Piccadilly Street made it easy for society
to attend the grand previews and sales, and the great exhibition hall displayed dignified grandeur in its proportions,
decoration, and tall, big, north-facing windows. The move
here had led to better consignments, higher bids, and notable
prestige.

She remembered the excitement she and her brother had
shared while they watched the building have a second floor
removed so the ceiling soared so high. Robert would bring
her over in the carriage almost every evening, to see what
progress had occurred. On those rides he regaled her with
his dreams for Fairbourne's. Papa sometimes still held minor
auctions, such as she had presented yesterday, or those of
libraries or inexpensive objects. Robert's plans aimed
higher, and he saw Fairbourne's competing with Christie's
in all ways and all things.

They soon were well on their way to that status. That first
year here, prior to Robert's disappearance, had been the best
year in her memory, full of optimism, good news, and a
stream of impressive consignments.

Her mind's eye saw her father and brother within the great room as clearly as if they had materialized. She realized suddenly that this must have been why her father sold Southwaite that partnership. This was how he had used that money. She had not seen the connection before.

She had been angry with Papa since she learned about that partnership from the solicitor. Now, with the memories of that glorious year filling her heart with sweet, aching emotion, she understood better.

She faced Obediah. "What say you, old friend? Either we go forward together, or Fairbourne's dies with yesterday's whimper."

Obediah's moist eyes suggested he had been dwelling in the past just as she had. "Seems we could try, at least, if you are determined," he said. "Your father paid for my license, didn't he? Seems right that I should call the final part of the final sale." He smiled softly. "I'll do my best to appear a man who knows more than I do, but I'm sure to be found out if anyone wants to unmask me."

"No one will try to do that, Obediah. Why would they bother?"

He did not appear convinced, but he did not argue. "I suppose I should unpack that silver that you put aside, so it can be listed." He walked away, back to the storage chamber.

Emma prepared to return home. She was relieved that Obediah would stay on, and that he would accept the new role she had devised for him. Nor should anyone question his abilities. He had called the auctions, after all. No one really knew how Fairbourne's operated, and who possessed what expertise in which area, when you got down to it.

Well, one person might know, she admitted ruefully. Southwaite might be aware of who knew what among the staff. He also possessed sufficient expertise of his own to spot a charlatan posing as a connoisseur.

She would have to prevent his visiting Fairbourne's again, if she could. With any luck he would remain too busy with whatever he did in Kent to much bother with them.

* * *

"He proposed," Emma said that afternoon, concluding her description of her unpleasant meeting with Mr. Nightingale after the auction.

Cassandra's blue eyes grew wide. The very dark lashes that rimmed those eyes gave additional drama to her surprise. So did the small parting of her full red lips.

Emma had seen the effect Cassandra's expressions of astonishment had on men. She wondered if they responded because it made her appear like an innocent, bewildered girl, when in fact she had not been anything of the sort for some years now.

"Did he profess love?" Cassandra angled closer, very interested in the story now.

"He tried. Imagine a voice droning like a fly's buzz, speaking the predictable words with the enthusiasm reserved for memorized school lessons. I stopped him and insisted we not pretend more sentiment than either of us has ever felt."

Emma lifted one of the necklaces laid out on velvet cloths on her dining room table and inspected it while she finished her tale. "All that was left after that was the most dreary and practical of offers. He finally threatened to leave his situation at Fairbourne's if I did not marry him."

Sympathy softened Cassandra's gaze. "Mr. Nightingale is very handsome. He cuts a good figure, and has an ease of manner with society. He probably thought his proposal would be welcomed."

"Welcomed? You underestimate his conceit. He assumed that I would *swoon* at such a catch, and count myself a lucky spinster, although I never gave him cause to think I favored him at all."

"You speak as if none of this mattered, yet your color is rising," Cassandra said. "I think his proposal annoyed you for reasons beyond his presumptions."

Emma rolled the tiny links of the delicate chain between her fingers. "He also assumed that I would claim my father's estate," she admitted. "He thought that he proposed to a wealthy heiress. When I disabused him of that notion, he tried to convince me of my brother's death, and spoke cruelly and harshly on the matter."

Cassandra's lips pursed the way mouths do when their owners are swallowing words. Since Cassandra did not have a small, bowed mouth, the effect could not be missed.

"Is there something you want to say? Do not hold back on my account," Emma said.

"I have nothing to say. Although, if I did, it might be a little scold that it is not fair to hold it against a man if he thinks someone who was on a sinking ship did not survive. There is an undeniable logic to that point of view."

"I explained to him—and to you, many times—that in this case the person in question did survive."

"Calm yourself, Emma. Pray, continue with the denouement of this proposal."

"It ended with merciful speed after that. He left with no employment and no wealthy fiancée, and I was left with no future husband and no exhibition room manager. I will sorely feel the latter loss."

Cassandra did not appear nearly sympathetic enough. "Emma, could you not have arranged to have him remain, at least until after the next auction? Could you not have put off your decision on his offer, for example?"

"Could I not have left him dangling, you mean."

"Could you not have left him *hopeful*, while you assessed your emotions, I mean."

"I knew my emotions already. It would be dishonest to allow him to think there might be a marriage."

"I suspect Mr. Nightingale would have settled for less. Even the possibility of winning your affection, if not your hand, might have induced him to stay."

"I hope that you are not suggesting that I should have flirted with him."

Cassandra laughed. "You say that like it is a crime. I know that you believe plain speaking is best, but a little flirting is harmless. You should try it sometime. Really, you should. It would do you good. Actually, Mr. Nightingale is reputed to flatter in the best ways at the right times, and some of his flattery might have done you good too."

Emma had not yet mastered how to decipher some of Cassandra's subtle meanings and entendres, and she interpreted them wrong at times. "You are not speaking of his verbal flatteries, are you?"

"As long as his lovers are left believing in his admiration, I doubt they care how it is communicated."

Emma felt her face warming. Cassandra now referred to things Emma knew little about. She was of an age when she found her own lack of experience annoying sometimes.

"I have no interest in that man's flatteries, of any kind. As for admiration, he made it clear that he had none. Please spare me the humiliation of describing just how clear."

Impish lights sparkled in Cassandra's eyes. "We must find you another man, then, one who knows better than to insult you when trying to win your favor."

"You will do nothing of the kind, Cassandra. I will be much too busy for such silly diversions. Now, enough of that. Let us talk about your exceptional jewels."

"If you insist. However, I look forward to the day when you learn there is never truly enough of that."

"Cassandra!"

"Oh, dear. I have shocked you. Yes, let us move on to a boring discussion of my financial misery, and my only hope to rectify the disaster." Cassandra gazed down on the collection that she had brought with her. The jewelry covered the table like a bed of deeply hued, glittering flowers. "I will cry when they are sold, but I have no choice unless I want to return to my brother's house and live the most dreary of lives."

"I know some of these were given to you by your aunt. Will she not be angry when she learns that you sold them?"

"I told her my plans, and she advised me on which items it would be best to consign. I hope that you can still get the two thousand that your father predicted."

"Since you allowed me to hold them back for the next

sale, I think we will. They would have been wasted yesterday, but will be one of the notable glories of the next auction
and should bring that amount at least."

Cassandra appeared skeptical. "You are very sure
that you are going to do another one, then? Even without
Mr. Nightingale?"

"Absolutely. Obediah has agreed to remain with Fairbourne's. I will begin preparing the other items for display
and also solicit more consignments. I will do everything
I can not to disappoint you."

Emma spoke honestly, but the situation only reminded
her of how much she had to do in the next few weeks. She
needed to fatten the auction with more consignments, and
find some rarities to pique the interest of the best people.
She needed it all ready before the Season ended too, so
society would still be in London when the auction was held.

"Do you want to take these home with you, and keep
them until we are closer to the sale?" Emma asked while
she rolled up the cloths that protected each item.

"It was hard enough bringing them today. I may lose my
resolve if I must do so again."

"Then come with me. I will show you how they will be
safe."

Carrying the little rolls in a box, Emma led the way
upstairs to her father's chambers. Her steps slowed as she
drew near the door. She did not like being in Papa's apartment now. Each brief visit sent grief slicing through her like
a newly honed sword.

As soon as she entered, she paused to collect herself.

She had rarely seen her father in his bedchamber, but she
had often visited him in this little anteroom. The wall of
bookcases made it a tiny private library, and Papa often used
the floor to spread out the large folios that held engraved
reproductions of paintings.

She had come upon him many times on his hands and
knees, hovering over several books opened thus, flipping
back and forth while he sought some tidbit of information
on an artist whose works had been consigned. More often

he would be at the small writing table on the opposite wall from the bookcases, his feather pen scratching on correspondence to his collectors.

It was in this small chamber that he had told her about Robert's ship going down, and promised her that despite that tragedy, Robert would one day return.

Softly and gently, Cassandra's arms came around her, reminding her too much of her father's embrace that day. Emma accepted the comfort but it made her more vulnerable to the memories, and for a while grief touched her deeply. Then she composed herself and carried the jewelry into the bedchamber.

The bedchamber was paneled in an old-fashioned style, and there was a good reason why new tastes in decoration would never change that. Going to one of the panels, she found the hidden latch behind a molding, and swung the wood away to reveal a locked case set in the wall.

The key hung on a long chain around her neck. She fished it out of her bodice, opened the case, and deposited the jewelry.

"See, all hidden and locked away now." She turned to Cassandra, and caught her friend studying her with speculative interest.

"You display such strength and inspire such confidence that it is easy to ignore the daunting task you have set for yourself, Emma. It is good news that Obediah will still call the auctions, since you surely cannot. However, while Mr. Nightingale was not essential, your father's passing made him more necessary than he was in the past."

"I think that you exaggerate his significance, much as he did."

"Emma, there were ladies who viewed the consignments only to have an excuse to view *him*, and to be flattered and amused by a handsome man of passable breeding."

"I hope that you mean flattery in the normal sense this time."

"Let us just say that you can no more take his place than

you can Obediah's at the rostrum. Despite his inappropriate proposal, you should have convinced him to stay on."

"I could not allow him to stay."

"Then you must hire another handsome young man of passable breeding to take his place," Cassandra said. "Let us go below and compose an advertisement to hire a new manager."

A half hour later Emma rose from the writing table in the library and carried her first version of an advertisement to Cassandra. "I do not want a public announcement that Fairbourne's is seeking inquiries, so I can only describe the requirements, not name the establishment or even its trade. However, this should do, don't you think?"

Cassandra read it. "It will do perfectly, if you have a situation available for a vicar."

Emma snatched it out of Cassandra's hand. "I think I did a fine job of it."

"You are not seeking just anyone for just any ordinary position, Emma. You must make this sound more appealing, so the sort of man who can do better will still find it interesting." She rose, took the advertisement back, and went to the writing table. She sat, tossed her long, black curls over her shoulders, and dipped the pen. "First, we must remove this word *industrious*. It sounds like hard labor."

"I only thought—"

"I know what you thought. A solid day's work for the money of the hire." Cassandra drew a line through the offending word. "Also, *sober-minded* must go. So must *self-effacing*. No man worth knowing ever thinks of himself as self-effacing." She tsked her tongue. "It is a good thing that I am here to advise you, Emma. Left on your own, you would have ended up with a very dull but dutiful man, and that will never do."

Emma thought it would do fine. "I am of two minds about mentioning the knowledge of art. It should be there, but

I want nothing in it to have people wondering if the advertisement is Fairbourne's."

"Why not?"

Because she did not want a certain earl to become aware of her plans, was why not. She did not explain that because even Cassandra did not know that Southwaite had that partnership. Both the earl and Papa had kept that very quiet, probably because, as she pointedly reminded Southwaite yesterday, it *did* smell of trade.

Emma did not know how she was going to manage the earl if he became aware of her intentions, but possibly his desire for discretion would aid her. It would be best not to ruin what might be an advantage.

"If it is known it is Fairbourne's, all sorts will show up at the door, cluttering the premises for weeks," she said. "Nor do I want our competition to have cause to use our current lack of a manager against us."

"We can remove the reference to art. You will only learn if a prospect truly knows anything when you engage him in conversation on the topic." Cassandra scratched one more long line with the pen. "Now, we must make it clear this is no ordinary situation. Young men suited for a haberdasher's shop need not apply." Cassandra tapped the feather against her chin, then scribbled.

Emma looked over her shoulder. "*Pleasurable employment*?"

"This man will attend your preview parties and mix with the ton. He will drink brandy with gentlemen and become an intimate friend with wellborn ladies. If he—"

"You have no proof that there will be, or ever has been, *intimacy*," Emma said crossly.

"He will become *a confidant* of ladies, if you prefer that word. My point is that you should make it clear that the situation has its pleasures if you want to attract the best that can be had."

"I begin to wonder why I would even pay this person. He should pay me, considering the opportunities that await him."

Cassandra laughed at that, then continued writing.

"There." She set down the pen. "What do you think?"

Emma read through the sheet that now held numerous deletions and additions. She could not deny that the resulting requirements described a replacement for Mr. Nightingale very well, mostly because they described Mr. Nightingale himself.

"I will give you the name of a solicitor who will act as go-between. He will ensure that obviously inappropriate prospects do not darken your door," Cassandra said.

"I think you will have to be with me when I speak with any man that he does send to me. Perhaps Mr. Riggles should be there too."

"I do not believe that he will contribute anything positive. We don't intend to lie about the situation, Emma, but I fear Mr. Riggles will not communicate the tone that we will want."

"Are you saying that he may not agree when I describe Fairbourne's future with boundless optimism?"

"He may also demur when we imply that a life of ever-growing prestige and wealth awaits."

Emma pictured Obediah at the interviews. Cassandra was correct. He did not dissemble well and would not contribute much that was positive. "I will have the advertisement printed early next week. Shall we agree to meet here a week hence, to discover who sees himself in this description?"

"A fair number shall, I think," Cassandra said. "I just hope that one of them suits you and also has the style that is needed."

"Suits Fairbourne's, you mean."

Cassandra absently wound a finger through one of her long raven curls. "Of course, that was what I meant. Absolutely."

Chapter 4

Darius swung off his horse in front of the house on Compton Street near Soho Square and approached the door. He did not relish the day's mission, but it should not be put off any longer. It was time to explain to Emma Fairbourne the reasons why her father's auction house had to be sold.

Not all of the reasons, of course. He saw no advantage in itemizing his suspicions about Maurice Fairbourne, suspicions that had crystallized during his visit to the coastline in Kent the last week. While there, he had visited the place from which Maurice had fallen during that evening stroll. Upon examining both the location and its prospects, he had concluded it was only a matter of time before rumors about that accident, and why Fairbourne was on that path, found their way to London.

There was no proof of anything untoward. If the auction house were sold or closed, there most likely never would be. The reputations of both Maurice Fairbourne and his business would probably remain unblemished, as would that of anyone associated with it. Like the Earl of Southwaite.

Memories of his last meeting with Miss Fairbourne made him pause at the door. He would make sure she did not distract him this time. However, he doubted that being forceful in his manner would serve his purpose well either. Firm and consistent, but gentle, might work best, much like dealing with a spirited horse. Even so, he expected resistance from her. A lot of it. A battle loomed.

He might feel better prepared if he had not endured some ridiculous dreams about that last meeting with her, dreams in which things ended very differently than they had a week ago in that storage room. As a result some very arresting images of Miss Fairbourne naked and in total surrender to him had stuck in his mind, and even now wanted to intrude.

That he was plagued by erotic night fantasies could be attributed to his recent abstinence, in turn due to realizing that his last mistress's sly manner of angling for expensive gifts had ceased being adorable.

That Miss Fairbourne played a starring role in the new fantasies had no explanation at all, however.

She was not the kind of woman that a man took for a mistress, even if he wanted to. Although not a girl, she was neither a widow nor the object of scandal, so hardly fair game. As the daughter of a merchant, she most likely had very conservative ideas about sexual congress and would expect it to be paired with matrimony.

She did not fit his idea of a mistress in other ways either. Sweet and accommodating, she was not. There was no evidence that she possessed the requisite sophistication for such affairs, either. Such dalliances demanded an acquired level of emotional superficiality in order to be fun, pleasurable, and intense, but also not entangling, and ultimately finite.

No, Miss Fairbourne obviously would not do, for numerous reasons.

He acknowledged with some chagrin that he had examined most of those reasons, from far too many angles and perspectives, and for all the wrong purposes. Fortunately, he would be free of such pointless rationalizations within the hour.

While he emerged from his reflections regarding Miss Fairbourne, a young blood, no more than twenty-two years in age, trotted his horse down the street, dismounted, and tied his gelding right next to Darius's own. He strode up the stone stairs, brushing his embroidered brown frock coat with his hands. He paused with his foot on the top step, and bent to rub at a scuff on the toe of his high boot.

He gave Darius a quick but incisive inspection, then flashed a cocky smile. Reaching around Darius he gave the knocker three sharp raps.

Displeased by this intrusion on his call, and wondering who the devil this fellow was, Darius waited, feeling the face hovering at his shoulder.

Maitland, the Fairbournes' butler, did not open the door. Rather Obediah Riggles, the auctioneer, did the duty.

Obediah appeared just as surprised to see Darius as Darius was to see him.

"Has Maitland gone?" Darius asked quietly after Obediah had taken his hat and card. The young blood busied himself primping the hair around his face, making sure the artful wisps of his Brutus fell just so.

"No, sir. Miss Fairbourne asked me to man the gate, just for today. I'm to turn away unsuitable sorts."

Presumably there were adventurers and even thieves aware that Miss Fairbourne was now a woman alone. Unsuitable sorts might well find excuses to impose on her, and it was unlikely she could identify who had been an associate of her father, seeking to offer condolences, and who had not been.

"I was told to bring visitors to the drawing room, sir," Obediah said, angling his head for a private word. "I think it might be better to escort *you* to the morning room instead. I will tell Miss Fairbourne that you are there."

"If she is receiving in the drawing room, take me there, Riggles. I will not have special accommodations made due to my station. I insist that you present my card exactly as you do the others. I can ask for a private word after her other callers leave."

Obediah vacillated. The young blood cleared his throat impatiently.

"The drawing room?" Darius prompted.

Bearing the salver with two cards, the auctioneer led the way up the stairs. He opened the doors to the drawing room and stood aside.

Darius entered into a most peculiar scene. Miss Fairbourne had not come down yet. She had a great many callers waiting, however. Ten young men lounged around the chamber.

The callers gave the newcomers critical examinations, then went back to doing nothing. Darius turned to ask Obediah the meaning of this masculine collection, but the doors had closed and Obediah had returned to his post.

Darius positioned himself in front of the fireplace and took stock of his company. All of them were of similar cut—young, fashionable, and handsome. Miss Fairbourne was an heiress now, and perhaps these were suitors, lining up to court her.

He pictured the earnest entreaties that would be made as each one pressed his case in turn. Considering his own experiences with Miss Fairbourne, these young men would likely get their ears burned. He was rather sorry that he would miss the show.

He strode to a divan and sat beside a polished blond swain wearing a striped red and blue waistcoat of considerable cost but questionable taste. The fellow smiled an acknowledgment but scrutinized Darius at the same time.

"A bit old, aren't you?" he said.

"Ancient," Darius replied dryly. Thirty-three probably did look old to a pup barely out of university, he supposed. It had to him when he was that age.

His new companion thought the response droll, but seemed to realize the question had not gone down well. "My apologies, sir. I only meant that I think she is looking for someone younger. Perhaps not, though, and your maturity will put us all to a disadvantage." He angled his body, the better to chat. "John Laughton, at your service."

Darius believed that etiquette existed for good reasons, but he prided himself on not being a stickler. Therefore he introduced himself in turn. "Southwaite."

Laughton frowned, perplexed. "Oh? *Ohhhh*." He glanced around the chamber. "You are not here—that is, it goes without saying you are not competition." He laughed. "I confess that is a relief to me."

Darius was about to reassure him that he certainly was *not* competition, when a door opened at the end of the drawing room and a woman emerged from the connecting library.

It was not Miss Fairbourne. Rather Lady Cassandra Vernham, the notorious sister of the Earl of Barrowmore, immediately garnered the attention of every man in the chamber.

A tumble of black curls fell around her face and neck from beneath a white lacy cap perched high on her crown. The palest green diaphanous cloth flowed around her body from where a white ribbon bound it high under her admirable breasts. Her large red mouth pursed and appeared shockingly erotic while she opened a journal book and peered at its page.

"Mr. Laughton."

Laughton sprang to his feet, smoothed his coat, and walked forward. He followed Cassandra into the library and the door closed.

Laughton had left behind a newspaper. Darius noticed that the page showing had been marked. He picked it up and read the advertisement that been worthy of John Laughton's attention.

Wanted: For a very special and most pleasurable employment, a handsome young man of amiable disposition and notable wit, with excellent manners, advanced education, and unquestionable discretion. Must possess a fashionable appearance, a strong physique, an enjoyment of female company, and undisputed charm. Inquire at the chambers of Mr. Weatherby, on Green Street.

It was a peculiar and somewhat startling notice. Someone clearly sought something other than a footman or secretary.

Darius looked at the very amiable and fashionable young men lounging in the drawing room. Presumably they had all been sent here when they visited Mr. Weatherby.

Evidently there was much more to Miss Fairbourne than he had surmised. Her judgment left much to be desired, however. What was the woman thinking? Maurice must be turning over in his grave.

He strode from the drawing room, to go and find Riggles. Out on the landing a sound made him pause in his tracks. Clear as could be, he heard two women speaking around the corner.

"He is definitely the best of the lot so far, and we should ensure he will pass muster, Emma."

"We can do that while he remains dressed."

"I only asked him to remove his coats so his physique would be visible. Much is obscured by coats, and strong shoulders can become quite narrow once a man is in his shirtsleeves and nothing more."

"He will be wearing coats all the time, so that does not signify."

Silence then. Long enough that Darius assumed the ladies had returned to the library.

"Emma, I fear that you do not comprehend the practicalities," Cassandra Vernham spoke again. "Do you really think that men forever remain in their coats when they charm and flatter to the extent you expect?"

Darius turned on his heel and returned to the drawing room. Standing at the door, he eyed the young men waiting to impress Miss Fairbourne with just how charming they could be.

"I say that you hire Mr. Laughton, and we send the others away," Cassandra said. "He was the best so far."

"He was, wasn't he? That is not the same as saying he

was superior, of course. I had no idea that so many conceited, self-absorbed, but somewhat stupid young men lived in London. I never guessed that my advertisement would be so successful when it came to the quantity of applicants, but so disappointing on the matter of quality."

Most of the ones Emma had thus far met looked the part she needed played. It was when they opened their mouths that she knew they would not do. They appeared incapable of talking about anything except themselves, no matter how much she and Cassandra prompted them.

They had shown a disconcerting tendency to flirt too. She supposed that men finding themselves facing female interrogators might conclude flirting would help. Mr. Laughton had at least been more subtle about that, and had known a thing or two about art as well. The others had not revealed familiarity with even the most famous old masters.

"I wish I could blame their youth or their class, Emma. I regret to say that most men of the ton are no more impressive. Less so, perhaps, since so many younger sons lack any purpose. And people wonder why I am in no rush to marry." Cassandra folded her arms. "So, will Mr. Laughton do?"

Emma weighed the decision. "I will give him credit that he even removed his coats with a certain aplomb, and hid his embarrassment well."

"That was because he was not embarrassed. He found it amusing."

So had Cassandra. That left only one person in the library suffering embarrassment. Her.

Mr. Laughton had not even found the request odd. Perhaps potential employers demanded disrobing with regularity, to assess whether a prospect was in good health.

"I believe that I should see any who respond to the advertisement today or tomorrow. If Mr. Laughton is still the best after that, and if Obediah finds him acceptable, he will have to do."

"Very well," Cassandra said. "Five minutes each. No more, unless one of them impresses us immediately as potentially more suitable than Mr. Laughton."

Cassandra picked up her journal, into which she had been listing names off the calling cards that Obediah kept stacking on a table just inside the door to the servants' corridor. She opened the door to the library.

She immediately closed it again. Her color rose. She appeared startled.

"They are all gone," she said.

"Gone?"

"Disappeared. There were at least ten prospects when I brought in Mr. Laughton, and now there are none."

"The drawing room is empty?"

"One man is waiting to be received, but he is not seeking your situation."

"How can you be sure? Obediah may have forgotten to bring us his card."

Cassandra marched to the table near the side door where a few cards still waited for entry on her list. "His card is here. For heaven's sake, Mr. Riggles should have warned us, and not merely stuck this with the others. Better to have used Maitland today. He would never have been so careless."

"I wanted Obediah to at least see these young men so he could consult with us. We agreed he would contribute nothing if he sat here with us, so having him at the door was an alternative." Emma held out her hand for the card. "Who is it?"

Cassandra gave it over.

Emma peered at the card. "The Earl of Southwaite? What an inconvenient nuisance for him to intrude today of all days."

"I did not realize you knew him."

"My father knew him. He has taken an interest in my welfare."

"He appears a little . . . stormy."

"That is probably because I have kept him waiting. I should not delay any longer, although I wish I could." Emma smoothed her black dress and brushed off some lint. "Will you join me? You probably know him better than I do, since I barely know him at all."

"I will leave unobserved, if you do not mind," Cassandra said. "Southwaite and I do not rub well together, and my presence will not make his humor improve."

"Is he a saint who thinks you are a sinner?" Emma teased.

"He is no saint. Nor do I believe he cares if I sin or not. He objects to the way society speculates about me, however. I am too notorious for him, and he is too arrogant for me." She gave Emma a kiss, picked up her reticule, and aimed for the side door. "I will return in the morning, so we can continue our great project."

Chapter 5

The drawing room dwarfed most men. The Earl of South-waite managed to make the chamber's proportions suit him instead. A tall man, with shoulders that did not look as if they would narrow much at all when he removed his coats, he wore the drawing room like it had been constructed to the measurements of his lean strength.

He did appear stormy, Emma thought as she walked toward him. A scowl marred his brow above his deep-set eyes while he gazed at a painting by ter Brugghen on the wall. He stood near the fireplace, arms crossed, chin high, chiseled profile severe, looking very lordly. From his dark hair's short, tousled cut to his impeccable blue frock coat, fawn breeches, and high boots, he exuded the kind of self-confidence that only breeding conferred on a man.

He did not uncross those arms right away when he saw Emma approach. She felt like a naughty schoolgirl called to task by her angry governess until he finally did.

He bowed while he greeted her, but his dark-eyed gaze never left her face and his expression appeared disapproving of something. The delay? Her uncovered hair while in mourning? Perhaps he merely had bad digestion, and his expression had nothing to do with her at all.

"It is generous of you to condescend to call," she said. She took a seat on a chair and he settled onto the nearby divan.

She noticed that one of the potential replacements for Mr. Nightingale had left his newspaper on a table right near Lord Southwaite's arm. His gaze followed her own to that folded paper. One of his eyebrows arched a little higher.

"You appear to be bearing up very well," he said. "First the auction, and now . . . an effort to move on with your life."

If there had truly been storms, he had banished them, or at least their visibility. He spoke calmly, in a quiet baritone that soothed like warm water.

"Day by day it gets better, as is the way with these things."

"We all find comfort as we can in such situations. Of course, as a mature woman of the world, you need less advice in doing so than a young girl might."

He smiled. It was a rather nice smile. Not a big one. Just an appealing slight uplift at the ends of his mouth. She thought it more truly charming than Mr. Nightingale's. Perhaps that was because warmth entered Lord Southwaite's eyes, and a spark of almost intimate familiarity, as if their prior conversations had created a bond of sympathy.

That smile lightened her spirits in a most pleasant way. It seemed to bridge all kinds of distances between them, those of class and purpose, and even physical space. His favorable change in disposition led her to speak more plainly than she might have.

"When you arrived, were there other callers in this chamber, sir?"

"There were. An assortment of them."

"May I ask how it is that they are all gone now?"

"I suggested that they leave."

"I apologize if Mr. Riggles did not alert me to your presence, so I could receive you at once."

"I insisted that Mr. Riggles not treat me differently, so do not blame him. I told him to present my card exactly as he did the others. Of course, when I told him that, I did not know your drawing room would be overflowing with young men." He lifted the newspaper off the table and gave it a good look. "I could not imagine who they were and why they were here until I saw this marked advertisement."

Her heart sank. She wished one of her callers had not left that paper behind. The earl had guessed that she was hiring someone. She had hoped to be further along on the new auction before he realized she was even planning another one, but advertising for staff made her intentions clear.

"You do not approve, I assume," she said.

"I haven't decided what I think of it, other than there are better, more discreet ways to handle such things." He appeared somewhat amused by the advertisement. Considering their last conversation, that gave her encouragement.

"I am only being practical," she said, gesturing to the paper. "I know that there are better ways to fill such a situation, but none that are as fast and which leave me as much choice. I want to move forward quickly."

He rested his arm on the divan's rolled end, and his chin on his fist, and looked at her. "That is understandable, I suppose. As I said, we all find comfort in our own ways when touched by grief."

"How kind of you to understand. Doing this does offer comfort, and I anticipate more as I proceed. Even planning for it has been a distraction." It relieved her that he was not going to complain and fight about her plan to continue Fairbourne's auctions. "Since you are so sympathetic, I do not understand why you sent all my callers away."

He did not respond immediately. Rather he subjected her to a penetrating, thoughtful gaze. One could almost hear his mind churning over his answer.

The longer he paused, the more uncomfortable she became. She did not sense anger in him, but something else just as powerful. His attention made the chamber rather small suddenly, and demanded something of her in return that she could not name. The sensation of a pending *something* was not unpleasant—even exciting—but it did make the silence awkward.

"I sent them away because they did not suit the situation you propose. They were all too green."

"How generous of you to worry for me. I wish you had not taken the burden upon yourself to do that, however. I am capable of making such a decision myself, and I had a dear friend's help as well."

"Ah, yes. Lady Cassandra. She has proven her expertise in such matters," he said sardonically. "Her involvement explains much."

She did not understand what he meant by that, but his tone indicated disapproval. Cassandra had been correct. Southwaite did not like her.

"Perhaps I also sent them away because I had an interest in the situation myself," he said in a musing tone of voice, as if he had not really decided either way yet.

"Surely not. You are making fun of me now."

"Not at all. The appeal is inexplicable, but I cannot deny the truth of its existence."

How very odd. Gentlemen did not engage in such work. It was beneath them. However, he *had* invested in the auction house. He collected the very best art. Perhaps he thought taking Mr. Nightingale's place would be fun? Rather like those lords who shed their coats to help with the sheep shearing on their estates?

Having him at Fairbourne's would create complications, however. He would probably try to take charge of everything. He would be in the way. He might well attempt to unmask Obediah, and he had the expertise to do so.

"Lord Southwaite, while perhaps you think you would find the situation amusing for a while, in the end we both know you cannot do this. It would be scandalous and demeaning."

"Discretion goes far in avoiding scandal, Miss Fairbourne, and I promise you that I am a master of it. Nor would

I be taking any pay, of course. I would not be an employee, such as you intended, so it would not be demeaning."

"Then you see the situation differently than I do, and the difference cannot be countenanced by me. If you are not an employee, you will forget your place. I'll not be having you whistle the tune, sir. It is my intention to manage things to my own way of thinking. Nor will discretion be possible, if you think about it."

"Let me worry about both the discretion and the scandal. As for your own way of thinking, I believe I can convince you we are of like minds if you allow me to. We will both whistle, in harmony, as it were."

"I think that is unlikely."

"Because you are less experienced at whistling? I promise not to drown out your efforts."

She laughed lightly, as if he had made a joke. "I fear that you really would not suit the situation at all, Lord Southwaite."

He appeared surprised. Perhaps even insulted. "Are you saying I do not fit your requirements? Am I too old? Not handsome enough?"

"You are hardly old, and your appearance is . . . acceptable." Actually, if he were not a gentleman, he would do splendidly. He even knew about art.

"Then why am I not suitable? I would think I am obviously preferable to the boys you had waiting here."

She wasn't even sure he was teasing her now. The conversation had become awkward.

"I trust that you do not expect me to remove my coats to prove that I satisfy the requirement regarding physique," he said. "I would find that undignified."

Oh, dear heavens. He must have overheard Cassandra. "Yes. Please, do not—that is, I am sure that— Your strength is undeniable. No one could doubt it. Demonstration is not necessary."

"I am relieved to hear it. And, I assure you, I require no similar proof of your physical attributes either. At least not in advance."

What an odd and shocking thing to even suggest.

She stared at him, dumbfounded. He smiled back. Warmly.

M iss Fairbourne appeared extremely surprised. Good. Darius trusted that she was comprehending the foolishness of that advertisement now that a man had actually taken her up on the offer.

She might think that she could control matters by being an employer instead of a lover, but as the woman in an affair she would ultimately be vulnerable in the worst ways no matter who paid whom. If the mere notion of disrobing for a lord left her mouth agape, she would not have fared well with one of those callow clerks who had come to call, especially once the bedroom door closed.

She appeared quite vulnerable when stunned. Very sweet, actually. Much as she had in those inconvenient dreams. He was only teaching her a lesson, of course, and protecting Fairbourne's reputation, but a small part of him, a totally physical part, argued for seeing if he could seal the deal instead.

Such were the dark voices of desire.

He could not resist teaching that lesson very well, since he finally had her at the disadvantage. "I realize I am not what you expected when you composed this advertisement. Nor, as I have told myself repeatedly, are you what I normally seek in such arrangements. However, I think we will be well matched. Your boldness suits my own preferences, and suggests that the pleasures you offer will not be only the predictable ones."

Still she said nothing. Her expression became even more astonished, to his satisfaction.

"Are you concerned that the change in your plans will put you at a disadvantage, Miss Fairbourne? That in not being able to whistle the tune alone, you will now be left without any voice? Or that, due to our difference in stations, and due to your original intention to pay, that I will be ungenerous either in my attentions or my appreciation? I promise that you will have no complaints, and if you do, I will correct the situation at once. Just as I am sure you will address any of mine."

She narrowed her eyes and frowned. "Lord Southwaite, what *are* you talking about?"

She appeared truly bewildered now, rather than surprised or frightened. Enough to give him pause. He picked up the newspaper. "I am talking about this, of course, only with appropriate alterations to make it less vulgar."

She stretched her arm to take the paper. She pored over the marked advertisement.

"You are not the first woman of mature years to look for a lover this way, Miss Fairbourne. You description is less bawdy than most, but you made your point well enough to be understood. I daresay all of London is enjoying the elegant directness with which you describe your needs."

A deep flush colored her face fast. She covered her mouth with her hands and stared at him. She returned her gaze to the paper but he saw fires enter her eyes. "Your presumptions are beyond the pale, sir."

"You think I am being presumptuous?" It was not a word that sat well with him, especially coming from a merchant's daughter who invited assumptions, if not presumptions.

"Unforgivably so."

"I think I am being unduly magnanimous." Damned high-minded, actually. She was willing to settle for buying a whore, and he offered her an earl's generosity, after all. This lesson could have proceeded much more crudely.

"I am sure you do think that. I am guessing you have no idea just how outrageous your presumption is."

"No doubt you will enlighten me, since you rarely hold your tongue when you would be wise to do so."

He trusted she would hear the warning. She appeared ready to detail the insult no matter how ill-advised it might be. Of course she would. What had he been thinking, to bother to try to spare her the indignities she had invited?

"First," she said. "You are presumptuous in assuming

that a woman advertising for a lover would want a lover who does not fulfill her requirements, the first of which is that he be an employee and nothing more."

"Actually I presumed that a woman seeking a lover would prefer a man of some skill, consideration, and breeding who bestows gifts, over some callow boy who thinks only of himself and then demands coin," he said. "Forgive me, however, for not seeing the benefits to such a woman of the more costly, indecorous, and less satisfying choice."

"*Second,*" she intoned, ignoring what he said. "You are presumptuous in thinking, with no encouragement from me, that I would be agreeable, no matter what the arrangements, to having *you* as the lover in question."

She stood. Her color rose. Her eyes flashed lightning. He half expected a spear to appear in her hand and for her to bellow a Celtic battle cry.

"Finally, you are *unbearably* presumptuous in thinking you know the meaning of this advertisement to begin with. The situation described in this notice was *not* for a lover, Lord Southwaite." She tossed the newspaper at him for emphasis.

He caught it, stood in turn, and glared down at the advertisement. "The *hell* it wasn't."

The potential for profound embarrassment suddenly loomed. *Damnation.* He *hated* that feeling, and this infuriating woman had all but lured him into experiencing it.

"I assure you that your interpretation is *totally erroneous.*"

"If so, you were careless in the extreme in writing this. Inexcusably so. Anyone who reads it would assume what I did."

"Only someone with a very lascivious mind." She had the audacity to say that primly.

He could not deny, much as he wanted to, that she truly looked insulted, and importuned.

Hell. He examined the advertisement yet again. Even in the light of revelation, it still read as though a woman sought a professional admirer. He was certain his embarrassment did not affect his judgment about that.

The awkwardness of his situation pressed on him. Explaining that he had not truly been trying to form a sexual arrangement would not rectify this either. He doubted that his intentions to teach her a lesson would find more favor with her than if his intentions had been to make her his mistress in fact.

"I must apologize, of course. However, I am obligated to say that if I thought it read that way, those young men did too. The presence of Lady Cassandra hardly helped since the allusions to her in the scandal sheets are read by all." It incensed him that Miss Fairbourne's poor judgment had him now making excuses and feeling like an idiot. "If there was any inappropriate flirting in that chamber back there, now you know why."

She hesitated one scant moment. Her eyes veiled with thought for an instant. Then she was all formidable indignation again. "There was no flirting. Everyone except you comprehended that the situation was other than . . . well, *that.*"

"The hell they did. And if not *that*, what *is* the situation? This *special* and *pleasurable* employment requires an interesting list of qualifications."

Another brief pause. She gathered herself into a pillar of hauteur. "I was helping Obediah hire a new exhibition hall manager. Mr. Nightingale has left, and Fairbourne's needs a presentable man to greet patrons and such. That is why Obediah was here today too." She gestured to the newspaper. "You will see that it perfectly describes the sort of person Obediah needs."

His annoyance abruptly shifted to this new information. It angered him even more, but at least did not leave him feeling like a complete ass. "There is no need for a new manager, and you know it, Miss Fairbourne."

She sat down and looked at him boldly. "I know nothing of the kind, Lord Southwaite."

"Mr. Nightingale left because he surmised the business must close. Without your father, it has no future, thus no need for Nightingale to be replaced."

"You may have invested, but you clearly remained ignorant of how Fairbourne's was managed. Obediah dealt with the finances and the catalogue. He is also duly licensed. As long as he remains, Fairbourne's can flourish. In fact, he is already well along preparing the next sale."

How like her to decide to have this conversation now, when he wanted very much to take his leave. "Your father never spoke of Riggles having such authority."

"It was not in his interest to reveal his reliance on others, least of all to you. Why, Obediah has an expertise to challenge Papa's, and superb eyes for attributions. I daresay that if he had possessed any fortune, Papa would have sold half the business to *him*, not you."

"Only he did sell it to me, and I gave no permission for another auction. Quite the opposite."

"Your permission was not required because it is more the second half of the last auction than a completely new one. Obediah decided to hold back the better works for another day."

Her fast retreat into self-possession aggravated his temper, just as it had the day of the auction. He saw himself during that last exchange, pacing back and forth in the storage room, barely able to move because of the paintings and table of silver.

She had so provoked him with her manner that he had not even wondered why such things would be in storage at an auction house that had just held its last sale. Now their presence there loomed large in his memory.

Those were the items held back from that auction, of course. She had spent the last week deliberately disobeying him, and continuing to plot a course that she knew he would not approve.

He had come here today to tell her that the auction house would be sold. It still needed saying. Unfortunately, the ridiculous misunderstanding with the advertisement meant he would be fighting a rear-guard action in the battle that would inevitably ensue.

While he composed a parting remark that would salvage something of his dignity, his gaze was distracted by the light coming from the west window and how it showed a variety of tones in the brown curls on her crown. Some streaks of hair appeared almost golden. That led him to observe how the light flattered her lovely complexion in a most becoming way too.

From this position he could also see the pale skin extending down prettily to the neckline of the simple black dress that covered breasts of admirable size. The high waist of her dress, and his current perspective, suggested that she would appear quite lovely if those breasts were visible. They would be very pale and perfect like the skin he could see, and firm and round, with pink—

It was definitely past time to leave.

"It has been an afternoon for misunderstandings, Miss Fairbourne. I think it best if I return another day to discuss our business, lest there be more of them. I will tell Mr. Riggles to expect me at Fairbourne's on occasion, so I can decide just where things stand there in light of this new information you have revealed."

"I agree that it might be wise to put off any discussion, Lord Southwaite. However, I should make it clear right now that Fairbourne's must not be sold." Her shoulders squared. Her chin rose. "It cannot be sold. It *will not* be sold."

He was not accustomed to women speaking to him in the sort of tone she had just used. Nor did he take well being the subject of the furious impertinence in her eyes. Her challenge was unmistakable and his blood urged him to answer it.

Instead he pulled out his pocket watch and glanced at it. "I regret that I do not have time to explain your errors on that topic right now."

"I do not require more time or conversation. I merely thought it best to explain just which tune I intend to whistle with you."

Several rude responses sprang to mind, referencing how she would whistle however he wanted before he was done with her. "I look forward to hearing more notes, at another time." He bowed. "I will leave you now. My apologies once more, for the misunderstanding today."

"We will never speak of it again, Lord Southwaite. By morning it will be as if it never happened, and we will forget it completely."

Chapter 6

The next morning Emma sat in the little chamber she used as a morning room, eating breakfast with Cassandra at a table near a back window that overlooked the garden. A small watch lay on the table among their plates and cutlery, showing the hour of nine thirty. Mr. Weatherby would send candidates for the situation at Fairbourne's beginning at ten.

Cassandra had set that watch there. Whenever Emma saw it, she thought about the advertisement. That in turn led her memory to the meeting yesterday with Southwaite. She had dubbed the entire disaster the Outrageous Misconception.

Cassandra set down her fork and demanded her attention. "You have been too quiet. I think you are deliberately teasing me with your silence. You know I am curious about your caller yesterday. What did Southwaite want with you?"

"It was a simple, brief social call. He did not *want* anything."

"I trust that you scolded him for sending away your young men."

"I did, politely but firmly. However, they were not *my* young men and I would appreciate your not calling them that. I am merely Fairbourne's agent. That advertisement has absolutely nothing to do with *me*."

"My, you are in a pique today. I hope that your disposition improves before we begin our meetings in the library. It will not be helpful if you present yourself as cross and unpleasant."

"And why not? It is not as if I am seeking this young man to dance attendance on me." She peered critically at Cassandra. "There can be no misunderstanding about that, I hope. I have wondered if including that requirement of enjoying female company was ill-advised. It seemed to me that most of those men yesterday were too bold in flirting."

Cassandra shrugged. "I did not find them over bold. I believe they merely hoped to prove they had the requisite charm."

"That requirement may have been ill-advised as well."

"Since both were added by me, are you now criticizing my advice? You are out of sorts today, but please do not turn your bad humor in my direction."

Emma bowed her head and tried to reclaim a better frame of mind. It was not fair to blame Cassandra for the embarrassment of the Outrageous Misconception. Surely Cassandra had not deliberately written the advertisement with the intention that it be interpreted in shocking ways.

Or had she? Cassandra's comments about flirting and flattery doing Emma good sprang to mind. So did the suggestion that they find her a man.

No, surely not. Lord Southwaite's accusations and presumptions were making her too suspicious.

Emma wished she had forgotten all about that humiliation by morning, the way she had told Southwaite she would. Instead she spent the whole night thinking about it. She had tried to give fair and honest thought to the misunderstanding with which it began.

In hindsight, she had to admit that his reading of her advertisement had not been entirely implausible. Their conversation, which had been a comedy of misconstruction, might have even given him reason to think she was amenable to his scandalous proposal. However, as a gentleman he should have made sure that she did not mind being propositioned before assuming that she would agree to *his* proposition. His boldness could not be excused.

The night being long and her thoughts being deep, she had inevitably pondered why an earl would be interested in Emma Fairbourne at all, least of all as a mistress. It really made no sense, unless Southwaite preferred women far below him in station and was not above taking advantage of a situation where one dropped into his lap. The lower born, the more grateful, no doubt. The more ordinary, the more in awe of him. The less wealthy, the cheaper to impress.

His interest was not to his credit, nor to hers. And so, when her sleepy thoughts had wandered into speculating what it was like to be such a man's mistress, she mostly managed to stop them before they drifted to the physical parts of such arrangements. Unfortunately, one thought snuck there anyway, and shocked her by provoking lazy titillations that slyly aroused her before she realized what was happening.

The memory of that made her feel ridiculous now. The entire Outrageous Misconception did. The only good thing to come out of the upsetting episode was that, once more, she had bought some time.

He had come to demand Fairbourne's be sold, she was quite sure. He would return to raise the question eventually. She counted on him being embarrassed enough by the Outrageous Misconception that he would not press his case for at least a few days.

"Cassandra, I know that you think flirting is as normal as breathing, and part of a man's charm when he possesses any at all. However, do you think . . . I found myself wondering last night if perhaps my advertisement might be misunderstood by some of these young men."

"Misunderstood? How so?"

"Is it possible that some of them believed the employment to be not only special and pleasurable, but also private? Very private."

Cassandra thought that very funny. She answered between giggles. "I suppose if a man were inclined to assume you were desperate, he might. Or that I was, come to think about it. After all, you might have been aiding me in the search, not I aiding you." She grinned while she patted Emma's hand. "Believe me, when women do write advertisements such as you imply, there is nothing subtle about it. Only an idiot would assume that your situation involved nothing more than private intimacies." She picked up the watch. "We should prepare. I fear it will be a long day."

While Emma walked with Cassandra up to her bedchamber, Cassandra regaled her with stories of advertisements she had seen by women seeking footmen or workers with strong backs, warm hands, and various other attributes that would ensure the fellow satisfied a most private situation.

Considering that her own advertisement had called for a strong physique, Emma was not nearly as amused as Cassandra expected.

She suspected Cassandra had indeed planned to encourage young men to assume such private pleasures, if not with Emma Fairbourne, then with ladies who patronized the auction house. The new man should not expect the situation to consist of *nothing more* than that, but Cassandra assumed that had been part of Mr. Nightingale's success, and had implied such duties when she revised the advertisement's words. Emma felt very stupid that she had, once again, not interpreted Cassandra's entendres correctly.

If she was right, then the Outrageous Misconception had not been nearly as outrageous as she had thought.

Not that she would ever admit that to the Earl of Southwaite.

* * *

At two o'clock that afternoon, Emma called for her carriage. She pulled on her black gloves, tied on her black bonnet, picked up her black parasol, and strode down the stairs of her house. On the second level she glanced into the drawing room. The empty drawing room.

Not a single applicant had been sent by Mr. Weatherby today. She and Cassandra had waited in vain all morning to see if Mr. Laughton could be improved upon by someone in today's batch of hopeful young men.

A half hour later she entered Mr. Weatherby's chambers on Green Street. After a brief wait, Mr. Weatherby received her.

She explained her surprise at the dearth of applicants today for her advertised situation. "Were there no inquiries at all?"

Mr. Weatherby, a solicitor who supplemented his fees by offering services such as he now provided to her, was a short, thin man composed of points, the most prominent being that of his nose. Pointed ears and eyebrows sung in harmony and, given the tune being played, even his shirt collar's ends seemed to hum along.

He responded blandly. "It happens this way sometimes. Most of the response comes the first day the advertisement runs in the newspaper."

"Most, you say. In this case it was all."

"I am not responsible for the success of an advertisement, Miss Fairbourne. I cannot imagine what you expect of me, but I am sure that I cannot help you." His nose aimed down to a paper on his desk. "My clerk will see you out."

He was rudely dismissing her, without even the courtesy of an adequate explanation.

She remained steadfast in her chair. He refused to acknowledge that she still sat there. Finally she stood. Positioned across the desk's expanse from the solicitor, she slammed her parasol down on the desk with as much force as she could.

The inkwell jumped. Mr. Weatherby did too. Then he reared back in his chair, eyes wide and mouth open, aghast at how close that parasol had come to his bent head.

"Mr. Weatherby, you were more than solicitous the day you sold me your services. You can remain courteous today as I ask the reason your services have halted with such abruptness. I am not so stupid as to believe that every single person in London even slightly suitable for that position came here all on one day."

He just stared at her, and the parasol, with astonishment.

She stood the parasol up on the desk and held it by its hilt. "Did even a single man come here today in response to the notice?"

Mr. Weatherby nodded.

"How many?"

Dumbfounded, he held up five fingers.

"Why did you not send them to my house?"

Mr. Weatherby hesitated. Emma readjusted her grip on the parasol. Mr. Weatherby cleared his throat, found his voice, and explained.

"I am thinking this must be it, Miss Fairbourne," her coachman, Mr. Dillon, said. "'Tis the one the fellow at the White Swan described."

Emma looked at the pale façade of the huge town house facing St. James Square. It certainly looked big enough to be an earl's home. She would have to trust that the fellow at the White Swan had gotten it right.

She alighted, and paused to fish a calling card from her reticule. She gave her bonnet a tweak on its rim to ensure it was straight. Calling up the blistering fury that had brought her here, and swallowing the sudden misgivings that assaulted her, she approached the door.

Although overwhelmed in her memory by thoughts of the Outrageous Misconception, Southwaite's parting comment about visiting the auction house had nagged at her all night too. It implied more interference than she had expected, or than she could afford. Southwaite was skeptical of her claims about Obediah, so it would not do for Southwaite to loiter around the exhibition hall. If he did, she could not go there herself and attend to the duties that she had claimed Obediah would be performing.

By morning she had convinced herself that he would probably visit once or twice at most, and that his words did not herald the trouble she feared.

Now she knew differently.

She was shown to a drawing room, one three times the size of her own. Paintings hung on the walls and she recognized several as having been purchased at Fairbourne's auctions. It was a very pale room otherwise, which set off the paintings quite nicely.

The furniture appeared finely boned, except for one rather large-scaled upholstered armchair near the fireplace. It had two gilt griffins flanking its sides, their legs forming the chair's base and their heads supporting the chair's arms.

She did not wait long before the earl arrived. He entered with a servant bearing a tray. Southwaite was dressed informally, as if he were visiting his country estate and had been riding. His circles would know what days he usually received callers, and apparently this was not one of them.

"Miss Fairbourne, I am happy to see you. Come and sit over here with me." His arm ushered her decidedly in the direction he required.

He guided her to the fireplace. She perched herself on an elegant, padded bench. He took the large chair. She realized it was there just for him. He would be uncomfortable on anything much smaller.

He sat like a king on his throne, with one fine boot forward and his arms supported by the griffins' heads. If she cared about such things, which she did not, she would have to admit that he appeared very handsome and noble today.

"You arrived just as I was about to have my afternoon coffee. Please have some too," he said.

She had much to say to this man, and intended to speak quite firmly, but she hoped to avoid another row. She held her tongue until the coffee had been served and the tray set aside.

She sipped some coffee. While she did the earl got in the first word.

"As I said, I am pleased you have called. My visit yesterday ended on a peculiar note, and there is no reason for us to be adversaries. You appear to be a sensible woman of some intelligence, and I am sure that we can cooperate instead of always arguing."

"I am flattered that you perceived some intelligence. That is rare praise, I am sure."

"Not so rare. I have met other women with intelligence. There are men who think the two things never go together, women and intelligence, but I am not one of them."

"How enlightened of you. The truth is, however, that I have come here today because our conversation yesterday was not only peculiar, but also incomplete."

"It was in several ways, I agree. Most lacking was your acceptance of my apology for the misunderstanding. I hope that you will accept those apologies now."

"Thank you. I shall. I have quite forgotten the matter already."

"It was also incomplete regarding the disposition of Fairbourne's, of course. May I assume that is what brought you here? I knew you would see what must be done once you thought about it. I promise you that I will take care of everything involved."

"I did not come here to discuss the disposition of Fairbourne's, Lord Southwaite. That subject is well settled between us. Any disposition is still out of the question."

He looked away but she saw exasperation flicker in his eyes. His attention returned to her. A tight smile formed on a face that had turned less amiable. "Then how can I help you, Miss Fairbourne? What other part of our conversation was incomplete? Ah, yes—I did not finish with my romantic proposition by discussing the usual details. Have you come here for that?"

She could not believe he made this reference to the Outrageous Misconception. He had just apologized a second time, hadn't he? They should be pretending it had never happened.

Instead he all but invited her once more to be his mistress, only without any misunderstanding as an excuse.

He watched her with dark humor. He was not flirting. Surely not. However, he observed her most specifically, as if he were truly interested in her reaction. She could not dispel the notion that he waited to see his reference fluster her, as if that would be some victory for him.

She managed not to reveal her surprise. However, she reacted to his gaze and insinuation, and not with the indignation that was warranted. Instead of disgust or anger, a very different emotion affected her. A thrilling sensation fluttered up to her throat, then spiraled down through her body, stirring her. Invisible sparkles danced on her skin and a foolish giggle bubbled in her brain. It was much like the taste of forbidden pleasure last night, only much less languid.

It dismayed her that her own femininity conspired against her by making her susceptible to this man, in that way, at this time. How incredibly unfair.

She reminded herself that Southwaite wanted to destroy Fairbourne's. She sought refuge in her anger, but was incapable of summoning its full force again, or of obliterating the new, discomforting awareness she had of Southwaite's masculinity, which saturated the air between them and made her nervous.

"I spoke with Mr. Weatherby today." She made her voice as crisp and unwavering as she could. "I know that you visited him after you left my house yesterday, and told him to stop referring applicants to me."

He calmly drank some coffee, then assumed a very cool expression. "Yes, I did. I had just proven how that advertisement could lead to misconceptions about the situation it described. I could not allow Mr. Weatherby to send prospects to your house all week, and risk the world knowing that the daughter of Maurice Fairbourne had written such a thing."

"You sought to preserve my reputation?"

"As best I could under the unfortunate circumstances, yes."

"Do you not find that in the least ironic, Lord Southwaite?"

He thought a moment, then shook his head. "I see no irony. Even if we had come to an arrangement yesterday, I would have used all of my power to avoid scandal for you."

He was speaking of it again!

"You will be relieved to know that I also paid off the men who were there when I arrived, and made them promise not to speak of where Mr. Weatherby sent them," he continued. "We will have to hope those you interviewed prior to my arrival are discreet. If they are not, I can only pray that you did not have any of them remove their coats."

He was scolding her. Obliquely, but it was a scold all the same. Worse, he did so as if he had the right to.

"Lord Southwaite, I came here to explain that Fairbourne's does not need or welcome your interference, only to learn just how much more you interfered than I knew. It was not your place to send those men away at all. Now I discover that you paid them for silence, as if I had committed a crime that needed to be obscured."

"You were not guilty of a crime, Miss Fairbourne. Only weak judgment."

"Forgive me for speaking plainly, but—"

"If I do not forgive you, will I be spared? No? I did not think so." He sighed with forbearance. "Pray, continue."

It was not easy to do so after he said that. Still, she managed to speak the message she had come here to give him. "Your meddling is not wanted. Your help is not needed. You were an invisible investor for years and should remain so."

"Miss Fairbourne, with your father's passing, the situation is much changed. We are two halves of a financial whole, and your half is now troublesome to mine. I will interfere as I see necessary and as I see fit."

He spoke like the lord he was, without the slightest note of apology or hesitation. Her mind formed scathing criticisms of his arrogant manner. Another part of her, the stupid feminine part giving her unexpected trouble today, was awed by his masterful presence and supreme confidence.

A slow smile appeared on his stunningly handsome face. It was a dazzling one that seemed calculated to appease the furious Emma and entrance the stupid one, as if he knew both existed and were at odds right now. To her shock that smile captivated her in ways she could not control. Almost immediately the remnants of her anger started slipping out of her grasp. She found it hard to look away.

"I do not require any particular behavior from you, Miss Fairbourne. I am not that much of a hypocrite," he explained, cajoling her to see the sense of it. "I merely require discretion such as I practice myself. Should the world learn about this partnership, our reputations will begin to leach onto each other. I would prefer not to get the worst of it, should that happen." That smile again. "I am sure you understand that."

"Your concerns are misplaced. I am too common and unknown to affect your reputation, no matter what I do. I am too insignificant to engender either gossip or scandal, nor am I accustomed to the kind of behavior that might incite either. Why, I even turned down an earl who offered to make me his mistress in a thoroughly discreet arrangement."

He cupped his chin with his hand and regarded her. "That earl's misunderstanding is cause enough for caution, don't you think? He might have made assumptions due to your friendship with Lady Cassandra, for example. More discretion would be wise there too, I think."

She was so entranced by how well he looked in that chair, and how handsome he could be when he was not stormy, and by how delicious her physical responses were, that she almost did not hear him. When she did she made a display of frowning, but it was a feint, a mere attempt to display the indignation that she should be experiencing instead of this foolish, pleasant stimulation that prickled in her.

"I will not insult my dearest friend to satisfy your oddly selective notions of propriety. As for the rest, if you do not interfere with Fairbourne's, no one will be the wiser about your investment, thus removing the reason you claim a need to interfere to begin with. I am sure *you* understand *that*."

She stood, to make good an escape before she did something that revealed how a hidden part of her had lost all claim to sense or strength. "Good day to you, Lord Southwaite. Thank you for receiving me so I could make my position clear."

"Are you finally ready to ride?"

The question, spoken with sharp impatience, pulled Darius out of his contemplation of Miss Fairbourne as soon as he opened the library door.

His friend Gavin Norwood, Viscount Kendale, did not wait for an answer. Already he was gathering his limbs and rising to leave.

"Five minutes, you said," Kendale muttered, raking his dark hair with his fingers while he reached for his gloves with his other hand. "I could be halfway to the coast by now."

"My caller's mission was not as friendly as I had hoped," Darius said. "It required some time to come to an understanding with the lady."

Not that they had come to one, he admitted to himself. He had put off this journey with Kendale and chosen to see Miss Fairbourne only because he assumed she had come to capitulate. It turned out that instead she had come to upbraid him.

No one did that. Women surely did not dare such a thing and remain unscathed, not even lovers who tried it while employing pouts or, more annoyingly, caresses.

At least he had not been at the disadvantage this time, even if she did have her say. He had also learned something about Emma Fairbourne. A smile could fluster her faster than a scowl, and a command could end an argument more surely than a threat.

He would not have minded exploring just where more smiles and commands could have led. Her extreme boldness today hardly encouraged the indifference he had sworn regarding her. In response he had experienced the urge to demand she bend to his will. Various ways of effecting that, most of them involving erotic subjugation on her part, had played through his mind vividly while they sat together. The remnants of those images still distracted him. There had been signs in her—a flush here and a stammer there, and the way her intense gaze never left his—that suggested her surrender was not out of the question.

"She?" Kendale asked, his stride to the door arrested by the pronoun when it finally penetrated his temper's storm. "You put off our duty because of *a woman*? You delayed a matter of dire importance to the realm, to dally with one of your lovers?" He cursed in annoyance. "You said that Tarrington wanted to meet in the morning."

"And we will meet in the morning. I stole no more than thirty minutes, and that we can spare. The woman is not a lover either, so please start no rumors."

"I don't know her name. How can I start a rumor? As for thirty minutes, I have seen men die because of a delay much shorter."

Darius opened the door to encourage Kendale to stride again, right out to the horses. Tomorrow morning's plans were important, but not nearly as significant as Kendale hoped. It was tomorrow night's meeting that would tell whether long-laid strategies had borne enough fruit to be successful.

Darius understood Kendale's preference for action over negotiation—Kendale had been in the army, after all—but it was the latter that might make their efforts work in the long run.

"Ours is merely an independent surveillance regarding movements on the coast, Kendale. It is not a military maneuver.

No one will die even if we are two days late, let alone half an hour."

Kendale walked by, brow furrowed and steely gaze straight ahead. "A lot you know about maneuvers, military or otherwise, or about the small mistakes that cause some men to die in them."

Chapter 7

Having fed Southwaite the lie about Obediah running things at Fairbourne's, Emma was reduced to complicated machinations in order to perform her duties at the auction house. She dared not just walk in the door, lest the earl be there to investigate his investment.

For all of her bravado, she knew that she had failed to obtain Southwaite's agreement not to interfere at their last meeting. Rather, the opposite might have occurred. She feared that she had dared him to do something he might not have done otherwise.

Worse, she suspected he knew about the sparkles and flutters. The more she remembered that slow smile and cajoling voice, the more she pictured the way he had looked at her, the stronger that suspicion became.

In order to make any progress with the catalogue, she devised a system of communication with Obediah. Doing so forced her to confide the news of the earl's partnership to him. Obediah took it very well, but then, the arrangement had not depleted *his* family business by half, had it?

For the next three mornings she sent a note to Fairbourne's

with a footman, asking if Lord Southwaite had come by. If Obediah responded in the negative, as he did each day, she had the carriage bring her over. Before entering, however, she checked the front window. Obediah had agreed to leave the Angelica Kauffman in the window if Southwaite still was not there.

She made good progress with cataloguing the silver while the workers cleaned the property and began hanging the paintings that she had held back. Patrons who walked by would see them, and could watch the next auction taking shape. Hopefully it would whet their appetites. In the least, the activity announced that Fairbourne's was not closing, as everyone assumed.

She worried about enhancing the offerings, and even turned to considering her family's own collections, to see what might be sacrificed if necessary. The best art was not in London, unfortunately. Papa had moved the most prized paintings to his cottage on the coast, where he would retreat for privacy and renewal. If she were reduced to selling any of them, she would have to transport them to London, which would involve a journey she would rather not make.

When she returned to her house on the third afternoon, Maitland immediately asked for a private word. Tall, thick, and black-haired, Maitland's size inspired a sense of safety in this house now that she lived here as a lone woman. Even his craggy face would discourage ne'er-do-wells.

"A person came, and is waiting for you," he said. "There is no card."

"Is there a name?"

"No name either, Miss Fairbourne."

"If there is no card, and no name, why did you allow this person to wait?"

"I thought I should, Miss Fairbourne. She said she had brought some items to consign at your auction."

"If that is the reason for her visit, you did not err in your judgment. Sometimes people, and especially women, do not want to have it known they sell their property thus, and seek private conversations." It was customary to keep such

consignors' identities a secret, and note in the auction catalogue only that the property was that of an *esteemed gentleman* or *a discreet patron*. "Where is she?"

"In the garden, Miss Fairbourne. She preferred to stay
out there, she said."

Emma walked to the morning room and to the French
doors that gave out to the back terrace. Despite their distort-
ing glass panes, she could make out her visitor sitting on a
stone bench near the terrace's low wall.

The woman wore a loose, full-sleeved, soft gray dress,
bound under her breasts with a broad red sash. A shawl of
gray and red pattern hung from her shoulders. Her long
auburn hair fell free in the current style, and a gray and red
turban had been tied in a full, carefree wrap around her
crown.

Emma envied the style with which this stranger wore that
headdress. She herself had tried many times to make such
a turban appear exotic and artistic on her own head. She had
managed only to appear like someone done up for the stage
in a silly costume.

She opened the door, and the image of her guest clarified.
The face under that turban turned to her, and she saw its
delicate beauty and captivating deep brown eyes.

Emma greeted the young woman as best she could, considering she did not have a name. "I am told you have
brought some items for consignment. Why don't you remove
them from your reticule so I can see what they are and assess
what they might bring."

"They are not in my reticule." The woman spoke slowly
and carefully, as if considering every word. Emma heard
the lingering accent that indicated her lovely guest was
French, but probably not a recent arrival. She was an émigré,
no doubt, a refugee from the revolution who had today come
to sell valuables carried out when she fled.

"They are there." The woman pointed a thin, elegant
finger toward the back of the garden. She wore no gloves,
and Emma saw dark smudges on her hand that marred its
cleanliness.

Her visitor began walking in the direction she had pointed.

Emma followed, perplexed, noticing again the willowy grace of this woman, but also seeing other things now. The dress, while presentable, displayed mending if one looked closely at its hem. The shawl had a smudge too, mostly obscured by its pattern. The woman wore old-fashioned mules, not slippers such as were common now.

They walked all the way to the back garden gate. Once they were in the little lane behind the property, the woman gestured lazily to a wagon next to the carriage house, her stained hand flowing up and down.

Emma loosened the tarp that covered the wagon's contents. She looked in, then slapped the tarp down again.

The old books and even the silver in the wagon were the sorts of things an émigré might well bring across the channel. However, this potential consignment did not consist only of household goods. Most of it was wine, and she had seen at once that the cases bore no customs stamps.

"Take it away. We do not accept smuggled goods at Fairbourne's."

"I cannot take it away. There is no donkey." The smudged finger floated toward the empty harness. "He took it with him."

"Who took it?"

"The man who paid me to come here with him. Four shillings, he gave me, to go to the house and say the wagon was here. He said you would understand about this wagon, and its importance to your winning the prize. But perhaps not?" She shrugged. The confusion of the situation bore no interest to her. She set her shawl higher on her shoulders and began walking down the lane.

"Stop. Wait," Emma said. "I do not understand its importance. I do not even know what the prize is. What was this man's name? Where is he?"

"I cannot help you more. I only rode in the wagon, and I told you it is here as I said I would. It was a strange request, but four shillings is good pay for a few hours. Now I must go."

"But I want to talk to this man."

"I do not know him. I am sorry."

"Was he English, or French?"

"English." She turned to leave again.

"Please, stop. If you see this man again, tell him that I need to speak with him. Will you do that for me?"

The woman considered it. "If I see him, I will tell him."

Emma watched the gray dress grow smaller as her guest walked away. Then she returned to that wagon and lifted the edge of the tarp again. She examined the silver and the books and the wine. Especially the wine. She counted fifteen cases. She felt inside a large trunk. Her fingers slid over satin and lace.

This wine must have been smuggled into England. Probably the cloth had been too. That was why it had been brought here, to the house, in a clandestine manner. It appeared that someone assumed that Fairbourne's would be willing to accept the contents of this wagon.

She did not want to imagine why such an assumption would be made. The disheartening conclusions pressed on her anyway, evoking a scathing disappointment that tainted memories she held in her heart.

How many of the consignments over the years described as "from the estate of a gentleman" had in fact arrived like this, anonymously and very quietly?

She tied down the canvas so the wagon's contents would be protected and also invisible. Then she returned to the house and sought out Maitland.

"Maitland, that woman today—have there been others? Strangers like her, who came to the garden door and asked for my father, and who left wagons near the carriage house?"

"There were some these last years. Not many." He paused, then added with earnest apology in his voice, "Mr. Fairbourne seemed to know when they would come. I thought you must know too. If my actions have distressed you, I am abjectly sorry."

"Do not apologize. It was wise for me to see her."

She retreated to her chamber before she did something

that revealed her shock and disappointment. If Maitland knew, all the servants probably did. She had been the only one in this house who had not guessed that Fairbourne's had been successful in part because Maurice Fairbourne dealt in smuggled goods.

Darius ran his finger down the row of figures, then glanced across the desk at Obediah Riggles. The older man tried to mask his discomfort at being subjected to this interrogation, but the way he kept blinking gave him away.

"I have duties to attend to, Lord Southwaite, if you can spare me now."

"Not quite yet, Riggles."

It was not clear what Riggles thought his current duties might be. That he had resisted being dragged back to this office, and had tried repeatedly to get away, could not be denied, however.

"There are consignments going back years for which there are no names," Darius said. "Does discretion extend to the accounts, if an individual requests privacy?"

Obediah's face tinted with a flush. "Sometimes. That is, Mr. Fairbourne would make that decision, as you can imagine."

"Yet Miss Fairbourne said that you kept the accounts. So Maurice would instruct you to leave off the names?"

Obediah's head dipped in what appeared to be a nod.

Darius found the last payment made to him as a partner. His name was not present either. He recognized it only from the amount.

He sat back and gave Riggles a good examination. The fellow looked to be a man who would not know how to be deceptive even if he wanted to be. That probably explained why being confronted with the extensive ambiguities in these accounts caused him such ill ease. A smile kept forming and fading on that pale face, but even at its broadest it could not hide the caution in Riggles's eyes.

"How much do you anticipate the next auction bringing in?" Darius asked.

Riggles sat straight, startled. "Next one, sir?"

"Miss Fairbourne has told me there is to be another."

"She has?"

"The paintings being hung on the walls today also gave me a clue."

"Oh. Yes, I see how that might make it obvious. I suppose since you know about it . . . We hope for many thousands, and should see it if the jewels remain with us."

"Jewels?"

"Lady Cassandra Vernham's jewels. Mr. Fairbourne estimated—that is, Mr. Fairbourne *and I* estimated—they would go for two thousand on their own."

Darius closed the account book and stood. Obediah jumped to his feet.

"I trust that you have learned what you sought to know, Lord Southwaite," he said earnestly.

"Hardly." Darius had learned what he feared learning, however. The accounts were vague enough, and possibly incomplete enough, that all manner of items could have passed through Fairbourne's without much documentation. That the total take could have been understated, and his own share as a result, did not concern him. That the auction house might have been involved in illegal activities did.

It would be a hell of a thing if a peer who complained publicly about an unprotected coast being vulnerable during this war with France were revealed to have profited from that vulnerability. The irony had not been far from his mind his last three days in Kent, during those meetings he, Ambury, and Kendale had held with the leaders of the volunteer units of citizens who had massed for drills near Dover.

He had even visited that cliff walk from where Maurice Fairbourne had taken his fatal fall again. There was nothing to recommend that barren strip other than its exceptional views of the beaches and sea in all directions. From that spot a man could easily signal to smugglers that the "coast was clear" of the few Board of Customs sloops that had not been requisitioned by the naval service.

Darius walked out to the exhibition hall with Obediah on his heels. He surveyed the paintings being hung in their long vertical rows on the tall, gray walls. One of the workers caught Obediah's eye and made an odd gesture.

Darius pointed to an oil painting that had garnered his attention when he entered Fairbourne's. "Andrea del Sarto?"

Riggles blinked. "Sir?"

"The painting is by del Sarto, it appears to me. Is that the attribution?"

"Uh . . . yes, quite so."

"The saints on the sides look a little weak compared to the Madonna." He bent and peered closely. "Another hand at work, perhaps?"

Riggles bent and peered too. "My thoughts exactly, sir."

Darius turned his attention to the rest of the wall. "It looks spare. Are you anticipating more?"

"Oh, yes. Yes, we are," Obediah mumbled. "Quite soon. Quite soon."

"From whom, Mr. Riggles?"

Obediah glanced at the front window before realizing another question had been asked. "Sir?"

"If you are expecting more paintings soon, who will be consigning them?"

Obediah paused. "Why, gentlemen, sir."

Darius doubted any more consignments would be forthcoming. Who would take such a chance with Maurice Fairbourne now gone? Miss Fairbourne said Obediah really managed this auction house, but even if it were true, no one knew that. The world assumed this ship had lost its captain.

He should have moved to sell the business immediately, before another auction proved its diminished worth, or others voiced suspicions about Maurice Fairbourne's purpose on that cliff walk.

The name Fairbourne's stood for something. Neither a lackluster auction nor rumors of smuggling would enhance its reputation or value.

"What else do you have, besides these paintings, Riggles?"

"For what, sir?"

"The *next auction*. Surely there will be more than these paintings."

"The usual sorts of lots, sir. Objets d'art. Silver. Some drawings. And, of course, the jewels. The last are in safe-keeping, and the rest is in storage here, being catalogued."

Darius walked toward a door at the back of the hall. Riggles scurried to catch up.

"Sir! I do not think— That is, the storage room is arranged most carefully, and visitors are not allowed to—"

"I am not a visitor, Riggles, and I have been in the storage before. I want to see just how sad a showing this second final auction will be."

The silver could not hold Emma's attention. Try as she might to concentrate on the silversmiths' marks and her notes, the arrival of that wagon yesterday kept interfering with her thoughts.

She had chewed over the reference to a prize all night. She had risen before dawn and sat at her window to watch day break, and in that silver silence a notion had come to her. Now she could not get it out of her head.

What if her father had accepted those wagons because he had no choice? It would explain behavior that she knew he abhorred in principle, and which he always believed would ruin Fairbourne's if it became commonplace.

If that had happened, what could coerce him to do it? She could think of only one thing. He would do it to protect that which was more valuable to him than Fairbourne's, or even his own good name.

He would do it to protect her.

Or Robert.

She gazed at her fluid reflection in a polished silver tray lying in front of her on the desk. Papa had always spoken with great conviction that Robert would return. He had been so sure that she had not dared doubt it herself, although everyone else thought they were both mad to believe it. That ship had gone down in the middle of the sea, but Papa had always said with certainty that Robert was not dead.

Was it possible that he spoke with such conviction because he actually knew it to be true?

Could Robert be the prize that must be won?

The notion had preoccupied her mind all morning. She had been relieved that Obediah was not in the exhibition hall when she arrived, because she wanted to be alone to sort it all out yet again. She kept trying to cast the idea away as a ridiculous speculation, but it fit what little she knew rather well.

A frightening emotion filled her heart. It was hope, and it wanted to burst free. She dared not allow that, but even contained, it had her on the verge of joyful tears. She proved unable to ignore its demand that she acknowledge that this idea might be correct. Robert might be alive but held by people who demanded that Fairbourne's pass their illicit goods.

If so, how long had her father been trying to protect him? It could have been since the day she last saw Robert. The wreck of that ship might have been only a tragic convenience that allowed Papa to create a false story about a false journey to explain Robert's absence to the world.

She tried to rationalize the criminal part of it. Under the circumstances, what father would refuse to include a few lots of questionable origin in his auctions? It was not as if smuggling were new or unusual. The Kent coastline had been a smugglers' lair for generations, and everyone knew it. Half that county's population must be involved in either bringing goods in or moving them on to London and other cities.

One might even say the wonder was that her father had not set up Fairbourne's specifically to enrich himself thus.

Only he had not, she knew. He prided himself on being a fair and honest man, and both qualities had distinguished his sales as well as his character. It must have sickened him to be required to debase himself, even if the reason was as good as they came. It would sicken her too, but if there were a chance she could see her brother again, if he might come home to her and Fairbourne's, and take their father's place, if she might laugh with him again, even one more time, she would do it too.

She had gone out in the morning and taken a better look at the contents of that wagon. All of it, even the wine, could be sold as if it came from someone in England. It should fetch a good price. Only she had no idea to whom she was supposed to give the proceeds.

She pondered whether to bring the wagon here, and what story to give Obediah. A plan was forming when abruptly the door opened, shattering her privacy.

Suddenly Southwaite stood there, looking at her with surprise. Obediah's head angled around from behind the earl's shoulder.

She managed a hooded glare at Obediah for failing to remove the Kauffman from the window. Then she greeted Southwaite with as bright an expression as she could muster.

"How good of you to visit us, sir. Were you riding by and decided to pay a very brief social call?"

"I have been here some hours and my purpose was not social."

"So you have chosen to interfere anyway, despite what I said at our last meeting."

"I have chosen to assess the situation here as I see fit, as I explained at our last meeting." He strolled into the chamber and looked at the deep shelves that held urns and old porcelain. While he distracted himself, she slid her catalogue notes under the silver tray.

"Lord Southwaite arrived early, and *immediately* went to your father's office, Miss Fairbourne." Obediah's expressions, invisible to Southwaite, communicated warning and distress. "He insisted that I accompany him *at once*, to explain what matters he might need explained."

That clarified why the Kauffman had not been removed from the window, but left other unfortunate puzzles. "Matters?" she asked, tipping her head up to smile at the earl.

Southwaite ignored her prompt. He gazed down at the table where she sat. "Do you have a fondness for silver?"

"Yes, I do. I possess an unabated passion for it. I always come here before auctions to admire the silver." It sounded stupid to her, but he had been the one to suggest such a possibility.

His right hand swung out sideways in a lazy gesture. Obediah rightly understood that he had been dismissed, and backed out of the chamber.

Southwaite sidled over to the table while his gaze examined its surface. "Some of it is handsome." He lifted a heavy candelabra and turned it to check its mark. "Is there more, or is this all of it?"

"For now, this is what has come in. Obediah told me that he anticipates another ten lots' worth next week."

He set the piece down. To her surprise he then sat on the edge of her table, his doeskin-encased hip and thigh supported by its edge and the rest of him still braced by his other leg. The casual position brought him alarmingly close to her.

"Ten lots will help, but the sale needs more than silver. It is not looking good, Miss Fairbourne. Better to retreat and be remembered as excellent rather than to let the world watch one's fall."

"I am sure that more is coming, including more paintings. Also books, I believe. And cases of very fine, very old wine." The lies trickled out with distressing ease. This auction had to be held now. More than pride and memories might be at stake.

"Wine?"

"So I hear. From the estate of a gentleman." She hoped she appeared blasé. "A gentleman who needs to pay creditors."

He examined her face, as if searching to see whether she merely put him off. She kept her expression innocent, she hoped, but his attention alone sent a series of tremors through her. She prayed she would not blush at the physical evidence that her reactions during that last meeting had apparently left her vulnerable in new ways to this man.

His gaze warmed and became even more direct. He saw the secret excitement in her. She just knew he did. His eyes carried a new intimacy that provoked alarming inner shudders. She worried that he did it deliberately, to distract her and make her pliable. To prove that he knew the Outrageous Misconception became less presumptuous with every contact that they had.

"You are not in mourning today." His examination moved down her body before finding her eyes again. His voice modulated in deep, quiet ways. He possessed a wonderful voice. Its sound affected her blood even when he vexed her. Right now she was helpless to its effects.

She self-consciously touched the pale rose muslin near her shoulder. "I am not in public. I am not receiving. No one is going to see me today."

"I am seeing you."

He certainly was. His attention overwhelmed her. So did the way his resting on the table made him loom large, too close and too *there*.

"Are you scolding me for inappropriate dress?" She wanted to sound haughty, but she spoke with breathless nervousness.

A smile. The disarming one. That smile was very masculine. Oh, yes, he knew the effect he was having on her.

"Far be it from me to scold you about wearing a hue that is so flattering to your complexion. As you said, no one will see you, except me. It is quite private here."

Very private. Obediah had left the door ajar a bit, but not by much. The workers sounded far away.

"Are you staying in town now, Lord Southwaite? You often prefer your country estate, I have heard, even during the Season." She spoke to fill the silence. Perhaps sound would help her evade the spell he was weaving.

"I was just there, for several days. I will remain in town for a while, I think."

That was not good news. "All is well in Kent, I trust."

"All is normal, at least. The volunteer units don their colors and drill, just as they do here in London. The tides still come in and the smugglers still run free. With the navy deployed to stop the French if they come, there is little to halt free trade on the coast now."

It took great effort not to react to this inopportune turn in the conversation. "Well, they are no real threat, unlike the French."

"If all that crossed were wine and lace, that would be true. However, spies also enter and information leaves." He sounded preoccupied, as if his mind did not really give much thought to his words.

Her mind, on the other hand, grew increasingly alarmed. *Wine and lace*. One might think he knew about that wagon.

She waited for him to say something else, or to move. Neither happened. He just sat there observing her with some private consideration apparent in his eyes.

Excitement danced in her chest, the beat increasing with each moment their gazes remained locked. She told herself she was reacting like a fool, but that did not stop the sensation.

She sensed him about to move. It was in the air more than his body, although the hand that rested on the table began to rise. Almost as quickly he halted the movement. One more look; then he broke the power he had been exerting over her as surely as if he had closed a door to his soul.

She found she was free and in possession of herself again, but not truly glad for it. She sought the thread of a subject that would set aside what had just happened.

"Obediah said you were asking about matters here," she said, remembering the way Obediah's face had contorted in wordless warning before he left.

"I thought that I should examine the accounts. Have you seen them?"

"Obediah deals with such things. What would I know about accounts?"

"They are not difficult to comprehend, if well-done. These are not very detailed, I am sorry to say. There are few names attached to either income or outlays."

She knew of what he spoke. She had tried to understand the books, but had given up. There were a variety of possible explanations for such sketchy bookkeeping, and she suspected the earl contemplated them. Considering what she had recently learned about her father's dealings, she did not want him doing that too much.

"I know that some consignors wanted privacy," she tried.

"So many?"

"My father had an excellent memory. All the rest of the information was probably in his head."

"No doubt." He pushed off the table and righted his coat. "I expect with some effort I will make sense of it all, even without his memory to guide me."

"Perhaps you should take the accounts with you, so you may study them at your leisure."

He thought about that, then waved the notion away. "I will do it here. It will give me a chance to see how Riggles is improving this sale, and whether it should even be held."

He took his leave then. As he did their gazes met once more, very briefly. During those few seconds she again could not look away, or move, or even breathe very well.

"Are you reading, Southwaite? Am I intruding?"

Darius looked up from his book. He had not been reading. His thoughts had been on a very nervous Obediah Riggles, suspiciously vague account books, and a pretty woman in a rose dress, surrounded by beautifully crafted old silver.

He had almost kissed Emma Fairbourne today. He would like to claim it had been a mad impulse. Only he never was a victim of such things, and today, in that back room, the decision to kiss her had been just that: a decision, one that had been very cool and not at all impulsive, and also very calculated.

His better sense had stopped him. He supposed he was glad for that. Mostly. Probably. That he really wasn't only forced the conclusion that he needed to end this alliance. He would do it very soon.

"You are not disturbing me, Lydia." He set the book aside while his sister sat down in a nearby chair. "That is a pretty dress."

She picked indifferently at the fabric on her lap and shrugged. Her maid had dressed Lydia's dark hair in the simplest of styles, a chignon on the nape of her neck. That had been Lydia's choice, not the servant's.

For reasons he did not understand, his sister did not care about her beauty, or about much at all. She had grown so quiet this last year, so nondescript and separate from the world, that he often feared for her health.

He wondered if he found her even more vague and devoid of warmth today because he had spent time with a woman full of spirit and vivid humanity. He looked in Emma Fairbourne's eyes and saw an active mind and frank disposition, and layers of thought and experience. He looked into Lydia's eyes and saw . . . nothing.

"You went down to Kent," she said. "You did not take me as you had promised."

Her voice carried a note of accusation. He was glad to hear anything that reflected some emotion. "I went with some friends. It would not have been appropriate to bring you."

She did not argue. She never did. She just gazed at him, her eyes shallow and opaque. "I want to go and live there."

"No." It was an old argument between them. Her relentless pursuit of isolation troubled him, like so much else about her.

"I will find a companion so I am not alone."

"No."

"I do not understand why you refuse me this, and force me to stay in town."

"You do not have to understand it. You only have to obey." He spoke with irritation, not at her rebelliousness but because this conversation was the only one they had anymore. He swallowed his resentment over that, and found a better tone. "You have removed yourself from society, from your friends, from our relatives . . ." *From me.* "I will not allow you to take the final step and remove yourself from even the observation of normal human activity."

Her gaze fixed on a spot on the distant carpet. He wished she would truly rebel, and start a row. Any evidence of emotion would be wonderful. Instead she wore the kind of manner a woman might don for a formal evening among strangers. It was as if she had put on a costume one day, and forgotten how to take it off when she returned home.

The insight distracted him. Put her at the right table with the right people, and her cool blandness would not look out of place at all. The peculiarity, and his worry, came from the mask never dropping, even with him. Especially with him.

"If I were a man, you would allow me to be whatever I needed to be." She said it quietly. Flatly. Then she left the library.

The chamber quaked for a moment with her sudden absence. Quickly, however, the shallow impression she had made on the space disappeared.

No chamber would dare obliterate Emma Fairbourne's presence like that. But then, her spirit did not whisper in a monotone, did it?

Chapter 8

"It will be a very small dinner party, Emma. Mrs. Markus specifically told me to bring you," Cassandra said, while she and Emma walked together on Bond Street the next afternoon.

"How small?"

"No more than twenty, I believe."

"It would be inappropriate for me to attend right now." She made a sweeping gesture at her subdued gray dress and lack of ornament, the evidence of her state of mourning.

"Mrs. Markus obviously does not think such restriction necessary for such a minor social event. Nor do I; nor would anyone else who will attend. I will bow to your choice, if I must, but I intend to arrange a full social agenda for you once it is acceptable."

Emma rather wished Cassandra would not do that. Emma had accompanied Cassandra to a few of her parties and dinners. She never felt comfortable at them. She so clearly was out of place that it was a wonder the other guests did not simply address her as such. *"The weather has been unseasonably warm, don't you think, Miss Whoever You*

Are?" Or *"Dear Social Clawing Friend of Lady Cassandra, have you decided how you will live now that your father's trade has been compromised by his death?"*

Even Cassandra's friendship was more a happy accident than a normal alliance. They had met two years ago while they both stood in front of a painting at the Royal Academy Exhibition. Emma had muttered to herself that the artist's handling of form was flamboyant but weak and Cassandra had taken umbrage because the artist was a friend of hers. They had argued for fifteen minutes and chatted for an hour more before Emma even learned her new friend was the sister of an earl.

"I will be much too busy for a social agenda, whatever that is," Emma said. "I have an auction house to manage. Remember?"

"I hope that you are not going to become like those men who attend to business and nothing else. With whom will I play, then? I know why you avoid my invitations, Emma. I promise that I will only arrange future ones to parties attended by the most democratic and artistic minds. Radicals and poets will never cut you. It would not be fashionable to do so in their circles."

"I am reassured that they would condescend to know such as me. I still will not fit in. That you think twenty is a small dinner party speaks eloquently to how our worlds are very different, and ne'er the twain will meet." They paused to admire some Italian cloth in a draper's window. "As for doing nothing but attending to business, I will try to avoid having it consume me. I currently can think of little else, however. Fortunately, I had a visitor yesterday and I believe she may be able to bring me more consignments and relieve me of one worry."

"Was it anyone I know?"

They walked on. "Possibly. She was French, although her English was quite good and not even heavily accented. She appeared poor, yet possessed a good deal of style."

"If she is French, it is unlikely that I know her. My contacts with the émigré community ceased once my interest in Jacques did."

"Surely your memories did not cease too."

"I have made progress in encouraging that they do, thank you."

"I think she may be an artist," Emma said. "She had smudges on her hands that appeared to be paints, or something else it would take time to remove, since she had not done so."

Cassandra turned her head toward Emma, interested now. "Might they have been ink stains?"

"Possibly. Yes, that makes sense now that I see them in my memory, but they were larger than one would get from carelessly blotting a letter."

"Then I may indeed know who she is, although I have never met her. I believe you were visited by the mysterious Marielle Lyon. What did she want with you?"

"She had questions about consigning items to auction." It was not a lie, although it was definitely one more deception. "I could use more lots, and I thought if I could find her, and offer a commission, she might point some of her countrymen toward Fairbourne's."

"It is said she is the niece of a count who was lost to the guillotine. Her family's fate is unknown. She escaped on her own during the terror."

"How horrible."

"Mmmm. Except some of her own people do not believe her story and whisper she is a fraud. Jacques was sure she was a shopkeeper's daughter who assumed another's past."

"Small wonder you called her mysterious. Do they all suspect her?"

"Only some. Others treat her like a princess. I am sure that she does know some émigrés who seek to convert treasures into coin."

That was what Emma hoped, but she had other reasons for wanting to find her mystery woman. "Do you know where she lives?"

"No, but perhaps I can show you how to find her."

A short while later Cassandra pulled a large mezzotint out of a bin at a print shop. She pointed to the inscription at the bottom. "This is from her studio. 'M. J. Lyon' is how she obscures that she is a woman."

Emma examined the mezzotint. It showed a rather tame view of the Thames near Richmond, and bore the name and address of the printer, M. J. Lyon. "The smudges on her hands could be the inks used in printing, I suppose. At least she has found a way to support herself, without going into service."

"It is said she makes others, with a fictitious name inscribed, that are less . . . formal." Cassandra carried the print to the proprietor, and opened her reticule for some coins.

"Scandalous ones?" Emma whispered. She knew there were very naughty images to be had, although she had never seen them.

Cassandra accepted the rolled print, and handed it to Emma. "Mocking ones. Humorous prints that poke at society's foibles and hypocrisies. Satires of government leaders. Jacques said he had seen them, and knew they were hers. He would not give me the name she uses, however."

"Why not?"

"It appears that one of her satires had my brother as its subject, wearing an ass's ears and tail. How silly of Jacques to think I would mind." Cassandra linked her arm through Emma's and guided her out of the shop. "Now, tell me about this idea you have, of offering commissions if someone brings consignors to you. I am insulted you did not think of me if you sought to recruit such agents, instead of some woman whose name you did not even know."

Before Emma had a chance to respond, they were distracted by a grand coach stopping in the street right beside where they walked. Even before the wheels stopped rolling, the door swung and Lord Southwaite stepped out, blocked their path, and bowed.

"Miss Fairbourne, how happy an accident to see you as I rode by. I was on my way to call on you." He added another bow in Cassandra's direction. "Lady Cassandra."

Cassandra bestowed the tightest of smiles. "It is always

a joy to see you, Southwaite. May I ask how your sister fares?"

Expression amiable, but eyes narrow, he maintained the pretense of friendship. "She fares very well. Indeed, she flourishes. And your aunt, Lady Cassandra? Has she been out of late?"

"My aunt finds that the comforts of her own home surpass those of anyone else's these days."

"I am sure that your company is a great comfort to her."

"I like to think so."

Emma all but groaned. She disliked when she was with Cassandra and was treated to these meaningless greetings. Neither of these people cared for the other, and it had been perverse for Southwaite to go out of his way to engage in such useless conversation.

"Lady Cassandra, I hope you will not mind if I steal Miss Fairbourne away from you," Southwaite said, still smooth and politely bland. "There is a conversation that she and I must have that should not be delayed."

Cassandra turned curious eyes on Emma, who now tried to appear as blasé as the two of them. She attempted a tiny shrug that only Cassandra would see.

"It concerns your father's estate," Southwaite said to Emma.

"Oh," Cassandra said. "I did not realize that you had a role in settling that, Southwaite." She peered at Emma with undisguised curiosity, and looked a little hurt.

"I am sure Lord Southwaite's conversation can wait until tomorrow," Emma said.

"It really should be today," he corrected. He opened the door of his coach.

Cassandra's eyebrows rose a fraction. "Southwaite, I am handing my friend over to your protection, not for you to subject her to scandal. You of all men should know better."

Southwaite did not so much color in anger as blush. Emma wondered if she would ever see such a thing again.

"You must stay with us, Cassandra," Emma said.

"Southwaite's instincts for discretion are telling him that would be worse. Is that not true, sir?"

"Then tomorrow will have to do," Emma said triumphantly.

"Not at all," Southwaite said. "Lady Cassandra, perhaps you would take Miss Fairbourne to the park. I will follow, and once there we can all stroll where we want and have conversations as needed."

Cassandra pondered the idea at length. She mumbled about such an outing not being in her plans and how she would rather not be diverted. Finally, however, with much muttering about the willfulness of certain lords who think the entire world should accommodate them, she agreed to his plan.

Emma had strong words for her once they were in her carriage. "You could have gotten me out of this. You almost did."

Cassandra turned those big blue eyes on her. "That would have been a disservice to you, Emma. Whatever the earl wants to say, it could have been said on any day. It could have been said by his solicitor, if you think about it."

"Quite true. That is why you should not have let him trap me into this, let alone become his accomplice."

"Darling, I do not care for him, but he is *an earl*. If an earl goes out of his way to spend time with a woman, she should at least find out why."

Emma knew why. He wanted to have that conversation about the auction house that she had thus far dodged.

"If you want my opinion," Cassandra mused, "I think Southwaite is pursuing you."

"What a mad idea. As you just said, he is *an earl*."

"He is without a mistress now. He sent the last one packing a month ago. So he has to pursue someone. Why not you?"

Emma thought the answer to that was obvious. She was not about to list the many reasons why men, and especially earls, did not pursue her.

"How delicious if I am correct," Cassandra said. "I hope

so. I am sure you will be unable to tolerate him, Emma, so he will pursue in vain. I would not mind seeing him get his comeuppance. I think, however, that you should practice your flirting on him before you reject him outright. Since you will not like him much, there will be no danger, but his frustration will be all the greater for it."

Emma avoided blushing only by keeping every memory of her experiences with Southwaite out of her mind. She managed that only by changing the subject. "I think that you understated the situation when you said the two of you do not rub well together."

"He has never forgiven me for befriending his sister. She is a dear young woman, but a bit odd. Since I am a bit odd too, she and I got on very well. Then Southwaite forbade the friendship." She made a face. "So now poor Lydia has no friends at all."

"How cruel of him."

"I am confident that the more you know him, the less you will like him. I anticipate that comeuppance with secure delight."

"You will be disappointed. He is not pursuing me."

Cassandra laughed, and patted Emma's hand like a mother might.

Chapter 9

S outhwaite was indeed waiting in the park, standing where his carriage had stopped on Rotten Row. He did not appear to be a man in pursuit. Emma thought he looked more like a man who had just eaten spoiled food. While evidence he pursued her would have been bad news, the true reason for his interest struck her as far worse.

Cassandra strolled with them no more than fifty feet before she saw a friend and diverted her path in that direction. Emma paced along beside Southwaite, taking two steps to each of his strides.

"It is time for us to address the reason I first called on you, don't you think, Miss Fairbourne? Whenever I raise the matter, you manage to deflect it. However, the future of your father's business must be settled. It gives me no pleasure to disappoint you or to thwart your carefully laid schemes, but I have concluded that the business must be sold as soon as possible, for your sake."

It all came out at once, as if he had rehearsed it in front of a looking glass to ensure he communicated his resolve in both tone and expression.

"For *my* sake? Are you so bold as to try to make this sound as if you are doing me a favor? That is rich, Lord Southwaite, when more likely you are seeking revenge for the embarrassment you experienced due to those presumptions you had."

"You will not succeed in distracting me with a row by dragging that up now. It will not work this time."

"I think we should wait to talk about this until after the next sale."

"Do not dare to treat me like a fool, Miss Fairbourne. I know what you are up to. After that sale, you will plan another, and another. Each one will decrease Fairbourne's prestige. I have no confidence that Riggles can manage the business as you claim."

"I do. He is very competent."

"Indeed? He seemed incapable of answering the smallest questions that I posed about the accounts, and reacted as if he had never heard of Andrea del Sarto. No, I have made up my mind. I will seek a buyer at once, and we will be done with it."

And that was going to be that, his tone said. The lord had spoken.

"The proceeds will ensure your future," Darius said, to emphasize the benefits of his intentions.

Miss Fairbourne reacted badly in ways that could not be missed. Brittle white lights glinted in her clear blue eyes. Unfortunate pink blotches marred her otherwise flawless complexion.

"You are welcome to sell your half if you choose," she said. "Indeed I hope that you will, for *my* sake, because you are becoming a pest."

He halted mid-stride at the bald insult. Miss Fairbourne calling him a pest was rich indeed, coming from a woman who probably spent hours each day plotting just how biting she would be.

"You should be grateful someone is looking out for you," he said.

"Dear heavens, is it not bad enough that you want to ruin my life and destroy all my memories and make me compromise my duty? Do not make it worse by pretending to be a protector. You have already shown your natural colors where that is concerned, and I would be a fool to think you had my welfare at heart."

He wished he had not seen her on the street and arranged for this talk in a public place. Emma Fairbourne's bluntness and high emotion were not in the least inhibited by her knowing she would be visible to others. He, on the other hand, was all too aware they were not alone in the park. He did not feel free to release or reveal his building annoyance in any way.

He forced a smile and a casual stance so anyone watching might believe this was a friendly chat. "I am sympathetic that you probably think of the auction house as embodying your father's spirit, Miss Fairbourne. However, his entire fortune was that business and its property. If anything of value is to be salvaged for you, if you are to have any income, it must be sold."

"You are wrong there. Fairbourne's itself will provide me with an income. Furthermore, that is my only option for having one. Selling it will do nothing to provide for my future, for the same reason it cannot be sold at all," she said. "The part of Fairbourne's that you do not own was not bequeathed to me, but to my father's oldest child. It now belongs to my brother, Robert."

Her stubbornness was about that? It was inconceivable that she held to this view. "I am aware that your father harbored a hope that your brother would return. However, you must know that will not happen."

"What I know is this—my father's heir is my brother, and it is my duty to preserve my brother's inheritance for when he comes back."

Darius controlled his simmering anger but it was becoming more difficult with each word she spoke. He had sought

this meeting after long debate with himself. He had concluded that it was time to resolve a simple matter, and, damnation, he would do so.

"You are determined to force me into being cruelly
direct, Miss Fairbourne."

"I have never objected to forthright speaking. I prize it."

"Then give this the value it is due. Your brother will
not be coming back. You must go and ask the courts to
declare him deceased and you must claim the inheritance.
Then the auction house *will be sold*. I advise you to put your
proceeds into bonds so you have an ongoing income. My
solicitor will arrange that purchase, and set it up with the
bank."

Her hard expression increasingly softened with each
word he said. Before he was finished she appeared sad and
vulnerable. Her glare suddenly sparkled and her eyes took
on new depths. Her bold, direct gaze mesmerized him for
a moment, during which, once again, he lost hold on his
anger, and even his thoughts.

Then he realized the effect had been caused by tears
flooding those blue pools.

Hell, she was going to weep.

She composed herself rather than succumb completely
to her emotion. That both impressed and relieved him, but
he was at a disadvantage now anyway. Again.

He narrowed his eyes on her, trying to see if she
had called up tears specifically to get the upper hand. He
had known too many women who were wont to do that. Miss
Fairbourne's struggle with emotion appeared true, however.
He cursed himself for speaking so severely.

She sniffed. "My father never had my brother declared
dead, and it is not for me to do so now, and show such little
faith. Robert is alive, I am very sure. I feel it in my heart. I
always have. I know it sounds irrational. Even Cassandra
thinks so, but there it is. I will not be claiming Robert's share
of Fairbourne's."

Darius did not relish what he was about to say, but Miss
Fairbourne clearly did not comprehend how vulnerable her

situation was. He tried to make his expression kinder than his words would be.

"I can force a sale. If I do, it will leave you destitute if the proceeds from your father's share are set aside for an heir other than you."

She turned those moist blue eyes on him, shocked. "Would you be so cruel as to remove a lone woman's means of support?"

He gazed in those sad eyes. Abruptly, and annoyingly, the wind went out of his sails.

He found himself battling the urge to take her head in his hands and kiss the tears away. "With your father gone, the business cannot provide support. Mr. Riggles cannot take his place. No one can, and I will not allow another auction that might result in unintended fraud. Furthermore, if we do not sell, Fairbourne's will become worthless within the year and there will be nothing for either you or your brother, should he indeed return."

She sniffed a few more times, and each one seemed to punctuate how heartless she found him. "I have heard every word you have said, Lord Southwaite. I appreciate and understand your concerns. Therefore I have hit on a compromise. I am going to tell Obediah to continue with the next auction. I will urge him to make it as grand as possible, so that we prove to you that you are wrong."

Had he not just told her that he would not allow another auction? Had she not heard that, or had she simply ignored it?

A man and woman approached on the path. Miss Fairbourne's dewy eyes would be visible to anyone who drew near. He quickly handed her his handkerchief, lest the scandal sheets be full of references to Lord S driving an unknown woman to tears in Hyde Park in midday.

She dabbed at her eyes, but did not do a very good job at it. Her liquid gaze remained on him as she waited for his response to her new plan.

Hell.

"When do you think Riggles will have this auction ready?"

"Three weeks, I believe." Her face lit with joy and relief. "Oh, thank you, Lord Southwaite, for being so kind and agreeable. You will see how well Fairbourne's will acquit itself. I have every faith in Obediah, and you can too."

He did not recall being agreeable. He had only asked—

"I should find Cassandra now." She began walking again. Almost jauntily. Nary a tear in sight. "Ah, there she is," she noted as the carriages came in sight. "She will be very disappointed that she was so wrong about you."

"How so?"

"She is not aware of your investment in Fairbourne's. I assumed you would not want it known, of course. So she— you will find this amusing—she thinks that you are pursuing me."

"What an amazing notion."

"Isn't it?" Miss Fairbourne giggled as they walked to the carriages. "She does not even know about the Outrageous Misconception that first day, so her imagination created this absurd idea out of whole cloth."

"I trust that you explained her error."

"Of course, but she thinks that I am too ignorant to see what is in front of my nose."

"She is a woman famous for enjoying romantic intrigues herself, and possibly believes the whole world joins in her pastime. As I have already warned, if you are known as her friend, there are those who will think that you do."

He received a sharp look for that. "I am sure that you think you are helping me with advice, Lord Southwaite, but I do not appreciate being warned off my friend. Please do not presume such authority. I am not your sister."

So Lady Cassandra had shared that story about Lydia, had she? Well, he would not scold again.

Miss Fairbourne was correct. She was not his sister, or even his responsibility. He had no duty to save her from anything, even scandal.

Darius handed Miss Fairbourne over to Lady Cassandra, whose eager eyes foretold the quizzing waiting for Miss Fairbourne once they were alone. After a happy wave out the window, and a smile that was only slightly self-satisfied, Miss Fairbourne rode away.

Darius climbed into his own carriage. The conversation had not gone well. Even harsh forthrightness had not succeeded with her. In fact, he suspected that she had herded him to exactly where she wanted him and had not even missed a step as she did so.

If he were to make any progress regarding the settlement of Fairbourne's, he obviously would have to change tactics. He had learned a thing or two about this woman during the last week. He was confident that there were better ways besides reason and talk to make Emma Fairbourne surrender to his way of thinking.

Chapter 10

Darius relit his cigar and gave it three sound puffs while listening to Ambury describe a recent adventure. Across the table, Kendale blew smoke back and downed a good gulp of brandy.

"Nothing more than fiddling while Rome burns," Kendale muttered, interrupting Ambury's tale. His green eyes shot the angry sparks that so often marked his expression. His free hand raked his dark hair in the habit he had when annoyed, which he seemed to be more often than not these days.

"I think that you should get on your horse and spend the next year riding up and down the coast, making sure we are all safe, Kendale. I know that I would sleep better if you did," Ambury said.

Kendale was not so absorbed that he missed the sarcasm. His glare said that he did not approve of Ambury's devil-may-care attitude when all indications said the devil did care, and was too busy these days. Kendale was among the overwhelming majority of citizens who believed the French would mount an invasion soon. Ambury was less convinced.

Along with Darius, however, both were of like mind that precautions were in order. They all had spent the last four months arranging a system of watches and surveillance on the southeast coast that focused not on spotting a French fleet, but on singular, insidious invasions.

Darius inserted himself so these old friends did not start an argument right here in Brooks's. "Kendale, we have done what can be done. It is too much for one man, or even three."

Or four or five. That their group was diminished from its size of several months ago hung there unspoken for a moment, and all of their glances met in silent acknowledgment of the fact.

"We have forged a chain full of weak links. I don't like being in bed with criminals either," Kendale said. "Unlike some people." He made it a point not to look at the *some people* he referred to.

"I only get into bed with female criminals, and even then most rarely, and for the best of reasons," Ambury said. "I think that your humor would be much improved if you got into bed with *anyone*, Kendale. If we work on your manners, you might see some success on that before Michaelmas."

Kendale uttered a crude sexual curse. Two gentlemen sitting close to them had been arguing about the rebellion in Ireland but ceased all talk on overhearing. They raised their eyebrows.

"See here, Kendale, this isn't an officers' mess," one of them admonished.

Kendale sucked in his cheeks. "More's the pity."

Ambury ignored him. "As I was saying before Kendale began being rude, my little investigation on the lady's behalf concluded successfully, and she now has proof that her husband was conniving with her trustee to sell off that land she inherited."

"I hope that she knows a good solicitor who has friends in Chancery," Darius said.

"I made a few recommendations there."

"I also trust that you were well paid, but discreetly so your father does not hear you are selling your services like some tradesman."

"Very well paid and very discreetly. The earl will be none the wiser."

"In coin, or in gratitude?"

Ambury did not respond.

Kendale laughed darkly. "What you were paid with won't keep the bailiffs away."

"I fear not. It seemed a very good bargain at the time, though."

Darius left Ambury to his memories of that bargain and Kendale to his eternal contemplation of whatever made him brood.

His own thoughts wandered to Fairbourne's, as they tended to do a lot these days. It was not long before those thoughts did not dwell on auctions or ill-considered investments or even vague accounts, but once again on a woman in a rose dress sitting in the dusty light, surrounded by glinting silver objects.

"You are distracted," Ambury said while he called for more brandy.

"I suppose I am," Darius said. "I am pondering a point of etiquette, if you must know."

Kendale laughed sardonically. "If I ever have the chance to speak my mind to my brother about breaking his neck in that fall and sticking me with this title, points of etiquette will figure prominently in my grievances."

"Stop complaining, as if the man sought to make you miserable by leaving a fortune and a title to you. The army has even more etiquette than we do, so you are ridiculous," Ambury chided.

"It is not relentless in the army."

"You mean that gentlemen can behave like scoundrels sometimes, on the field? Spare me the details." Ambury pointedly turned his attention to Darius. "I have never met another man who can show the world such perfect behavior while privately living as he wants, the way you do, Southwaite.

I would think that your talent means never needing to ponder anything regarding when to bow to propriety, and when to ignore it."

"It has to do with a woman."

"Kendale is no use to you, then. Your only hope of advice is me."

Kendale did not disagree. He sat back in his chair and smoked, removing himself from the conversation.

Darius put the question to Ambury, but felt foolish doing so. "Is it appropriate to pursue a woman who is in mourning? I almost kissed one recently."

"Full mourning or half mourning?"

"Full. But . . ." Darius felt obliged to give a bigger picture in his own defense. "I have good reason to think she is not prostrate with grief any longer. I daresay she is not the sort of woman to lose her wits at any time, even this."

"I expect one should be careful, as you concluded. Although I would let the lady have some say in it. She might find a kiss very comforting."

Kendale decided his advice was needed, after all. "If you stood down, Southwaite, it was because you knew you should. You are only trying to rationalize taking her when you know it would be dishonorable, seems to me."

Ambury sighed heavily at their friend's lack of tact. "He spoke of a mere kiss, Kendale. I knew the army would coarsen you a little, but really—"

"If speaking what is what, instead of meaningless witty nonsense, makes me coarse, so be it. As for the *mere kiss*— when was the last time any of us kissed a woman without a conquest being the goal? Hell, we aren't schoolboys anymore."

Darius would have demurred with some of that meaningless witty nonsense, except that Kendale was correct. Kendale's bluntness derived, ironically, from a mind that saw the world most sharply.

"Hell," Kendale muttered again, sitting upright, his attention suddenly diverted from their table. "I thought the bastard had gone up north."

Darius turned his head, but he already knew what had set Kendale cursing again. A man had just entered the room, and was joining a party down near the door. Tall, elegant, and deliberately old-fashioned in silk brocade waistcoat and dark queue, the man glanced once in their direction, caught Darius's eye, and reacted enough to acknowledge the party down the way noting his arrival.

"Penthurst?" Ambury asked without looking. He received no response, which was answer enough.

Kendale's eyes might have been throwing daggers, his glare was that sharp. "I've half a mind to—"

"You will not," Ambury said. "Call up the other half of your mind, like Southwaite and I have learned to do."

"It was a duel, Kendale," Darius said briskly, hearing his voice sound masculine and tolerant even if he still harbored other reactions. "I was his second, so I know all was correct."

"It was murder."

"Lakewood issued the challenge." Ambury almost sounded bored, as if reminding Kendale, and himself, of this had grown tiresome. "Hell of a thing, though. Who ever thought Lakewood would die in a duel over a woman."

Who ever, indeed. The Baron Lakewood had not been a man quick to lose his head or heart over a woman, let alone his life. Yet that was what had happened. As a result, they all had lost a good friend, and their circle had never been quite the same since.

Actually, they had lost two good friends.

Darius felt the presence of Penthurst at the other end of the chamber, casting a pall over their own little group. *You should have stopped him.* The words flowed inaudibly, echoing the only ones spoken between Darius and Penthurst since that tragic morning.

Yes, they should have.

"Damnation," Ambury said, peeved that his good mood had been spoiled. "Hell, but I miss him."

It was not clear which lost old friend he meant.

* * *

Emma's coachman made it obvious that he thought this call ill-advised. While he handed her out of the carriage, he kept most of his attention over his shoulder, surveying the crowd that thronged by on this narrow street near London's wall, eyeing their rough garments and cringing from their loud calls and shouts.

"I best come with you, Miss Fairbourne." He glanced at the horse with regret. He patted its rump, as if saying good-bye.

"I am going to that building right there, Mr. Dillon. The one with the dark blue door. The windows are open, I see, and there are a good number of them. Perhaps you should remain with the carriage, and listen. I will call you if there is any trouble, or if I need your protection."

Mr. Dillon remained skeptical. She reassured him that she could not afford to lose the horse any more than he wanted to lose his employer. Before he could object further, she walked the thirty feet to the blue door.

A stout woman dressed in a simple fawn dress, white cap, and apron, opened the door. Emma explained that she wanted to speak with M. J. Lyon.

Not bothering to accept the offered card, the woman turned on her heel and walked away. Emma did not know if that had been a dismissal or an invitation. Deciding to assume the latter, she followed the old-fashioned full skirt into a room that must have been intended as a dining room for this house.

An assortment of tables cluttered the space, and stacks of papers filled the bookcases. Women bent over those tables, dipping brushes and little bundled rags into pans of colors, then daubing at engravings set in front of them.

Murmurs filled the chamber as the women spoke to one another. Emma heard enough to know the women were all French. Some very sumptuous garments and wigs could be seen beneath their aprons and caps. She guessed they were all émigrés, aristocrats, and other wellborn women who had fled a France that had become dangerous to them and their families.

Her guide left her and squeezed between tables and chairs to the back of the chamber. She said something and pointed. Another woman had been bending over one of the tables, talking to a worker, and her head now rose. Marielle Lyon, the woman who had delivered that wagon to Emma, peered across the space at her visitor.

She made her way to where Emma waited. "How did you find me?"

Emma opened her reticule and removed the folded mezzotint that Cassandra had purchased. "A friend knew who you might be from my description. Once I said your hands were stained with inks, she guessed you were the woman behind the name on this print."

Marielle made a face. "I did not think the whole world knew that this studio belongs to me. I must find another name."

"She has been friends with some of your countrymen. That is how she knew your identity. It is not the whole world that knows."

"Enough know. Too many, perhaps. Soon the print shops will not take the images made by so many French women." A question from a nearby table regarding color distracted her. She stepped over, scrutinized the print, and shook her head. *"Plus ici."* She pointed at the paper.

She returned to Emma.

"The rags put the color on evenly and well," Emma said. "I did not realize it was done like that."

"It is our way. We call it *a la poupee."* She paused, to translate. "With the little doll."

The bundled and tied rags did look like little dolls. Emma watched while feminine hands dabbed away. She wondered if any of the satirical prints were being made.

"So, you are here," Marielle said. "If you come to ask about that man, I have seen him. I do not think he can tell you anything. He is—how do you say—a lickey. One who does as another bids."

"A lackey. Did you learn nothing at all from him?"

"*Rien.* I told him you want to speak to him, and would pay him well." She smiled impishly, and suddenly looked much younger. "Your house is very fine. I think you will not mind a few coins, if necessary, yes?"

"Not at all." Emma dug into her reticule and plucked out a few shillings, assuming the mention of a few coins was a hint as well as a report. "Thank you for your kind help. Please write to me, if he tells you he is willing to meet me. Tell him that I need to know the details of the arrangement. Say also that I want to resolve the matter of the great prize, and request instructions on how to do so."

Marielle accepted the money without comment, then turned away to return to her work. "I will inform you if he agrees. I think I will see him again. He is about sometimes." She waved toward the street beyond.

"I have come about something else too," Emma said, stopping her.

Emma explained her idea that Marielle might recommend some of her countrymen to Fairbourne's, if they had good paintings they wanted to sell. "I will give you ten percent of whatever is Fairbourne's commission," she said.

Marielle thought it over. "Twenty percent. You will have these paintings not at all without me."

Marielle might claim to be of aristocratic blood, but she could bargain like a street peddler. "Twenty, then."

"You must promise secrecy. They are proud people often, and do not want it known that they must sell their heritage to eat."

"Fairbourne's is well-known for discretion."

"Some come here at night across the sea. They will have no documents for what they bring. Like that wagon."

Indignation jumped inside Emma, but expressing any feelings of insult would be comical, with this woman of all people. Fairbourne's had accepted that wagon, hadn't it?

Who was she to start getting particular about documents of paintings smuggled in by refugees?

"Good paintings have recorded provenances," Emma said. "I will need the history of ownership up until the current owner. The best collectors know to ask for it, and to be suspicious of old masters that suddenly appear with no references or pedigree."

"Much like some people, you mean." Marielle gave one of her little shrugs. "Eh, *il est compliqué le faire*, but I will see what can be had."

Emma left, hoping she had struck some kind of bargain with this young woman who, according to Cassandra, had appeared suddenly, with no references and suspect pedigree. She prayed her message would get to the man with the wagon. She also hoped that Marielle would cajole some good art out of the émigrés.

She could not be sure either would happen, however. In fact, she might never see or hear from Marielle again. She would need to enhance the auction in other ways too, and soon.

Chapter 11

Emma was not able to go to the auction house for two days. Obediah sent messages both mornings to say Lord Southwaite had come, so she should stay away. Obediah added to both notes his worry about being able to play his new role persuasively with the earl. It seemed that Southwaite had taken to inviting conversation about the attributions and qualities of the paintings now hanging in the exhibition hall.

Vexed with the catalogue's delay, Emma turned her mind to other problems, such as whether to include that wagon's contents in the auction. She would prefer to know more about her father's arrangements before committing such a crime. In particular, she desperately wanted some indication that her theory regarding the "prize" was accurate. If no further information came to her, she would have a hard decision to make.

If she considered it necessary to auction the wagon's contents, she would then have to find a way to do so without Southwaite suspecting what it really was. She could not avoid him seeing all the wine once the auction's preview nights were prepared, but until then she preferred not being quizzed on it.

Deciding that she might solve two problems with one solution, she had Maitland carry in the books and objets d'art from the wagon so she could spend her Southwaite days, which were becoming annoyingly numerous, working on a potential part of the catalogue at home.

"I may have a new patron for Fairbourne's," Cassandra announced the second afternoon while they pretended they were going to order hats at a milliner's. Neither of them could afford this shop's fine wares right now, but Cassandra always received groveling service due to her position in society. Emma was not above having some fun by hanging on to Cassandra's skirt hem.

"I hope he has a good collection," Emma said as she picked through a basket overflowing with sumptuous ribbons. "Who is it?"

Cassandra studied a fashion plate showing an exotic turban. "Count Alexis von Kardstadt of Bavaria,"

Emma lost all interest in the ribbons. "Do you mean it? You know him? I read that he was sending his collection to England for sale, since France is not hospitable these days, but I just assumed that Christie's—"

"As did Christie's assume. However, his man called on my aunt soon after he disembarked, and she actually received him—it has been months since she accepted a caller—and it turns out Alexis's servant remembers meeting me when I traveled with my aunt. I took advantage of the connection and suggested that he consider Fairbourne's for selling the collection." She glanced over. "I do get ten percent, correct?"

"Of course."

Cassandra removed a bonnet that she had donned and tossed it aside. She primped her raven curls in the looking glass. "Unfortunately, I am going to have to remove one of the jewels from my consignment. The ruby necklace with the tiny pearls."

"You dangle the chance of rarities with one hand while snatching away a certain sale with another, Cassandra. Why are you taking away one of the best pieces?"

"My aunt needs it. That was why the factor came to call, and why she received him. Count Alexis has asked for it back, so she needs it back from me too. It is a family item that the count should not have given away." She picked up a lustrous raw silk cloth patterned in blue and red and began trying to tie a turban cap around her crown. A shopgirl hurried over to help.

Emma waited until the elaborate folds and turns were done and the girl had left. "Are you saying that your aunt and the count were . . . good friends?"

"It appears so."

"Isn't he much younger than she is? He only wed recently."

"Mmmmmm. Family jewels given impetuously in passion are now needed for that young wife." Cassandra kept turning her head while she admired the turban from this angle and that in the looking glass.

"Is that intended as a bawdy double entendre?"

Cassandra looked startled, then burst out laughing. "In both meanings my aunt is sympathetic, and I cannot refuse her, since she is generous enough to allow me to live with her. So I need it back. Hopefully you will get a wonderful collection that will far surpass my jewels in attracting the best of society." She touched the red and blue silk lovingly. "I think that I will have this made."

"You cannot afford it."

"Once the count's man visits Fairbourne's tomorrow, and you convince him to consign with you, I will have expectations beyond what comes from my jewels."

"Tomorrow!"

"I told him that Mr. Riggles would meet with him tomorrow morning. I decided there should be no delay. We don't want him talking to Mr. Christie first, do we?"

No, they did not. Only Mr. Riggles could never convince this factor to entrust the collection to Fairbourne's, and

Emma was not sure that her participation would help or even be agreeable to the man.

For the first time, she seriously doubted whether she would be able to keep Fairbourne's alive. The loss of her father's connections and reputation had effects both large and small, and she could no longer ignore them. He would have met with this agent of the count, and impressed him with his charm, expertise, and manner. He would have entertained this man in ways that she, a woman, never could.

Nor could another man take his place. That truly discouraged her. Even Mr. Nightingale would have been overwhelmed tomorrow, and young Mr. Laughton, if she sent for him and he came, would appear a schoolboy struggling to learn a foreign language in such negotiations.

Her heart thickened while she lined up all the circumstances that weighed against her chance for success. They overwhelmed her resolve and confidence. She was going to fail, and Robert's birthright would be lost when she did. Maybe Robert himself would be too.

She normally held back considerations of all that might mean, but the weight on her spirit sent her mind in that direction now. If Fairbourne's closed, Robert's disappointment upon returning would be horrible to see, especially if her own inadequacies had caused it. Even if the money from the sale waited for him, it would take years to rebuild the business.

Would their deep bond even survive it? She and Robert had always been very close, partners in play and in crime when children and mutually sympathetic to life's hurts as they got older. He had comforted her during her first tendre for a man who never realized she existed, and she in turn had understood his disappointment when Papa had forbade his pursuit of an actress. Robert had understood the awkwardness of having regular contact with society, all the while knowing society would never accept them as equals. Papa had walked that odd line with aplomb, but both she and Robert had felt the chasm deeply.

She ached for some proof that Robert still lived and she might have him back one day. Images of that reunion tortured her with their impossible hope for happiness. She hated not knowing for certain that she was right, and dreaded placing one foot in the wrong place on the perilous path she felt she was walking. And now, with this opportunity to succeed with at least one part of her plan, she worried deeply that it would disappear because she could not hide that Fairbourne's survived as only a shadow of its former self.

Unless . . .

A possible solution entered her mind. It became a faint flame illuminating the darkness of her mood. It flickered while she watched the shopgirl pin the turban's fabric and fit it to Cassandra's head.

The idea was outlandish. It would never work. She had no choice except to try, however.

*   *   *

My lord,

I write to you on a matter of mutual interest and some urgency, since you are a part owner of my brother's auction house. I have reason to believe that Herr Ludwig Werner, a representative of Count Alexis von Kardstadt, will visit Fairbourne's tomorrow morning. He will come to discuss placing part of the count's collection on consignment with us.

Such a collection will bring the next auction much fame and attention, and greatly enhance its offerings.

Mr. Riggles has informed me that you have been at the property quite a bit lately. It could be awkward if you were there again tomorrow.

While the presence of a man of your stature would impress the count's representative, I am sure that you would find the haggling that is likely to ensue distasteful, and the public evidence of your investment in such trade demeaning.

I am convinced that you must obey my directions on this, and absent yourself, so that we will avoid any gossip or difficulties.

It is my intention to be present, to welcome him in my father's name. I will be sure to inform you of the day's outcome.

I have the honor to remain, my lord, Your Lordship's faithful servant,

Emma Fairbourne

The letter arrived by evening post, along with several from the coast that Darius had been awaiting. He left it for last while he read the surveillance reports. Finally he broke the seal and read Miss Fairbourne's "directions."

He examined the penmanship afterward. The woman who had written this possessed a straightforward hand that had banished most flourishes and affectations from its lines. The letters flowed clearly, even elegantly, but they did not angle much. Rather there was a tendency for the *H*s and *T*s to stand upright, and oblige the letters around them to aim for the vertical too.

It was just the sort of penmanship he would expect of Miss Fairbourne.

How unexpectedly thoughtful of her to warn him to stay away so his interest in Fairbourne's remained a secret. She rightly pointed out that hawking the auction house's service to a potential consignor was not something an earl should be known as doing.

However, her concern was also odd. If she truly cared about the auction house surviving, she should be begging him to attend in the morning, no matter what an earl should be seen doing. She should want him to help Riggles cajole this collection out of the count's factor by flaunting another lord's patronage of the establishment.

The more he thought about it, the more he found the letter suspicious.

Perhaps someone other than a count's factor would be visiting Fairbourne's, someone whom it was vital that her father's partner not meet. He would prefer not to suspect her along with her father, but if illicit goods had moved through Fairbourne's in the past, they might in the future too.

Nor did he care for her command that he "obey" her directions. His faithful servant, hell. Miss Fairbourne could be over bold. Unwisely so at times. That she did not know her place did not concern him too much. Her misunderstanding of *his* place needed to be corrected, however.

He had not yet decided what to do when he called for his horse in the morning. Once he mounted, he turned in the direction of Albemarle Street, however.

Partly he did so because it was in his interest to see if a count's factor really thought to consign the collection to Fairbourne's today. If no such appointment took place, he needed to find out what else Mr. Riggles and Miss Fairbourne were plotting that required his absence.

Mostly, however, he admitted that he went because he did not like the implications of that letter. Miss Fairbourne appeared to believe that if she wanted a certain earl to dance to her tune, she need merely command it.

The paintings in the great hall at Fairbourne's had been hung differently when Darius arrived at eleven o'clock. From the sweat on the brows of the workmen, he gathered most of the changes had just been made.

The new arrangement made much out of little. Paintings did not hang so high or so low or so close to one another, and therefore filled the center of the towering walls more completely. It had been a shrewd solution, one that he might not have noticed if he had not seen the obvious holes a few days ago.

Riggles appeared dismayed when he saw Darius. "My lord, I did not expect you. Miss Fairbourne said that we should not anticipate a visit today."

"I decided to call while on my way to elsewhere. I trust that my presence is not ill timed."

Riggles's frozen smile and strangled silence suggested it was.

"I can make myself scarce if I am interfering," Darius soothed. "I will secrete myself in the office, and continue perusing the accounts."

"I regret that the office will be needed soon, sir."

"Then I will nose around the storage, and see if anything has come in that I want to bid upon for my own account."

"Regrettably the storage room is too full to allow comfortable previews."

Just then the door to the storage opened and Miss Fairbourne emerged. She wore mourning clothes today, very fine ones. Her hair, long and free in the current fashion, fell in little curls and waves down to her breasts. She froze briefly upon seeing him talking to Riggles in the great room, then joined them.

"I think all is as ready as it will ever be, Obediah," she said.

"Except perhaps me, Miss Fairbourne." Riggles shifted uncomfortably.

Miss Fairbourne laughed lightly. "What a modest man you continue to be, Mr. Riggles. True, this may be a most illustrious collection owned by a famous and noble man, but in the end it is the same trade as you have excelled in for years."

Riggles flushed and nodded none too firmly. He appeared to age and shrink by the moment. Darius doubted a count's agent would be impressed.

The auctioneer drifted off, presumably to collect his persuasive abilities. Miss Fairbourne surveyed the new arrangement of paintings on the wall.

"You chose to come today, I see. Since you did, we need to decide immediately how to accommodate your interference." There was no umbrage in her tone, but her eyes communicated some exasperation, and the word *interference* all but asked for a row. "Do you want us to introduce you as a frequent patron? Shall we pretend you just happened by this morning?"

"That might be best."

"It will be deceptive, however. I think it would be better to let him know that you are an owner."

"Hardly better."

She walked over and straightened one of the paintings. "Consider it, though. If we are honest, you can be more direct."

He joined her at the wall. "I did not come here to take your father's place. That is Mr. Riggles's duty, and, according to you, also his experience."

"He almost never persuaded alone. Mr. Nightingale would aid him, both with consignors and with patrons who bid."

"Perhaps you should replace Mr. Nightingale with another man."

"I have tried. Remember? A Mr. Laughton was a good prospect but, alas, someone both warned him off and bought him off."

"Laughton was a cub. He could never match wits with a count's man."

"You, however, surely can." She looked over her shoulder to the entrance. A carriage was stopping in the street outside. "Please appear impressed with our expertise. This auction will be held with or without this collection he comes to discuss, so it is in your interest, and that of your investment, for Fairbourne's to get it."

He began to explain that he had never actually agreed that the auction would be held. She heard not a word, however, because the door opened and the count's servant entered.

Herr Werner was neither tall nor broad, but his arrogance gave him stature. He posed inside the doorway like a man who knew his worth too well. Blond curls neatly dressed and coat embellished with braid and buttons, he sniffed the air as if taking its occupants' measure by scent alone.

His pale blue eyes swept the premises and came to rest on Darius, whom he sized up in every way imaginable.

Riggles appeared out of nowhere, advanced on their visitor, and introduced himself.

Herr Werner's gaze never left Darius.

Riggles brought him over. "Allow me to introduce you to one of Fairbourne's most esteemed patrons, the Earl of Southwaite."

Chapter 12

Emma tried to find distraction in the garden behind Fair-bourne's. She strolled its paths, and took note of work that needed to be done before they held the grand preview night.

She tried not to imagine the conversation taking place in her father's office. She prayed that between Riggles playing the manager that he truly was not, and the earl playing the disinterested patron, which he definitely was not, the two of them would persuade Herr Werner to consign that collection to them.

She fretted that she should have stayed, and joined them in their discussion. Herr Werner had barely bothered to condescend to her, however. Once he met Southwaite, all attention had focused there, not on Maurice Fairbourne's ordinary daughter, who, as a mere woman, could not begin to understand a count's financial and artistic concerns.

The danger, as she saw it, was that Southwaite might be too honest, and point out that currently there were few consignments of sufficient prestige to buttress the count's own in the next auction. He might even openly discourage Herr

Werner. He wanted to be done with Fairbourne's, and would prefer if the auction could not go forward.

Her contemplations caused a good deal of agitation in her heart. The waiting seemed to go on forever.

Her self-absorption caused her to startle when she looked up from some shrubbery and saw Southwaite standing not twenty feet from her.

His back rested against a tree trunk. Arms crossed, he regarded her. His sudden appearance took her aback, but so did his expression, so much that she stayed in place even though her heart began pounding with excitement at the hopes that he brought good news.

No, that was not the only reason for the way her heart did a jig in her chest. His gaze struck her as invasive, much as it had in the storage room the other day. She was not accustomed to being watched like that by anyone, let alone a handsome man. It frightened her, but also proved very titillating.

Time pulsed by awkwardly when he did not speak. She collected herself and forced her feet to move. A flush warmed her as she drew near. She prayed that she did nothing to reveal how foolish her reactions were.

"What are you looking at? The sad state of the shrubbery, or that of the rose hedge?" She glanced over her shoulder as if to guess which neglected part of the garden concerned him.

"I am looking at you. Do not pretend you do not know it."

"I can think of no reason why you would, so I do not know it at all."

He settled against that tree more comfortably. "There are several reasons why, and I think you know that too. However, mostly this time I was deciding if you are really as sly as I suspect."

"No one has ever called me sly, so your suspicions are unfounded."

"Are they?" He pushed away from the tree and advanced to where she stood. He peered down at her, somewhat amused but not entirely so. "I think that you sent that letter advising me not to come here this morning because you calculated it was the best way to get me here in fact."

"I am flattered that you think I am that clever."

"Oh, you are very clever, Miss Fairbourne. That has been clear for some time."

"Clever enough to know that your actions would be deliberately contrary to my advice? I barely know you, Lord Southwaite, so I could hardly predict such a thing."

"Perhaps you know me well enough to guess, or know men well enough to suppose your direction would not be well received."

She looked at the building. "I trust that my worst fears did not come to pass, and that you were able to keep your investment discreet?"

"Herr Werner only wanted my honest appraisal of Fairbourne's from a collector's view, and believes that is what he received." He moved to her side and they strolled through the garden. "Just as well that I came, whatever your true intentions. Riggles performed so poorly that I wonder whether he ever attended such a meeting before."

His suspicion hung there, waiting for a response. Emma decided to ignore it. "Is the collection as prized as rumored?"

"Very fine. A large Titian. Rubens, Poussin, Veronese—if they are of as high quality as reputed, it will be a notable sale."

"A Raphael?"

"No."

That was unfortunate. Raphael was very popular among collectors.

"He did not miss that the paintings now on your wall are not of the caliber that he has," Southwaite said. "He opened negotiations with Riggles on a lower commission. He guesses that you need him far more than he needs you."

She performed some quick calculations of the likely income if Herr Werner paid less, and she also then had to pay Cassandra ten percent of their commission. Fairbourne's share would not be what she had hoped then.

"Did you tell him that more paintings were coming?" she asked.

"Are more coming?"

"Yes." She made a decision that she had been avoiding. "Among others, a Raphael is coming. A very fine one, with excellent provenance."

"Riggles did not mention a Raphael. How curious."

A slight pressure on her arm caught her attention. She looked down at the fine masculine fingers touching her, stopping her stroll. Her gaze moved up to the dark eyes watching her most closely.

"There will need to be authentication of the collection if he consigns it," Southwaite said. "Someone who knows a true Titian from a fake will have to examine each lot. I will not be party to a fraud."

"That goes without saying. Obediah will carefully—"

"Obediah will not, because he cannot." He released her, but blocked any further progress on the path with his body. "I admire that you are clever, but I warn you not to be too clever with me now."

Not feeling at all clever at the moment, she held her tongue.

His head dipped closer to hers. "Answer me clearly, Miss Fairbourne. Is there anyone associated with the auction house now who has the expertise to replace your father?"

He stood inappropriately close to her. That thought slid through her mind while her nose quivered as it absorbed his scent. Masculine and individual and clean, with undercurrents of leather and horse and wool, it surrounded her like a manifestation of his presence, invading her sense.

"Yes." The affirmation slipped out without much thought. His thorough attention left no room for lies. She no longer thought clearly enough to deceive effectively anyway.

His head dipped closer yet, and his dark scrutiny penetrated deeper. "But not Mr. Riggles, I assume."

"No, not Mr. Riggles."

"You, then." It wasn't even a question.

She barely found the ability to nod. Speaking was now beyond her. The oddest thickness filled her chest and throat, and lively tingles teased her cheeks.

"I do not like being lied to." He did not sound angry. Rather, his quiet statement breathed over her as if carried on a gentle, warm breeze.

"I—That is, it was not really a—"

His finger came to rest on her lips, silencing her. "You have been found out. Do not attempt to cover one deception with another."

His gaze did not reflect much interest in whatever she would have claimed or attempted. His finger stayed on her mouth, warm and firm, making her lips tremble. Then it moved, in a tiny caress of her lips.

Her reactions astonished her. Frightened her. Her body and her essence grew achingly aware of him, and of that touch. Quivers moved down in a sensual blush. It was far more powerful than the sensations that had confused her thus far.

He is going to kiss you. The thought came to her one second before his finger left her lips.

Then he did kiss her, as if her thought had been a request.

The kiss enchanted her. She did not even think about resisting for what seemed a long time. Then his hands cradled her head and the kiss deepened and a cascade of wonder defeated any attempts at forming words of denial.

He pulled her into an embrace and the tiniest part of her mind knew she had erred in not speaking. She should push away now, but oh, the warmth, the human touch and masculine strength and scent seduced her into compliance. The pleasures streaming through her were distraction enough, but the poignant intimacy was what really made her heart sigh.

She did not have to stand alone in that embrace, or be strong. There was no sorrow while those kisses pressed her lips, her face and neck, and no worry or calculations. No thought at all, just the delight of new, fresh sensations, much like feeling the first warm spring breeze after a hard winter.

She did not kiss him back, or embrace him in turn. She merely accepted, awed by how he transformed her world for a few moments. Only when his hands moved, and his embrace became caresses, did her sense reassert itself. She knew then that she had proven too compliant, and that this man assumed more agreement than she had realized she gave.

Still, she could not stop it. She did not want to. His hands did not shock her. Instead they felt wonderful. Necessary. Their firm pressure formed connection after connection that raised compelling, almost frantic urges inside her, especially very deep and very low where a heaviness full of delicious anticipation grew.

He moved her from the path, but she had no awareness of how. She noticed only the leaves above her head now, and the privacy afforded by shrubs and trees. Most of her senses centered on his shockingly intimate kisses and his hands and how both drove her to the brink of insanity again.

A new embrace, encompassing. A new kiss, burning into her neck. A new caress, finding her stomach and side and finally closing on her breast. Madness truly beckoned then. She succumbed when he intensified the pleasure with artful touches that made her gasp. She surrendered to a luscious sensuality full of excitement and need and deepening passion.

She thought she might dwell there forever. She hoped it would never end or change, but even as she accepted it, the urges increased, driving her, demanding more. An overwhelming ache began transforming the pleasure into a primitive, carnal hunger.

She sensed the danger, but even so she was not the one to stop it. Rather, a voice did, calling her name. The sound penetrated her daze.

She recognized Obediah's voice seeking her. Southwaite heard it too. That voice served as a strong slap that forced them both to find some control.

One sweet final kiss, and Southwaite set her away from him, releasing her. One deep look in her eyes, then his gaze lowered to her body. The angles of his face hardened.

His fingertips brushed the black frill at the neck of her black dress.

Her glorious arousal had not yet faded, but she stepped away, because of course she must. She walked into the sunlight and sought Obediah's face at a window. "I am here," she called. "You must tell me every word that Herr Werner said."

*W*hat the devil was wrong with him? The question shouted in Darius's head while he trailed Emma into the building, and kept chanting while Riggles gave a report and answered Miss Fairbourne's many questions.

Thwarted desire did not sit well with him, and he heard little of what she said to Obediah in response. He had to make an effort to keep his eyes off her.

You have been an ass with her and now you are being an idiot. Had he not sworn to himself, repeatedly, to close Fairbourne's? Had not long thought always led to the conclusion he should, even must? Instead today he had played the knight to a lady in distress and all but bribed Herr Werner to consign those damned paintings here. And instead of laying down a few laws when he met her in the garden, he had come very close to seducing her, and still wished Riggles had left them alone.

Arousal led his thoughts to places they really did not need to go now, if ever. He could not help but reflect that she had not seemed very experienced. That was bad news on several counts. It indicated apologies were in order, when he could summon no inclination to make them. It suggested that he should feel guilty, when he did not in the least.

What was wrong with him? Even now, as the conversation between Riggles and Emma began to penetrate his brain, most of his mind was back under the trees hearing her surprised gasps of pleasure and feeling her supple warmth against his body.

"You will write to him," Miss Fairbourne said to Riggles. "Tell him that after deliberation, you are prepared to take a smaller commission on the sale. Make it very clear that you rely on his discretion in the matter. We can't have him telling the world about that. Other collectors will want the same terms, and it will ruin us."

She was no longer pretending that Riggles managed things, now that her secret was out. If Riggles himself thought that odd, he did not show it. He nodded dutifully, and went to the office to compose his letter.

Miss Fairbourne in turn strode to the storage. Darius followed because he had things he was supposed to say. However, a part of him—the dishonorable, hungry, larger part—instead calculated how to continue what had started in the garden.

She plucked an apron from a wall hook and put it on. "I confess that I am almost happy that you know the truth, Lord Southwaite. I have much to do during the next weeks, and it has been very inconvenient evading you while you interfered here."

"How much did you do while your father lived?" The question came from his better half, the half not picturing this woman out of those mourning clothes, and lying naked on the surface of that desk, her blue eyes filmed by the ecstasy of pleasure the way they had been mere minutes ago.

"I helped with the catalogue of large auctions. Silver and objets d'art mostly. I consulted with him on paintings, however. He did not dismiss my views, if you are wondering if I overstate my abilities."

"And the management? The accounts and the consignments? Did you help there as well?"

"That was my father's role alone. Especially the consignments. That was too public for me to be involved." She faced him with an expression both severe and exasperated. "I deceived *you* because I need to deceive the world. You know that no one would accept that my expertise is good enough. No one would patronize Fairbourne's if they knew a woman's judgment made the decisions on anything, especially authenticity."

He was glad that she had not been aware of the past consignors, since he was sure some of those lots had been suspect at best. "There is no law that says a woman cannot have a good eye for art."

She moved some silver to the table and pulled a sheaf of papers from under a tray. "Oh, tosh. If you had known the truth during our first conversation, I could never have convinced you not to sell the business at once instead of allowing this sale."

"I do not remember your convincing me to allow anything. I said I would decide after determining if Riggles was up to the management."

She froze. She glared at him. "And now you have concluded he is not. Well, *I am*."

Desperation entered her eyes. If he had not kissed her less than an hour ago, that might not have touched him as it did. Since he had, the urge to reassure her swept him and he came close to promising her whatever she wanted to hear.

He feigned a connoisseur's interest in the objects piled in the storage room, but in truth he saw only her, felt only her. Wanted only her. "There will be a Raphael, you said."

Her expression softened with relief, beautifully. "Yes. A superb one."

"From the collection of an esteemed gentleman, I assume."

"Most esteemed." Her conspiratorial smile lit up the chamber, and his damned blood began heating again.

He reached for the door latch, lest he reach for her instead. "Perhaps I will buy it, if it is as good as you say."

He finally left, too long after he should have. He was on his horse before he remembered that he had lingered in order to apologize for what happened in the garden, but had neglected to say the words.

Just as well. He was not opposed to saying the right things for the right reasons. This time, however, if he had expressed apologies or remorse, it would not have rung true at all. Reassurances to behave better in the future would have definitely sounded hollow, since he already doubted he could carry through on the promise.

Chapter 13

"I may get the count's collection," Emma confided to Cassandra.

"You required a meeting at nine o'clock to tell me this? In a damp park? I dare not step off this path lest the dew ruin my skirt."

Emma kept them hugged to the Serpentine's edge. Cassandra had been sweet to agree to this walk at all and had a right to her annoyance with the hour. Given a choice, Emma would have done this differently.

They strolled along a deserted path in Hyde Park. Even as she chatted with Cassandra, Emma's gaze swept the surrounding park land. At this hour, very few visitors could be seen, and all appeared to be men. Most rode horses, taking advantage of the open spaces to give their mounts exercise. Over near the chestnut trees men in uniform clustered, probably preparing for the spectacle of the volunteer unit review planned for midday. Back near the start of Rotten Row, a small collection of riders gathered for what looked to be an impromptu race.

One of them, on a large white horse, caught her eye. Was

that Southwaite? She fancied that the man held himself much like the earl. She could not tell for certain from this distance, but the mere possibility had her all but stumbling.

It was very annoying that she could not even think about him without getting flustered. She had probably flushed too, and hoped that Cassandra would think it was because of the crisp breeze and the exercise. The problem was that thinking about the earl meant thinking about the garden, and that only confused her.

She had not gotten far in sorting out what had happened, and why. The latter part was the bigger conundrum. She could not deny she had enjoyed every kiss, but she had no confidence Southwaite had been swept away by pleasure and passion too. He wasn't inexperienced, was he? He was not likely to be mesmerized by the sheer novelty of all that human warmth and sensation. She suspected that when she finally mustered the courage to analyze why he had kissed her, she would not much like the conclusions she would draw.

In the meantime, she would rather not see him.

"I apologize, Emma. I should rejoice at your news, and not notice how the air chills me. I have been hopeful for your success with Herr Werner, but I confess I thought it unlikely that Mr. Riggles could convince him," Cassandra said.

"He had help."

Cassandra lowered her head and gazed up through her dark lashes. "I thought you were not going to allow anyone to know that you now managed affairs there."

"It was not me. Southwaite was visiting the auction house when Herr Werner came by. His patronage reassured Herr Werner, I think."

"I am sure Herr Werner dared not be other than impressed, if Southwaite required it."

Cassandra's tones and words never spoke well of Southwaite. Emma ached to confide more about that day Herr Werner had visited, but it would be embarrassing to describe how she had succumbed without a murmur of protest to a man she was not even sure she liked. Worse, Cassandra might want to start scheming for Southwaite's comeuppance.

"You really do not like the earl at all," she said.

"Nor should you. He is a hypocrite, like most of the rest. For example, everyone knows he has had a series of mistresses, but he makes very sure his affairs never fuel more than vague whispers. Hence he feels free to criticize others for their scandals, but he really is no better."

Cassandra referred to her own scandals, Emma assumed. After Cassandra refused to marry a man who had compromised her when she was a girl, society had noted every one of her subsequent diversions off the virtuous path through life.

Emma could not disagree with her friend's assessment of the earl, even if she inexplicably found herself wanting to defend him.

Southwaite had said he was a master at managing discretion and avoiding scandal. He had *not* said he did not *do* anything scandalous. Indeed, he had even lured her into bad behavior. Yet he had raised an eyebrow over her friendship with Cassandra.

"You sound bitter, Cassandra. Has someone been cruel to you recently? You know that you only have to return to your brother's household to avoid such cuts. All will be forgiven once he takes you back."

"I could not bear being the prodigal sister. He and his wife would watch me like hawks if I returned, and make me know I was dependent on them for my reputation as well as my board. He would probably want to marry me off to some dull man in order to make all the gossip go away. No, as long as my aunt will have me, I will stay with her."

Part of Cassandra's notoriety came from those living arrangements, however. Cassandra's aunt had collected a few scandals of her own. That she now lived as a recluse meant that Cassandra had too much independence.

"He is radical, so one would expect less rigidity on the social rules," Cassandra said after they had walked a bit more. "I am speaking of Southwaite. He is a Whig, and has spoken for reform in the past. With the war, no one does

anymore, lest they be seen as sympathetic to the revolution-
aries in France."

"Perhaps he bides his time." Emma rather liked hearing
that the earl had spoken for reform, even if he no longer
dared. It suggested he was not a slave to expected ways of
thought even if he conformed to those regarding behavior.

"Or perhaps he has changed his mind. More recently his
voice has called for better guarding of our coast. He pesters
the admiralty about it. With property in Kent, he knows too
well how vulnerable that coast can be, I suppose."

Mention of Kent turned Emma's mind to her father's
property there, and its contents. She would have to visit there
very soon.

That thought led to others about the auction. She trusted
that her plans today were progressing well. A certain wagon
was moving from her house to a building on Albemarle
Street this morning. By noon its contents should be mixed
with the other items, and the wine hidden out of view in
storage.

A movement up ahead caught her thoughts up short. A
figure had appeared as if by magic on the path. Swathed in
brown cloth, it seemed to merge with its surroundings from
this distance, but Emma recognized the willowy form.

"Who is that?" Cassandra asked.

They drew closer, but the figure did not move.

"That is Marielle Lyon," Emma said. "I think perhaps
she wants to talk to me."

"How odd that she guessed you would be here," Cassandra teased. "Go to her, and see what she has for your
auction. I hope it is worth the chill we both risked with this
rendezvous. I will wait for you here, and be jealous that a
woman who is wearing a dull sack dress twenty years out
of style manages to appear so fashionable."

Marielle waited in the shade of a tree that overhung the
path.

"You have come," she said when Emma reached her. She

gave brief but sharp consideration of Cassandra, then ignored her presence. "I have found some things for your auction. A big roll of drawings. Old things. The owner says they are by artists sought after in England. I told him you wanted paintings, but he said you would know their value if you know anything at all."

"Where are they? I must see them in order to know they are good enough for the sale, and authentic."

"He said to learn if you wanted them first. If so, he will bring them to you." She toed at the soil flanking the path with her mule. "Twenty percent, you said."

"It will be yours if all is in order, after the sale. Tell this man that I do want them, if they are as good as he thinks. Ask him to bring them to my house tomorrow morning."

Too conscious that Cassandra watched with unguarded interest, Emma started to walk back to her.

"Do you not want the rest?" Marielle asked.

"There is more? Are they also drawings?"

"I do not speak of art. That man, the one who brought the wagon. He will see you."

Emma's heart leapt. She glanced back furtively at Cassandra, who knew nothing about that wagon.

"When?"

"He said Thursday afternoon. At the east entrance to St. Paul's. You should bring some money. I promised him good coin."

Emma did not miss the reminder. She retrieved two shillings out of her reticule. "I will be there. Thank you."

Marielle tucked the coins away. Her gaze sharpened on the path behind Emma. She tsked her tongue in annoyance. "I must go now. I have been followed, and you do not want it misunderstood why we meet."

Emma glanced over her shoulder. A horse approached Cassandra's spot at a slow walk. The man riding it did not appear interested in them, or in anything except the fine day.

Marielle laughed. "It is amusing. The English worry that

I spy for the French, and some of the French think I spy for the English. In truth, I spy for no one but you."

Then she was gone, melting into the dappled shadows below the nearby trees.

D arius visited the auction house the morning after Herr Werner had called there. He went the following afternoon as well. His detailed perusals of the records and accounts were yielding nothing of value. Their vagueness defeated any efforts to see what Maurice Fairbourne had been doing the last few years.

Miss Fairbourne did not grace the establishment with her presence either day. He thought that odd. She no longer had to pretend she was not writing the catalogue, and she had said she had much work to do.

He wondered if she avoided the premises in order to avoid him. Since he haunted the same spaces in part to see her, that was not acceptable.

He rode east to Compton Street after leaving the auction house the third day. Maitland brought him to the dining room. Miss Fairbourne stood at the table, flipping sheets of paper. As he approached he saw that she examined a stack of drawings.

"They were brought to me today," she explained. "They are much better than I had dared hope. I am sure this is a Leonardo. I also accept the claim that this silverpoint portrait is by Dürer. What do you think?"

He admired the drawings, and her excitement over them. She appeared very animated today, even flushed. She wore a fashionable pale yellow dress, and appeared very fresh and pretty in it.

"These must be from the same consignor as the other new items that arrived," he mused, while he bent to get a better look at the details in the Dürer.

Did he imagine that she stiffened beside him? For a moment she stilled, at least.

"You have been to the storage again, I see," she said. "I hope that you did not move anything. It is all arranged to my liking, so that I do not miss anything as I complete the catalogue."

He straightened. "I touched nothing at all. It has become so crowded that I wonder how you get to that desk, however."

"I told you there would be more, and it is arriving. All I need is to hear from Herr Werner." She turned two more sheets, and revealed a large drawing in ink and wash. "For all the other great names attached to these drawings, I think this one will be the prize among them. It is a magnificent Tiepolo, and a study for a ceiling painting. You should tell your friends that it will be offered. Any good collector would want to know."

"Are you suggesting that I sell your sale, Miss Fairbourne?"

"I would never ask such a thing of you. However, if you found yourself expressing interest in it while you attended parties and dinners, and described some rarities you have heard it will contain, that would help."

"If I am not careful, you will have me in Mr. Nightingale's coats and shoes, greeting the ton as they arrive at the preview night."

She began rolling the stack of drawings carefully. "Well, someone has to do it." She tied a thick ribbon around the roll. The flush had not left her face, and her fingers trembled at their task.

"You were not at the auction house today. Nor yesterday."

She did not look at him. "I had other matters to attend to."

"And tomorrow?"

"More matters. Other ones."

"Eventually the catalogue must be written."

"I will complete it in time. And you, Lord Southwaite? Are you quite done with examining the records and accounts?"

"Almost done." More than done, in truth. He should just say so, and see her again at the auction. "Have you stayed away because you fear I will be there? Has what happened in the garden caused you to hide?"

"I truly have other matters to which I must attend. However—" Her gaze met his with all the directness that could so easily undo him. "I have chosen not to think too much about that afternoon. I fear that if I do, I will only blame myself for the what, and you for the why."

"Allow me to blame myself for both. I should have apologized that day."

"Yet you did not. Because I am not a lady?"

"Your birth had nothing to do with it. I did not because I was not truly sorry." Lies, lies. Deceptions and omissions. He had not apologized because his darker side was hoping for more, and her birth probably had more to do with that than he wanted to contemplate.

"Are you sorry now?"

"No, but I am not a man to take advantage of a woman." More lies. Damnable ones. "There is no reason for you to be afraid of me."

"I am not afraid of you."

The hell she wasn't. The caution showed in her eyes. He saw other things in them too. Vulnerability, as if she expected this conversation to insult her before it was over.

"Perhaps your restraint is better with wellborn ladies due to more practice. I doubt you have had much experience with ordinary women in these things," she said.

"You have it backward. To me you are not ordinary. You are very unusual to my experience, and that may be what disarmed my restraint." Some truth at last, but a flattery given with self-interest.

"What an odd world you must live in, Lord Southwaite. One so full of pretense that my lack of sophistication becomes intriguing in comparison." She held the roll of drawings in front of her like a shield, but did not avert her intense focus on him. "Let us speak the truth we both know when we can, sir. Whatever your reasons or impulses, you took advantage of my surprise, but nothing more. I will not pretend that I behaved well, so we are both aware the blame is not wholly yours. I trust that you know, however, that I will never be that surprised again. Not ever."

Wouldn't she now? Damnation, he had come here to make peace, and she sounded like she was lining up her knights to engage his again, and had just issued a challenge.

That raised the devil in him, and the devil was far too glad to stretch his black wings. "Are you saying that if I should try to kiss you again, you will find the fortitude to deny me?"

He did not intend it as a threat, nor did she take it as one. His words opened the possibility of more kisses, and other things, however. She knew it, too. She could hardly miss how it altered the air and forged an invisible link between them.

"While I have every faith in my fortitude, I thought it was clear that I assumed you would *not* try to kiss me again."

"What an impractical and naïve thing for you to expect."

"You apologized. I had every reason to expect it."

"If ever a man's apology revealed where his thoughts really were, mine did."

"Then allow me to speak more plainly. I do not assume or expect you to resist such impulses. I *require* it. In fact, I would like your word on it."

She did not plan a battle, after all. She wanted a diplomatic victory instead. Unfortunately for her strategy, he had learned that Emma Fairbourne well pleasured was much easier to deal with than Emma Fairbourne self-possessed.

"I never give my word of honor when I know that I am likely to break it, Miss Fairbourne." He gently pried the roll of drawings from her arms and set it aside. "And I have known since I left that garden that I would try again."

He cupped her face with his hands. She startled, but she did not pull away.

Her skin felt like silky velvet under his palms. A flush rose in her and its warmth passed into him, joining his own heat. Her eyes widened in surprise at her reaction and arousal, revealing the same astonishment he had sensed in the garden.

As soon as his lips touched hers, he knew he would pay dearly for this kiss. As Kendale put it, he was not a schoolboy anymore. She was very sweet, and adorably artless, and despite her announcement, she was still very surprised at the way a kiss could affect her. His desire urged that he try for yet more, argued forcefully for it.

He ravished her mouth, but managed to keep his hands off her body. When that became unbearable, he released her and stepped away. *Not here. Not now. Not in her own household with her servants about.*

It seemed they stood there forever, the passion and want still binding them. Pulling them. That could be a sweet torture, but only if ultimately it ended the right way.

He assumed that she saw it in him, what he wanted. Just as he saw her suspicions about the "why" and her fear of the "what."

She executed a careful, slow curtsy. He made the requisite bow, and left.

Chapter 14

Emma walked around the corner of the western façade of St. Paul's, heading for the yard to the east. She had worn black in the hopes that the man would recognize her from that, if he did not know her face already.

The visit from Southwaite yesterday repeated in her head as she examined the people she passed, hoping for a sign that one was her quarry.

Southwaite had apologized without the kind of embarrassment one might expect under the circumstances. The very correct earl had said the very correct words required, with exactly the right tone and the appropriate, if insincere, self-recrimination. He might have read a little pamphlet that served as a guide in such things.

The part about her not being ordinary had been a kindness, she assumed. She had challenged his motivations, hadn't she? She had implied that he treated her with less respect than he did better-born women. It would have been insulting for him to admit it. What could he say? That the rules did not apply to a lord's treatment of such as her, but only to his behavior with daughters of peers and gentlemen?

It would be stupid to be angry that he had lied to spare her the insult. And she had lied too, after all, in saying she was not afraid of him. He had always overwhelmed her, and now she found herself at an additional disadvantage. She had not trusted herself to show "fortitude" should he ever kiss her again. Now he had, and once more she had succumbed like a . . . a what? A wanton? A harlot?

She almost wished those damning words applied. She knew better. She had succumbed like an ignorant woman of mature years who knew little about men, and even less about her own sensuality. Perhaps she should ask Cassandra how long it took a woman to learn to master her own body's reactions, to the point where she could enjoy or reject pleasure according to some objective calculation.

She was very sure that she did not overwhelm Southwaite in turn, so his excuse for those kisses in the garden did not ring true to her. The kiss this morning most certainly had not been the act of a man undone by passion. He had announced it first, for heaven's sake. If a man had the mental faculties to map his path and point to the signposts, he had sufficient control to walk a different road entirely.

The real reason for all these kisses, she feared, was much less pretty than some poetic passion. He had made clear that first day that he sought a new mistress and thought she might do for a while. As she had suspected then, central to his mastery of discretion was probably choosing lower-born women whom the ton did not care about.

He also still wanted to persuade her to sell the auction house, of course. He had probably chosen to use sensual delights to make her pliable once he saw all those stupid flusters and sparkles in her. There were all kinds of ways to bend a person to one's will. To make a woman whistle in harmony, as it were.

Her gaze snapped from person to person lingering in the cathedral yard, and finally came to rest on a man standing beside the eastern portal. He appeared average in every way except for the manner in which he also examined those passing by. Dark coats, old hat pulled low on his brow, ill-fitting breeches—he looked like a less-than-prosperous tradesman.

His squinting eyes turned to her. Acknowledgment passed between them, and she walked to where he stood.

"We can go in the church, if ye like," he said.

"That would be disrespectful, since we will speak of criminal things."

Her bluntness took him aback. "See here, now, I take coin for delivering this an' that. I'm no criminal."

She did not want to argue about morals. "I need to speak with the man who paid you to deliver the wagon to my home. I have questions that must get answers."

He shifted and chewed on his lip. He turned his gaze to the yard. "Could be I have the answers. I don't just deliver wagons."

"Are you saying that you have a message for me?"

He shrugged. "Depends on why we are here."

"Something is expected of me, in terms of payment. I do not know how much. The proceeds from auctioning those goods? Nothing more? I am not aware of my father's agreement. He never told me about this. I also want to end this for good. Tell your master that I want to know what to do to ensure that I win the prize."

"Win the prize? The'nt no prize to win."

"The woman you sent with the wagon said—"

"Ye'll be wantin' to *redeem* the prize, I told her to say, not win it. Stupid for'ner. No luck to it, if ye know what I mean. Just payment, as I understand it."

Her heart beat so hard it pained her. She could barely contain her hope. "Do you know what the prize is?"

"Could be I do. Don't you?"

"No. I must know what is at risk or I will throw that wagon and its contents in the river. So tell me now—is the prize a person?"

He gave her a big wink as an answer.

She had to step away, to maintain her composure. She closed her eyes hard so tears would not flow. *Oh, Papa, why did you not tell me all of it? Why did you not prepare me so*

I would know what to do? She knew the answer in her heart. He had not told her because he did not know if he would ever succeed. He had not prepared her because he never expected to die so soon.

She returned to her messenger. "I must have him back."

"My employer guessed as much, seems like, since what I was told fits that which you ask. He said to tell you a hundred pounds on account, to be sure the prize is kept safe for ye, in addition to what the contents of the wagon brings. Or, for three thousand silver to settle, and you can have him now."

"Three thousand!" The high ransom shocked her. Where was she to find three thousand pounds? She would never be able to pay it. Even the hundred would slice a goodly amount out of her proceeds from the auction.

That was the goal, she realized. The ransom was set too high for her father or her to reach. Why release Robert when holding him ensured an endless stream of payments and a sure way to sell smuggled goods?

"It is too much," she said. "Tell him that. I am not going to be bled forever either, if that is the thinking. I want proof that my brother is alive and well too. I am not such a fool as to take a blackguard's word for it."

"He won't take well yer calling him that, now. Ye've a sharp tongue and best ye think what ye say, since there is more I am to tell ye, and it is not ungenerous."

She held her sharp tongue, so the "more" would be revealed.

"I was told to say that the settling was three thousand, but could be half that if you did a small favor."

"What favor?"

"That, I was not told. Ye would learn of it soon, was all that was said."

The favor was probably auctioning more bad goods. Probably twenty carts' worth would arrive after she paid the ransom, for a grand finale.

"Is there anything more?"

He nodded. "Some lord goes to that building ye have.

I was told to warn ye not to tell him anything." He inclined his head and gave a conspiratorial wink. "Most stern, my employer was on this. I think that lord has him suspicious of ye. Maybe ye play a two-sided game? He said that lord has interfered of late with free commerce on the coast, he did. Yer friendship with such as him is of concern."

The warning made her neck prickle. Was this kidnapper watching her, and Fairbourne's? The notion made her very uncomfortable, as if unseen eyes peered at her even now.

Worse, the warning implied that Southwaite concerned himself with smuggling more than she had known. Perhaps it was part of his interest in the vulnerable coast, which Cassandra had mentioned. No matter what the motivations, a new reason for why he showed such interest in Fairbourne's, and her, suddenly presented itself.

Perhaps he had paid more attention to her father's business than she knew. Maybe he had even guessed about the special lots, the ones that arrived at home, hidden beneath canvas.

He might not merely be an investor seeking to ensure the efficient disposition of a business. He might be investigating Fairbourne's, and her father, and now her. He had spent hours, *days*, examining the accounts, hadn't he?

The idea saddened her, for reasons she did not have time to decipher now. She gathered her wits and tried to appear formidable. She caught the messenger's gaze with her own and pinned him in place.

"I want to know where you meet this man who told you what to say to me."

He shrank back, scowling. "I'd be a fool to say, now, wouldn't I? Would be no one to be a messenger for then, is how I see it."

She dug into her reticule and took out a few shillings. "You could be *my* messenger."

He accepted the coins fast enough, but smiled smugly as he tucked them away. "Sounds like ye won't have much to pay with soon. Maybe that lord will swear against ye, and ye'll be in gaol soon. I'll keep the situation I have now, thank ye. It keeps me in ale well enough."

He walked away, whistling. Emma made her way back to her carriage.

Three thousand pounds. If Herr Werner consigned the count's collection, and if Marielle found a few more émigrés with good items, Fairbourne's commission on the auction might raise half that at best. She could not depend on bidders taking prices to their highest levels, however. She needed something more to ensure that she at least raised the fifteen hundred she would need after she performed the favor.

The Raphael that her family owned would surely tip the balance. The entire sale price would be hers too, not only a commission. It would break her heart to sell it, but she would have to add it to the auction.

Of more interest to her right now were the messenger's explanations about his employer. It sounded like conversations were held. Perhaps whoever had sent this messenger was close by. Perhaps Robert was too.

For all of her distress, that thought excited her. She pictured herself throwing open the door of some dungeon or cellar room, and seeing his astonishment and joy at being rescued. She imagined bringing him home and showing him how well she had done preserving his legacy, and watching as he took his place in his best coats at the spot where Papa had stood during the auctions.

She needed to find out if Robert was all but under her nose. She would not wait on her mysterious kidnapper, or his demands for payments and favors. She had no reason to trust him. She dared not sit still while her brother was his victim.

Emotions churned in her all the way home. Excitement mixed with very real fear. She wished she could hand all of this over to someone in authority, who would use more force to find Robert than she could ever muster. Kidnapping was a serious crime. Surely if she went to a magistrate and explained what she knew, some help would be forthcoming.

The problem was she did not know very much at all. She did not know why anyone had settled on taking Robert in the first place. She could not ignore that it might not have been a random choice.

Perhaps Robert had been doing things that were illegal too. If he had somehow been involved with the smuggling that now tainted Fairbourne's, she could not seek help. She could not trust another person to turn a blind eye to the crimes that might possibly be behind all of this. It would be a fine thing if Robert were released from one gaol, only to land in another.

No, if anyone were going to discover if Robert was in England, or uncover the identity of who held him, it would have to be her. She should at least try.

She felt much better after she reached that decision. Less helpless, and less a pawn of persons unknown. The fear became quieter, but that only allowed her to recognize another emotion that had settled in her heart, making her slightly sick. She thought about Southwaite, and the sickness swelled.

She could not trust him either. She certainly could not ask *him* for any help. In fact, she would have to pray that he never asked questions about some of the lots in the next auction.

Chapter 15

"Where are we going?" Ambury asked loudly, with annoyance. He aimed the question at Kendale's back.

Kendale did not reply, but continued leading the way while they walked their horses through the crowded streets east of Hanover Square. His strict posture spoke eloquently, though. This sojourn had an Important Purpose.

"All will be revealed soon," Darius said to Ambury. "I hope."

"I do not know why he has to be mysterious," Ambury muttered. "It is vexing when he gets this way. I am not a soldier under his command, and do not care for cryptic notes ordering me to muster at five o'clock."

Kendale heard that. He pivoted his horse until its nose faced the heads of their mounts. "I am not being mysterious. Conversation would be difficult even if we rode three abreast."

"It isn't difficult *before* you ride," Ambury pointed out. "Nor will it be so now. Before you take the lead again, I demand to know where we are going, and why."

Ambury's prickly humor today surprised Kendale, who

looked at Darius quizzically. Darius considered, not for the first time, that Kendale's single-mindedness had probably made him an excellent officer, but it made him a trying friend at times.

"He is hoping to meet someone in the park today," Darius said, to explain Ambury's pique.

"Are you saying that I am interfering with a romantic rendezvous? Damnation, Ambury, why did you not say so? I would hate to delay the frivolous matters with which you occupy your life during the Season by diverting you to a mission of potentially great consequence."

"I do not mind the delay. I only want some small indication it is even of minor consequence. So, yet once more I will ask, where *in hell* are we going?"

Kendale moved his horse forward so that it flanked Ambury's, and he could speak confidentially. Unfortunately that did put them three abreast, and now they blocked the street. Darius kept one ear open for the forthcoming explanation, which he would not mind hearing himself. The other ear began being assaulted by the rising calls and curses of coachmen and teamsters unable to move around them.

"I have been investigating a rumor, and believe I have learned something alarming," Kendale said. "Have either of you heard of a woman named Marielle Lyon?"

"I have," Darius said. "She is a French woman, a refugee a few years ago from the Terror. She is the niece of the Comte de Beaulieu."

"What are the rumors?" Ambury asked, interested now. The objections from the men in the blocked vehicles began to roar.

"Some say she is a charlatan, and not who she claims to be," Darius said. "This is hardly news, Kendale. Nor are the rumors likely true. There have been efforts to unmask her, and all have failed. That suggests there is no mask to remove."

"That the rumors come from her own people interested me," Kendale said. "So, sometimes, I have been watching her."

"That sounds unfair," Ambury said. "I would not like to think that someone spied on *me* because of a rumor."

"I do not do this out of idle curiosity, or to play at investigating the way you do sometimes, Ambury. If a woman lives in England as a refugee, claiming to be the niece of a count when in fact she is someone else, that is too suspicious to leave alone. How better to hide a spy than in plain sight, but with a false identity that would make her sympathetic?" Kendale asked. "If that kind of rumor attached itself to you, I promise that you would be followed too."

"Thank God England has you, Kendale. I am sure the ministers add you to their prayers each morning," Ambury said. "Did one of them give you this mission, or did you take it upon yourself?"

"We know the answer to that, and considering our own unauthorized activities, you can hardly object on that count, Ambury," Darius said. "Furthermore, his suspicions are not unique to him. Some in the government have two eyebrows raised regarding this woman. It is possible others are watching her too."

"Not that I have seen. Careless, that," Kendale said. "I know for certain that no one was about when she held an early-morning rendezvous in the park the other day. She met with the daughter of that man who had that suspicious fall from a sea walk in Kent."

Darius just stared at Kendale. He saw where the man's mind had been going the last few days. His own now raced to catch up and get ahead.

"Are you taking us to arrest her, for daring to speak to another woman in a park?" Ambury asked.

The sarcasm was lost on Kendale. "We don't know enough yet for that. I'm taking you to see where that other woman lives so you can help me. We must scout the property and street, and see how best to do it. I have been using some trusted servants to aid me in this mission recently, since I can't handle my list of suspicious persons alone, but even so I am shorthanded."

"You have involved your servants in this?" Darius said.

"Are you mad? Satisfying your own curiosity is one thing, but establishing a network of vigilantes is another."

"Of course he is mad," Ambury said. "You cannot trust servants to be discreet, Kendale. Word of your doings should reach Pitt any day now. You should anticipate an unpleasant meeting with the home secretary within the week, I would say."

"My servants are trustworthy, even if yours are not. My household is more disciplined than a unit of the Horse Guards. If either of you can even identify one manservant who is loyal, you might consider using him too, since it is impossible for one or two men to watch a person all themselves."

Having completely ignored their rebuke, Kendale turned his horse and moved on. Darius and Ambury fell in behind him, riding side by side. The blocked coachmen began passing around them, throwing out their final curses as they sped by.

Darius wanted to strangle Kendale. The man acted as if he alone would save the realm. This particular investigation of his promised to create awkward complications.

It had been inevitable that someone would eventually wonder about that accident Maurice Fairbourne had, and why he had been on that cliff walk at night. Darius had never expected it to be one of his own friends, however.

"He is going to drive me to drink," Ambury said quietly. "He resented having to sell his commission, and he was too eager to help set up that web of watchers on the coast. He enjoys this much more than I do, and if we do not stop this latest excess, he will soon have some of those trusted servants spying on *us*."

"I think he has found an excuse to avoid the social expectations attached to his title, by occupying himself with more serious concerns."

"If we find him a woman, he will not mind the social expectations so much. We must put our minds to that, and soon."

Kendale held up a hand, stopping their little march at the

end of Compton Street. He moved his horse so he could see them. "It is the fourth door down from the next crossroad. The other woman lives there alone now, with only her servants. When she returns, it would help if you two would arrange to keep an eye on her, to see if she meets with the Lyon woman again, or anyone else suspicious."

"When she returns?" Darius's gaze swung from the familiar door to Kendale, sharply.

"There has been no carriage in the carriage house all day, not since dawn. I looked again right before I met you. She has taken a journey, I believe, and I curse myself that I did not call the two of you to the task sooner so we knew where she has gone."

"No doubt she is only visiting a friend in town," Darius said. "She does have some, of course."

"Possibly. However, I have been wondering if she went to her father's property in Kent. If so, well, think of it—she meets with the Lyon woman, and a mere two days later travels to the coast." Kendale's expression assumed its most military severity. "I think these two women are up to no good."

"I think you are making much out of nothing, and boring me while you do so," Ambury said. "It is all too vague."

"I do not deny it is vague, but you can't deny it is also more than a little coincidental, and peculiar."

"*Only if it happened.* There is no proof it did, except in your imagination," Ambury said.

"As it happens, I knew Maurice Fairbourne, the man who fell from the cliff walk," Darius said. "I frequented his auction house. His property in Kent was not far from mine, so we had further cause for acquaintance."

Ambury, who had evidently not made the connection between the other woman and Emma Fairbourne until this moment, turned his attention on Darius with unabashed curiosity.

"Do you know his daughter too?" Kendale asked.

"We have been introduced."

Kendale chewed that over.

Ambury sent Darius a slow, sidelong look. "I expect that this other woman is still in mourning, Kendale?" Another sly glance let Darius know that one of his friends had not forgotten his concerns about kissing and pursuing a grieving woman.

"She is, which is why her long absence today causes concern. It is unlikely she has a full social agenda now. It is convenient that you have met her, and knew her father, Southwaite. You can keep that eye on her without it being too obvious."

"Now, that *is* convenient," Ambury muttered under his breath.

"I will turn my attention to her if you insist, Kendale, although I believe your suspicions are the product of a warrior's mind in search of a battle."

Kendale frowned. "If you think it would be wrong . . . ignoble, since you have a social connection already, I suppose that Ambury could—"

"No, better if I do it. I am less likely to misunderstand things, since I know the lady already. I will turn my mind to it at once, and start by discovering if her absent carriage means she has taken a journey, and if so, where she has gone." Darius moved his horse forward.

"How will you do that?" Kendale asked. "Damned hard to track a missing carriage."

"Only if it is indeed missing," Ambury pointed out with exasperation.

"Have no fear, Kendale. I have my ways," Darius called back.

His first way was the easiest. He would go question Maitland, the butler, and no doubt receive assurances that Miss Fairbourne was doing nothing more suspicious than spending the evening with Lady Cassandra and her aunt.

Chapter 16

The house had been closed for more than a month, and held the odor of stale air that spoke of absence and dust. Emma immediately threw open some windows upon her arrival, glad to have something to do so she would not succumb to her emotions.

She had not been here in close to a year. This property hugged the coast about halfway between Deal and Dover, where the Downs gave way to the Straits. It had been Papa's retreat, and not a family place. She had not even come after he died. Rather, he had been brought back to her in London, for a proper burial next to her mother. Now the sea breezes flowed into the kitchen, carrying memories of the few times she had accompanied her father here.

"I'll be washing these curtains," Mrs. Norriston said, as she held one to her nose. "Was meaning to do that when he was here last time, but he—" She caught herself, flushed, and looked at Emma with apologies.

Mrs. Norriston lived in the nearby village of Ringswold, and served here on occasion when her father was in residence. Emma had stopped by and picked her up on the way.

She did not really need a servant for the brief visit she was making. She wanted Mrs. Norriston with her for other reasons, which she now broached.

"I am here on a mission, Mrs. Norriston. I hope that you can help me with it."

"It is not likely I can help such as you, Miss Fairbourne. I am a simple woman. You need cooking and cleaning, that is fine. But a mission sounds too important."

"You have lived in these parts your whole life, my father once said. It is exactly such as you from whom I need help. You see, I want to talk to some of the smugglers who work this coast. I thought perhaps you know someone who knows them, and who could get word to them that it is important I have this conversation."

Mrs. Norriston quickly shook her head. "No one knows who they are. They like it that way, don't they? 'Tis their business not to be known and seen."

"Some of them are well-known, and their faces have been seen by those who aid them. I am not a magistrate. I am not seeking their arrest. There are those in the village who could do this for me, I am sure. Why, when I visited the village last year there was a man hawking French soap from a cart in the village green."

Thick and sturdy, with a large white cap that covered most of her gray hair, Mrs. Norriston lumbered back and forth in the kitchen, putting away the cheese and ham and bread that Emma had bought on the way. She checked the larder for staples and smelled the dripping jar's contents.

Emma waited a solid five minutes for Mrs. Norriston to say something. When it became obvious the housekeeper chose to ignore the request for help, Emma changed the subject.

"Do you know how far away the Earl of Southwaite's estate is? It is near Folkstone, I think."

Mrs. Norriston tapped her chin while she thought. "Six or seven miles south, that would be. Said to be a hard man, he is. Smiles enough until he is crossed, I've heard." She reached for a pan. "I'll warm the ham for supper. Your coachman will be glad for a bit of hot food, I think. I'll get him fed, then call you when I have it all set for you."

Knowing she had been dismissed, Emma left the kitchen and went up the stairs, noticing as she did how her steps sounded overly loud and the shadows seemed to stir as she approached.

She had not come here very often, so the house did not feel like her home. Yet she could not escape that the entire cottage reminded her of that anteroom to Papa's apartment in London. His presence seemed to have impressed itself on this place in ways that time had not obliterated yet. Maybe his retreat and isolation here caused something of him, something almost tangible, to remain.

The sensation that she was closer to him here than she had been since his death pressed on her as she opened the door to his bedchamber. It did not frighten her or make her uncomfortable, but it seeped into her soul and demanded acknowledgment.

A small painting graced the north wall of his bedroom, and her gaze went there immediately when she entered. Its vivid colors could not be obscured by the gathering shadows. They glowed from painterly light, the reds like rubies and the blue as pure as the lapis lazuli from which the pigment had been made.

She could see the subject very clearly. St. George, clad in Renaissance armor, speared a fantastic-looking dragon in a mountainous landscape. A lovely woman in an ancient gown stood to the side, watching her protector with love and gratitude. It was not Raphael's only painting of this subject, but her father had always insisted it was his finest.

She glanced away from the painting, to the bed and chair, and the stack of books on a table. Her chest thickened painfully until it felt as if a weight had lodged above her heart. She strode over to the painting and removed it from the wall. She was about to carry it out when her surroundings captured her attention again.

Where were the other paintings?

There used to be two others in this chamber, a small

mythological scene by Botticelli and a portrait of a cardinal by Sebastiano. Papa had sold the bulk of his collection to raise the funds for the move to Albemarle Street, but he had held back those two because they were his favorites.

She set down the Raphael and looked under the bed and in the wardrobe. She went down to the sitting room to check there, but neither painting could be found. In fact, the walls were bare.

They had not been stolen, if the Raphael remained. No thief would take them and leave the bigger prize. Her father must have sold everything else, however.

She returned to the bedchamber to retrieve the Raphael, sure now that Papa had been trying to help Robert. Perhaps the demand for the money to keep Robert safe had arrived at a time the hundred pounds was otherwise not available. As for this last painting, she knew why it had been spared. He had not sold it because he believed it was not his to sell. He had bought it for her mother, who in turn had said she wanted her daughter to have it upon Papa's death.

In her own chamber, she wrapped the small panel in a long linen and nestled it at the bottom of her valise. Then she spent the evening deciding how to arrange a rendezvous with men who were expert in never being seen.

That night she slept alone in the house. Mr. Dillon's presence in the outlying carriage house allayed any misgivings, but could not keep the ghosts away. Memories of her father and brother kept haunting her thoughts.

She remembered the last time they were all here together, not long before Robert left on the journey from which he never returned. There had been a small row between him and Papa, now that she thought about it. She had been in the garden but she had heard their voices raised. The next day Robert had confided to her that he would be making a journey to the Continent soon, to purchase his first collection to sell at Fairbourne's on his own account.

Only he never got there, it appeared. Nor was he returning from Italy on that ship that went down.

Where had he gone instead? Had he even left England.

That was what she wanted to find out. Tomorrow she would go to the village and find a way to talk to those who might know, even if she had to bribe someone.

Mrs. Norriston had returned by the time Emma went down the stairs the next morning. The old woman served breakfast, then positioned herself at the side of the table while Emma ate. She frowned, and her eyes glinted with displeasure.

"He will reach out from the grave to smite me if harm comes to you," she said. "So you do this the way I say, do you hear?"

Emma nodded obediently.

"Eleven o'clock tomorrow you go to the village, to the Prince's Sword there. Don't wear your weeds and don't look too fine. No carriage and no coachman either, I was told to say. Just go there and wait."

"Yes. I will do that. Just as you say."

"A conversation, you said. There'll be nothing more. Best bring some coin. Weren't clear if you would need it, but best if you expect so."

"I will bring what I have." She reached over and took Mrs. Norriston's hand in her own. "I thank you. Do not worry about being smitten. It will be broad daylight, in the middle of a village, and no harm will come to me."

Mrs. Norriston did not look convinced. Shaking her head, she aimed her heavy steps back to the kitchen.

The next day Emma donned an old brown pelisse over her rose dress, and tied on a simple straw bonnet.

Both items had been left here from a visit more than a year ago, and as she put them on she remembered the scents and sounds in this house when she last wore them. The memories came to her so vividly that she thought she really heard her father's step on the floorboards in the chamber next to hers.

Gritting her teeth against a flood of emotion, she left the house and walked the mile inland to the village.

The buildings displayed the ravages of sea air. Some badly needed new paint and whitewash, but others had been better maintained. The houses had gardens and were small in size. Families of fishermen lived in most of them, but the village possessed a store too, and was big enough to support the living of a tradesman or two.

Her walk down the main lane garnered some passing attention, and also a few greetings from people who recognized her from her occasional visits to her father. She stopped outside the Prince's Sword and looked through the window. It was too early in the day for a tavern to have many patrons, and the tables were mostly empty. A man sitting near the window peered up at her as she peered in at him, then lost interest in her presence.

She had never entered a tavern before. It was not a place for women like her at any time. She wished her smuggler had set this meeting for the churchyard. He had not, however, and if she hoped to learn anything about her brother, she must enter.

Enter she did. The few patrons inside barely noticed. The proprietor merely glanced her way. She chose a rough table away from the window, and sat down to wait.

The unmistakable odor of beer and ale filled the air. It mixed with other smells, of food being cooked. Somewhere out of sight a meal was being prepared, perhaps for selling along with drink. Her nose twitched. Mutton stew, she decided.

A long ten minutes passed while she sat alone beneath the timbered ceiling. Then the door to the street opened and a man entered. No one paid him much mind. He strode over to her table and slid onto the bench so he faced her.

In her mind she had expected to meet with an old, grizzled fellow, one very coarse and red-faced from the sea winds. Instead her smuggler appeared no more than his mid-thirties in age, and thin in a wiry way that spoke of some strength. He looked almost stylish in his long brown frock coat and loosely tied neckcloth. The only odd part of his appearance was his facial hair. A neatly groomed mustache and short beard hid most of his face, and thick dark eyebrows framed his blue eyes.

"You are alone." His quiet voice made it both a statement and a question, enough of the latter that she felt compelled to nod.

"That was foolish," he said.

"You left me no choice. Would you have entered just now if I brought an escort?"

"I shouldn't have anyway. Some woman pled your case to a good friend of mine, though, so here I am for a few minutes. No more."

She took that as an invitation to speak. "I need your word that you will not repeat anything that I tell you. I cannot risk anyone in authority learning these things, and—"

"For a woman I am seeing as a favor, you have conditions?" He laughed softly.

"I am sorry, but I must make them. I must ask for your word as a . . . as a gentleman."

He did not laugh at that. Instead his blue eyes examined her with curiosity. He nodded.

"I am Maurice Fairbourne's daughter. He owned the property down on the—"

"I know of him."

"My brother, Robert, went missing two years ago. I think perhaps he is being held by smugglers."

"Not by any that work this stretch of coast."

Her heart dropped. She had been stupid to hope this would be simple, and that the answers just waited for her questions. "Are you sure? There might be others besides you who thought to make easy money this way."

He looked at her with some exasperation, and also, she thought, some sympathy. "There are some who put in here at times, who are not from these parts, the sea being what it is. It is discouraged, though."

She wondered how, but guessed she should not ask. "Have you ever heard anything about this, then? About my brother, or if those from other parts are holding a young man? You see, everyone thinks he is dead, but now I am sure he is not, and I must try—"

A gesture from him, a raised hand, abruptly commanded her silence. His attention shifted from her to the window. The man sitting there also gestured, calling for attention while he peered intently out the window, craning his neck to see something on the street. Everyone in the tavern, even the proprietor, stilled like animals alerted to danger.

Another gesture from the man at the window, a calming one, and a quick glance in their direction spoke reassurance.

Her smuggler relaxed. "Would be a hell of a thing to find myself in gaol for letting your story touch my heart," he said. "As for your questions, I've heard nothing about a man being held."

"Do you think you would have learned about it? Do you all speak among yourselves?"

"I would know for certain if it were near here. As for the rest of the southeast coast, there's gossip, just like in your drawing rooms. A man drinks and he talks, and such as that can become known. Or not."

She hated asking the next question. The disloyalty of it sickened her, but she really should find out what she faced. "Did you . . . Did my father or brother ever trade with you or the others?"

She thought she saw pity in his eyes, enough that she was not sure he would be honest. "I would not have minded it. Things come to us that would do better in a place such as his. But he did not trade with such as us. Not me or my lads, at least. However, it is a very long coast, and I don't know about any of the others."

That was something, at least, and it gave her some heart. As for the rest, she sadly accepted that she would have little to show for this small adventure. "Learning that you know nothing is learning something, I suppose. I will not wonder if Robert is easily within reach, but languishing due to lack of effort on my part. I thank you for the kindness of seeing me so I could discover that much, at least."

She stood to leave, and her smuggler began to as well. It was then that she saw that another man had entered the tavern, probably from a door at the rear of the building, near where he now stood. She froze, staring at him. The glare he returned made her catch her breath.

Her smuggler looked over his shoulder. He did not run as she expected. Instead he cast a sharp gaze at the other men in the tavern, then sank back on the bench. "Southwaite," he muttered. "Are you his woman?"

"No! I did not bring him either. I swear I did not." She settled down again too.

Southwaite walked over to them. His blue riding coat contrasted starkly with the simple clothes of the other men, and the pistol tucked visibly beneath it could not be missed. Their companions in the tavern rose and quickly left. Even the proprietor decided to take some air outside.

The earl made his presence known, forcefully, by the way he loomed beside the table. He looked at her smuggler. "Tarrington."

Tarrington merely nodded acknowledgment.

They knew each other.

"What are you doing here, Miss Fairbourne?" Southwaite asked.

"Waiting for some mutton stew to finish cooking."

Tarrington smirked at her arch response. Southwaite did not find it clever at all. He turned his questioning gaze on Tarrington.

Emma expected the whole story to come out at once. Tarrington was in a bad spot here. If Southwaite recognized him, he was probably a well-known smuggler. She feared he would end up in gaol for letting her sad story touch his heart, after all.

To her surprise Tarrington met Southwaite's gaze with a steady one of his own, and said nothing.

"Honor among thieves, I see," Southwaite said.

Tarrington smiled. "There are no thieves here. Just a man looking for ale, and a pretty woman waiting to bring home some stew." He looked toward the street. "I think you should leave the way you came, pistol or no, and without me. I would not want my lads' affection for me to put you in harm's way."

"I did not come here for you." He turned to Emma. "If you will do me the honor, Miss Fairbourne, I will escort you home."

She did not want him to escort her home. For all his politeness, it had not been a request, however. She held her seat for a few rebellious moments, trying to find a way out of this.

Tarrington watched, amused. He was not going to break his word about their conversation, but he was not going to interfere with Southwaite on her behalf either.

"I will carry you out if I must," Southwaite warned. "It will be more dignified if you obey me willingly."

He had no right to expect any obedience. She almost said so. The air had turned heavy with his anger, however, and it was not clear how long Tarrington's lads would remain on the street.

She stood. Southwaite took her arm in a firm grasp and guided her to the back of the tavern, and out a door.

He moved her down the lane to where his horse waited.

"I will walk," she said, pulling her arm free.

In response he physically lifted her and set her up on the saddle. "Don't move."

She dared not, perched like this sitting sideways. Suddenly he was behind her, astride behind the saddle, his chest pressing her shoulder and his arms surrounding her as he took the reins.

"I can *walk*," she complained. "Stop this now."

"Once we are out of this village, you can walk," he said, moving the horse to a trot. "Now, not another word of objection, Emma. Not one word, if you are wise."

She tried to angle herself so there would be less contact. "I will not object, but not because you warn me. I will not because I have other things to say. You, sir, continue to be an interfering nuisance. I thank Providence that you are the only earl I have ever had the misfortune to know if such presumptions are—"

"You would also be wise not to call me presumptuous unless you are eager to see just how presumptuous an earl can be."

"Then I will find other appropriate words. High-handed. Conceited. Arrogant . . ." She burned his ears with every other descriptive she could think of while the horse bore them away.

Chapter 17

Southwaite did allow her to walk once they were well outside the village. She had to demand it of him twice, however. Finally he stopped the horse and slid her down, his arm crossing her body and breast to support her until her feet hit the ground.

She found her balance and shook off the overwhelming intimacy of being encompassed by him. "You can leave now, Lord Southwaite. There is not a soul in sight, so I am totally safe." She strode down the road, and hoped he would move on past her.

He did not. That horse paced alongside slowly, its master silently providing the escort he had offered. The air remained heavy with his mood, however, and she did not feel protected so much as vulnerable.

It seemed a longer walk home than it had going to the village. The hovering force behind her only partly explained that. Her resentment at her helplessness regarding Robert stoked her anger. She had gained so little from her conversation with Tarrington, and he had dashed her secret hope to learn Robert's whereabouts.

A little fantasy of a daring rescue had played in her head during the last few days. What a goose she had been to indulge in such a childish dream. She had no choice but to do as she had been ordered, and try to find the money to pay the ransom and hope for the best if she did. Her better sense rebelled against being such a pawn.

She stopped at the edge of her father's property and turned to Southwaite. "Thank you." She tried to make her voice one of firm dismissal. He chose not to hear that note. While she trod to the house, that horse kept pace behind her.

Mrs. Norriston's face appeared in the doorway. Her gaze shifted from Emma to the horse shadowing her, and up to the man riding it. With a deep flush she rushed out with apologies. "I did not know how to refuse such a man. He said if harm came to you, I would share the blame."

"Why would he think harm might come to me? I could have been taking a turn on the property and nothing more."

Mrs. Norriston lowered her gaze to the ground. "I might a' said that you were at a meeting. I may a' mentioned your need to speak to smugglers. He frightened me, and I could not think of ways not to answer."

"Really, Mrs. Norriston, you should not have told him my business. Nor should you be frightened just because a man happened to receive the good fortune of being born a lord's heir. He only told you I was in danger in order to get his way."

Looking very sorry, Mrs. Norriston bobbed a vague curtsy in the direction of the horse, then disappeared inside. Emma followed her, and closed the door on the dismounting earl. If Southwaite did not understand *that* dismissal, he was stupid as well as arrogant.

She strode into the sitting room. She did not even get her bonnet untied before she heard Southwaite rap on the door. She ignored the summons. He rapped harder and slower, in a steady rhythm that reflected both his insistence and irritation. Well, he could stand out there all day if he wanted to. She would be damned before she let him in. He had no right to keep inter—

To her horror, she spied Mrs. Norriston's skirts floating past the sitting room. Before she had a chance to forbid it, she heard Mrs. Norriston open the door again and greet his lordship like the good servant she was.

Boots strode toward the sitting room where she had taken refuge. His dark humor preceded him into the chamber like an ill wind.

When he finally darkened the doorway, he appeared very stern. Magnificent too, she had to admit, although that did little to placate her annoyance with him, or with herself for even noticing the figure he cut. Still, she resentfully acknowledged that he appeared very handsome in his riding coat and high boots, and his hair a little wild from the breeze. He no longer glared, but his dark eyes conveyed the sort of displeasure that only men feel entitled to.

"Mrs. Norriston erred in allowing you entrance, so please leave," she said.

"There are things I must say first."

"Often that which must be said is better left unsaid. I am sure that is the situation with the words you are urged to spill."

"That is a fine lesson coming from you, of all people. You had your intemperate say on the horse, and I must insist on mine now."

"I will not hear it. I did not require your interference today. I was in no danger and—"

"You have no idea how much danger you might have been in. None at all. If any other man had heard about your housekeeper's request for your meeting, I might have had to use this pistol." He removed it and set it on a table. "That whole damned village is involved in illicit trade. Everyone knows it."

He crossed his arms and regarded her with no sympathy. He reminded her of the way he had appeared when she first approached him before the Outrageous Misconception. She was in no mood for whatever he wanted to say, but she knew she would end up hearing it. With a heavy sigh of resignation, she sank onto a chair, set aside her scathing disappointment in her failed adventure, and gathered what strength her indignation might afford her.

"Why did you want to meet with *any* smuggler, Miss Fairbourne?"

"I am not obligated to submit to an interrogation. You have no right to—"

"The hell I don't. You have been too willful from the start and my tolerance of that has led to this. Did you think to arrange a special consignment from them, to enhance that damned auction? Yet one more set of lots from the estate of an esteemed and discreet gentleman?"

Her heart pained her, it beat so heavily. "What are you implying? I'll not have you impugn him."

He exhaled an impatient sigh. "Those accounts are incomplete and vague for a reason. I thought to spare you my suspicions, but I do not think that is necessary any longer. Is it?"

She refused to answer. She bowed her head, gritted her teeth, and prayed he would just go away.

He did not. He stood there, overwhelming the chamber and her.

"You appear to know at least one smuggler yourself," she said. "That is one more than we are sure my father knew. If my father had any doings with them, perhaps you led him into it."

A mistake, that. For a terrible moment his fury crackled through the air. He paced away from her and stood there, a tight, tall figure exuding power and intensity. She braced herself for the slicing words sure to come.

Instead he reined in whatever had broken in him. He turned back to her, his eyes flaming. He was still angry, but he had composed himself.

"I know Tarrington because he does a bit of work for me. He is the king of his kind here, and he knows others of his stature all along the coast."

"I am told you take a particular interest in the coast."

"I and others. The Royal Navy does not have the ships to patrol it all, or even most of it. Even the sloops that make up the Prevention Service stay near the major ports. The bulk of the naval fleet sits at Portsmouth, to be ready if the French invade. Meanwhile, they can come in other ways short of a fighting force. Spies enter with impunity, as easily as French brandy. Information leaves the same way."

"Are you saying English smugglers help them?"

"Some do. Better use is made of others, though. They watch and report activities that are suspicious. There is a chain now, all along the southeast coast, made up of such as them, and fishermen and landowners."

"And lords?"

"There are some lords who remain at their coastal estates for this purpose."

"Not you, I know."

"I and a few others coordinate this surveillance, and ensure the links do not weaken."

She guessed that meant he had helped put this in place. "What do the smugglers get in return? A blind eye?"

"They get nothing, except the satisfaction of aiding England. If Tarrington or another is ever caught, his efforts might speak for him and procure some leniency, but it has not been promised."

"Why not? It would be only fair for the government to do that."

"One does not bargain with thieves. Loyalty bought with such a promise could be just as quickly bought by another for a higher price."

That made sense, she supposed. However, she wondered if the government had made no promises because the government was not involved, at least not officially.

Of larger concern to her was what this bargain revealed about himself. He would give no quarter with these men, should he catch them in their crimes, even though they aided this network of watchers that he had arranged.

Her spirits sank yet more on accepting how rigid Southwaite would be in matters of honor. That spoke well of him, she knew. It indicated that he would give no quarter to Robert or her either, however. She thought about the wine hidden deep in the storage room of Fairbourne's, beneath obscuring swaths of canvas.

"You must make no attempt to meet them again," he said firmly. "There are some of them who would kill you for the coin you carry. Do not let Tarrington's manner fool you. Better if you stayed away from the coast entirely, now that you made the grievous error of being seen with him. This adventure was inexcusable, no matter what you hoped to achieve by it."

She did not miss the ambiguity he gave her motivations. She assumed he attributed the worst to her, and believed Fairbourne's was in league with Tarrington. She also heard the tone of a man who still had much to say. The storm clouds reappeared at the edges of his mood and blew in fast. Their winds puffed him up. She knew what was coming.

On a different day she might have defended herself, or tried to deflect his reprimand by being witty, indignant, or shrewd. Right now she felt too sick at heart that she had failed so spectacularly today. Worse, the longer she was in this house, the more she felt the presence of her father. His scent seemed to surround her now, and she sensed that his spirit reproached her as clearly as the earl did. Images of him kept invading her mind, distracting her from Southwaite's lecture.

D arius could not hold back his profound irritation with Emma. An equally profound relief wanted to temper his ire, but he was not a man accustomed to biting his tongue.

His brain had been rehearsing this moment since Maitland opened the door to her London home and explained that Miss Fairbourne had gone to the coast. Maitland had appeared worried about that, or perhaps about Darius learning it. Neither the information nor the butler's expression had encouraged an innocent interpretation of Miss Fairbourne's behavior.

He had contemplated the possible reasons for this unexpected journey during his ride to the coast, and well into the night. Ridiculous visions of her digging up loot on a beach taunted him. While he doubted she would be that bold, she was up to no good, he was sure. The only question was whether she embarked on something merely foolhardy or truly dangerous.

Damnation, but he should have ridden to this cottage at dawn today. Noon had clearly been too late for such as this woman. Thank God the housekeeper poured out the whole story once she heard his title. Mrs. Norriston had reacted like an accomplice being threatened with the rack.

He explained most of this to Emma while he gave her a sound dressing-down. He did not mention his sickening worry, but he itemized the rest of it, the elements that pointed out she had a lot to answer for. Describing his pursuit only made the emotions fresh and chaotic again, and they fed the fire in his head.

While he reiterated her danger, he pictured that cliff walk from which her father had plunged to his death, and the fetid chambers at Newgate prison where women were housed, and the fate that could befall a woman at the mercy of men with nothing to lose. The last became a hot iron in his head and he heaped more admonishments on her.

She said not a word. She sat there, hands clasped on her lap and gaze fixed on the carpet, while his words rained down on her. Her silence only annoyed him more, but then he found it troublesome. Her manner was uncharacteristic of the Miss Fairbourne he knew.

He began to sound too forceful to his own ears. He wondered if the way he paced back and forth frightened her. Her refusal to defend herself, to have a decent row, put him increasingly at a disadvantage.

"Have you nothing at all to say?" he demanded, at wit's end with her docility. "Not even one word?"

"You had so many that I thought to give you the stage."

He would have preferred if she said that with more spirit, instead of a quiet, almost dejected voice. He angled a bit to try to see her face better. Hell, she wasn't weeping, was she? He thought he heard a sniff.

He cursed himself. Dismayed, he dropped to one knee beside her. "Forgive me. My worry for your safety almost drove me mad and I have perhaps been too vigorous as a result in expressing my—" His what? Anger, but not the normal sort. Fear, perhaps, but not for himself and not only for her, but also about a situation that might leave him faced with a terrible choice. "My concern."

She turned her gaze on him. He saw tears and sadness, but little that indicated contrition. "That is good of you, to be concerned, especially since I am not your responsibility."

Her statement carried a rebuke of its own. Since she was not his responsibility, she was saying, he had no right to scold her like this, or to even question her behavior.

His essence rebelled at the claim. She had occupied his thoughts and time enough these last weeks that he possessed some rights, damn it. He remained ensnarled in that auction house too, and whatever she plotted no doubt involved it, and hence him. She could not really expect him to remain uninterested in her meetings with known smugglers.

He began to explain that, but her eyes and expression arrested his attention so completely that further words seemed unnecessary. She already knew all that he might say, he was sure.

No more than two handspans separated their faces. She was so close that her sweet breath feathered his skin. So close that he felt the shadows burdening her. Something dark weighed on her right now. It occupied her mind more than anything he might say.

You unbearable ass. Admonishing himself more violently than he had her, he withdrew his handkerchief. He dabbed at a tear that began a tiny path down her cheek, and battled the impulse to use his lips instead.

Southwaite did not ask her why she wept. Perhaps he assumed his long, hard scold caused it. Yet as he knelt there, too close, closer than was wise, she believed she saw in his eyes that he knew her tears were not in reaction to him.

He pressed the handkerchief into her hand and stood. He hovered for a long moment, standing right beside her, before stepping away.

With the absence of his close presence, other forces had their way again. Thoughts of her father evoked almost palpable manifestations of his person. The ghost was not in the house, she knew. It was inside of her.

"I did not spend much time with him here," she heard herself saying. "I do not think anyone did. This was all his, and nothing intrudes to dilute the lingering sense of him." She used the handkerchief to blot her eyes. "It is different in London, except in his apartment."

"Have you entered that apartment much since you received the news of his accident?"

She shook her head. She rarely went there.

"You were remarkably composed at his funeral," he said. "Less than a month later you were busy taking up the threads of your life. Perhaps you have not mourned him."

"Of all you have said today, that is the most cruel."

"It is not uncommon, Emma. I did not truly mourn my father until two years after his death. It is not an emotion one can command, so those accustomed to command might well avoid it."

She wished she could say he spoke nonsense, that of course she had mourned. Yet she realized now she had avoided the worst of it, and busied herself whenever grief threatened to break in her. She had not wanted to acknowledge the frightening emotion that had been gathering in her since she arrived at this house.

"Will I go mad?"

"No. You will just accept the truth of it."

She understood what he meant, in ways she would not have a week ago. She understood well enough that she now considered what would have been unthinkable even yesterday.

"I want to see where it happened. Do you know exactly where?"

He hesitated, then nodded.

"Will you take me there?"

"Acceptance does not require that you torture yourself with the details."

"I should like to see, all the same."

He did not agree right away. Perhaps his protective inclinations debated against it.

"We will take your carriage," he finally said. "I will speak with your coachman and tell him to prepare it."

Chapter 18

Mrs. Norriston served a light supper before they left. Southwaite excused himself as soon as he was finished, to see that the carriage was ready.

Emma noticed as she stepped into the carriage that the earl's horse had been tethered to the rear. He would come with her and show her the spot in question but she would return alone.

It took them no more than ten minutes to arrive at a rise along the coast where the shore began the climb that would end in the high cliffs at Dover. Southwaite helped her down, and they walked the hundred yards to the path that snaked at the top of this bluff.

"He walked here from the house, I was told. There was no horse or carriage," she said.

"Apparently he walked along this path often. It goes all the way along the coast, and he could access it not far from his cottage."

She stepped cautiously from the path to where the ground dropped away. It was not as steep as it would become farther south, but it was steep enough. "I suppose he was right here when it happened."

"So I am told."

She raised her gaze and looked out to the sea. The height and location of this spot gave good prospects of the coast. Far in the distance to the north she spied a massing of lines and forms. It was the Thames fleet, she realized, guarding the sea route near London.

"I was told he fell in the evening but was not found until morning."

"The justice of the peace learned at the inquiry that he was seen walking the path around eight o'clock."

"Late evening, then. Almost twilight. Did you attend the inquiry?" She had not. She had not wanted to hear the details then, or ever, until now.

He nodded.

Southwaite left her to her thoughts. She appreciated that, but she also found his manner very reserved. The man who had revealed his emotions so vigorously a couple of hours ago had become a cipher.

She looked up and down the coast again.

"He was here fairly late," she said. "It would be dark when he walked home. Perhaps he fell on the way back, at a later time, when it was dark and he could not judge the path as well."

"That is possible."

"One wonders why he would take a turn along a dangerous path like this at such a time. Do you have any ideas about that, Lord Southwaite?"

"No doubt there are many possible explanations."

She could think of only a few. One in particular made too much sense. She pondered it, and suspected from his closed and quiet manner that Southwaite had pondered it too.

Her father could have been watching the coast for someone. Smugglers had such watchers, who would signal if the way were clear to bring in boats at night. She did not know if Southwaite believed her father had been doing that, but he was not stupid and the possibility would not have been dismissed by him.

She looked at him, standing there with the sea behind him, waiting patiently for her to finish with this cliff walk. He commanded this deserted, windswept rise just as he had her drawing room that first day. His handsome profile, backed by the graying sky and shadowed by the setting sun in the west, defined his nobility in its expression as surely as its features.

He had proven himself shrewd enough, and very clever in seeing her game. He had probably guessed much about her father and Fairbourne's before she had known anything at all. He had most likely been suspicious from the start, upon hearing where her father had fallen. He had come to her house that day to rid himself of an investment that might compromise his reputation and his duty.

She wished she could tell him his suspicions were wrong. She wanted to explain that her father had accepted some illicit goods, true, but had never played an active role. The admissions and excuses caught in her throat.

She was not sure herself anymore, of what her father had done and not done, so how could she convince him? A reference had been made to her providing a favor in order to secure Robert's release. Perhaps her father had been doing such favors too, by watching the coast one night.

Even that was putting the best light on it. There were other explanations that did not acquit her father so well, or make him so innocent, weren't there? He had not been in league with smugglers right here, near his cottage, but, as Tarrington had said, it was a very long coast.

They returned to the carriage. She believed there had been some usefulness in seeing this bit of coast. It removed some of the vagueness about that evening, and helped the acceptance that her heart was experiencing.

She only wished that what she had seen had not raised more questions about her father, and left her even more worried about her brother.

* * *

"Where are we going?"

It took Emma a good while to ask that question. She had been lost in her thoughts and not noticed the carriage's direction, or anything at all. Now she stuck her face to the window, and recognized nothing that they passed.

"We are heading south, and not returning to my house," she said.

"It is not safe for you to stay there tonight."

"Do you think Tarrington will murder me in my sleep?"

"He is not the only person who knows you have questions and sought a meeting with a smuggler."

She wondered what questions he thought might be attributed to her. He did not know Robert was alive, so it would not be the real ones.

More likely his own suspicions had provoked this move. He thought he had interrupted a bit of trade at the tavern, and was not going to give her the chance to finish it.

"I expect there is a decent inn in one of these local villages," she said. "I wish you had told me of this plan, so I could have packed a valise at least."

"Mrs. Norriston provided yours, and packed your belongings. It is up with your coachman."

"It was very thoughtful of you to see to that."

"You are welcome. Regrettably, there is not a decent inn in one of these villages. Nor would you be any safer in one if there were. Therefore, you will be my guest tonight at Crownhill Hall."

He might have been informing her they would attend the theater this evening, he spoke so blandly.

"I think that you should have mentioned this idea before we left the house."

"You were distraught. My decision might have only upset you further."

"Surely it should have been my decision, not yours."

"As it happened, it was not."

"Since it was not, you have abducted me."

"Do not be dramatic. I am doing this for your protection. If you think about it with a calm mind, you will agree that you will be safest at Crownhill, and that there was no other choice."

He conveniently ignored that she was going to be at Crownhill with *him*. "Is there a female relative there, or another mature woman?"

"The housekeeper is quite mature."

"She lacks any authority. You are playing loose with my reputation. If it is learned that—"

"It will not be learned. Have no fear of that." Despite his charming smile, he managed to appear a little wounded. "I only seek to ensure your safety, as is my duty as a gentleman."

Yes, he was a gentleman. One with an expertise in discretion, according to Cassandra. He was a gentleman who privately broke the rules while presenting himself to the world as a man who obeyed and upheld the most stringent social conventions, and even demanded the same of others.

A fraud, in short. She had quite forgotten that. She never saw him in the ton's drawing rooms, and he had dropped most of the pretensions typical of his kind with her.

Except now he was plying his smooth charm just as he might with a duchess. His wonderful voice soothed and his smiles reassured. It was a type of seduction, with the goal probably nothing more than her submission to his will.

"And if I insist that you not be so presumptuous as to require that I acccpt this protection that you have decided I need, what then?"

"As long as you are near the coast, you will be where I can keep an eye on you. I will not tolerate the risk of Tarrington or any of his kind coming near you again, Emma."

So there it was. Not plainly said, but said all the same. He assumed she had indeed been in search of more lots to sell, of an illicit nature. If he believed that he was stopping that by keeping an eye on her, she would never convince him to allow her return to the cottage.

She formed an argument to attempt to persuade him anyway, but gave up on it. The truth was that she did not really want to go back to her father's house and face the memories and questions about him. She did not want to fret the night away, worrying about Robert and whether she could find the money to ransom him.

By the time the carriage turned up the drive to Crownhill Hall, she was half-convinced that nothing ill would come of this decision of his. She was almost sure that she would indeed be safe. Even from him.

Chapter 19

The housekeeper took Emma in hand at once and brought her up to a chamber. Darius handed the carriage and coachman over to the servants, and went to the library.

There truly had not been any choice but to bring her here. The only alternative was to put her in an inn and sit outside her door. He had interrupted something at the tavern today, and try though he had, he was not able to convince himself that she would not pursue her little adventure if given the chance.

It all depended on why she had met with Tarrington, of course. Her emotion had distracted him from discovering the reason. One tear and he had been vanquished.

Just as well. She had not taken well his insinuations about her father. She would have hardly appreciated him quizzing her about her own activities, especially since she had certainly met with Tarrington for the most likely reason.

By now she had most likely pieced together enough to at least be dubious about all those vague entries in the books, and about her father's time here on the coast. She had even alluded to it while they were on the cliff walk, and invited him to give voice to his own suspicions. Well, if she had come here to follow in Papa's footsteps and throw in with smugglers herself, he trusted he had thwarted that in time.

He poured himself some brandy and carried it out to the terrace. She would remain up above in her chamber, he assumed. He doubted she would be brave enough to join him this evening.

His body did not like that idea at all. Hunger coiled quietly inside him and ached for encouragement. He drank his brandy and watched the shadows gather in the garden, knowing it would be a long, wakeful night.

A few faint splashes of light from windows above gave the terrace a golden wash, as if a thin glaze of pale paint had been brushed over the dark. While he finished his brandy he noticed that the illumination closest to him dimmed.

He turned and looked up. Two levels above, Miss Fairbourne stood at the window, looking out.

"Is the chamber to your liking?" He did not have to raise his voice at all to speak to her. The night was so quiet that one could hear even distant sounds like the surf clearly. "If you require anything, you must tell the housekeeper."

"It is very comfortable, thank you. Luxurious." Her head tipped up a bit, as if matters more interesting than he absorbed her attention. "I think that I hear horses."

"They are bred on land to the west of here. We drove past them as we arrived, but you did not notice." She had not noticed because she had been weighing the danger of being alone against that of being with him.

"They are yours, then? There must be a lot of them, if they make enough noise to be heard here."

He listened. "Two stallions are facing off, so more noise than normal is being made. We can go see them tomorrow if you like. One field is reserved for thoroughbreds that are impressive."

"Since we passed on our way here, I expect we will pass on our way back west. If it will be no inconvenience, I would enjoy seeing them."

She remained at the window, a silhouette backlit by the chamber's lamp. *She is only taking some air, you ass. Bid her good night and be off.*

"The night is fair," he said. "You are welcome to enjoy the garden if you want, or to read in the library. You are not obligated to remain up there."

"That is kind of you. It is early yet, and I have much on my mind and am unlikely to sleep for a while to come."

"Allow me to assist you. I will give you a tour of the public rooms. The portraits of my ancestors in the gallery will bore you enough to make you nod."

She said nothing. Her hesitation encouraged him as much as agreement would. He did not wait for her to reach a conclusion not in his favor.

"I will meet you halfway, at the top of the main stairs." He strode into the house before she had a chance to demur.

No sooner did Southwaite disappear than Emma knew she had been foolish. She had rather counted on him not noticing her at the window, watching him. She had allowed herself to be bedazzled as she spied, however, and words of refusal had stuck in her throat because her heart kept rising to block their path.

It had not been only his appearance on the terrace that undid her, although the night flattered him and the vague light washed the planes of his face in the most appealing way. Rather, she had been amazed at how she could feel him from this distance, could be captured by his presence even when he was unaware of her, as if an invisible tether bound her. That kept tugging at her, creating an unbearably delicious sense of danger and . . . exhilaration.

She pictured him walking up those stairs. She could remain in this chamber. She could hide from him. He might think it childish, but it would be the sensible thing to do now.

The lure of being sensible could not stand against the bigger ones. Bedazzlement was far nicer than the other emotions that had owned her today. It had refreshed her more surely than the night breeze while she stood at the window. The forbidden excitement lightened her spirits and distracted her wonderfully. To her mind the choice was not between danger and safety, but between lonely worry and enlivening human stimulation.

She composed herself before she moved. She built a little wall on her side of that tether, lest it pull her in entirely. Then she left the chamber and walked down the stairs.

His expression when she saw him gave her heart. She might have been his cousin, he acknowledged her so casually. That tether was all on her side, it seemed. Of course it was.

"This way," he said. "The gallery flanks the ballroom. Let us visit that first."

He carried a candelabra into the ballroom. Large mirrors on the walls caught the flames and multiplied them a hundred times, so the huge room appeared to sparkle. There was enough light from those reflections and the row of long windows to see the silk-covered benches and chairs, and the heavy molding on the ceiling high above.

The room ran the length of the house. She gazed up at the hovering chandeliers. The center one would hold dozens of candles and sported hundreds of crystals. "How many people attend a ball here?"

"I do not know how many. Hundreds, I think. My mother hosted the last one, and it was some years ago."

"She is gone now? You are alone?"

"I have a sister. She does not care for balls, so there is no incentive to have another one."

He did not speak of his sister with much joy. Rather the opposite.

"I suppose balls are noisy, crowded affairs even in a chamber of this size. Perhaps your sister just doesn't like the chaos."

"You suppose? Have you never attended a ball, Miss Fairbourne?"

"I have enjoyed assemblies and parties, but if balls are held in ballrooms, then I have not."

"We will have to have you invited to one."

Emma tipped her head and gazed at the towering ceiling, and the chandelier with places for a hundred tapers. She turned, making a secret little dance step out of it, and the mirrors duplicated her form over and over. She pictured this room full of women in gorgeous gowns creating a riot of color.

"I am not sure that I would enjoy such a night. I might feel horribly out of place," she said. "And I think this room, full of people and all the candles lit—I think it might be ruined. I like it just as it is now, with tiny flame lights dancing all over the mirrors and gilt, creating this very pale golden glow. It is a magical place when it is empty and mostly dark."

"Then you must enjoy the magic as long as you like." He carried the candelabra to the center of the chamber and set it on the floor.

The candles' new position increased the effect. The crystals above picked up the reflections, and the room sparkled all the more.

Southwaite walked into the shadows. A scraping noise preceded his reemergence. He pushed a satin chaise longue toward the candelabra. "You can even sleep here if you like."

"If I did, perhaps I would dream of faeries."

He took her hand and backed up slowly, cajoling her into the center of the room as well. "I was hoping that you would dream of me."

He lured more than pulled. She had only to keep her feet still to stop herself, and him. The dim light hid nothing of his intentions. If anything, the flickering pale gold emphasized his eyes, and the magical glitter almost appeared to emanate from them.

Caution whispered in her, but the danger titillated more than frightened. Various ways to end this marched through her mind, but every objection died on her lips. Thrill after thrill coursed up her arm from where he touched her. The power he could spin ensnared her without mercy.

It was a slow path to the candles. She ceased to notice

that she even moved, he so captivated her. The more she entered the light, the more the chamber shrunk. The dark corners disappeared, and the far ends, and all of it except the center beneath the hundreds of crystals dangling over the ten tapers of the candelabra on the floor.

She found herself in the center, her hand still in his. It was magical here. Unearthly. She might be immersed in water that reflected a thousand stars. It appeared like no place she had ever seen. She felt like someone she had never been.

His arm lowered, drawing her closer to him. Her heart rose and began beating desperately. She stopped a foot away, but it was already too close. She felt him. Sensed him. Her body reacted as if they embraced.

He appeared too wonderful in this light. All darks and golds and eyes that burned. The magic suited him too well, and made him handsome and mysterious and commanding.

He laid his palm against her face, then cradled her jaw and chin with his hand, looking at what he held. She wondered if, perhaps in these twinkling dim reflections, she might be beautiful.

"Are you thinking of seducing me, Southwaite?"

A slow, small smile formed. "You are nothing if not direct, Miss Fairbourne."

"If you think to seduce me, perhaps you can call me Emma."

"In truth I have not been thinking about much at all the last few minutes."

"Not about much, but about something?"

The space between them disappeared and his sudden closeness caused her body to tremble. His head lowered and his lips brushed hers. "Yes, Emma. About something." Another teasing kiss, one that made all the glitter dance. "About you, and about how I have wanted you ever since you cut me at your not-so-final final auction."

If he had said anything else, she might have called up some fortitude. If he had murmured that he had been thinking about how the light transformed her, or how the chamber obliterated the real world, or made a magic he could not resist—if he had said anything at all, other than admit he had wanted the ordinary, not very beautiful, and sometimes headstrong Miss Fairbourne, she might yet have denied him.

Instead his words touched her profoundly. Even if he lied, it was the right lie.

He pulled her into his arms. She knew there were things she should consider and weigh about the why of this, and about the what that would come later, but she proved helpless against the excitement he created. The sparkles on the walls and floor entered her blood. The fearful masculine power of his will and caress overwhelmed her.

The manner in which he kissed her and handled her said he knew she had surrendered. He knew she was his now.

She released her last hold on reserve. She embraced him and felt the tension rise in him as he ravished her mouth with demanding kisses. She abandoned herself so thoroughly to the magic and to him that she did not even startle when he began unbuttoning the front of her brown pelisse.

Who would have guessed that getting undressed could be so erotic? Wonder after wonder amazed her as the pelisse fell to the floor, then his coats. He kissed and caressed while he worked this service effortlessly. He embraced her, and the tapes on her dress's back loosened.

He drew her to the chaise longue and sat, with her standing in front of him. He lowered her dress so she could step out of it. She finally experienced shyness then, standing in only her chemise and hose. Even the magical lights could not hide that she was almost naked.

He kissed her body through the chemise and she startled. He did again, right below her breast, and a shriek of pleasure astonished her. Then his mouth moved to her breast itself, and it felt too delicious to bear. He caressed while he kissed her, his hands smoothing on her thighs high beneath her chemise. He seemed to know what would shock her, and let her accommodate one invasion of her modesty before assaulting another.

She did not know how they came to lie together on that

chaise longue. A kiss drew her to his side, then an artful turn, and then she was looking up at the crystals, and him. His mouth closed on one breast and his hand on the other and he drove her to distraction with a wonderful torture. He enticed her breasts to increasing sensitivity until the slightest touch or breath created fluid thrills inside her. She was beyond modest soon, and did not mind at all when the chemise slid up and off and floated away.

She lost sense of time then, of what came first or later or which seductive art did what to her. She sensed movements, then the new feel of his body against her, skin on skin everywhere. With a series of devilish kisses on her thighs and legs, he bent to remove her hose so the connection was complete.

He took control of her after that, with touches and intimacies intended to madden her. His caresses covered all of her without restraint. She accepted each one, and reveled in the tightening, climbing pleasure. Her arousal kept getting more intense, more focused, more aching. Desire became a series of thrills never quite finished, never resolved, always building one on the next and reaching for more.

In a long caress he stroked up her body and between her legs until his hand cupped her bottom and his lower arm pressed against her mound. She pressed down hard, finding brief relief from the hard contact. Then a burst of intensity sent a hundred tiny trembles through her body, making her breath catch. He pressed more until she squirmed against him shamelessly. Rich, deep pleasure quaked through her over and over, each one stunning her more.

His hand slid forward in a long stroke that sent a cry through her head. Then another intimate touch, and another, each provoking more intense feelings, each one moving her further from any thought except an unending, frantic song of need.

He moved over her and settled between her thighs. With his weight braced on an arm pressed against the furniture's rolled side, he slowly entered her. Her breath caught again and again as a series of shocks split through the pleasure.

The raw intimacy of this act stunned her. A stark awareness of her vulnerability would not abate. Even so she accepted the masculine power taking possession of her.

He moved. Within the soreness, despite it, the pleasure returned. Not the same as before. Not desperate and mad but poignant and deep. More than physical, the new sensation permeated all of her, body and heart, while she clung to him and watched countless tiny lights dance on crystals above.

Chapter 20

Emma woke up naked in the middle of a huge, bright ballroom beneath a massive chandelier. The shock of her situation brought her to full attention fast. She took stock, breathless at her own audacity.

She might have accommodated the starkness of both her nudity and the morning's reality if she were not also nestled against a totally unclothed Lord Southwaite.

She lay there silently, trying not to move at all, while her senses took in how very everyday the morning seemed except for her current situation. She tried mightily to reconcile their shocking embrace with the utter ordinariness of everything else.

She closed her eyes again, and was able to capture some of last night's magic. The problem was that she could not keep her eyes closed all day, could she?

She spied her clothes in a heap on the floor right beside her. Ever so carefully she eased her arm free. If she could reach her dress, or his shirt, or *anything*, she might be able to at least cover herself somewhat, or, better yet, cover him.

With painstaking care not to move too much, she

stretched out her arm and grabbed the edge of her dress. Ever so slowly she dragged it toward her and—

The skin of a hard male chest pressed her shoulder. Southwaite leaned over her, grabbed the dress, and draped it over both their hips. That solved the worst of it, but still left her breasts completely exposed.

He turned on his side, propped his head on his hand, and looked at her. She glanced his way enough to see his expression. She could not avoid the thought that he appeared to be wondering how in the world he had ended up here with her, of all women.

"The servants . . ." she said, imagining some poor maid finding them like this.

"They will not enter," he said. "Not if they want to live, that is."

She looked around the massive ballroom. Their bed in its center was diminished by its proportions this morning. She caught her reflection in one of the mirrors. Then another and another. All she saw were her breasts, over and over, everywhere she turned her gaze.

He kissed her cheek, as if to reassure her. She took a deep breath and managed to avoid seeing the mirrors at all.

"You are probably thinking that we were quite rash last night," she said.

"Not at all. I am thinking that I am grateful that *you* were rash last night."

"Oh, thank goodness. I would hate to think that I led you into that which you might regret."

He smiled at her irony, but responded most oddly by lowering his head to kiss her breast. "I am also thinking that you appear as lovely in the light of dawn as you did in that of the candles."

"It is going to be hard to blame you for ruthlessly seducing me if you keep saying things like that."

"Is that what you are thinking about now? My ruthlessness?"

"I do not know how I feel about this yet, Southwaite. It is all too new to me, and quite startling at the moment.

Perhaps when I am not naked beneath a ballroom's chandelier I might know my mind better."

"Are you saying that I must allow you to dress?"

"I think that would be wise, don't you?"

"I am not in the mood to be wise."

She almost asked what mood he was in, but she guessed from the way he looked at her. She rather wished the notion did not stir her the way it did, although those sensations helped the night and morning connect more, and not seem two slices from separate worlds and lives.

He stretched over her body again, covering her while he reached for his breeches. He sat and, somehow, put them on. She took the opportunity to use her dress to cover herself better.

"Hand me your chemise, and I will get you dressed if you want," he said.

"It would be better if I rode back to London with some clothes on, don't you think?"

"I think it would be better if you did not ride back to London at all today." He sat on the edge of the chaise longue and sorted through the garments, eyeing hers with a bit of confusion. "I can see that removing them is easier," he mused.

"I will do it. I can be dressed in a few minutes."

"I would not hear of it. I put you in your current state and I will get you out of it. Now, stand here and we will figure this out."

He urged her to her feet and once more she stood in front of him as she had last night. Only no shadows obscured her and no dancing lights softened her. Or him. He sat there, still half-naked, his chest and shoulders right below her chin, acting as if what had transpired last night made this normal.

Perhaps it did for him, but she remained awkwardly aware that she wore nothing at all. She gripped her dress to her body while he fussed with her chemise. When he had it untangled and ready, he turned his attention to her and must have noticed her dismay.

Smiling to himself, he gently tugged at the dress, pulling

it away. "Surrender it now, Emma. You are giving me nothing that I have not already had."

The dress slipped away, leaving her stark naked to his view in the morning light. And to her own. The looking glasses sheathing the walls displayed her without mercy, over and over. Her face warmed. Her whole body did.

"Do not be embarrassed. You are even more beautiful this morning than you were last night." He rested his hands on her hips and drew her closer, then gently kissed the side of one breast, then its other side, then its tip.

She stirred, violently, as if the night's pleasures had not ended but only subdued to rest. He looked up at her, seeing and knowing her reaction as surely as if she had described it. Teasing lights entered his eyes. Carefully, ruthlessly, he closed his teeth on her tight nipple.

A sensual shock shot down her body, fast and hard. She had not expected such an intense reaction with so little preliminary love play. He used his tongue, wickedly, to make it even worse. She grasped his shoulders so she might not lose her balance as her legs turned liquid.

Closer now, one hand on her hip holding her in place. The other ventured between her legs. She tried to back away.

"I know you are sore. I will not hurt you," he murmured, not letting her go.

He did not caress the slight soreness that still felt the echo of his fullness. Instead he sought another spot of shocking intensity and began torturing her with touches designed to madden her.

She no longer cared that she was naked. She clutched his shoulders and lost her sense of any other part of her except where he aroused her. Shameless, she arched so that her breasts begged for more, and she moaned when he flicked his tongue over their tips again and again.

Pleasure upon pleasure coursed through her, pooling where he caressed, turning urgent and needy with frightening quickness. The most primitive hunger soon owned her consciousness, making her ache, making her cry. This time no pain interfered; no shock brought her back to the world.

Erotic abandon broke in her like a storm and the pleasure turned frantic and tight and desperate. It kept getting worse until she wanted to scream for relief.

Then she did scream, in wondrous shock when a glorious burst of sensation exploded in her. He pulled her close as it happened and held her to him, his face buried in her breasts, his arms wrapping her tightly. She opened her eyes and saw herself in the large looking glasses, naked and wild like a maenad, embracing his dark head while she surrendered to ecstasy.

While Darius drank coffee in the morning room, he frowned over a letter that had been brought by messenger at dawn. He had no choice but to heed the call in it. However, today of all days he did not want to be riding all over the county for the sake of duty. He wanted to stay right here.

Emma had dressed and retreated to her chamber, to wash and dress again, he assumed. She would be down soon.

There was much he needed to say to her and demand of her. About Fairbourne's. About her meeting with Tarrington. About last night. Most of it should wait for another day now. If things between them progressed as he expected, some of it might not have to be said at all.

She entered the morning room, wearing a simple black dress and carrying a black bonnet. He would have preferred she wear another color, but perhaps that was his conscience looking to pretend last night had been other than it was. There had probably been nothing other than black for Mrs. Norriston to pack in her valise anyway.

He bid the footman serve her breakfast from the food on the breakfront. She ate heartily. He had been prepared for dawn's awkwardness again when she came down, but perhaps her renewed abandon had made the day less strange.

"I should start back to London," she said. "Please have your people tell Mr. Dillon to prepare my carriage."

"I think that you should stay here another day. I have someone I must see this afternoon, and if you wait, I can ride back with you tomorrow."

"If you will be busy this afternoon, there is little point in my staying longer."

Miss Fairbourne said that, but Emma immediately emerged and realized the error of that logic. "Oh." She glanced at him and colored. "I wish that I were clever and sophisticated, Southwaite, so I could bandy your intentions with witty double entendres."

"Your usual forthrightness suits me better."

"That is fortunate because it is all I have at my disposal this morning." She looked at him very directly. That had always captivated him, but now it also brought forth vivid memories of her astonishment last night, and how her gaze forced a pervasive intimacy in the ballroom.

"It was a beautiful and touching night, and an amazing morning," she said. "However, it would be unwise to do it again."

She did not hesitate or falter as she issued her rejection. She did not even blink.

He reacted badly to her bluntness, but he managed to swallow his sense of insult. He had asked for forthright, hadn't he?

Apparently her mind had spared neither herself nor him during the time upstairs while she washed and dressed. He pictured her, weighing it all, putting the pleasure on a scale and stacking all the potential costs against it.

She had surrendered herself to him last night, but not forever. Hell, not even for an entire day, it seemed.

Which meant he now had a choice. Either he could dismiss the servants and persuade her with pleasure right here in the morning room, or some of those things that should be said would have to be said right now.

He stood and offered his hand. "Let us take a turn outside, so that I can explain my thinking on what is wise or not."

* * *

Southwaite's hard expression surprised Emma. Perhaps she assumed she should be so bedazzled that she would melt at the insinuation that he wanted this tryst to continue?

She was not untouched by his interest, or unmoved by the way he looked at her. The familiarity in his manner kept her blood simmering with the remnants of this morning's heat. She was not so conceited as to think that this attention was her due either. On reflection it had impressed her that she did not wake up alone in that ballroom, with her packed valise waiting outside the door.

He could not really expect an affair, however. He had to know that the risks were too high for her. Nor could she consider it for her own reasons. For the real reasons, she ruefully admitted.

She had finally shaken off her sensual daze while she washed, and acknowledged the impossibility of being the lover of a man from whom she needed to keep secrets of a potentially criminal nature.

The terrace was shaded this time of day by a large elm that hovered overhead. The edge of the back gardens bordered an expanse of grass dotted by other trees and shrubs, and the sounds of a brook twinkled in the air.

He took both her hands and drew her into an embrace. The contact moved her all the more. The thought entered her mind that he would not play fair, and would just seduce her again to get his way. She more than half wished he would. Then she could succumb for another night and another morning, and live for a while in a place of magic where there were no duties and no secrets.

"Emma, you were correct this morning. I ruthlessly seduced you. Nor am I at all sorry for it. You were an innocent, however, and I cannot even claim I thought otherwise. Therefore—"

"I am not sure the word *innocent* ever applies to a woman

of my age. I was, however, a virgin; that is true. Now I am not. I am not regretting it yet, and do not expect to later."

"A gentleman who compromises a lady is—"

"Are you feeling guilty? Is that what this is about? Well, I am not a lady, so I think that absolves you of the rules your kind has about these things. Doesn't it?"

For a man facing logic that favored him, he appeared exasperated.

"Damnation, Emma, I am trying to—If you would stop interrupting—" He took a deep breath. "I will not treat you differently due to our different stations, although you keep assuming that I will. We will marry, and very soon at that."

That deep breath tickled her memory. It reminded her of something. Ah, yes, Mr. Nightingale, as he braced himself to speak words he did not mean so that he might get his hands on Fairbourne's.

Southwaite did not want Fairbourne's, although he might not mind having total control over its future. But this was not about that. Like Mr. Nightingale, however, he was making a proposal for all the wrong reasons.

She did not respond right away. She allowed herself to experience the flutter of excitement that filled her on hearing this proposal, despite its motivations. She permitted a series of rapid fantasies to fly through her mind, of her being the Countess of Southwaite.

Unfortunately other images followed them, of this man's reaction when he confirmed his wife's father had cooperated with smugglers. Of his cold silence when he learned that she had continued that right under his nose. Of his anger when her brother returned and revealed their father had not been coerced at all, but had used the auction house thus for years.

She set aside those sadder pictures and focused on the face in front of her eyes. She gazed hard and deep so she might never forget what he looked like right now, and how he made her feel anything but ordinary, even if he was only doing the right thing as gentlemen were taught to do.

"I am honored, of course. I dare not be," she said.

"However, I know you do not want to do this. I am not suitable, and we both know it."

"I know nothing of the kind. You are suitable if I say you are."

He really believed that. How adorable his conceit could be sometimes. "I cannot accept. I think you already know most of the reasons why."

She eased out of his embrace. An unexpectedly deep disappointment and pain in her heart said that she would indeed pay dearly for their passion, but not in ways assessed by the world.

He paced away, stopped to look at her in amazement, then paced some more. "You are impossible sometimes."

"I like to think I am practical, not impossible."

"How is it practical for you to choose scandal over marriage to an earl? It is so impractical as to put your sanity in question."

"There will be no scandal. No one will find out. Your famous discretion will see to that. So there is no reason to swallow the bitter medicine and do the right thing."

"You are most understanding. Oddly so. If you hăd not been moaning with pleasure mere hours ago, I might take offense at all your practical consideration."

She was trying very hard to keep this civil but he simply would not allow it. "What is odd is your insistence on having a row about this, when instead you should be rejoicing in your close call."

Something passed through him that brought a poignant warmth to his eyes. "If you will not accept my proposal, then be my lover, Emma."

Ah, now they were down to it. She *was* suitable for that.

"Please do not be insulted, but—I think not. Please know that my decision in no way reflects on . . . your amorous skills."

His eyelids lowered. "I am heartily relieved to hear it. Your good opinion of me is so very important. Can I ask what your decision does reflect on? Perhaps there is some other area in which I can improve."

"You do not have to be sarcastic. I thought you would want to know it was not due to . . . that. I would if I were a man. As for the rest, there are many areas in which you can improve. There are for all of us. However, my decision mostly reflects that your pursuit of me, beginning with the Outrageous Misconception, has never made any sense."

"Who said such things make sense? Hell, if they made sense, or had to make sense, I—"

"You would have never kissed me, let alone the rest. No, do not object to spare me a truth that I already know. I am sure I am not typical of the women you have had as lovers before, and we rarely converse without arguing. That is why your pursuit has been, well, suspicious."

"*Suspicious* now."

"Yes, *suspicious*. I would have to be stupid not to wonder about ulterior motives."

"Do not impugn *my* motives just because *you* think you are ordinary, Emma."

Oh, for heaven's sake. "I will speak plainly since your pride will not allow you to hear anything less—"

"Heaven spare me. I think you have been plenty plain already." His furious eyes settled on her, darkly. "Fine, explain my motives that you know so much better than I do myself."

"I think that you used your flirting and pursuit to try to make me pliable so I might bend to your will about Fairbourne's. If something resembling true desire eventually moved you, I am flattered. However, I would like to keep last night a fond memory, and avoid ever wondering about your motives in the future. For that reason, and because of our frequent rows and . . . everything else, I do not think any kind of intimate alliance between us would be wise."

He gazed in her eyes deeply, directly. "I'll be damned before I accept a fond memory and nothing more."

She did not miss that he did not disagree with a single word she had said. "Then I fear you will be damned, Lord Southwaite. Now, please, call for my carriage. I must return to London. I have an auction to prepare."

* * *

The woman was infuriating. Maddening. Irritating as hell . . .

Darius released his anger while he galloped up the coast. Did she really expect him to stand down? *Now?*

"You do not really want to do this." Hell, no man wanted to marry but most did eventually. Not because they wanted marriage itself, but because they wanted a woman. Some marriages came about because a man seduced a woman and it was the right thing to do. She knew that, damn it, but acted as if the rules did not apply to her.

Just as she ignored that a woman once seduced was supposed to *stay* seduced, especially if it was her first time with a man.

She had expected him to be relieved at her refusal. And he was, in a way. Not entirely, which was odd. All of which was beside the point, damn it.

"I am not suitable." No, she wasn't. If he were willing to overlook the ways in which she wasn't, including the potential scandal looming about her father, why should she feel obligated to be "practical"?

Hell, Emma Fairbourne was not a woman to care if she was not suitable anyway.

Both rejections had probably all been due to the "everything else." She knew that he was suspicious that her father had been in league with smugglers. She might be too. Well, he would take care of part of the "everything else" today, and the rest very soon.

Head still pounding with curses, he followed the slope of the cliff path north of Fairbourne's cottage, where it dipped down to the sea. Before it leveled again, he turned his mount right onto a rocky path that took a more precipitous route to the shore. Fifty yards before it met the water, he dismounted, tied his horse to a ragged, bony tree, then walked along a narrow ledge. Almost like magic one of the deep shadows on the cliff face turned into the mouth of a cave.

Tarrington lounged against its edge, calmly honing a very large knife against a stone. He looked up on hearing Darius's footfall.

"Good that you came," he said. "I don't want to be paying for their board another night."

"Of course I came. Why wouldn't I?"

"I thought maybe you were still busy protecting that lady." He grinned. "To say your face looked black yesterday is putting a fine point on it. Not that you appear any friendlier today."

"I would be much friendlier if you told me what she wanted with you."

Tarrington shook his head. "Gave my word as a gentleman not to say."

"You are not a gentleman, so you are free to talk."

"Gave my word as a cutthroat, then."

Darius assumed a cutthroat could be persuaded. He would take care of that later. Right now he would make sure one thing at least was understood. "I warn you now to have nothing more to do with Miss Fairbourne. If I learn that you meet with her again, or discover that you are providing her with special consignments, or even send others to her for that purpose, you will answer to me."

Tarrington laughed. He sheathed the knife and gestured. "Come meet our guests. We saw them coming by the light of the moon, and waited onshore and took them there. They landed not far south of here."

Darius followed him deep into the cave. A fire burned there for light, and five men sat against the cave wall. Most were dressed well, even elegantly. All wore expressions of disdain. Some of Tarrington's lads lounged about, their pistols at the ready lest their guests decide to bolt.

"They are émigrés," Darius said to Tarrington. "You did not need me at all."

"They are indeed, each with his bag of gold and jewels and most with a sack of items of value or sentiment. It is impressive how they can grab two handfuls that are worth hundreds, even thousands sometimes."

"Let them go. *With* their bags and sacks. Where is the crew?"

"They ran for it, and what with keeping this lot together . . ." He shrugged. "Just paid hands, nothing more. No danger from them, so it is not a loss."

The hell they had escaped. Tarrington must have known them and let them go. "Where are the goods the crew brought over?"

Tarrington scratched his ear. "Goods? There were very few. Not worth your worrying about. So little that I found it odd. Normally the cargo is the reason for the run, and these Frenchies are just ballast. Peculiar that so little for sale came across." He pointed over his shoulder. "That one there might be able to explain it. He is why I sent for you."

Darius glanced over to a man sitting a little aside from the others. He appeared more roughly dressed, and his coats fit as if they had been made when he was less hearty. "Why do you think he has anything to tell me?"

"He brought almost nothing with him. No gold. No miniature of his dear mother. Just some clothes that do not look so fine as those he wears. He speaks English better than they do too. I thought you might want to have a word with him before we set him loose."

Darius examined the man, who refused to acknowledge he was the object of interest. He was young and fit and his dark eyes served as iron doors guarding his thoughts. A soldier? Possibly. If he were a spy, he would never admit it now.

"I believe you are correct, Tarrington. Since you probably are, it is just as well that you held the others too. Keep a close watch on that one. I will return once I arrange what to do with them all."

Darius walked back to his horse, cursing anew. Damnation, it might be days before he was able to follow Emma to London.

Chapter 21

By the time Emma returned home her emotions had dulled to the point of melancholy. Even going to Fairbourne's the next day could not raise her spirits.

On the second morning, when she arrived at the auction house, Obediah greeted her with the announcement that Herr Werner had written to say he would be consigning the count's collection to Fairbourne's. She pretended more joy than she experienced on hearing the news.

She tried to blame herself for her mood, and for her shocking willingness to be seduced. The guilt would not stick. She could not drum up enough regret to support her efforts at castigating herself. Rather the opposite. At the least convenient moments, memories would slide into her mind, of touches and sensations, of Southwaite's eyes in the candlelight, of standing naked in the dawn. At night while she drifted to sleep thoughts about that night would own her completely, and her body stirred again, as if she had returned to the ballroom and could feel him in her arms.

On the third day, a letter came, but not from him. It was

delivered at dawn by a young boy who had been paid a penny to knock on the door. Her pulse quickened as soon as she touched the letter. She tore it open and wept when she saw the familiar hand that had penned the few lines.

Emma,

I am told that you require evidence that I am alive. How like you to make demands of the devil himself.

If I had a choice I would not write this, but have you think I am dead. It amuses them that I tell you this. Yes, it is being read, so I cannot reveal where I am. I am also told to warn you to tell no one that I have written to you.

Better if you forgot you had read this too, dear Emma. I am here through my own failed ambitions, and do not want your future to be ruined too.

I hold you in my heart, and knowing that you are safe is my only comfort. Remain so, for me.

Robert

How like him to warn her off, to rebel against the plans that ensnared her now. She could not obey him, of course. She could never just forget about him. Now that she knew her heart had not lied to her for two years, she had to buy his freedom.

She called for her carriage and had Mr. Dillon take her to the house where Cassandra lived. Cassandra knew at once that something important had happened. She made her sit and demanded to know the reason for her flushed excitement.

Fortunately Emma had news that would satisfy her friend, even if it would not be the really important news. "Herr Werner has agreed to give me the count's collection," she said. "I want your help in planning the grand preview. I want it to be the finest we have held."

* * *

"I am sure that Miss Fairbourne is not involved in anything that interests us," Darius said. "I cannot speak for Marielle Lyon, however."

Darius gave his report, such as it was, while he smoked a cigar in his library. Ambury nodded sagely and risked a small, knowing smile. "That is a relief to know."

"How so?" Kendale asked, his sharp gaze shooting from one friend to the other.

Ambury blew smoke toward the ceiling. "We hope not to discover trouble of that nature that involves our citizens, correct?"

"I did not mean how so is it a relief, but how so does Southwaite know for sure that she is not up to no good."

Darius had not said she was not up to no good. "I asked Tarrington if he had cause to think she should be watched. He said this was her first visit to the coast in a year, and that there was no evidence she had any involvement with either spies or information."

It had been all he had gotten out of Tarrington when he forced the question yet again before leaving Kent. Emma had extracted that promise from Tarrington not to speak of her meeting with him. Damned if Tarrington hadn't insisted on keeping his word to the end, even when offered a bribe.

"Well, of course, if the king of smugglers vouches for her, who am I to be suspicious?" Kendale said.

"You will leave her alone now," Darius said firmly. "You will no longer watch her or have her watched."

"I have not watched her. That was to be your duty, for all the good that did."

"Damnation, Kendale, do not take it as yours again, is what I am saying. Turn your attention elsewhere."

Ambury raised one eyebrow at his tone, but kept whatever clever retort had sprung to mind to himself. "What did you do with the boat Tarrington stopped?"

"I left it with Tarrington. I brought the spy back with me. He is a guest of the Home Office now," Darius said.

"He may not be a spy," Ambury said.

"The boat held little of value on it. A few kegs of brandy to pretend it made the journey for trade. Four other refugees came, who are dismayed to find themselves guests of the Home Office now too. As for the man in question, he brought nothing personal with him. That is what made Tarrington suspicious. Who would flee his home, perhaps never to return, and not pocket at least one item of value or sentiment?"

"You should have just hanged him," Kendale said.

"We still have a government, Kendale. It has the authority to hang people, not us." Ambury spoke casually but anyone who knew him would hear the pointed notes of disapproval. "Your bloodlust against the French is why we do not allow you to do anything on your own. None of us relish the notion of being tried for murder."

The word *bloodlust* seemed to check Kendale. He even appeared momentarily chagrined by the lecture.

Ambury became all smooth amiability again. "It was convenient that you were on the coast, Southwaite. It spared me another journey."

Yes, most convenient to their mission. Most inconvenient to his private purposes for being on the coast in the first place.

He had not seen Emma since her carriage had rolled away from his house. His own return had been delayed two days while he arranged for the transport of the boat's passengers. Upon finally arriving yesterday, he had flipped through his mail looking in vain for her plain penmanship on a letter.

What had he expected her to write? That she had erred? That of course she would entertain the notion of marriage? It had been a proposal of obligation. In addition to her "everything else," she was not a woman to accept the obligation that such a marriage would create for her in turn.

"All of this duty is making me feel old," Ambury mused, while he poured some wine. He looked at the decanter and cocked an eyebrow in Darius's direction. "It is French. From your cellar, I assume," he teased.

Kendale looked down at his own glass.

"It is very old, like you feel."

"We must do something fun, before we forget how," Ambury said. "Perhaps we should all go to Penthurst's ball. Were you invited? That was bold of him."

"Damned bold," Kendale said.

Darius had been invited. That letter had been waiting upon his return too. It was not clear whether Penthurst had sent it as an attempt at rapprochement, or as a perverse, sardonic whim. He was capable of the latter.

"I say we go," Ambury said. "We will clean you up, Kendale. If we put you in formal dress and teach you to smile, you should be presentable, at least. I will introduce you to some young ladies who, rumor has it, find you attractive in a somewhat barbaric way."

"I am not looking for a wife."

"Nor are they looking for husbands, since they already have them."

They all laughed, but thoughts of his own ballroom filled Darius's mind, and of a woman who had never danced in such a chamber, but whose eyes and body and sensual embrace had enchanted him beneath a large chandelier.

"Here he comes," Cassandra whispered with excitement. "I cannot believe we pulled this off, Emma."

Nor could Emma believe it. Evidence that they had walked in the auction house door. Herr Ludwig Werner, bedecked in his braided coat and military in his bearing, approached them and bowed.

Obediah bowed even deeper. "We are extremely honored that you have entrusted us with the count's consignments. We will not disappoint you."

Herr Werner raised a hand in a gesture to invisible people. A small army of servants began carrying in paintings.

Emma wetted her lips and stepped closer to Obediah. "Titian," she whispered as a large mythological scene paraded by.

"What a magnificent Titian," Obediah exclaimed loudly.

Herr Werner smiled indulgently.

"Giovanni Bellini," she whispered as a small oil passed. "The headdress says it is a Doge of Venice."

"Ah, Bellini!" Obediah clasped his hands together in joy. "I think that is the finest portrait by him that I have seen. That is a doge, is it not, Herr Werner?"

"Rembrandt, but questionable," she whispered as an Old Testament scene sped by a tad too fast.

Obediah stopped the servants and peered severely at the painting, then waved it on. Herr Werner would not be surprised if they gave it a less illustrious attribution now.

And so it went for half an hour, as twenty-five paintings came in, were given a first, cursory inspection, then propped against the exhibition hall walls. When all the paintings had entered, three soldiers did as well.

"You will not mind, I am sure, if a few of the count's house guards remain here until after the auction," Herr Werner said. "One does not leave treasures without protection."

Obediah appeared perplexed. Emma inserted herself between them. "We expected nothing less, Herr Werner. I think one of them should stand outside the door, to announce to anyone thinking of theft that a sword waits if such an attempt it made."

Herr Werner nodded with approval, and said something in German to the guards. One of them retreated to the door to take up his post.

Emma retreated to Cassandra's side.

"Very shrewd," Cassandra said. "That uniform standing guard will be more intriguing than all the advertisements and invitations you could arrange."

"I thought so."

The delivery completed, Emma expected Herr Werner to leave. She and Cassandra needed to finish planning the grand preview, and she wanted to give these paintings a much closer look.

Instead Herr Werner studied the walls, and the paintings hanging on them. "I am confused," he said to Obediah. "Where are Lord Southwaite's contributions?"

Obediah pasted a smile on his face, but glanced to Emma desperately. "Lord Southwaite's contributions . . . Yes—that is, they are . . ."

"I expected them to be here by now. Perhaps I misunderstood when he would bring them."

"Uhh . . . yes, I think that perhaps you—"

"You have been in communication with our esteemed collector, Herr Werner?" Emma asked.

He kept frowning at the walls. "He wrote to me and said he intended to consign four important paintings. The patronage of such a man reassured me, of course." He looked over his shoulder at Obediah and smiled slyly. "Our special arrangements on the commission helped too."

"We have added a Raphael to the auction recently. It did not come from the Earl of Southwaite, but rather an esteemed gentleman who requires anonymity," Emma said. "It is an exquisite work, one more than worthy to keep company with the count's collection. Would you like to see it?"

The mention of a Raphael suitably impressed Herr Werner. He was about to speak when something caught his eye. He abruptly turned toward the door and broke into a big smile. "Ah, here he is. I wrote to say I was bringing the paintings today if he wanted to see them first."

Southwaite entered like the lord he was and greeted Herr Werner with the hint of condescension expected. He bowed formally to Emma and Cassandra, then turned to Obediah.

"Mr. Riggles, the paintings that I mentioned are being removed from a wagon outside. I trust that you will have a corner where they can be hung, even with the count's impressive collection in your sale."

Obediah did not show his surprise, but Emma could read it well enough in his eyes. This was the first he had heard of any consignments from Southwaite.

Herr Werner had eyes for no one except Southwaite now. "You intend to auction more current works, I believe you wrote, Lord Southwaite." He rubbed his hands together. "A good mix, then. We will not compete with each other."

The two men chatted while those current works were carried in. A Watteau that Southwaite had bought here at auction came first, then a Gillot and an Italian primitive of great charm that Emma could not attribute. Finally a large, beautiful Venetian scene by Guardi arrived, carried by three men.

Obediah sidled close to Emma. "Did Lord Southwaite tell you about these consignments?"

"Not one word." She wondered when he had written to Herr Werner with his intentions. Before they went to Kent, it appeared.

Southwaite had not approved of this sale. He wanted the business sold. She knew now that he even suspected Fairbourne's of criminal activity. Yet he had taken a step to ensure she received this collection.

Herr Werner came over to take his leave. With a flourish he marched out. Southwaite turned his attention to the count's paintings.

"I will prepare the papers for these consignments, sir," Obediah said to Southwaite. "They should be in order in a quarter hour, if you would care to wait, or I will bring them to you if you prefer."

"I will wait." He lifted the Bellini to get a closer look.

Cassandra caught Emma's eye. She nodded her head in Southwaite's direction and rolled her eyes. Then she walked away and sat in a chair near the entrance and proceeded to flirt with the house guards.

Emma approached Southwaite. She could not blame him if he cut her now, or dismissed her the way he might a servant. He appeared capable of either. She had come to know him so well that she forgot sometimes just how hard he could appear, and how his face and carriage were marked by the prerogatives of his birth and breeding.

"It is a stunning portrait," she said of the Bellini that he held.

"It is amazing. The clarity of the light makes it very lifelike."

"Perhaps you will buy it."

"Perhaps I will." He set it down and turned to face her with an expression most cool. "When will the sale be?"

"Ten days from now. The invitations were sent this morning for the grand preview. It will be the night before." The letter from Robert had made holding the sale as soon as possible an imperative. Her fingers had almost bled last night from all the invitations she had written.

"The count's collection is better than I expected," he said. "You should do very well."

"Your help will make it so. Thank you."

He shrugged. "Except for the Guardi, I had tired of them."

"I do not mean your paintings, but your correspondence with Herr Werner."

He strolled slowly along the wall, and resumed viewing the paintings lined up at its base. "Well, you were determined to go forward. If it were going to happen at all, Fairbourne's should make a good showing."

Of course. He had an investment here, after all. He would indeed want Fairbourne's to acquit itself well, so its value would not be diminished.

She paced along with him, admiring the collection, proud of just how good a showing it would be and relieved that she might well raise the money to ransom Robert.

"You are being very cool, Emma," Southwaite said. "Have you nothing to say to me except things about your auction?"

"Forgive me. I do not know the etiquette. I cannot imagine what women and men would say to each other in situations such as this."

"In your case, you might say that after some thought you realized that only a madwoman would turn down a proposal from an earl."

She had counted on him never mentioning that. His pride was hurt, still. "It was mad, wasn't it?"

"Idiotic."

"But also wise, unfortunately." She did not like having to say that again. She resented that he required it.

"I disagree. However, for the moment it is convenient. It makes what I am about to say easier to broach."

"What is that?"

His gaze scanned the exhibition hall, then came to rest on her. "How many lots in this auction will be from esteemed gentlemen who demand discretion?"

She swallowed hard. "Not too many."

"Make it none."

"That may not be possible."

"Make it possible. Return what you cannot attach to a name. It must all go. Today."

"The consignor of the drawings will not agree to have his name used. Also there is one painting—you have not seen it yet—which must remain even if all else is returned. The Raphael. Word has unaccountably spread that there will be one."

"Has it, now? Unaccountably, no less."

"I will not give that up. I promise that its provenance is in order."

"You can keep the Raphael, and the drawings, but you must obey me on the rest. Do you understand that, Emma? The Guardi alone will replace whatever you might have earned off what you return."

She nodded, not because she was sure the Guardi would do that, but because she could not find the courage to refuse him. He had taken some pains to arrange things so she would not have to sell illegal goods. She could hardly announce that she would do so anyway, even if a part of her wanted to, in order to prove that she had not surrendered more than she guessed in the ballroom.

She had, however. That was obvious to her now that she was with him again. His closeness affected her body and her heart. With one look and one word he could spin his spell. She hated to admit that she had little defense against it.

He took her hand and bent over it in a bow of farewell. His warm breath titillated her skin and sent trembles up her arm.

His lips briefly touched her skin.

She glanced around, worried that someone might see the deep flush that she felt warming her face, and the rest of her too. Cassandra still sat near the door. The two guards now stood near her, laughing.

Again his lips pressed her hand. He looked up at her and triumph showed in his eyes. He knew about that flush even if no one else did. It was all there, his awareness that she was hardly immune and the power that her surrender had given him. He did not appear to be a man who had accepted her rejection, but then, he had given her fair warning that he would not.

One more kiss, then he walked away.

Cassandra received a bow too. After the earl left, she hurried to where Emma stood. She looked at Emma with anticipation.

"We need to complete the planning of the grand preview," Emma said, walking toward the storage. "We must decide on the food and drink."

Cassandra followed. "What a surprise, to have Southwaite bring those paintings."

"It was very surprising."

"It will be the finest auction of the year, I think."

"Your jewels will have the best audience possible." Emma moved aside the roll of drawings that came to her by way of Mariélle Lyon, then set a sheet of paper on the desk. "What should we feed the guests?"

"Better turn your mind to the drink first. That is the costlier provision. Punch?"

"Punch will do, but . . ." Emma rose and squeezed between the tables toward a far corner where canvas covered a blocky tower.

Southwaite had commanded she return anything without a named consignor. She did not know how to return the goods that had come in the wagon. Nor would she do it.

She needed to raise a good amount of money from this auction. Herr Werner had demanded a much lower seller's commission, and she would owe Marielle and Cassandra payments too. She would make sure that those books and silver and even the silk and laces had a consignor, though, so he was not exactly disobeyed.

As for the rest, she could always throw it in the river, she supposed. Or . . .

"Fairbourne's has some cases of old wine here, Cassandra. Perhaps we should serve that." She fished under the canvas until her hand felt a bottle's neck. She pulled it out and made her way back to the desk, holding it high.

"Serve the punch, but definitely offer wine if you have enough."

"I have enough." She nipped over to the office and found a screw. "Are you experienced in using one of these?" she asked Cassandra upon returning.

Cassandra went to work on the bottle. "I heard that Southwaite was down in Kent again. At the same time that you were there."

"Do tell."

"Did you see him?"

"Kent is a big county and we hardly have the same circles. We were unlikely to cross paths."

"It is not so big." Cassandra put her strength into pulling out the cork. "He kissed your hand when he left."

"He can be very gallant."

"It seemed a long kiss to me. Very long. I would describe it as lingering."

"Tosh! You could not even see it."

"I could see you blush. That was very apparent to me. As was the way he looked at you when he left."

"You are boring me now." Emma wiped out two silver goblets borrowed from the consignments. "Let us taste this, to make sure it will be worthy of my guests."

They tasted. Cassandra raised her eyebrows, impressed. "It is a very fine claret, nicely aged."

Emma enjoyed her cup immensely. "It does not seem to have suffered any damage, or turned."

Cassandra poured them each another cup. "You must bring one bottle home and have Maitland decant it, to be sure. After it breathes it should taste even better. Let us try a bit more, though, to make sure our initial impressions hold."

Emma's impressions improved with the second cup. It warmed her, and brought the gentle peace wine could imbue.

"Emma, forgive me for asking, but if I do not, I will burst. Have you been a little naughty?" Cassandra asked between sips. "With Southwaite, I mean."

"No, I have not been naughty, Cassandra."

"Oh, that is a relief." Cassandra pressed her palm to her heart. "When I saw the two of you together today, well, the most astonishing notion came to me." She laughed at herself. "I am happy that I misunderstood."

Emma cradled the goblet in her two hands and gazed over its rim at Cassandra. "You certainly have misunderstood. I have not been a little naughty. I have been very, very bad."

Cassandra's eyes widened in shock, then narrowed fast. She scrutinized Emma hard. "When you say very bad, do you mean very bad for Emma, who is never bad at all and thus very bad might only mean quite naughty, or do you mean very bad in a generally understood sort of way?"

"I mean very bad the way you might mean it."

"Emma, are you saying that Southwaite *seduced* you?"

Emma nodded, drank her wine, and waited for Cassandra's congratulations.

"Oh, dear," Cassandra muttered, stunned.

"I thought you would approve. You encouraged me to practice with him."

"*Flirting*, Emma. I encouraged you to practice *flirting* with him."

At six o'clock that evening, Emma still remained at Fairbourne's. Other than the house guards, she was alone.

Cassandra had left in a state of shock. Emma refused to give the details of that tryst with Southwaite, but Cassandra had surmised enough to know just how bad Emma had been. After swearing her to secrecy, Emma had revealed the proposal too, but only because Cassandra had taken umbrage at Southwaite's behavior and called him a scoundrel.

Cassandra had understood why Emma could not accept such an offer. At least, she claimed she had. If Cassandra had thought the reasons less than clear, it was because she did not know all the reasons.

Emma gazed at the bottle of wine they had shared. If she did not auction the wine, or the other contents of that wagon, could she claim she had not done anything wrong? In providing those paintings that would cover the loss of commissions if she obeyed Southwaite, had he also provided a balm to her conscience? It would be nice not to betray him by passing illegal goods right under his nose, through a business in which he possessed a troublesome partnership.

If no more wagons arrived secretly, if she could win the prize with a favor that did not compromise Fairbourne's or him, if she could be done with all of this in a week, perhaps—

The second cup of wine had made her merry, but its effects were fading fast. All of her "ifs" sounded foolish to her mind. They were the voices of a woman grasping for hope that perhaps she might finish this game unscathed. She did not really think that would happen. Her own character and honor would be stained, even if no one else ever knew it.

She went out to the exhibition hall. The house guards still stood at their posts, and the third remained outside. Perhaps they waited for her to depart so they could sit down.

The paintings faced her from where they had been set against the wall. She had a lot of work to do in the next week. She would be very busy. Too busy, perhaps, to think about Southwaite.

The door to the street opened. The guards immediately flanked the threshold. A man in an ill-fitting coat and flat-brimmed hat entered. The guard posted outside grabbed him by the collar and began to pull him back out.

"Allow him in," she called. "He is here to see me."

The guard released her caller. The man whom she had met at St. Paul's walked to her, head tilted so he could see the paintings high on the wall.

"I was wondering how to find you again," she said. "I will have the payment soon, but do not know how to deliver it."

"That's what I am for. Deliveries and such, back and forth. I'm here to explain how it is done, seein' as how yer father doesn't seem to have told ye."

"I hope you are not saying that I am supposed to hand the money to *you*."

He drew back, insulted. "I do not like the way ye said that. Ye will do it just as I say when it happens."

"Then tell your master that I'll be wanting that prize immediately."

"Ye expect to be that rich so soon?" He pushed back his hat and stared up at the paintings in wonder. "Are these daubings worth so much? That is why ye have those soldiers here, I guess."

"That is why. So deliver my expectations to whoever sent you. Tell him that I will be waiting to hear his plans for receiving the payment and delivering the prize. The auction is ten days hence. I want to settle this two days after that."

He turned to her with a perplexed frown. "Did ye not hear me the last time, about watching that sharp tongue? I'll say it nicer for ye, so it ain't taken wrong."

"Say it however you like, as long as you say it plainly enough to be heard right. Now I must lock this building, and those guards appear to think thrashing you would be fun, so you should probably leave."

He left quickly enough, skirting around the guards as best he could while keeping a cautious eye on them. Emma waited until the door closed, then ran to it and opened it a crack to peer out.

She saw her visitor walking down the street at a casual saunter. She bid farewell to the guards, then nipped into her waiting carriage. She opened the panel behind the coachman.

"Mr. Dillon, do you see that man that just left, walking up ahead of you? Can you follow him, but at enough distance that he does not suspect you are on his trail?"

"I can try, Miss Fairbourne."

"Then do try, please. I would like to know where he is going."

They plodded along at a very slow pace. Emma resisted the urge to hang out the window to keep the man in view.

She saw the buildings of the Strand for a long while, then those that indicated they were in the City. It seemed to her that they turned north, but it was hard to tell in the winding streets of the old sections of London. She also saw the light changing, as evening stretched on toward night.

It must have been almost two hours of incremental movement before the carriage stopped completely.

"I fear that I have lost him, Miss Fairbourne. He turned down this street, then disappeared. Could be he entered one of these houses," Mr. Dillon said.

Emma finally stuck her head to the window and looked out. Mr. Dillon angled around from his seat at the ribbons.

"You are sure he came here?" she asked, studying the houses.

"I'm sure. He might have suspected us, and nipped through a garden to another street, of course."

She supposed so. She wished something about one of these houses indicated he had entered, though. They were average homes, narrow and tall, and appeared familiar in a general way. The people walking this street looked like so many others in the City—not poor, but far from comfortably situated too.

"Not as crowded this time," Mr. Dillon said. "Even ne'er-do-wells have to eat supper."

She looked up at him. "This time? Have you been here before?"

"Not here exactly. The next street over. Remember? That house with the blue door that I took you to—it is right down there, over one street."

No wonder this neighborhood looked familiar. She was sitting within two hundred yards of Marielle Lyon's print-making studio.

Chapter 22

Torches flamed on both sides of Albemarle Street, illuminating the carriages lined up to release their occupants. Inside Fairbourne's, Obediah Riggles prepared to perform as both auctioneer and exhibition hall manager.

Emma kept reassuring him that he would excel at the latter role, but a grand preview was not the night to find out if that were true. She hoped the presence of Herr Werner, who was not too proud to do a bit of hawking of his master's paintings, would avoid having Obediah ever be stumped by questions he could not answer.

Society began entering the auction house. First a trickle, then a stream. Ladies in artistic turbans and narrow, diaphanous evening dresses posed on the arms of gentlemen dressed with more variety. Some wigs could still be seen among older men, as well as colorful frock coats. The younger ones sported the subdued garments and the short, classical Roman–cropped hair promoted by republican sentiments.

Emma wore a dress of dusty lavender with long full sleeves, and no jewels or feathers. This was not a social occasion for her, as such. Mourning did not prohibit her attendance, but she sought to appear appropriately sedate.

Cassandra had not been so constrained. Her jewels were a highlight of the auction, and she wore one of the most magnificent on her neck. The reds and blues of her new turban wrapped her dark crown, all of it set off by a huge white feather. She stood near the case holding the other jewels, smugly enjoying how society's matrons had to acknowledge her in order to peer at the riches.

Emma spied a large party outside the door. A man with them entered first. Tall, dark, and unnaturally beautiful, he held the door for the rest. He shared smiles and laughs with them while he eased the happy knot toward the walls, then turned and signaled for a member of the staff to bring them wine.

Leaving the party as smoothly as he had joined it, he approached Emma and bowed.

"Miss Fairbourne, you look to be triumphant tonight."

"How nice of you to say so, Mr. Nightingale."

He turned his attention to the mosaic of paintings. "They are as fine as your father ever procured." He cocked his head, still watching that wall. "Mr. Riggles is having difficulties, however. I just heard him refer to the small portrait as by Gentile Bellini, not Giovanni."

"An understandable error."

"Not with a crowd such as this. I think that you badly need an experienced exhibition hall manager tonight."

Pride made her want to disagree. She did not want Mr. Nightingale to be right about anything he had said to her after the last auction.

She looked for Obediah, and saw him surrounded by patrons. A most respected collector pointed at the Titian while he spoke. Obediah tried valiantly to appear confident and expert, but Emma could read the desperation in his eyes.

"Two guineas," she offered. "For tonight and the auction. Also, while I may need a manager with this crush, I do not need a husband, Mr. Nightingale. I trust that your return means that you understand that."

He laughed as if she had made a great joke. He appeared to have forgotten that he had ever proposed.

He turned and welcomed a viscountess who had always been one of his favorite rich birds. The flatteries flowed like molten sugar in both directions, but Emma suddenly lost all interest in the show. A most illustrious collector had just entered the auction house, and he commanded all of her attention.

Her heart rose to her throat. It remained there, blocking her breath. She had been waiting all night for Southwaite to arrive. She realized she had been waiting all week to see him again. The excitement that had maddened her today had not been only because of this party.

He was not alone. Two men accompanied him. One was the handsome man with blue eyes from the first auction. The other looked familiar too, but Emma could not remember where she had seen him.

Cassandra left her post by the jewels and hurried over. "You must be very charming to him, Emma, no matter what you think of his scandalous behavior toward you. He has brought two of his friends, and elevated the party in doing so."

"Who are they?"

"The friendly one is Viscount Ambury, heir to the Earl of Highburton. The scowling, unpleasant one is Viscount Kendale." Cassandra froze, and quickly turned her back on the trio. "Oh, dear. He is coming this way. Be brave, Emma." She glanced over her shoulder. "Oh, dear." She hurried away.

Oh, dear. That was what Cassandra had said after learning about the ballroom. Three times she had said it. *Oh, dear, oh, dear, oh, dear.*

Southwaite moved in Emma's direction. He made slow progress. His name was on the catalogue sheets as a consignor, so he was one of the actors in this show even if the absent Count von Kardstadt was the leading man. Everyone wanted a word with him.

With each of his steps, a delicious anticipation took a stronger hold of her. *Oh, dear.*

"I trust you are not going to cut me this time," he said when he finally greeted her.

"I never cut patrons who consign four superb paintings."

"You only cut partners with a vested interest in what you are doing, then."

"Only partners who might interfere with what I am doing." She looked out on the crowd in the hall. "It may be the finest grand preview Fairbourne's has seen. The count's collection helped, as did the house guard standing outside all week, but I think many thanks go to you. Did you encourage attendance tonight?"

"I may have mentioned the auction in the course of conversation with some people, but curiosity about the doings here had a life of its own." He accepted a glass of wine from one of the servants offering it to the guests. He sipped, and raised an appreciative eyebrow. He glanced to his left. "I see Mr. Nightingale has returned."

"Only for tonight. He arrived when it was apparent the attendance would be in the hundreds, and poor Obediah could not manage, so I hired him on the spot."

"You do not have to explain to me."

As if he heard their conversation, Mr. Nightingale looked their way, caught Southwaite's eye, and nodded, as if answering some question.

"That was odd. Did you tell him to come here this evening, Southwaite?" Emma asked.

"I might have suggested that he show up, and grovel a bit."

"I would have preferred if you had spoken to me first. He left for a reason and—"

"Oh, good. A row. I have missed them." He took her arm and guided her to the terrace door. "But not here, Emma. Discretion, remember? Come with me."

She should have insisted that she could not leave, that she was needed in the exhibition hall. The flutters in her chest defeated any such objection. She allowed him to spirit her outside, and into the garden.

They were not alone. Patrons dotted the walks, taking some air, and conversation buzzed in the night. The lanterns on the terrace did not provide much light amid the plantings, however, and the dark offered some privacy.

"You needed Nightingale tonight. Since you were too proud to call for him, I devised a different strategy," he said.

"I did not ask you to devise a—"

"I did not require your request, Emma. I am an investor, remember? A partner. My equal interests in this auction permit me to devise whenever I choose."

His words penetrated her silly excitement. They entered her head and just sat there, in their fullness, with all their implications. She stopped walking and looked at him. She almost burst out laughing at her own astonishment. At the same time, however, deep discouragement killed her joy and turned her spirit tired and leaden.

"My own interests." He was not only speaking of his four paintings. *"I am an investor."*

She could not believe she had been so stupid.

In all of her plotting and calculations, as she estimated the auction's income and subtracted the payments to consignors and agents, she had neglected to account for the most obvious and largest cost. Him.

Her father's accounts had shown no such payments to his partner, but there had been many with no name at all. She should have assumed some were to Southwaite. If a man invested in a business, he anticipated some income from it.

Whatever Fairbourne's made off this auction, Southwaite would receive half. More than half, since she had never given him his share from the last sale.

A glint moved in the dark, as he set down his glass on a stone bench. Emma rather wished she had not served the wine tonight. She could have sold it somehow, even if not at this auction. She could have gotten good money for it if its quality impressed both Cassandra and this earl.

"You are suddenly subdued, Emma."

"I am reconciling myself to admitting that you were correct in anticipating that I would need Mr. Nightingale tonight. Within a half hour Obediah was a drowning man in that crowd."

"Then you forgive me?" He said it as a tease, which meant he did not really require her forgiveness.

"You are an *owner*. I cannot even claim the rights of one myself. It is not for me to forgive." Her mind kept racing through figures and likely commissions. She would not see three thousand, she was certain, after Southwaite was paid. She would possibly have fifteen hundred, however. She would just have to agree to do that favor.

Southwaite pulled her into the shadows behind some shrubbery. His arms surrounded her and all thoughts of auctions and figures flew from her mind.

"I am not only an owner and an investor, Emma. I was your lover. Have you forgotten that so quickly?" His forehead touched hers, then his lips brushed her mouth. "Do I need to remind you?"

"I need no reminders about the past. However, you are not my lover now." It needed saying, much as it pained her. He was pretending some understanding had been made, when she had agreed to nothing. Quite the opposite. Speaking plainly was much harder when your heart and blood urged you to say something other than what your mind decreed, however.

She felt his lips smile against her mouth. "My, how formidable you sound, Emma. If words won such engagements, you would always be the victor. I should retreat immediately, but that is hard to do when my arms are full of lovely, supple, feminine warmth."

He had a good point. It felt very good in his arms, however. Friendly and safe and, yes, pleasantly arousing. The last purred lowly. "I am just proving that I can resist you."

"This is not the way to prove it."

To prove it better, to herself as well as to him, she placed her palms on his chest and slowly pushed back against his embrace. It was harder to do than she thought it would be. The purr did not like it at all. Nor did her heart, which ached with disappointment and resignation.

He released her. They shared a few awkward moments facing each other in the dark, saying nothing. She wondered if he weighed just how serious her resistance would be if he were more aggressive. She wondered too.

"I must return to the preview," she said, lest she find out just how weak she was.

They emerged from behind the shrubs and aimed for the hall.

She stepped up to the terrace. She paused and cocked her head. "That is odd. It is suddenly very quiet in there."

The exhibition hall might have been a church, it had grown so still. She noticed that they were all alone on the terrace now, and no patrons remained in the garden.

A sweet, plaintive sound snaked out the open window. It grew into a melody much like a cry from a human heart. Someone inside was playing a violin.

"It is my friend, Viscount Ambury," Southwaite whispered. "He rarely plays for others. Perhaps once or twice a year, and it is never known when and if he will. But all who have heard him know that he rivals the best to be had in a concert hall."

They could not enter without disturbing the performance, so they listened from the terrace. The music touched Emma deeply. It plucked at her composure until she could not resist the way it moved her. The notes seemed to become part of the breeze, and form a web of sentiment between her and the man at her side.

She closed her eyes, so only the music would affect her senses. She knew Southwaite did too. They stood there in the night while the music spoke to their souls. She sensed how they shared this as surely as she felt his warmth.

It was not a long piece. Silence held for a few moments when it was over, then accolades rang in the exhibition hall. Emma opened her eyes, and realized that her hand was held by Southwaite.

"He is technically as proficient as anyone. He never misses a note." Southwaite's voice came gruffly. He made a little cough to clear it.

"It was not technical expertise alone that produced such sound. He is a magnificent musician in every way."

"So women say. Men do not notice the sentimental effects as much."

Cassandra descended on her as soon as they rejoined the party, and pulled her away from Southwaite. "What a triumph, Emma. It will be all the talk tomorrow. Why did you not tell me of this entertainment when I expressed concerns that you had not hired enough musicians?"

"I kept no secret from you. I am as surprised as you are. Perhaps he thought the count's collection deserved a special homage."

Emma sought Ambury's blue eyes in the crowd, and went to him to express her gratitude.

Southwaite had probably pressed his friend into this. Like Cassandra, he had known it would be all the talk tomorrow. Which meant that the auction itself would be on everyone's lips too.

He was ensuring Fairbourne's success in every way he could. When it was done, she will have arranged and managed one of the most illustrious auctions in Fairbourne's history. It would be a triumph to remember for the rest of her life.

She could not ignore, however, that Southwaite's motivations were not all pure kindness. He might be giving her this one great victory and wonderful memory because he still intended there to be no others.

Chapter 23

D arius watched two men carefully remove the Titian from the wall and hand it down to two others. Once it was propped on the floor, Mr. Nightingale moved in with his journal. He marked the buyer's name on the back.

"Leave it here," he instructed. "It is too large for the worktables, and we will box it where it stands for delivery." He gestured to the Guardi. "That one next, and it also must remain here in the hall."

Darius left Mr. Nightingale to finish one other task that he clearly did very well. He walked into the office.

Herr Werner sat there, frowning. His expression probably had to do with Emma's presence in Maurice Fairbourne's chair. She scribbled furiously on a sheet of paper, all the while consulting her notes from the auction.

"Lord Southwaite," he said, jumping to his feet. "Thank goodness you are still here. This woman—" He gestured with an agitated hand at Emma.

"She is unnaturally sharp with figures, Herr Werner," Darius soothed. "I have confidence that you will find her calculations clear and precise when you check them yourself."

Herr Werner looked down at his catalogue, and seemed reassured. Emma kept scribbling. Finally she sat back in the chair.

"Herr Werner, most of the purchase money will arrive tomorrow. Solicitors will bring it, and other agents of our patrons. We do not expect them to carry such amounts with them when they attend auctions here." She pointed to a high stack of banknotes. "However, some did pay at once, for items of smaller value. The drawings, for example. Much of the silver. Here is the amount on hand now. I will give you part of what is due you tonight, based on your percentage for those paid for items that you consigned."

Werner did not like her logic. Since he had consigned very few items of small value, the amount to be handed over to him would be minimal.

She gave him her figures and he scrutinized the columns. "The rest will be here tomorrow, you say?"

"Two days hence at the latest."

"And if someone does not pay?"

"He will not receive the painting. Fairbourne's does not extend credit. Is that not so, Lord Southwaite?"

"That is correct, Herr Werner. Fairbourne's is very strict about payments. Even from me."

Emma counted out three stacks of banknotes, and handed him the smallest.

"I will leave the guards here until all is settled," he said by way of farewell.

With his departure, Emma exhaled a deep sigh and closed her eyes. She appeared distant and exhausted. It had been a trying few weeks for her. During the last four days Darius knew she had all but lived at the auction house, preparing for the party and sale.

"Congratulations are due, Emma. Fairbourne's will be long remembered for today's auction."

She opened her eyes. No longer distant, and anything but

tired in appearance, she smiled broadly. "It was good, wasn't it?"

"Very good. Impressive. As smooth as the best-rehearsed opera."

"Did you see that crowd? We did not have enough chairs. Mr. Nightingale reported he counted more than three hundred." She flushed with excitement. "And the bids! Cassandra is in heaven over what her jewels brought. The drawings went for much more than I expected, and I cannot believe that the Duke of Penthurst paid so much for your Guardi. That was the biggest surprise of the day."

"He has always admired it." It had been the surprise of the day for Darius; that was certain. He hoped Penthurst had not purchased it out of nostalgia for better times between them. They had been together in Venice during their grand tours, and Guardi's view of St. Mark's Square captured nuanced impressions of that experience. "Fortunately, his pursuit of it distracted him from the Raphael."

"I am glad that is going to you, Southwaite. The man who consigned it will be very glad to know it will have such a worthy home."

Still smiling, and restless in her happiness, she stood. She pointed at one of the stacks of banknotes. "That is yours." She picked up the other and began stuffing it into her reticule.

He eyed his stack, then picked up the accounting she had given to Herr Werner. "This is not clear in naming the costs."

"Of course it is." She came around the desk and pointed at the figures. "See here. This is the auction's total, but these down here address the amounts received today. This is Fairbourne's costs and payouts, and this—"

"I do not understand the need for some of these expenses. The amounts are very large." He folded the accounting. "There is much to discuss here, Emma."

She groaned, audibly. "I will sit and explain every line to you, but not right now, please. I want to store this money safely in my house, then celebrate how brilliant I was today."

"You should not do either alone. Are you done here? Can you leave the rest to Nightingale and Riggles? Good. I will call for my carriage."

Southwaite ushered Emma out of the auction house with a surprising lack of ceremony. In no time at all she found herself in his carriage with her bulging reticule on her lap. He climbed in and sat across from her. She stuck her face to the window. "Mr. Dillon—"

"I just sent him home. I will see you returned to your house once matters are settled between us."

He was still curious about the accounting. She knew why. She just did not want to match wits with him over it now. "What is to settle? I calculated everything on the assumption that you were to get half." She held out her hands. "All done."

He gazed at her reticule. She had stuffed in so much money that it would not even close properly. It looked like a fattened chicken.

"Were you going to ride home with that much money with no more than your coachman as an escort?"

"Mr. Dillon is capable of protecting me. Nor are there highwaymen on the streets of London."

"There must be at least a thousand pounds there. A member of your staff could have told a friend to lie in wait. That reticule would be far gone before Mr. Dillon even climbed down from his perch."

"That would never happen."

"It won't now, since I am here."

It was thoughtful of him to offer protection, but she suspected that his fascination with her reticule had nothing to do with thieves. He had noticed that her stack of banknotes had far exceeded his own in height; that was all. He wondered to whom all that extra money would be going. Perhaps he even thought that payments for consignments of smuggled goods were included. If so, he would be right.

She decided it would be best to immediately tell him about Marielle Lyon's twenty percent, and Cassandra's ten, and her decision to put off paying him for the first auction until she received all the money from this one. All of that might keep him from probing too deeply on what else was in her reticule and why.

"Let us go to the park and take a turn and I will explain the accounting while we walk," she said.

"I do not think a park is the appropriate place."

She leaned toward him and whispered. "I will talk very softly like this and no one will ever know that our conversation is about something as terrible as money."

"There is a successful auction to celebrate, Emma, and we cannot do that in the park. Far better if we go to my house, where we can enjoy both discretion and comfort while we congratulate each other."

She looked at him. He looked right back.

"Southwaite, are you being sly? Are you just trying to get me alone?"

"Absolutely, but you have nothing to fear. Your formidable resistance should protect you from me if seduction enters my mind." He smiled. "I have no suspicious, ulterior motives today, however. I want to toast you and praise you, as you deserve."

Emma viewed the façade of Southwaite's townhome with some trepidation. The last time she had entered one of his properties, she had ended up naked in the middle of a ballroom.

He claimed he had no ulterior motives, however. He had not even tried to kiss her in the carriage.

He brought her to the library, a vast comfortable room on the second level that overlooked a charming side garden. A dark-haired woman sat near those windows, reading a book. She did not even look up from her page when they entered.

Southwaite excused himself and went over to her. He said a few words and the woman looked down the chamber at

Emma. Face expressionless and eyes as opaque as an iron door, she rose and accompanied him back to where Emma stood.

Southwaite introduced her as his sister, Lydia. The family resemblance was obvious in the dark hair and even more in the form of their eyes. However, while Southwaite's normally showed something of his inner self, Lydia's revealed . . . nothing much at all.

"Will you be good enough to sit with Miss Fairbourne while I speak with the steward about ferreting out the wine cellar's best champagne, Lydia? It should only be a short while."

Lydia nodded. Southwaite left the library.

Emma and Lydia sat on two divans that faced each other. Emma smiled. Lydia did not. Silence reigned. Lydia regarded Emma but made no attempt to do more than she had been asked by her brother.

"The day is fair, is it not?" Emma asked.

"Most fair," Lydia said.

More silence. "This is a handsome library."

"I like it well enough."

Emma made a few more efforts. For each she received the minimal response and no effort in return.

"I think that your brother assumed you would not mind company," Emma finally said. "He erred, did he not?"

"I do not mind company as such. I merely do not like idle conversation. I say very little, because it is more polite than speaking most of the time."

"I doubt anything you say could be less polite than making no conversation at all."

Lydia's eyebrows rose. Depths formed in her eyes, as if a soul had just been breathed into her body. "I dare not share my thoughts most of the time, because they are almost never proper enough for polite discourse."

"Nor are mine. That does not stop me. I believe that plain speaking can often save one much misunderstanding and time."

Lydia found that amusing. Little lights danced in her eyes. "Should I speak plainly and tell you what I am thinking? You must promise not to tell my brother."

"I promise."

Lydia glanced to the door, as if expecting Southwaite to fly in and smite her. "I am wondering if he brought you here to seduce you."

Emma did not know if appearing shocked or blasé would acquit her better. She believed in plain speaking, but not about this.

"Of course he didn't. He seeks only a business discussion with me."

Lydia frowned. She picked absently at the white fabric of her dress while she gazed at her lap. "That is disappointing. I had rather counted on him seducing you today. The mention of champagne—" She shrugged.

"He does that often, does he? Bring women home to seduce them?"

"Oh, never. He does that somewhere else. I live here, and he would never scandalize me that way."

"Then history says I am safe, am I not?"

"I expect so. What a nuisance." She looked up. "I do not suppose you would consider seducing him instead?"

"I would not want to scandalize you either."

"I would not mind. Truly. I am two and twenty, and am almost never scandalized anymore, least of all by my brother's affairs."

More silence. It had been an odd conversation. Emma had difficulty swallowing her curiosity about just how peculiar it had been.

"Why did you even think he had those intentions?" she asked.

"He has been too interested in that auction house. He invested on a collector's whim, like a boy buys a toy, and now it is troublesome to him. He feels obligated to make conversation if we have a meal together, and recently I have heard a lot of Miss Fairbourne this and Miss Fairbourne that. I assumed he had some fascination and, being a man, he would do what men are wont to do when they are fascinated."

"I am flattered that he spoke well of me to you."

"Oh, no. He didn't. Not at all. It was never the *wonderful* Miss Fairbourne. More the annoying Miss Fairbourne and the exasperating Miss Fairbourne."

"Do tell." Emma could not help but laugh.

Lydia laughed too. "He was so beside himself with astonishment at your refusal to conform to his will regarding that business that I almost fell in love with you." She giggled. "'The woman is impossible,'" she mimicked, matching Southwaite's voice quite well. "'Negotiating with ten men would be easier.'"

Emma laughed hard at Lydia's imitation. She wiped tears from her eyes. "If he was so critical, why would you think he might seduce me?"

"It was the paintings. When he had them taken down the other day, to put in the auction, I thought perhaps he favored the exasperating Miss Fairbourne and wanted to impress her. So I made some plans on the assumption that when that auction was done, he would seduce you." She made a face. "All in vain, though."

"I am sorry. I hope that your plans can be rearranged."

Lydia shook her head. "I do not think so. I am doomed to a life of boring parties with dull people. My brother never lets me be friends with the interesting ones."

The door opened and the brother in question reappeared then. Lydia cast Emma one more lively, conspiratorial look, then put her mask back on.

Darius paused outside the door of the library. The sound coming from within halted him in mid-step with his hand already on the latch.

Laughter. Feminine peals of joy. Emma's laugh sounded hearty and loud, but a softer, more delicate one wove in and out of its notes.

He resisted the impulse to stride in. He had not heard or

seen Lydia laugh in a very long time. Even her smiles were halfhearted, and at best private reactions to personal thoughts. At worst they were the calculated stage business of an actress forced to play a part for which she had no sympathy.

The sound died away. He waited, lest he interrupt a moment that his sister might be enjoying. He heard the distant drone of conversation, but no more chortles or guffaws penetrated the door.

When he entered the library, merriment could still be seen in Emma's eyes. Lydia, however, showed no humor at all. Or any other emotion. As always.

It delighted him that Lydia had found secret enjoyment in Emma's company. He would make sure that they spent time together in the future. But not today.

"Miss Fairbourne, will you excuse me for a few minutes more? I need to speak to my sister."

Emma cradled that fat reticule on her lap while Lydia took her leave.

Darius brought Lydia outside the library. She gazed up at him blankly.

"Aunt Hortense has written to me," he explained. "She claims the Season has exhausted her. Her headaches have returned and she wants to retreat from town for a spell. She asks to go to Crownhill for a few days."

"I suppose the sea air might help her."

"She also asks that you accompany her. You have been wanting to go down to Kent, so I thought you might agree to it."

"It will be dreadful with her there too. When I spoke of a companion, I meant someone more my age. Aunt Hortense will treat me like a child, and want to know what I am doing every minute."

Which was exactly why Aunt Hortense would be the ideal companion. "At least she will let you ride. It will not be as bad as if it were Aunt Amelia."

"That is true." She made an indifferent shrug. "It will be boring, but at least a different boring. I suppose I will go."

"She plans to leave at dawn. Have your maid pack and I will call for the carriage. You can stay with Aunt Hortense tonight so her departure tomorrow is not delayed."

"That would make great sense. You are sure that you will not need me here, to help with Miss Fairbourne?"

"Help?"

"I know how disagreeable you find her."

"I will muddle through."

"You are very brave, since she vexes you so. I will go pack, then. Tell them to have the carriage outside in half an hour."

She drifted off, to make her preparations. Darius gave instructions about the coach, then returned to the library. The champagne had arrived. He sat down beside Emma on the divan and handed her a glass.

"Won't your sister be rejoining us?" Emma looked at the door expectantly.

"She is otherwise occupied."

"That is unfortunate. I like her."

"I will encourage her to call on you. Now, let us toast your—"

"If she does call, does that mean that you find me dull? She said that you only allow her to be friends with uninteresting people."

Darius thought it astonishing that Lydia had confided her thinking on that, or anything at all, in such a brief time. "I discouraged a few of her friendships—that is true—but I do not restrict her to uninteresting people. She restricts herself. She makes no calls; she shows no emotion; she is—" He threw up his hands. "I confess that she is a worry to me. A cipher."

Emma sipped her champagne. "Perhaps she is hiding something."

"What could she have to hide? And if she did have something, why hide it from me? I am her brother."

"You are more than ten years her senior. She probably has no memories of you as an accomplice during her childhood. Maybe she sees you as more of a parent. I would if I were her."

That was a ridiculous idea. Except it really wasn't, he admitted in the next thought.

"This is very good champagne," she said. "I expect it is very old."

"Some years. Now, about that toast—"

"Before you praise my victory, I need to explain something," she said. "You were correct. There are large expenses that will affect the actual profit that Fairbourne's sees. I have the money for some of them with me, which is why my share looked so much bigger than yours."

He did not want to talk about this now. She had decided that she did, however. Why did he think that meant he would not be hearing the whole story?

"What kind of expenses?"

"Commissions. I paid someone to find the drawings for me, for example, and I must now give her twenty percent."

"You paid someone twenty percent to find you those lots? That is ruinous." He did not care how thick his stack of banknotes ended up being, but giving out 20 percent of the income would close Fairbourne's within the year for certain.

"It was necessary. Nor is it a practice that I will continue. Why, I only paid ten percent for the count's collection, for example."

"Ten percent of the amount of the final bids, or of the count's commission paid to Fairbourne's?"

"Of the commission, of course." She laughed at him like the question had been too stupid to endure. Then a small frown formed. "I am sure I explained it that way to Cassandra. She knows how auctions work and she would never misunderstand." A bigger frown. "Yes, I am certain she knows it is ten percent of the commission and not the final bids."

He stood and walked to the front windows. Down below the coach waited. "You had better hope she does, or you will see very little from today."

Lydia's bonnet came into view as she left the house. A footman hefted her portmanteau onto the carriage, and another handed her in. Before her head ducked inside, she glanced back at the house.

Her expression surprised him. She looked happy. It seemed Lydia preferred a boring aunt in Kent to a tedious brother in London.

The carriage moved, taking Lydia away. Free now to contemplate the evening's privacy, he looked back over his shoulder at Emma.

Her frown remained, deeper now. She reflected hard on something. She appeared worried. Desperately so.

"I am sure that Lady Cassandra has no illusions that she is getting all of Fairbourne's income from those paintings, Emma," he said, going back to her. "That is what it would be if she received ten percent of the total take."

"I wish I were as confident as you are. Now that you raise the chance of it, I am scouring my memory to recall exactly what we said to each other on the matter."

"If she misunderstood, I will make sure that you are not out anything for the error of her thinking."

She turned her attention to him. "I am sure it will not come to that. Anyway, I thought that I should explain the commissions, since you noticed so quickly that the expenses were too high. Is there anything else that you found suspicious and want me to explain?"

Suspicious had been an odd word for her to use. Unfortunately, it had also been an accurate one.

In accordance with his instructions, there had been no lots consigned by discreet anonymous gentlemen except for the drawings and the Raphael. Instead there had been lots of silver and sumptuous silks and lace consigned by Emma herself, on her own account. Emma had obeyed the letter of his command, but not the spirit, he suspected.

The proceeds from those lots now rested in Emma's reticule too, if his quick reading of her preliminary accounting had been correct.

If he asked her about them, what would she say? That they were family items she decided to turn into coin? He could never disprove that, even if he felt sure it were not true. As had happened often since they had met, he did not want to accuse her outright. There was little reason to, when he could not prove his suspicions. She would never just break down and confess it all. Nor did he really want her to confess it, he realized. If the sale of illicit goods became a fact instead of a suspicion, it would have to change everything.

Still, he should mind those lots more than he did right now. But then, she appeared very lovely and vulnerable sitting here. The dove gray of the dress she had worn to the auction flattered her hair and emphasized the subtle rose tint on her cheeks.

Confronting her about the source of that silk could wait. Perhaps forever. The sum total of those lots was not very large, and after today she would not do it again. He would make sure of that.

He rested his hands on the back of the divan and bent over her shoulder to pluck the champagne glass from her fingers. The faint scent she had used today teased his nose, and the skin of her neck and face, so close to his own, lured with its promise of velvet softness.

"You can explain the rest at the final accounting, Emma. It is a different matter entirely that we need to settle today."

Chapter 24

She could not say he had not warned her. That was Emma's thought as she turned around to look at the man standing behind her divan.

Her gaze moved up his frock coat to his face, hoping she would see humor in his eyes that indicated he was teasing her now.

His expression made her breath catch. It was apparent that at least one of them did not question what would happen now.

"Lydia . . ." she tried.

"Gone. To an aunt who requested her company on a journey."

She found it impossible to conquer what his closeness did to her. His desire might be speaking directly to hers, urging it to wake up and enjoy itself. Her reactions came fast, without mercy.

She turned away and closed her eyes and tried to sort out her good sense from those delicious, insidious sensations. It was both fascinating and horrible how alive sensuality made one feel. The mere anticipation of pleasure created shivers and pulses in parts of her body that she normally forgot existed.

Still, she should not do this. Nothing had really changed since she left him in Kent. She should reiterate her reasons for rejecting his offer. They still stood, whether he sought a wife or a lover.

Other reasons did too. She wished she could explain all of them. She wished that she could be the plain speaker she always claimed to be. If she told him everything, and how badly it might all turn out, he would lose interest at once.

He came around the divan and sat beside her. With careful fingers he turned her face toward him. He was going to kiss her now, and once he did she knew in her soul that she would not stop him.

She should speak at once if she wanted to claim anything other than immediate surrender had occurred. The words formed in her head, but his lips took hers and the discouraging sentences broke apart and scattered into so many unspoken sounds.

She said nothing. Not one word of objection. She made no effort to resist. She admitted, as he embraced her and the kiss deepened and desire broke free and ran through her, that she did not want to give up the chance to feel extraordinary one more time.

Darius was not too good to seduce Emma again. He was glad he did not have to, however.

She joined the kiss and embrace as equally as she knew how. It pleased him to see her forthrightness manifested in this new way, and the part of him still capable of thought pictured her more experienced soon, less artless, not waiting for him but demanding passion as she wanted it.

Her tongue finally ventured some equality too. Her attempt at boldness intensified his arousal abruptly. His body reacted as if he had been starved for years, and not only a fortnight. His imagination already explored her body in ways his body would not for days or weeks.

He held her breast and kissed the unbearable soft swell along the top edge of her dress. Her breaths shortened to a series of surprised inhales when he caressed the fullness he held. His fingers sought the tip and rubbed, and increasingly frantic, anxious cries flowed out on each of her gasps.

Lips parted and her eyes glistening, she looked down at his hand and what he was doing to her. Her acknowledgment of her arousal caused his own to soar.

She licked her lips, as if she were going to speak. He pressed his mouth to her neck, below her ear, so her scent surrounded him. "What is it?" he asked. "Do you not like this?"

"Yes. It is . . . unearthly. But . . . can you do again what you did last time?"

Her impatience surprised him. He stood, bringing her with him in his arm. "Not here. Come with me."

He took her by the hand, and led her out to the hall, then sped her up the stairs. Doors closed softly as they approached while the servants made themselves scarce.

The damned stairs seemed to go on forever. He looked back, and the sight of her so captivated him that he impulsively swung her against the wall and kissed and bit her mouth and neck while he pressed her there.

"Surely not here," she gasped. His hands sought her breasts and thighs. He barely heard her as he pressed to feel her, know her.

He wanted her helpless and so pleasured she wept. He wanted her now. He wanted— He grabbed her hand and dragged her the rest of the way up to the level that held his chambers. Blood flaming and mind darkening, he brought her into the bedchamber and pulled her into a kiss of triumphant possession.

When he released her she fell back on the bed. He looked down on her breathless surprise while he shed his coats.

* * *

Emma's senses could barely settle after Southwaite absorbed her into his whirlwind. Views and sounds and emotions fractured into pieces and became a jumble within the sensual turbulence.

Kisses first sweet, then commanding . . . trickles of pleasure submerged by a coursing river of need . . . stairs and a wall and a hard body and devastating hands . . . a chamber with books and chairs, then another with a bed draped in whites and blues . . . a kiss, a frightening kiss, that did not request surrender but claimed it, as if she had no choice.

She floated alone, slowly, through air heavy with sensual scents. Her skirt billowed from a breeze. Her outstretched arms were empty now. She drifted down until her back hit a mattress and a blue coverlet stretched beneath a sapphire tent.

Her senses righted a little. Enough. She peered through the gathering dusk that still lit the chamber. Southwaite stood near her feet, tall, lean, and strong. His frock coat slid away. Then his waistcoat and cravat. Each movement seemed a taunt, a dare, and a warning. He seemed to strip away his gentility with the garments. Deep in her, a primal thrill said there would be no etiquette at all left in him soon.

Suddenly he stood there naked, his body like marble in the gray light. Then the statue moved, until he knelt on one knee beside her, his body and face braced on taut arms that flanked her. For one lucid moment she admired him, his face and hard shoulders and the intensity that desire gave his dark eyes. Then he came down to her and filled her arms and overwhelmed her, and plain thinking was lost to her again.

He caressed her as if she had ceded everything to him— her body, her privacy, her everything. He created unbearable pleasure that became torturous, so much so that she resented the garments that made a barrier to the body she embraced. When he kissed her breast, the fabric between them became an agony.

He shifted his weight so he could turn her. She hugged the mattress while he unfastened her dress. Each small release sent a tremor down her center, as sure and focused as an arrow. After that her clothes disappeared with astonishing speed, spirited away while she hung on to him and obeyed his words and touches that helped him release her from their bindings.

Free then. Shockingly so. Pleasure and madness did not dim the astonishment of their bodies touching. The closeness awed her again as it had the last time.

He caressed her breasts and they swelled and rose. His tongue flicked at one tip and it tightened even more. Each contact, each breath, sent the most delicious charge through her.

"I promised more, didn't I?" he said. "Like last time, you asked."

She was too aroused to be shy or embarrassed. She nodded, and anticipation alone increased her sensitivity.

He moved away from her. "Come here, then." He reached for her and rearranged them both until he sat with his back against the bed's headboard and she faced him, her knees flanking his hips and her bottom pressing his thighs. She felt him beneath her, felt the base of his phallus snug in her cleft, teasing that spot he had used to unhinge her at dawn the last time.

He could touch her freely while he kissed her now. He could tease and titillate both of her breasts and he showed no mercy. She loved it. She closed her eyes and let the exquisite pleasure build and fill her until she knew nothing else.

He knew just what to do to make it even better, even more maddening. She rocked for relief. As she did her stomach kept brushing the top of his arousal where it rose between them. He took her hand, finally, and moved it there, so that she might give him pleasure too.

She was groaning soon. Crying and impatient and splitting apart. The edge of desperation began to preoccupy her. He lifted her hips so he could use his mouth, but that only made it worse. She clung to his shoulders, her head back and her mind begging for more, for something, for everything.

He touched her where she pulsed and a shock of pleasure streaked to every inch of her. Another subtle touch, then another. Her essence reached toward a frightening place.

He moved her hands to the headboard. "Stay here like this. I am going to kiss you here."

She nodded, too dazed to care or even hear, a silent begging for more being her only thought now. She did not care when he moved down or when he spread her legs and lowered her hips. She did not comprehend what he was doing until a most devilish thrill replaced that made by his hand.

She thought she would faint from it. For all its intensity, it also shocked her sane for a moment. She looked down and realized what was happening.

Her confused moment of rationality could not survive what came next. He did something that made her cry out. Another sensation, too intimate to believe, forced a groan from her. Then the insistent and building cravings spread until that was all there was, all she was. She clung to the bed while pleasure pushed her to desire's ragged peak.

She crashed through the barrier to completion. She seemed to hover, suspended for a long, incredible spell of pure sensation. Then the need itself snapped, creating a scream of pleasure that owned her, body and soul.

She found herself straddled atop him when her own voice and thoughts could speak again. He entered her, stretching her and filling her and claiming her anew. She had neither will nor strength nor even a secure sense of her own body still. The remnants of her self-possession offered no protection at all from the pervasive intimacy of being encompassed by his tense arms and body while he thrust hard and deep.

She should insist that he call for his carriage and have her brought home.

It took forever for that very sensible idea to come to

Emma. Far too long for him to take her resolve seriously should she make the demand.

She sat on the disheveled bed in the glow of fifty candles. Southwaite had lit them himself when he finally rose from the bed. They flickered like fifty exclamation points that required no sentences to communicate their meaning. They burned atop tapers long enough to last all night.

Sounds from a flanking chamber spoke of the meal being set out. She gazed down at the silk robe she wore, provided by the earl. Her state of undress required that they dine in privacy in his dressing room. She had not objected to that plan, or to its implications regarding the hours that would follow.

She had been more herself after the ballroom. For all the magic and astonishment, she had left then, hadn't she? She could not find the resolve to do so now, perhaps because dawn had not yet come to burn away the sensual dream of the night.

Hopping off the bed, she plucked her dress off the floor, folded it, and set it on a chair. She did not want to appear a waif when she left here. She would have to be vigilant about the time too. She had things she must do, important things, and she dare not allow her heart to delay them.

She sought her reticule. She had not let go of it when he dragged her up here, but it was nowhere in view now. She dropped to her knees to look beneath chairs and furniture. She cursed herself for being careless. Allowing herself to dally for pleasure was one thing, but completely losing sight of her duty could not be excused, not even for love.

She froze on the floor, with her hand under the bed where it had been feeling for the silk and lace of her reticule. Her thoughts had called this love without her choosing the word. She had no right to think of this passion in those terms. Southwaite had been kind, and had even made the obligatory proposal, but she had no reason to permit her heart such sentiments.

She kneeled, sitting on her feet, and looked into her heart. For the first time in her life it was not an easy thing to do. An odd emotion tried to block her reflection. Her inner voice warned that illusions and lies had their place in the doings between men and women, and honesty would bring only pain.

Contemplating Southwaite's thinking and feelings indeed provoked a fearful anguish. She set the attempt aside. She could never really know what he was about. It would be ridiculous to attribute motives or emotions to him. She could and would expect nothing there, nor blame him for less affection than she might wish.

Honesty with herself was all she could hope for. Once summoned, it did not take long for her to face the fullness of it. She had become accustomed to Southwaite's attention and the excitement he could create with his mere presence. She had reveled in the new sensations he woke in her. But she could not claim her true emotions were very sophisticated. She was still here, wasn't she? In his bedchamber now that night had fallen, agreeing without saying so to stay with him while she could?

It would be harder to leave this time. Terribly hard. The mere thought made her composure wobble.

"What are you doing there, Emma?"

Southwaite's question jolted her out of her reverie. She looked over to where he stood at the door to his dressing room. His own robe, of brown brocaded silk, made him appear both dissolute and exotic.

"I cannot find my reticule."

He came over and helped her up. "We will find it later. It has not gone far. It is among the sheets and garments somewhere. Come and eat something."

The servants had set a table in the huge dressing room. Silver and fine porcelain bedecked exquisite linens. Two comfortable armchairs faced each other. The food had already been served, and no servant could be seen.

She marveled at how discreet it all was. Also at how expertly arranged. Even the food on her plate, some fowl and sauce and a compote of warm fruit, would not suffer too much should the earl get distracted before he dined.

Perhaps it came together so well because there had been

much practice. Lydia could be wrong about where her brother seduced his women. How would his sister even know whom he spirited up here and sent out again at dawn?

A spike of jealousy speared her at the thought. She tried to laugh the reaction off as ridiculous. It needled for a while longer all the same.

Southwaite poured some champagne. "Finally, at last, we must make that toast to your triumph today."

She almost made a joke about whether the champagne had been smuggled in, but bit her tongue. The impulse only reminded her of the way she had disobeyed him on those lots. To gain the prize, she might be required to do so again.

"It is unfortunate Cassandra is not here," she said. "I think she is celebrating too. She will see more than she expected from those jewels. Your friend Ambury was very aggressive on the sapphire and diamond earbobs."

"I tried to stop him, but he would not hear me."

"Perhaps he intends them for a special lady."

"If so, she had better be ready to feed him for a spell. His father keeps him on a limited income, and he can ill afford such indulgences, even for special ladies."

"I trust that he will pay up. I would not like to tell Cassandra that—"

"If he does not, I will." He raised his glass. "To eyes both expert and beautiful, to a mind most extraordinary and exasperating, and to a body wholly captivating and deli—"

"Why, thank you!" she quickly interrupted.

He laughed. "Forgive me, but I thought you preferred plain speaking."

Her face was already hot and now it burned even more. "I have decided there are some things better left unsaid."

"That is an unexpected complication. How am I to know which things those are?"

She narrowed her eyes on him. "You know already, I think."

He appeared ready to tease her more, but instead he ate his food. "I have been thinking about your eyes. Fondly, of course, but also about the expertise they have, as learned from your father. You must have seen more art pass through Fairbourne's over the years than I did on my grand tour. You would have learned much from that."

"There was more than the consignments," she said. "When we journeyed anywhere—Father would be asked to visit estates to give estimates, so we did at times—he would bring my brother and me to the private galleries along the way. Other travelers might request to tour the gardens of those manor houses, but he would speak to the housekeeper and beg that his children see the art. There are some amazing rarities tucked away in the collections of England."

"Then your brother had the same education, and had the same expertise, I expect."

Had. He spoke of her brother in the past tense. Only she and Papa had not.

She wanted to correct him. She wanted to explain she was not some madwoman who refused to accept the truth of Robert's fate. She fought the unexpectedly strong urge to blurt out that she had received proof now that vindicated her belief, and would soon have him back as well.

The desire to share this with him, the weighing of it all, immobilized her for a long count. If he found her reaction either visible or noteworthy, he did not say so. He ate his meal and did not seem to notice that she had stopped eating hers.

"English collections are very fine, but you will still be impressed when you go to the Continent and see the abundance of riches there," he said. "You can walk into an obscure, humble church and find an old master to rival the best we have here."

"Is that how you spent your grand tour? Visiting obscure churches to seek out old masters? I thought young men used those months to pursue bad women and drink too much wine."

"I confess that I wasted my tour just like the rest of them. That is why I need to do it again. Here is a thought—when this infernal war is over, you will come with me. During the days you will advise me as I buy a collection to rival the one

Arundel amassed. During the nights I will teach you everything I know about sharing pleasure."

He was teasing her again. Probably. She could not tell. She dared not take him seriously, but fantasies of those distant cities and monuments wanted to occupy her mind. The woman who had surrendered too much to this man wanted to believe he wished it to be true too, that at least tonight he did.

He reached for her hand and raised it to a kiss. "No? Too scandalous a journey for you?" He stood, and guided her to her feet too. "Then the lessons will have to take place here."

Emma broke her hand free when they entered the bedchamber. With a frown she climbed on the bed and groped amid the sheets and coverlet. She flipped pillows around. "It must be here somewhere," she muttered.

She was looking for her reticule again. He lounged on his side and let her. Her expression, a little worried and a lot determined, reminded him of how often her private thoughts revealed deep considerations that she did not share with him.

There had been moments in the dressing room when he saw that in her. Thoughts besides games of pleasure would create little flames in the tenth layer of her eyes. She had been a woman with much on her mind these last weeks, but tonight, at least, if ever, she should be relieved of concerns about Fairbourne's and the future.

He had a passing notion that this reticule's contents meant more to her than he knew. The idea did not last long because the erotic potential of her position could not be ignored.

She paused, on her hands and knees, and examined him in turn. She crawled over and stuck her hand under the folds of sheet on which he lay. She yanked, and held up the plump reticule.

"You were lying on it," she said accusingly.

"So I was." He reached out and cupped the back of her head, and pulled her forward for a kiss. "Do not move." He took the reticule from her, turned, and hung its strings over a knob on the footboard. "You will find it when you need it now."

She began to sit.

"No. Stay like that."

She appeared puzzled until he reached under her and loosened the robe. The sides fell in silken drapes from her back, offering mere glimpses of her body. He reached between her hands and her knees, beneath the silk, and softly rubbed the tips of her breasts as they hung there.

She closed her eyes and the pleasure transformed her. She always looked so beautiful when aroused. He could see how she concentrated on the sensations, and how she reacted in nuanced ways to what he did to her.

He moved his caress to her thigh. Tension flexed through her when his hand rose higher on its inner flesh. Her lips parted and her tongue rested there, its tip visible against her upper teeth while she tried to control herself.

He caressed higher, to remind her that she could not contain this now. His own arousal made him ruthless and he stroked her until he brought her to the edge, until her gasping whispers both groaned for more and begged for help.

Hunger ruled him then. He knelt and moved behind her and threw off his own robe. She looked over her shoulder, her eyes slitting to reveal confusion amid the glistens of passion's daze.

"Stay like that," he said. "That is how I want you. I will show you what to do."

He lifted the silk that flowed over her hips. He did it slowly, teasing himself, and his phallus swelled harder and larger with each inch of the fabric's rise. It affected her too, so much that her stance wobbled. He pressed against her back and she dipped her shoulders until her arms and head lay on the sheet.

The pose made her hips rise. He uncovered them completely and let the silk slide down her back. Her bottom rose even more, rounding erotically. The more he caressed those soft swells, the more she angled herself to invite his touch and thrusts. He tortured himself as long as he could bear it, his desire coiling ever tighter as her scent filled his head and her cries filled his ears. He waited as long as he dared so the rest would be all the more intense.

Finally he could deny himself no longer. She hissed an assent when she felt the first pressure at the lips of her vulva, then a loud, groaning one when he entered her fully. He withdrew, and the perfection of the sensation, the intensity created by her snug hold on him, almost caused him to lose control.

He knew little restraint after that. He was not aware of much at all except her body's velvet hold and the way her bottom rose to his thrusts and the desperate feminine cries that rang through the night until her finish turned them into a scream of ecstasy.

"What do you think she is hiding?"
His question came softly in the dark, as if he knew she was not asleep. They still lay where they had landed, a tumble of limbs and spent bodies too sated to move. She had drifted in a half sleep, but had never lost awareness of him.

"Who?"

"My sister. You said she was probably hiding something."

A man, most likely. Perhaps a lover. She pictured him getting angry that some scoundrel had dared seduce his sister. Under the circumstances, that would be too comical, and too sad. "Something she thinks you would not approve, I suppose. Another friend like Cassandra, perhaps."

"Perhaps it is a man of whom I would not approve."

So much for being sly. "Would she not then embrace social opportunities instead of avoiding them? She is not going to have any time with an inappropriate man if she never leaves the house."

Unless she sneaks him up to *her* chambers and feeds him fowl and champagne in *her* dressing room. Emma doubted

Lydia would risk such a thing, or that the servants would cooperate, but for all she knew, such games happened all the time among the haut ton.

"I suppose you are right," he said drowsily. "Still, it bears some consideration." He rearranged himself, and her, in an embrace. He breathed the deeply contented way people did as they fell asleep.

She allowed herself a brief, thorough enjoyment of the tender contentment binding them. She tried lying to herself, that this sweetness could last a long time. Until morning if she allowed it, at least. She knew that she should not indulge even that long, however.

Forcing down a swelling sadness, she tried to lift the arm he had draped over her. "I have to leave."

"I told my valet to rap on the door at six o'clock. I will get you out discreetly."

"It is not discretion but duty that demands I leave now. I have things that I must do early in the morning. I do not want to arrive home and immediately leave again."

That arm did not move. The other one did. He propped his head on his hand and looked down at her. "Those duties distract you often, Emma. I see it in you. Even tonight Miss Fairbourne lapsed into deep thought sometimes. Much deeper than one would expect today of all days, when current duties are finished and current responsibilities will be easily settled."

He spoke in a speculative tone, even a concerned one. There was no accusation, but she feared again that he had surmised much more than she knew.

She was grateful that most of the tapers had burned out. She doubted she could hide her surprise from him.

"Do you need my help in any of these duties, Emma? We are partners, after all, but I could not refuse you anyway."

The offer touched her deeply. He did suspect something. She knew it now. He was offering to help her rectify it. An earl's voice and influence could do far more than any other person's to fix most normal problems. He might be making the offer out of passing sentiment, or even obligation, but he had voiced it all the same. She would remember forever that he had thought her important enough to do so.

For the second time tonight the impulse to confide in him almost overwhelmed her. Fear held her back. Fear and also love. She did not want to entangle him in something she did not completely understand herself. Even if she got Robert back, there might be embarrassing revelations regarding her father and brother. And now her too. She could not ask Southwaite to look the other way when it came to criminal matters, or count on him doing so.

She forced her voice to sound light, even mocking. She stretched to kiss him. "That is good of you to offer, Southwaite. However, you have only been seeing the preoccupation of a merchant's daughter with handing over money in her safekeeping. Such unfinished business creates heavy weights to such as us. Once I disperse the contents of that reticule and settle the auction payments, I will no longer be distracted."

His hold on her tensed and tightened a little. Then he raised his arm, freeing her. "Go if you must. I will have the carriage bring you to your house."

Chapter 25

Emma rapped on the blue door at ten o'clock. Mr. Dillon stood guard at her side. Until she entered this house, she would not risk the reticule that she had tucked under her arm.

She wondered if Mr. Dillon knew that she had not arrived home this morning until close to four o'clock. Maitland knew because he had sat in the reception hall waiting to let her in. Her maid did too, and probably all of the other servants now. Her arrival home in the earl's carriage must have them all wondering what she had been doing. With any luck they would assume that Southwaite had hosted a dinner party and her social life was reaching new heights.

Mr. Dillon retreated once the door opened, to watch the carriage and horse. The same old woman greeted her, but this time she was expected. They did not go to the studio, but Emma could hear the women working there. Instead she followed the old woman to the back of the house, to a chamber that looked out over a garden.

As arranged by recent letters, Marielle Lyon waited for her with the old man who had consigned the drawings. Emma greeted them, then opened her reticule.

"As you may have heard, the auction proved very successful. People came for old masters' paintings and jewels, but they bid well on everything."

The old man nodded, but he had eyes only for her reticule. With no further ceremony, Emma pulled out the banknotes and counted out seven hundred pounds. Then she slid one of the catalogue sheets to him. "The amounts realized for each drawing are noted there. It was a public sale, so there is no way for me to cheat you. If you want to add it all up to ensure I am paying you correctly, I will not be insulted. Of course, ten percent goes to Fairbourne's, as a commission."

He said something in French to Marielle. She shook her head, took the catalogue sheet, and ran her finger down the figures. "He trusts you. I, however, prefer to add."

Emma waited until Marielle put down the paper and nodded to the old man. He scooped up the money, stood, bowed, and left.

"It embarrasses him," Marielle said. "Your discretion with his name—" She pointed to the catalogue line that designated the drawings as from the collection of an esteemed gentleman. "He is grateful. He will tell others, and perhaps more such things will come to you."

Emma withdrew more money from her reticule. "Twenty percent to you, of what Fairbourne's received in commission." She counted out fourteen pounds. Marielle slid it away.

"Where is the other man? I have part of his payment as well," Emma said. "The proceeds from the wagon."

"I know nothing of that."

"I think you do know something of it. He frequents this neighborhood, does he not?"

Marielle shrugged. "Perhaps. Sometimes. It is here that I have seen him, and he me, but not often."

Emma studied this lovely young woman who had so mastered French insouciance. Marielle appeared bored with the conversation.

"Do you know his name?" Emma pressed. "Do you know if he lives nearby, or only visits these streets? Have you seen him enter any house?" She paused, but risked the insult. "Does he enter this house?"

Marielle turned her brown eyes on Emma. "You think I have lied to you? If I have, why would I now tell the truth?"

"Because perhaps you have surmised that this is about more than a wagon of wine and silks."

Marielle turned her gaze to the garden. Her lips pursed, then she clucked her tongue. "So much trouble for four shillings," she muttered.

"But perhaps not for fourteen pounds."

Marielle laughed, then shook her head. "I should not like to meet you in the market. I think I would spend twice for my meat than it is worth." Her inner debate was visible. Finally another shrug indicated a decision. "He is a stupid man. You know this, I think, if you have met him. The stupid ones are the most dangerous."

"How is he dangerous to you?"

"His stupidity is what is dangerous, not him. He comes here, mmm, two weeks ago. He wanted to have a chamber above. Good pay he offers, like he did with that wagon. Too good. You understand?"

"He wanted to live here?"

Marielle rolled her eyes, as if Emma were now the stupid one. "Not for him. For another who would come to London soon. He thinks he is very clever in this. He does this a lot, as if he and I share a secret." She winked one eye, again and again, with gross exaggeration. "I know then that this stupid man will get me hanged if I am not careful. He has heard stories about Marielle Lyon, and he thinks he knows what he does not know at all."

"What did you tell him?"

"I said we are all women here, and we do not have any chambers for men. I tell him to leave and to stay away from me. I throw him out."

Emma rather wished the man had been less stupid, or that Marielle had been less shrewd. "For whom do you think he wanted that chamber?"

"Is it not obvious? Someone who needs to hide, and who dares not go to an inn or to an Englishwoman's house. Perhaps it is the man who sends over the wine that was in that wagon. I only knew the stupid man was pulling me into trouble I did not need." She shook her head. "Other stupid men watch me. As if I would do in broad day what they suspect! This stupid man did not think that if he had heard stories, others had too, so no one could hide here anyway."

Emma laughed at Marielle's exasperation. "At least he has a name now. Stupid Man."

"But there are so many with that name. How do we tell them apart?"

"Fat stupid man? Tall stupid man?"

Marielle giggled. "There is one who follows me sometimes who has too much beauty to avoid notice. I do not know whether his name should be Handsome Stupid Man or Very Stupid Man."

They laughed, enjoying their irreverence. Emma pulled the strings on her reticule and stood. "I had hoped you knew where to find him. Then I would have been done with that wagon and perhaps with more important matters, very soon. Instead, with your warning him to stay away, I have no way to try to contact him."

Marielle pointed to the reticule. "You have money for him, no? You do not need to contact him. He will find you very soon. He is the kind of man who will risk a noose for a shilling."

Emma had wanted to do it her own way, at her own time, however. Like Marielle, she did not want to be seen with this stupid man who might bring her trouble.

"I will go now. Perhaps one day you will visit me. We can sit in the garden and talk about better things."

Marielle's expression softened. She appeared neither shrewd nor cautious now. "You are very kind. Perhaps I will do that." She petted the money she had received. "I will look for more art for you too."

* * *

Darius was still dressing when the card came up at two o'clock. Ambury had called.

He had him brought to the dressing room. He accepted the final ministrations of his valet while he waited. As his watch was attached and his cuffs tweaked just so, he turned his head and looked into the bedroom.

It had been serviced. All signs of last night were gone. The scents he had breathed while he slept and the impressions they had made in their passion—it had all been obliterated by the precise cleanliness that the best servants imposed on a household.

It was just as well Emma had left when she did, although her insistence had angered him. If she had stayed until six, he would have kept her until ten, however. Then until one and eventually until night came again. He would have tried to keep her until he had his fill of her, and that might have been many days or weeks.

Ambury strolled in just as the valet left. He tossed a newspaper onto the dressing table, then threw himself into the high-backed armchair that Emma had used at supper last night.

"I was summoned by the earl this morning," he said. He pointed at the newspaper. "You owe me two hours of my life back."

Darius had not yet seen the morning paper. He read the story that described the auction at Fairbourne's. It mentioned that reports said Viscount Ambury had entertained at the grand preview with a violin performance.

"I apologize for pressing you into it. At least he cannot threaten your allowance, since he gives you almost none already."

"I mentioned that to him every chance I got this morning. I enjoyed reminding him that he has already played all his aces," Ambury said.

"All of which makes your purchase of those jewels peculiar. You ignored my efforts to hold you back and now you have a large bill of sale due."

Ambury pretended bravado. "They captivated me. I am a fool for sapphires."

"Please tell me you were bidding for someone else."

"Regrettably, no. A good night at the tables last week will save my reputation, however. I will merely be in dun to everyone else again, but that is not new."

"If I had not pressed you to perform, you would not have seen those sapphires."

"Do not apologize. I like to play for others every now and then. I noticed that you were absent, however."

"I heard every note. I was right outside." Darius did not have a strong affinity for music. He appreciated a maestro's artistry enough, but he sat through most concerts with only an intellectual engagement. Ambury's playing was different. He found it embarrassing, just how much it affected him.

"I did not come to talk about the newspaper story, or my enthusiasm for jewels," Ambury said. "I thought you would want to know that your prisoner finally talked yesterday. I heard about it from Pitt last night."

Darius had been waiting for news, but his contacts in the Home Office had been annoyingly silent. "What induced him to do that after a week in gaol?"

"Perhaps the week itself. Pitt only said he was persuaded to confide."

"As gentlemen we would rather not know how that persuading was done, I think. Please tell me Kendale was not involved."

"He was not. He was with me all afternoon and evening, although he fought me every minute. I introduced him to a lady who finds dark, rough, brooding men attractive. She simpered soulfully at him and he ignored her, increasing his appeal. The result is she has fallen in love but he can't even remember her name."

Darius pictured it and chuckled. "Do we know what our persuaded prisoner said?"

"He is insisting he is not a spy, but a common smuggler. He was to be met by a man who would take the brandy and give him lodging. Then together they were supposed to seek out Englishmen of the same profession, and forge an alliance."

"I wish I had been there to hear this tale, so I might better know if I believe it."

"I do not believe it." Ambury stretched out his legs and crossed them. "There are problems with his story and it does not ring true."

"How so?"

"What are the chances that any smuggler, even a French one, would not know how Tarrington reigns in that area of the coast? That suggests this man is not a smuggler at all, or that he left the farm a week ago with a grand plan and no knowledge of his new trade. Yet he said he had someone to meet once he landed, which implies he is an old hand at it, so—his story does not make sense."

Darius was inclined to give Ambury's views considerable weight. Ambury had more experience with such matters, what with those quiet investigations he undertook to supplement his very small income. As a result Ambury had also developed the disconcerting ability to put himself in a criminal's shoes and see things through a criminal's eyes, which broadened the realm of possible theories when they speculated like this.

"If you are correct, another will be sent when it is learned this one was caught," Darius said.

"I would say that is likely. I fully expect it."

"I wonder if he revealed whom he was supposed to meet."

"Pitt did not say. If they accept his story, he will be left to languish in gaol. If they do not, I expect more persuasion will be brought to bear. I doubt it will matter. Most likely this prisoner did not bring information, but was to receive it. Whoever was to hand it over is probably aware things went awry. He will disappear if he can now, but he will be wanting to get his information to France."

Ambury had lined up the possibilities with calm precision. Darius did not like how many of them revealed the holes in their attempts to prevent such things happening. If they could not prevent one man from entering and leaving England with impunity, they were wasting their time.

"I will write to Tarrington and the others, and tell them to be alert for unexpected boats going in either direction," he said. "We will find out if our chain has too many weak links to be effective, at least."

By five o'clock two days after the auction, Emma had seen enough numbers to make her loathe the sight of them. It was not that she disliked the notion of accounting for the consignments and sales. She merely tired of the rows and rows of calculations, and came to resent the expressions on the faces of the factors, solicitors, and stewards who filed in to make the payments.

Money showed up in every way imaginable. Piles of coin and bank drafts abounded. The rents on properties were pledged in two cases. A baroness came herself and removed a gold necklace right in the office. Emma was not too proud to weigh it on the spot and agree to take it in lieu of traditional payment.

The paintings left as the money flowed in. So did the rest of the drawings and the other objects, even, she noted with relief, the silks. As she crossed off the art removed and checked off the money received, she noted that only three people still had to settle. One was with her in the office when the penultimate tally was completed.

Cassandra sat waiting, a spark of avarice in her eyes. Emma carefully moved two stacks of coin and drafts toward her.

"This is the twenty-three hundred from your jewels. And this is the commission from the count's collection."

Emma watched Cassandra closely, looking for either confusion or surprise at the size of the latter amount. She was almost certain that there had been no misunderstanding about this commission, but Southwaite's raising the possibility had plagued her ever since.

"Ten percent of what came to Fairbourne's, as agreed," she added, so any confusion would be clarified now.

Cassandra hesitated a fraction of a moment. If surprise blinked over her expression, at least there was no obvious shock, and certainly no objection. She eyed the various forms of lucre. "All that coin will be very clumsy to take home. I had no idea this was done with other than bank drafts."

"If you are willing to wait, we can arrange a bank draft for tomorrow or the next day. Many consignors are rather in a hurry to have the money."

"No more than I am." She picked through the pile and lifted a round object. "What is this?"

"Viscount Ambury requires a few days to pay. He leaves that as surety, and the jewels with you. He will deliver payment, and take delivery directly, if you are agreeable."

Cassandra peered at the gold ring and red stone. She squinted to examine the inside for inscriptions. "It sounds like a lot of trouble," she muttered.

"If you prefer, I will take the payment here, and hold the earrings until then," Emma said. "Or if you cannot consider the delay, Southwaite has offered to advance the amount in full. Then Ambury will repay him."

Cassandra looked up. "Now it is sounding like even more trouble. I will hold the ring as surety. I suspect it is worth more than the earbobs anyway." She tucked it in her reticule. "I don't suppose you provide sacks to transport the coin."

"If you take it this way, we will also provide an escort. Allow me to talk to Obediah."

Emma left Cassandra and entered the exhibition hall. As she did, another of her final patrons entered.

"I expected you earlier," she said.

"The delay was unfortunate," Southwaite said. He looked around to see who else might be in the hall. "Then again . . ." He pulled her into an embrace and a lazy, luring kiss.

She permitted it for a while because it made her heart

both sing and ache. It summoned the mood of their celebration and the familiarity built that night.

They would not be alone long, and Cassandra might come out of the office at any moment, however. Gently but firmly, Emma pushed away.

He accepted it, for now. He reached in his coat and withdrew a paper. "For the Raphael." He paced to the wall to admire the painting, now the only one still hanging on the gray expanse.

She took the draft and examined it. "You did not deduct your share of the commission."

"I thought to, but realized that might complicate things. Better to treat all the lots the same, so there is no confusion."

She rather wished he had been one of the ones to bring coin. It would take time to deal with this draft. Unless—"Is it possible to sign this to Cassandra? Then she would not have to carry so many bags of hard coin home. It will be far easier for Fairbourne's to handle such inconvenience."

"I do not see why not. The bank knows my hand, and should accept the change."

They went to the office and Southwaite made the change. Happy with her drafts and replenished fortune, and still in possession of the sapphire earbobs, Cassandra left.

Emma grabbed some papers from a drawer, and she and Southwaite returned to the hall, and the painting. "Do you want it delivered? Or boxed?" she asked.

"That is not necessary. I will carry it. It is small, and I have my carriage."

He admired his new possession. She admired him. As she did, a movement at the north windows caught her eye. What she saw horrified her.

The last person to require payment stood outside the windows, gesturing to her. Stupid Man had indeed found her in order to get his money, but he had arrived at the most inopportune time.

Southwaite began to turn away from the wall. She saw him move as if time had slowed. Stupid Man was right in the middle of the north windows. He kept pointing in one direction, then the other, and shrugging, asking where to go.

In mere seconds the earl was going to see a peculiar fellow of questionable purpose making a pantomime that implied familiarity with her.

Frantic, Emma grabbed Southwaite into an embrace and kissed him hard. He reacted with surprise, but did not mind at all. Arms circling his neck, she kissed him aggressively while she gestured behind his back, trying to tell Stupid Man to go to the garden.

The papers she held fell to the floor as she lost her grasp on them. Southwaite did not seem aware of anything except the increasingly heated kisses they shared.

He moved his mouth to her neck, and she had the chance to see the north windows. Her visitor had made himself scarce. Her lover took her deep sigh of relief as something else.

"Come with me," he said, between kisses she found more tempting than she would have thought possible in this situation. "Do the rest of this another day."

"I will not be able to give you due attention if I leave it unfinished now."

"I will take that as a promise that you will give me due attention at another time."

She had made no such promise. He knew it too. It broke her heart that she could not know her own mind yet. Until she spoke to the man waiting in the garden, she did not have the freedom to offer herself under any terms.

He did not appear to notice that she left his assumption twisting in the wind. He held her and looked down at her, and she saw no expectation of a response in his eyes. Rather, the knowing of the night was there, as if he perceived much more than she could guess.

He kissed her forehead. "You are right. You must finish it. I do not want to share you with it any longer." He released her and stepped back. His boot landed on the papers she had dropped.

He picked them up.

"Those are the documents on the Raphael," she said.

He stuffed them into his coat and reached to lift the painting from the wall. "If ever a painting did not need provenance to prove itself, this is it. Be sure to thank the esteemed, discreet gentleman for me."

As soon as Southwaite left, Emma called for Obediah. He emerged from the storage.

"I need you to do one more thing for me today, old friend," she said. "There is a good deal of money in the office. Please find a sack and put the large pile into it. Bring it to me. Then you can leave."

Obediah displayed no surprise at the instruction. He wandered back to the storage room to look for a sack.

After Obediah returned and handed her the heavy sack, Emma strode to the northwest corner of the exhibition hall, and let herself out through the garden door.

Her visitor was not visible when she entered the garden. She was halfway down a path before he revealed himself by whistling from behind a large shrub.

"I thought it best to stay back here," he said when she went to him. "Didn't want that man of yours wondering about us."

She heartily disliked this man on several counts, but his lascivious smile now made him repulsive. "Do not insult me with your insinuations, or I will tell that man all about it, to your sorrow."

"I will be glad to be done with ye; that's for certain. I've known fishwives with more sweetness."

"Then let us be done." *You must finish it. I do not want to share you with it any longer.* "I intend to ransom the prize so this will be over."

"You've the whole three thousand?"

She set down the sack. "I have fifteen hundred here. I'll be needing to hear the favor." She prayed it would not be passing shiploads of wine or something equally visible.

"Well, now, that be interesting," he said, rubbing his chin

thoughtfully. "It were expected to be like this, but I said you would get the whole three if anyone could."

"It appears those you work for understand more about the finances of auction houses than you do. Now, tell me the favor, or else tell me where to learn about it. Do not put me off, or you will take back not a penny."

He looked over his shoulder and stretched to see the house. Neither caution was a good sign, and Emma steeled herself for a demand that she would not like at all.

Satisfied that he would not be heard, he spoke more clearly and soberly than he ever had previously. So clearly that Emma realized that Stupid Man was not nearly as stupid as she and Marielle thought.

"The favor would've been required, no matter how much ye pay, so in picking the fifteen hundred ye've cut yerself a bargain. Ye need to finish that which your father started," he said. "It is to do that which he was doing when he took that bad step and fell."

Chapter 26

D arius was half a mile from Fairbourne's before he set aside the Raphael. A small painting, it rewarded close study. He decided that he would not hang it, but set in a case in the library so it could be held to close view just as he had held it for the last fifteen minutes.

The bulge in his coat crackled when he placed the panel on the opposite bench. He sat back and pulled out the packet of documents that Emma had given him.

It was a very complete provenance. Step by step, from the middle of the sixteenth century to that of the current one, the pages described the history of the painting's ownership. There were references to documents and letters in support of the early claims, and to English inventories from the seventeenth century on.

The last entry, scribbled at the bottom of the final page, required deciphering because the ink had become blurred and faint, as if a liquid had dripped on it. It appeared to note that the painting had been offered at auction at Fairbourne's fifteen years ago.

He held the paper to the window to make out the writing.

It had been bought by count . . . No, it had been bought *in on account*. That meant the auctioneer had bid against his own patrons, to purchase the work himself.

He set down the documents, surprised, and lifted the panel again. Maurice Fairbourne had owned this. He was the esteemed gentleman from whose collection it came.

Why would Emma sell such a treasure? Prior to the count's collection being consigned, it might have made some sense if she sought to enhance the auction's offerings, or if she needed funds to maintain her household. By the time the auction was held, however, she knew that she would see enough from its proceeds to be secure for many months, and the Raphael, while a significant addition, was not essential anymore to garner prestige.

There was only one explanation that made sense. Like Lady Cassandra, and many of the other people who sent family heirlooms to auction, Emma must need money. A lot of it, if she sacrificed this painting.

He doubted she needed money for the normal reasons. There was no indication she gambled. It was possible she had run up debts at modistes and milliners, but he had not seen evidence of extravagance.

He could not ignore that she had been very secretive about this too. She might claim she sought only privacy in her personal finances by creating the ruse that an anonymous client consigned the Raphael. It was a lot of trouble to go through without a better reason than that, however.

He did not think he would enjoy this painting as much now. Something had coerced her to sell it, and he would think of that each time he viewed it.

He told his coachman to turn the horses and return to Fairbourne's. He would give it back to her, as a gift. If she tried to refuse it, he would leave it at the auction house, so she had no choice.

He would not ask why she had done it either. Although he badly wanted to know, he suspected the answer would not reflect well on Fairbourne's, or her father, and probably not even on her.

He called for the coach to stop before it arrived at Fairbourne's door. Something had caught his eye that needed to be addressed first.

He put his head to the window and looked out. Tucked amid the horses tied nearby was a large chestnut. Its rider calmly hand-fed it pieces of an apple that he lazily cut with a small knife. The presence of that horse and rider here, ten doors down from Fairbourne's, infuriated Darius.

"I told you not to follow her," he said. "I told you to leave her alone."

The owner palmed the rest of the apple under his horse's mouth. When it was gone he walked over, set his elbows on the windows lower edge, and looked in. "I am not following her. I am not even watching her. That was to be your role, remember?"

"Then what the hell are you doing here, Kendale?"

"Maybe I am having a new coat made at that tailor there." He jerked his thumb over his shoulder.

It was Kendale's way of pointing out that it was a public street and he could be here if he chose. Which it was. But Darius doubted Kendale had ordered a new coat in many months. Other things occupied his time and mind.

"Are you saying that you are not here because of Fairbourne's?"

"I'm saying I did not come here because of *her*. If you are angry because she matters to you in some way, it may be good that you are here now too, though."

"Why? Is she having another rendezvous with Marielle Lyon?"

"She did that yesterday. If you had been watching her like you are supposed to, you would know that." A frowning scold formed. "You and Ambury have proven useless."

Darius opened the door and stepped down. "That is because you are on a fool's errand. It would be impossible to keep watch on every person in England around whom the vaguest rumors and suspicions fly. I will not insult law-abiding citizens to satisfy your—"

Darius broke off his speech when Kendale abruptly tensed and all but pointed like a hunting dog.

Darius followed Kendale's sharp gaze to Fairbourne's. A man walked along the side of the building, carrying a sack. The fellow wore ill-fitting clothes and a flat-brimmed, low-crowned hat.

"Who is he? A thief?"

Kendale shook his head. "He is very nonchalant for a thief. I do not know his name yet."

"Why do you know him at all?"

"He visited Marielle Lyon two weeks ago. From the sharp words exchanged as he left, she threw him out. Since she spends most of her days in that studio she runs, I've left a footman to watch her and took to following this fellow instead some days."

"Why?"

"Mostly because he smells wrong," he said. "However, when Mam'selle Lyon threw him out, she castigated him soundly, in French. She said he was too stupid if he came to her, and would bring her nothing but more trouble. I thought that of interest. So I pick up his trail some days. He moves through town a lot."

And now he had come here.

"Imagine my surprise to see him visit Miss Fairbourne," Kendale added with exaggerated blandness. "It is probably just another coincidence, though."

"You do not know he visited her. She may not be there."

"She has not left since you did, and her carriage is still down the street. She is there." The man in question was far down the street now. Kendale untied his horse and swung up into the saddle.

"You saw me leave?" Darius said.

"I did. Now, move, please. I think I will see where that sack is going."

Kendale angled his horse away and proceeded down the

street at a slow walk. From his height on horseback he would be able to see his quarry from a good distance.

Darius told his coachman to move down to Fairbourne's. He reached in the carriage, removed the painting, and walked the short distance.

He had intended to require no information when he returned this, but he doubted he would be able to avoid a few questions now. For one thing, if Kendale had seen him leave half an hour ago, that meant Emma's final visitor had led Kendale to this street before that. The man had not been visible at Fairbourne's while Darius settled his account, however.

The revelations troubled Darius more than angered him. Apparently Emma kept more secrets than he had guessed. Worse, perhaps whatever had been preying on her mind now preyed in other ways too.

The door to Fairbourne's was unlocked. He looked down the street. Kendale was still visible, slowly pacing along. Emma's carriage waited there too.

Darius let himself in. The exhibition hall, so recently crowded with paintings and luxuries, quaked with total emptiness now. He heard no evidence that anyone was here. Riggles had gone, it seemed.

He looked in the office for Emma, expecting to find her at the desk pouring over accounts. Instead he saw only the remnants of the auction's revenue, a small heap of coins and drafts left out for the taking should he be a thief. He could not imagine Emma being so careless.

He set the painting against a wall in the hall and let himself out through the garden door. He saw her then, standing in the garden, unmoving and unseeing. Her expression reminded him of the passing preoccupation that claimed her at times, even in the aftermath of pleasure. Only now it owned her totally.

His questions about the Raphael did not matter much anymore. Nor did the coincidences that Kendale kept finding. She looked lost there, as if she did not have a friend in the world.

"Emma," he said, so that maybe she would decide she had at least one.

She did not hear him. She did not notice him. She stood in the waning sunlight, her black dress stark against the backdrop of verdant leaves, frowning with dismayed worry. It was obvious something had happened within the last hour to distress her beyond her ability to contain her emotions.

What did she contemplate? Nothing happy. It affected her whole body and the way she hugged herself for warmth. It showed in her eyes. She saw nothing of her surroundings, but only her own thoughts, and those thoughts made her afraid. Very afraid.

He knew, just knew, that whatever haunted her right now was much bigger than a few lots of illicit goods auctioned at Fairbourne's. And it had something to do with that man with the sack.

He did not call her name again. He did not think she would welcome his seeing her like this, or be relieved to share her burden. She had been carrying it for a while already, after all, and had never asked for his advice or help. She did not trust him with it. Perhaps she dared not.

He returned to the exhibition hall and hung the Raphael on the wall. Then he let himself out, and told his coachman to catch up with Kendale.

Emma did not move from the garden for a long while after she brought the money to her visitor. Waves of nausea plagued her and would not stop. Unpleasant shivers wracked her, but she did not feel cool. Rather the opposite. The illness centered in her heart, but it affected her in physical ways.

She would never call her visitor Stupid Man again. He had proven very shrewd. If anyone had been stupid, it had been her.

Not about everything. She had been smart enough not to share her problem with anyone. Even when tempted again and again to confide to Southwaite, she had held her tongue. Thank God for that.

This was turning out very badly. Any cooperation with smuggling would look like child's play when it was done. Even if she did not miss a step, even if she had Robert in a reunion embrace a fortnight hence, she would never live down agreeing to what had been demanded.

A favor, they called it. Hardly a favor. She should have given more weight to Marielle's revelations yesterday. The young French woman's experiences had honed her perceptions well. What had she said? *This stupid man will get me hanged if I am not careful.*

If Southwaite learned of it, he would never forgive her. Should her acts be discovered, his alliance with her would instantly become the most dreadful mistake he had ever made. Even worse, Robert himself might turn from her. He would not want the guilt of being the reason for her actions.

When Robert wrote to her, had he guessed that his captors used him to lure first Papa and now her into crime and compromise, then betrayal and disloyalty?

She sat on a stone bench and hugged herself so perhaps she would not shake from the fear that would not fade. She heard her own thoughts and question. Already her mind tried to avoid naming what she would be doing.

Betrayal and disloyalty were hardly forthright descriptions of this "favor." She would be bargaining for Robert's life with nothing less than treason, and she would not spare herself the truth of that.

Twilight came while she sat there. Finally, Mr. Dillon walked into the garden.

"Will you be wanting to go home now, Miss Fairbourne? The horse needs feeding and water."

She forced herself to her feet. "I have been inconsiderate. It has been a long day and we can all use feeding and water."

Mr. Dillon thought that very funny. He followed her into the exhibition hall through the garden door, and waited while she went to the office and scooped what was left of the money into her reticule.

"Should I bring this?" he asked when she rejoined him. He pointed to the wall.

A painting hung there. Even in the dim light its blues and reds shone from an internal light. St. George slew his dragon once more, while a princess watched.

She looked around the exhibition hall, half expecting to see Southwaite emerge from a dark corner. He must have returned the painting and left at once.

He had probably deciphered the provenance, despite her efforts to make that hard to do. He would have realized this had been Papa's and that she had sold it for herself.

Had he returned it out of sentimentality, so she might not lose one of Papa's prized paintings? Or did he suspect where the money would go, and wanted to distance himself from being touched by it all?

"Yes, please bring it, Mr. Dillon. It is too valuable to leave here unguarded."

In the carriage, she admired the Raphael for a few minutes, thinking it would be nice to have a St. George to slay her dragons. Then she set it aside, and began composing the letter she must write to Southwaite, to tell him that their personal alliance was over forever.

Chapter 27

Darius approached the massive house on Grosvenor Square at ten o'clock the next night. He would rather not knock on this door, but he could think of no other way to get answers to his questions quickly.

The first question would be settled in mere moments. Would he even be received?

A servant took his hat and another accepted his card.

"Please tell His Grace that I come on a matter of government," Darius said.

He waited in the reception hall. The house seemed quiet. No sounds of a dinner party broke the silence, nor even those of footsteps. The duke must be at home, however, if the card had been borne away.

He fought to conquer his impatience. There was the chance he would be left here a long while with no response to his calling card. It would be a childish retaliation for all the cuts and silence, but dukes were allowed to indulge in pique.

It seemed like an hour before the servant returned, but on checking his watch he saw it had been only fifteen

minutes. He was told His Grace would see him. He followed
the periwigged servant up to the public rooms.

The Duke of Penthurst received him in the library. It
appeared his host had been enjoying a quiet evening alone,
reading in the company of two of his hounds.

He set aside his book as Darius was announced, then
gestured to a chair facing his own. He stretched out his legs,
crossed his boots, and dangled his hand to give the closest
dog a scratch. He subjected Darius to a scrutiny that made
his dark eyes appear even more hooded than normal.

"A matter of government, you said. Last I recall you were
on the back benches on the wrong side."

"I did not send up word that I brought you information
about the government."

"You want it to go the other way, in other words."

"Yes."

Penthurst found that amusing. Even as he smiled, his eyes
lit with brittle lights. "Why would I be agreeable to that?"

No reason. Not anymore, at least. Not long ago he would
do it in friendship, perhaps.

"It touches on that chain we were establishing on the
coast."

"Ah, yes, that. Did you ever manage it? That was a very
ambitious plan."

"You are nothing if not an ambitious man."

"As I recall, it was a joint effort."

"It still is, and it is now in place. It has been for more
than a month. It has seen some success."

"You refer to the prisoner you brought back from the
coast with you, I assume."

"You know about that?"

"Of course. Is that why you are here? I would suggest we
toast your role in his capture, but he freely admitted only to
being a smuggler. I could nab any fellow walking along a
road in Kent and have an even chance of capturing one of
those."

"I had heard of that confession. I thought perhaps he later
was more forthcoming."

Penthurst gathered his limbs and leaned forward so he could scratch the head of his dog. The candles on the table with his book caught the sheen of the yellow silk ribbon that bound his old-fashioned queue at his nape.

"By *later*, I suppose you mean after he was tortured." He looked up. "We might as well call it what it is."

"Was it called that when you heard about it?"

"Of course not. We are a civilized people, so we never admit to such things." He made himself comfortable again. "Officially, on his own, after due deliberation of his situation, the prisoner chose of his own free will to make a confession that would get him hanged as a spy. Your chain indeed worked, Southwaite."

"It is not his confession that interests me, but his explanation, if he gave it, of how he expected it to go if it went well. When he claimed to be a smuggler, I am told he said he would be met onshore, for example."

"In assuming I know anything more, you are assuming much."

"I know you share my concerns about our special vulnerabilities. If you heard a spy had been taken, you would ask for the details, and get them."

Penthurst rose and walked to a table behind his chair. He lifted a brandy decanter with an offer in his eyes. Darius nodded, and soon two glasses had joined them in their conversation.

"I am told that by the end he was cursing the decision to send him over at all, with no more protection than the pretense of fleeing France. It seems they had a more secure way of doing it that fell apart recently, perhaps a few months ago. Your chain may have caused that disruption, I suppose."

"Did he describe the old way of doing it?"

"Someone watched from the coast and sent a signal into the night that the way was clear. The French boat would put in not far from where your people found his, and its special passenger was met and brought to a house that was safe. As soon as possible, he would be moved on to London, or whatever town or city he aimed for, where another safe abode waited. Information would be given to the special passenger, and he would leave the same way."

"He was a courier, then. Did he say who sent him, or who was to meet him? Did he give names of who passed him information?"

Penthurst drank some brandy. "Regrettably, he was not in the best of health. A bad heart, I am told. He unexpectedly expired before he shared those details."

Darius glared at Penthurst. *"Damnation."* He stood and paced away to relieve his outrage. There was much about this story that raised profound concerns. That the most important pieces had been lost maddened him.

"If it helps at all, I have expressed my displeasure to Pitt," Penthurst said. "I suggested that if England is going to dirty its hands thusly, we should at least find men to do it who get all the information before their darker natures get the better of them."

"He probably expressed shock that you would think such things happened at all."

"Of course he did. Still, I was heard."

"Well, I'll be damned before I hand over another one to them."

"You will do it yourself instead?" He ruminated. "You could use Kendale, I suppose. Do it the army's way. Just put a pistol to a temple and ask the questions. The poor bastard has only to look at Kendale to know he would pull the trigger."

As would you. Darius almost said it, but swallowed the words along with more brandy. If Penthurst had killed a friend, he could kill a spy.

Penthurst looked over with the vague smile of someone who knew Darius too well. "Yes, I would, if necessary. As would we all." He set his glass aside and stood. Both dogs rose up in unison. "Come with me. I will show you where I hung the Guardi."

Darius had not intended a social call, and did not care to do anything that would make it one. Still, he had been received and had been given the information he sought. He had no choice except to follow Penthurst and the hounds out of the library.

"That woman at the auction house. Fairbourne's daughter," Penthurst said as they made their way to the gallery. "Have you had her?"

Six months ago the question would have been normal, even expected. Tonight, under the circumstances of both their estrangement and the recent conversation, it was startling.

"Why would you ask?"

"Curiosity. Nothing more. She has a certain something to her. I thought you might have found out just what it is."

It was well past midnight when Darius returned to his house. He immediately went up to his dressing room. "Open it," he said through the door.

The latch moved. Kendale opened the door and stood aside. "There has been no undue curiosity from your household," he said. "Our guest is so contented with the accommodations that he is asleep."

Darius paced into the dressing room. Ambury looked over from a chair where he read a book. Snoring came from a divan, where the man with the sack had stretched out.

Darius was in no mood to behave like a gentleman. He had hoped to learn from Penthurst that the spy had talked long and fast and revealed the name and location of all the others he would meet while in England. Instead this fool on his divan might be the only chance left to discover that information.

Darius walked over, grabbed the front of the sleeping man's coat, and jerked him upright.

He woke up fast, with a yelp. After a moment of confusion, he righted himself and turned his body so his boots hit the floor. He glanced askance at his company, each man in turn.

Darius pulled over a chair. Ambury set aside his book.

Kendale hovered behind the divan, which made their guest very nervous.

"I am going to ask questions again, and this time you will answer them. What was your business at the auction house?" Darius bit out the words, but his anger was not so much with this man as with a situation that was slipping out of his grasp. He silently prayed that what he suspected was not true, and waited for this man to say something to relieve his sickening worry.

The fellow's response was to tighten his lips hard.

"What is your name?" Kendale asked. "I can find out within a few hours if I have to. It might go better for you if you do not put me to the trouble."

He thought it over and decided he could reveal that much without endangering whatever or whomever he sought to protect. "Hodgson."

Still standing behind him, Kendale leaned over so his mouth was very close to Hodgson's ear. "Now, Mr. Hodgson, you will answer my friend's questions. You have already wasted too much time. We are with the government. Your body will never be found, and no one will be the wiser if we kill you."

Hodgson twisted his neck to stare at Kendale in astonishment. Hodgson proved Penthurst correct. Hodgson clearly concluded that at least one man in the room would indeed kill him.

"I was only negotiating a little private business at that auction place," he said. "I stole nothing. The money in the sack is mine."

"We do not suspect you of theft," Darius said. "Did you leave town for a few days recently? Did you visit Kent?"

Hodgson's eyelids lowered. "What if I did?"

Ambury groaned with impatience. "Listen to me. We know enough to hand you to men who will surely learn the rest from you. They will use ways that will make being killed a mercy. If you went to Kent, you went by stagecoach and we can learn about that too, from the staging inns. You are facing the noose and worse, Mr. Hodgson, and your only hope is to speak plainly. If you do, perhaps we can use our influence to keep the worst from happening."

Kendale glared his disapproval at the last part of that. Hodgson's eyes grew wide at the word *noose*.

"I'm only a messenger. I deliver this an' that, is all!"

"Why were you in Kent?" Darius asked.

"I was to meet a man, and bring him to London. He never came, though."

"This was not the first time you met men. You have been to the coast often before on similar errands, haven't you?"

"A few times."

"Tell us about your business with Maurice Fairbourne, and now his daughter."

"Ah, hell. Ye already know about that?" Hodgson flushed. His expression fell into one of miserable worry. "I would bring him messages. I'd also bring him some things, wine and such, for his auction house to sell. That is where that sack of coin came from." He coughed and rubbed his mouth with his sleeve. "He has a cottage on the coast, and a few times these men I met—usually they do come, not like the last one—would stay there a night or so before we went to London."

"Did you kill him? Push him from that cliff? Was that one of the messages that you delivered?" Darius asked.

"No! That fall was nothin' but trouble for me. No cottage after that, and no help. The fool went and fell on his own." He shook his head. "What a bad night that was. See here, I keep telling ye, I am just a man who does errands. I deliver things. Now, I'll admit that it entered my head now and then that I was being hired by them that smuggle, what with that wine and such, but that ain't a real crime. Most everyone does it." He tried a smile. "Most likely your lordships have drunk some of it, at those fine parties you have."

"Who gave you the messages that you gave Fairbourne?" Ambury asked. "Who instructed you on these deliveries and who paid you?"

"Sometimes the men I met gave me the messages to deliver. And sometimes . . . there might be another one who came too, and made me explain how it had gone, and might give me messages or even notes to deliver, or I would deliver such to him. That one did not stay with me. I think he would go back, though."

"You knew this was not about smuggling," Kendale said dangerously. "I hope they paid you well for your treason."

"Treason! Goods came in those boats and goods is what I brought to Mr. Fairbourne."

"Goods and spies," Kendale snarled.

Hodgson turned to Darius. "M'lord, you surely do not think that—"

Darius held up a hand to stop him. "Fairbourne was convenient to your duties. Once he died, that must have been a problem."

"Hell of a problem, truth be told."

"Were you told to replace him with his daughter? Is that why you were at the auction house?"

"Replace, hell. Same family. It was thought she knew what to do." He shrugged. "Was easier for it to be her as someone else. She was happy enough to do it."

Darius saw red. He was on his feet and halfway to Hodgson before Ambury caught his arm, hard, stopping him. Hodgson reared back at the threat, visibly shaken by Darius's reaction.

Darius found some restraint, barely. He did not sit, however. Nor did Ambury. Mr. Hodgson looked up at the three of them now hovering over him. Darius's fist still had not unclenched.

"You blackmailed Fairbourne and his daughter into this," Darius said. "Why else would you have that sack of money and all this help you claim they gave? Fairbourne did not need whatever goods you brought him."

"I keep telling ye. I did not do anything. I was only a messenger!"

Impatient now, Darius grabbed him by the coat again. "What message did you give that would make Maurice Fairbourne help you?"

"His son!" Hodgson yelped. "I was told to tell him his

son was being held, and would only live if he helped. He was to signal to the boat if all was clear, and take in a guest that I might bring now and then."

"You fed him a lie, then. Did you ever see his son?"

"Of course not. Where would I see him? I was told to tell him that and I did, and I explained it to the daughter when she proved ignorant. She wanted to pay a ransom and be done with it. It was so high she had to help anyway."

"Damn you." Darius made to hit him again.

Ambury pulled Darius away and warned him off with a glare, then went and sat beside Mr. Hodgson. "You are in a bad spot here. There's two men here ready to hang you now, and others who will be more than happy to do it later. Your only hope is if you can help us find some of these men whom you met on the coast and aided in entering England."

"But I don't know where they be now." Hodgson was sweating badly, and appeared desperate. "I'd help if I could. I swear it."

"That is unfortunate. However . . . perhaps you know if another one is coming soon," Ambury suggested. "Are you expected to meet anyone on the coast again soon?"

Hodgson shot him a cautious look. He glanced over his shoulder at Kendale, and quickly checked Darius's demeanor too.

"I was planning a journey to the coast again next week. That is how it is done. If the man doesn't meet me the week he is supposed to, I go a fortnight later again."

Darius did not want to hear more, if more was coming. He would not stand there while this bastard described how Emma would be signaling from the cliff walk and opening her cottage to spies looking for very discreet lodging.

He strode from the dressing room before he thrashed Hodgson bloody. He went to his bedchamber and slammed the door in his wake. His head filled with a fury so black he could barely contain it.

Damnation. He should have seen it. Should have guessed. Smuggling, hell. He had been an idiot. Emma would never risk so much for so little. Of course the "everything else" had to do with graver matters than a few wagons of illegally imported goods.

She should have told him. He would have found a way to get her out of it. He would have shown her how her father's refusal to accept Robert's death had led to this, and how she must not allow herself to be coerced with the same stupid lie. He would have explained how holding steadfast on that belief created a vulnerability that anyone who knew of the belief could exploit. He would have—

His mind saw her in the garden, looking so lost after Hodgson left her. Was that when she had learned the real price? His memory of her there, so torn and confused and unbearably unhappy, made too much sense now. It touched him despite his chaotic thoughts and raw emotions.

She could not tell him, of course. She could not ask for his help, no matter what she thought was at stake. She did not trust him to spare her if he learned about it, either.

He strode to a table that held some books and took out a folded letter tucked in its drawer. The paper's condition reflected the way he had crumbled it in his fist on first reading the words on it yesterday. His reaction had been immediate and explosive. If there had been a fire lit, he would have tossed it in.

He read it again now, and its meaning did not anger him nearly as much. He saw it was not the harsh repudiation he thought. Actually, it had little to do with him at all.

My lord,

After much thought and much honesty with myself, I have realized that our alliance is as unwise and ill-advised as I first thought it would be. Forgive me for not having the fortitude to act accordingly after the auction. I can only blame my girlish excitement in the day's triumph, along with your winning ways.

As the Season ends, so do auctions of note. Fairbourne's will have no forthcoming business to conduct for at least two months. Therefore I am leaving London.

Perhaps a visit to the lake district will offer me retreat and solitude.

Upon my return, I trust that you and I can treat each other as respected business associates. We should, however, permit nothing more to exist between us.

Emma Fairbourne

Ambury entered the bedchamber just as Darius was folding the letter again. He just stood there, as if expecting Darius to say something.

"I am sorry to learn that she is as involved as she is," Ambury finally said.

It was the sympathy of a friend, but it was also a reminder of her betrayal.

"She thinks her brother is alive, just as her father did," Darius said.

"Yes. However, that doesn't make a difference in the end, does it?"

No, damn it. His fear for her had become a burning coal in his chest.

"Kendale wants to use Hodgson and have him meet his man as planned. He thinks we then can follow the courier and find the men he meets with in London and elsewhere." Ambury tried to sound skeptical. "You know Kendale—he is picturing an entire network brought down."

Darius said nothing. There was great sense in Kendale's plan, and Ambury knew it. The only flaw was that having Hodgson meet that boat and its special passenger would require allowing Emma to make her signal and give the spy refuge. They would use not only Hodgson, but also Miss Fairbourne. Instead of stopping her, they would let her play her designated role.

Ambury looked at him with eyes too aware and too concerned. "If you say the word, we will not do it. I think that I know what she means—"

"No. It must be done. If it is another courier, he might lead us to five more. Ten perhaps."

Ambury did not reply.

"When does the game start?" Darius asked.

"Monday, Hodgson said. We can take him to the coast. Kendale has created a little army out of his household staff, it seems. His own private citizens' unit. They will help. You need not be there."

"Of course I will be there. I will go down to Kent tomorrow, and send my sister and aunt back to town so we can use Crownhill. I will inform the other gentlemen watchers of what is happening. I expect that most of them will join us, so your plans can assume plenty of eyes and pistols being available. I will also talk to Tarrington and alert him too, so he does not move on that boat until the man Hodgson is meeting has left the shore and moved inland."

Ambury nodded. "We will come to Crownhill directly from town."

Darius turned away. "Please get that man out of my house, Ambury. Let Kendale deal with him until you make the journey."

Ambury left. Darius looked at the letter still in his hand. His mind saw Emma again in the garden. The memory of her distress pained him.

She thought she was saving her brother. It was, he supposed, the most noble reason imaginable for the most ignoble act. He was not at all sure, if he were in her place, that he could have chosen differently.

Chapter 28

Emma let herself into the cottage. She set down her valise and immediately opened the windows to air out the space. A breeze blew in, bringing with it the scents of the coast and the sounds of her hired carriage rolling away.

She set about unpacking the two baskets of food that she had purchased on the way. There would be no Mrs. Norriston to cook on this brief visit, and no Mr. Dillon to feed, so she had kept the provisions simple. Some ham and a few fresh eggs. Some bread and, as an indulgence, some peaches. She should probably eat something now, as it was evening, but she was too sick with worry to be hungry.

Once all had been sorted and stored, she went up the stairs and did the same with the garments she had brought. Then she went down again and searched for lanterns.

She found one in a kitchen cupboard, and two in the horse stable. Lining them up on the kitchen worktable, she fitted them with candles that she had brought with her. Then she lit one.

She sat with a book near that light. No pages turned, however. She kept watching night come, and checking the time. She noted the hour when the last of twilight's glow had faded. No clock chimed the time, but her heart and fear did.

In exactly twenty-four hours she would begin her mission to redeem her brother. Once it was over, surely she would reconcile herself to what she had done. The prize would surely be worth the price. Right now, however, she could muster no excitement or anticipation over seeing Robert again. She knew only a dread that left her unable to do anything but wait.

She slept well that night. So well that she wondered if already she had lost her soul. She made some preparations in the cottage for the guest she expected. She also loaded and hid the pistol she had brought. It had not passed her notice that in acting outside the law, she would be unable to expect laws to protect her.

At noon she left the cottage and trod the three hundred yards east to where the land fell away to the sea. She noted her path carefully, and even kicked aside some large rocks that might not be visible at night. She found the path that formed a long cliff walk, turned to her right, and followed it south to where it began its slow, long rise toward Dover.

She stopped finally, standing where she had stood one time before, at the spot below which Papa's body had been found. She could see up and down the coast. She had not realized that if she could view so much of the sea from this spot, those on the sea could view her too.

Right now the prospects of the churning waves did not interest her. The ground around her feet did. It could be treacherous ground, as Papa had learned that night. There were places where the cliff walk veered too close to the edge, and other spots where time had weathered and weakened the edge itself.

She sat on the ground, and forced herself to contain the panic that wanted to rule her. If that happened, she might make a mistake. She might even run away. The only way to control her composure, however, was to remain forever alert and to permit no wild images of either failure or retribution to invade her head.

She closed her eyes and clenched her whole self against the fear. She tried to let the sea breeze refresh her, but it seemed only to worsen the unending shivers that had begun in the garden that day.

Annoyed at how these unknown men had robbed her of herself, she stood and brushed off her dress. It was then that she saw the carriage down the rise to the west, like a blot on her vision as she squinted west into the setting sun. Her eyes adjusted a bit, and she noticed the dark form of a man walking toward her.

As he neared, the sun's glare no longer obscured his features. Southwaite!

Guilt urged flight. She swallowed the impulse, and tried to find a face that would not appear desperate.

He came up to her, and stopped no more than an arm span away. He smiled.

"Hello, Emma."

"I thought you were going to the lake district," Darius said while they walked north. Down at the bottom of the hill his carriage moved along too, at the same slow pace.

"The intention of my letter was not to inform you of my plans to retreat for some rest. I had not decided yet where I would go. I did not feel compelled to explain my choice once I made it."

Darius welcomed her testy tone. She had appeared so pale when he first saw her face. Pale and drawn and confused by his presence. At least now she had mustered enough of the Emma he knew to be annoyed.

He pretended not to notice how agitated his presence made her, but he saw it in her stiffness and in the haunted expression in her eyes. And in the way she did not look at him directly, as if she knew she could hide nothing if she did.

She stopped walking and frowned. "Since you have made

reference to my letter, I know that you received it. Considering its content, your insistence on this stroll and conversation is perplexing."

"Forthright as always, I see. Yes, I read it. I did not care for the contents. I am not used to being thrown over with so little ceremony, and with no reason."

"No reason? That is rich, Southwaite. The reasons are so obvious as to not need enumeration. You felt obligated to offer marriage because of all the excellent reasons for me to end such a liaison. Now, please, go seduce someone else and leave me in peace."

Face flushed with exasperation, she marched away. He caught up. She spied him falling into step again, closed her eyes, and groaned.

"I cannot leave you in peace, Emma. I am sorry."

"Then you are more conceited than I knew."

He stopped her, and pulled her into his arms. She startled at the abruptness of his movement, and struggled to break away. He held her firmly in a tight embrace and her resistance slid away, but she would not turn her face up to him.

"I cannot because I will not give you up so easily. I refuse to believe that you know your own mind on this yet. Not completely." He tipped up her face with a finger below her chin. Her expression touched him. She appeared so distraught that tears flooded her eyes.

He kissed each damp cheek, then her mouth. "I must insist on the right to try to change your mind, Emma." Arm around her, he guided her down the hill.

It took several steps before she fully understood what he was doing. "What are you—Do you expect me to go with you? I cannot." She tried to squirm out of his arm's embrace.

He held firm and sped her forward. "As always, I promise the highest discretion."

"Discretion be damned. I insist you stop this." She tried to dig in her heels but her feet slid along with him. She hit him on his arm to try to break his hold, and began lowering herself to the ground so he could not force her to walk. "If you desire a discussion on the matter, I will engage in one after I have rested for several days."

"I would much prefer it be settled now." He lifted her physically into his arms and walked toward the open door of his carriage. His coachman and two footmen did not move or flinch, but stood in place like blind statues.

Emma's eyes widened. She twisted and flailed and hit him again, this time on the face. "You do not understand. I *cannot* go with you now." She glared with shock and fury when he did not stop walking. When he reached the carriage she hit his shoulder and pushed against his hold. "Stop at once, or you will be guilty of abduction!"

"Then abduction it will be, Emma."

Emma clung to the window's edge as the world sped by. Each minute took her farther from where she needed to be tonight.

Her mind raced. If she did not signal with the lantern, it would be interpreted as a warning that the coast was not clear. How often could that happen before there were other interpretations, and she was suspected of betrayal? And Robert—how horrible if night after night they put him in that boat headed for home, only to bring him back each time because his sister had not done as she was told.

She sank back on her seat, too frightened to think. Southwaite reached for her hand. She slapped his away.

He tried to gather her into his arms and she hit him again and again while she wept tears of helplessness. "Stop. Do not touch me. You do not know—this is just a game to you. A man's prideful game. I am just a game to such as you."

"You are no game, Emma." He retreated, however, and moved to the seat facing her.

She refused to look at him. She gazed out the window until the coach stopped in the drive of Crownhill. As soon as she was handed down, she strode into the house. She ignored the servants and mounted the stairs, seeking the chamber she had used the last time he brought her here.

She found the room easily enough. She entered, slammed the door, and rested against it while she turned the key. Then she ran to the window.

The terrace below looked terribly distant. There was no way to jump or climb. She would have to give him the slip somehow, if not today, then tomorrow. She wondered how long it would take to walk back to her father's cottage.

"Emma."

She froze. He spoke through the door but she heard him clearly. "Go away, Lord Southwaite. There will be no seductions in ballrooms this time."

Silence. She prayed he had left. She did not want to insult him. She wished . . . She wished he had accepted her letter for what it said, and not conceived this game. He had no way to know how dangerous this delay that he created for her could be, and how terribly confused his presence made her. *Go away, go away, so I do not have to break my own heart by being cold and cruel.*

"Emma, I know."

The wood of the door did not muffle the warm resonance of his voice. Nor its inflections. He did not say, "I know," as if he responded to what she had yelled at him. He said it like *he knew*.

Her heart beat so hard that she felt it in her head. She walked halfway back to the door. "What do you know?"

"I know why you are at the cottage, alone, without even your coachman. I know why I found you on the cliff walk, at the spot where your father fell."

Each word he said chilled her more. She experienced the worst fear then. It was the terror of a person in flight who had just been caught.

"I know almost everything," he said. "Open the door now. I am no danger to you. You have no reason to be afraid. You have not done anything wrong."

Not yet, but it was not for lack of intention. Had he not stopped her— Even now, if she could escape—

She was not sure she had the courage to face him, if indeed he knew almost everything.

"Open the door, darling. I cannot bear that you are alone with the unhappiness I have seen in you."

Her vision blurred and her eyes stung. She could no longer hold her composure together. Defeated, and miserable with grief that she would fail her brother, she stumbled to the door and worked the key.

One look at Southwaite, at the sympathy in his eyes, and she fell into his arms sobbing.

"I thought it was about smuggling. That is wrong, of course, but it is a very commonplace crime."

Emma whispered while her head lulled on his shoulder. Her outpouring of emotion had given her some peace. He felt little strength in her while he held her on his lap on the edge of the bed.

She wiped her eyes. "I knew that you could not excuse even that. When I learned much more was involved, I dared not tell you, or even see you again. Even now, just knowing what I planned to do compromises you, doesn't it?"

That remained to be seen.

"You must let me go, Southwaite. Please, I beg you. These people have Robert. Once I have him back, once I see him, I will find a way to undo this. I will—I will shoot the man who brings him over, if you want. Just please, let me do what I must so they will bring him back."

He did not know what to say to that, so he said nothing. Both Maurice and Emma had been badly deceived, however. No matter what they paid or what they did, Robert Fairbourne would not be restored to them.

"You do not believe me," she said. "You do not trust me either."

"I trust you, Emma. I think you would shoot him, if that was the bargain you struck with me. And I believe that you and your father truly thought you were saving your brother."

"I not only think it. I *know* it. I insisted on proof, and they let him write a letter to me."

"Emma, I do not think—"

"*It was from Robert*. I know his hand. I could hear his voice saying the words as I read them."

"They could have—"

"It was not a forgery." She pushed off his lap and stood. She looked at him as if his lack of belief made him less of a friend. "Do you think I would agree to do such a thing for anything less? Do you believe I would not recognize a letter written by someone else in his name?"

He took her hand and cajoled her back to him. She sat beside him, distressed once more.

"Tell me what you were told to do, in order to get him back."

"I thought you knew everything."

"Almost everything."

She weighed what she would say. He knew her well now, and he could almost hear her thoughts.

"Am I a prisoner? If I confide, is it a confession? I know that you concern yourself with doings on the coast. You have made it your mission to catch people like me."

He tried to swallow his sense of insult. He told himself that she was afraid, and for good reason.

"You do like your plain speaking, Emma. I have brought you here, and will keep you here, to ensure that you do not do anything that will leave me with an impossible choice between my honor and the woman I love. You must accept that you will not complete this mission. I have stopped you now, and if you manage to leave here, I will stop you again."

She looked at him, her gaze penetrating the way that could make him forget himself. He wondered if she searched for evidence of his resolve or for proof he would protect her.

"This week, every evening, I am to go to the cliff walk on that high rise," she said. "I need to be there in late evening, right before night falls, so there is still light to see the coast and the sea."

"You were to check that there were no ships?"

She nodded. "And that the sea is calm enough. Papa was doing this that night." She blinked the thought away. "If there are no customs' cruisers visible, I am to wait for night to fall, then take my lighted lanterns and walk back and forth on that walk. For an hour I am to do that. Then I can return home and wait."

"Wait for what?"

"For Stupid Man—that is the name I gave the man who delivered instructions—to bring Robert to me. And to bring someone else too, perhaps. A guest, for a night or so. That was how I knew for certain this was not only about smuggling—when the chance of this secret guest was broached." She wiped her eyes with her hand. "I know what you mean about a horrible choice, Southwaite."

He embraced her with his arm. "That guest would have come, but not your brother. Even if he is alive, they would not have given him back. After you did this once, they would have demanded it again and again. The night your father fell was probably not the first time he spent an hour on that cliff walk."

She neither agreed nor disagreed. She looked around the chamber. "How long will I be here?"

"I do not know. Until I am sure you are safe."

"Will you be here too?"

"Some of the time. I would like your word that you will not try to leave."

"I cannot give it."

"Then I will have to keep a close watch on you."

Her color rose in a lovely flush. "Did you mean it, when you spoke of me as the woman you love?"

"I meant it."

"Then I must make sure you are never faced with that horrible choice, Southwaite. That may require some plain speaking that is not in my own interests."

"How so, Emma?"

"You must know that if I ever tried to escape from here, it would be at night. I wish I could swear that the idea has not entered my mind, but I regret that it already has."

"I will have to keep a very close watch of you at night, then."

"I think that would be wise." She leaned into him, until

her face was an inch from his. "I think that you should kiss me now, if I am not only your prisoner, but the woman you love. It would bring me great comfort if you did. I might not feel helpless and alone and so afraid if you held me in your arms."

He was happy to kiss her and hold her, for whatever reason she wanted him to. His worst fear upon reading that letter she had sent was that he might never be able to do so again.

It could never be a simple kiss anymore, even if it were only one. There was too much between them now. She thwarted his intention to be very careful with her, however. She responded to his kiss with a fierce outpouring of passion that finally released her fears.

She destroyed his restraint with fevered kisses and impatient caresses. She clawed at his cravat and shirt until she bared his chest to her teeth and tongue. Her aggression incited an unbearable hunger that darkened his mind to anything except having her, taking her, and possessing her forever.

He cast off his coats easily enough. He loosened her dress closures and they both stripped off her garments while managing to remain bound together with grasping embraces and furious kisses. As soon as her chemise flew away, she lay back on the bed and pulled him with her.

"Now." She gasped. "All of you. I want all of you with me, so I feel something besides worry and fear."

He rose above her on outstretched arms so he could look at her. He reached down and moved her legs until they bent and her knees hugged her body. He caressed the soft flesh that her position exposed. She moaned with pleasure again and again, and each sound pierced what was left of his mind and urged him toward a violent release.

She reached low and devastated him with caresses of her own, then guided him to her body, making her desire clear. He entered her slowly. Her long inhale, full of wonder and relief accompanied the silent groan that his soul made at the perfect sensation.

He was relieved then that she had not wanted him to be careful, and thankful that her wildness matched his. In her abandon she relinquished all control, all modesty, and exposed her heart even more boldly than her body.

He took her hard and she urged him on until they shared a rare union, one of joy and fear and of pleasure so intense it almost made him insane. When his climax broke it was a lightning bolt, splintering his awareness, and she was the only part of the world that remained in the deep thread of consciousness where he momentarily dwelled.

Chapter 29

Emma leaned against the rough fence, watching South-waite ride a young stallion in the large pen attached to the long, half-timbered stable. She admired the animal's lines and spirit, the latter of which Southwaite coaxed into submission through subtle control. She also admired the rider, who appeared very rustic in his muddy boots and shirtsleeves.

The last two days had been erotic. Seductive. Loving. Their passion had dulled her fear, but it had not obliterated it. Whenever she thought about Robert, her failure to help him saddened her. There were even times, like right now, when she contemplated how she might still get away so that boat came to shore the way it had been planned.

Escape would do no good, of course. Southwaite knew exactly where she would go, and why. She knew that he had abducted her so she could do nothing that would be seen as treason, no matter what her intentions. If she went near that cliff walk now, he would have to hand her to the authorities himself. He still might have to, if anyone else knew what she had planned.

She had decided not to contemplate the future, or whether she might find herself soon with a real gaoler, instead of this one who offered protection and sanctuary as well as restraint.

Southwaite made the horse stop and stand still. It wanted to bolt. He said something that she could not hear and its ears went up, then back. It gave up the effort to rebel, and seemed to smile when he patted its neck. He let it move, but only at a walk. He paced it over to her.

"We will go back to the house soon," he said.

"I do not mind. I enjoy watching the horses. Do not leave because of me."

He nodded, then rode over to a gate on the enclosure. He lifted a latch and rode out. One subtle signal, and the stallion broke into a gallop across the field beyond.

She went to a wooden bench set against the stable and waited. Her feet dangled a bit, sticking out prominently from below her hem. She looked down and laughed at herself. She had forgotten how odd she looked today.

She wore low boots loaned by one female servant and a dress from another that was a little too short. Her bonnet had been found in Lydia's chamber and, since it was very plain, fit her ensemble nicely. How she and Southwaite had laughed when she dressed in this assemblage of borrowed items.

She had suggested he just send someone to the cottage for her own things. He had refused, saying she would do fine for him as she was. That had been charming, and the kiss he gave her distracting, but that refusal had come with a finality that suggested those clothes would remain in that cottage for a reason.

He did not intend to stay here with her forever and let this idyll spin out for weeks. She would remain here until he knew she was safe, he had said. She guessed they were waiting for something to happen so he would know that.

He rode the horse in her direction, teaching it to trot. The stallion made it clear he did not like the silly gait. She heard Southwaite laugh as the horse rebelled in clever little half steps. Then he stopped, and his attention was on neither the horse nor her.

Another rider galloped on the field. He was close enough that she guessed he had been heading to the stable when he saw Southwaite on the field. They met out there and talked, then rode back to where she sat. The other man was Viscount Ambury.

Southwaite dismounted and called to the grooms to saddle his bay gelding. Ambury greeted her.

"I trust your visit has been restful, Miss Fairbourne," he said.

"Quite restful, thank you. Have you come to rest as well? I expect the Season was exhausting."

Ambury smiled oddly and nodded. "Southwaite has been boasting about a young racehorse he bought. I came to see it put through its paces."

A groom brought out the gelding. "Ambury and I are going to ride back to the house," Southwaite said. "The carriage will bring you." He took her hand and led her to the carriage and handed her up.

He appeared serious and thoughtful. Rather suddenly, he had hardened in many small ways, and it even affected how he spoke to her.

She looked to where Ambury waited. "Has something happened?"

"Nothing. I will explain later." He raised her hand and kissed it. Ambury managed to be looking elsewhere right then.

Southwaite swung into his saddle, and he and Ambury rode away.

"What are you looking at?" Darius asked. He and Ambury slowed to a walk as they rode up the lane to the front of Crownhill. Ambury kept looking his way with disapproval. Darius guessed why, and it was better to have it out now. "You look like a man who has something critical to say."

"It is not for me to criticize your handling of this matter, especially as it concerns Miss Fairbourne," Ambury said. "I will leave that to Kendale, who, I should warn you, is going to be in rare form when he learns that she is here, and not where we expect her to be."

"I will deal with Kendale." Damned if he knew how. Kendale would accuse him of jeopardizing the entire mission. Which he had.

"I also will not mention that it is apparent the lady does not know you intend to interfere beyond stopping her. She certainly did not expect to see others arrive."

"I will explain it all to her soon."

"Nor is it for me to point out that your letters made demands on me that I loathed accommodating. Calling on Penthurst to ask him to intercede with the home secretary was particularly distasteful."

"We both know Kendale would have never agreed to do those things."

"How fortunate I am to be so agreeable, then. I am heartened that you find my character convenient to your purposes."

Darius assumed that having itemized his annoyances, Ambury would be contented. He caught his friend giving another sharp look in his direction, however.

"Disapproval does not suit you, Ambury. You look too much like my aunt Amelia when you purse your mouth like that."

"I am not pursing my mouth. I am not even disapproving. I will admit, however, to being confounded. Even, perhaps, astonished."

"By what?"

"You and Miss Fairbourne."

"I am never judgmental of your affairs, but then, I know it is dangerous to tell a man that his lady is not suitable."

"*An affair?* I was not criticizing an affair that I was not even aware of, I assure you. I assumed you spared her due to having a tendre for her, true, but I did not guess you had seen such success as an affair would necessitate."

"Perhaps you think that I should not be showing her the consideration that I am, affair or not. Perhaps you want to hand her over to the Home Office's brutes for her role in this. I am prepared for Kendale telling me I should have let it play out so we were sure to capture the whole of the web, but—"

"Again you presume to know my mind when you do not. I expect us to capture them all anyway, with only slightly more danger to it, and I would never countenance handing a woman over to—that."

They pulled up their horses in front of Crownhill, and dismounted.

"If you must know, Southwaite, I am appalled that you would allow that poor woman to be dressed like she was. It is to her credit that she wore that hideous and ill-fitting dress as if it were the finest silk and refused to be embarrassed by your thoughtlessness."

Darius had not thought Emma looked hideous. He had not even noticed the dress after they laughed over it. "We had to make do."

"You should have done better." Ambury shook his head. "The poor woman."

They immediately went to the library. Kendale waited there. So did a small arsenal. Pistols, muskets, and bags of powder cluttered the tables.

"There are three of us and five muskets," Darius said, examining the display of arms.

"I like to have extras, all loaded, ready, and well placed," Kendale said. "There are more in my carriage, if you want some too."

"I am much better with a pistol," Darius said.

"You will remember that the goal is to take them alive, I hope," Ambury said to Kendale while he lifted a musket and sighted along its barrel.

"I'm the least of your worries. And if we are not careful, whoever gets off that boat will be the least of ours. I don't like having to worry about my back while I am charging forward."

"You have no reason to believe Tarrington and his lads will betray you," Darius said.

"You have no reason to believe they won't, except the sworn word of a criminal."

"I happen to have had experience with how well Tarrington keeps his word."

"He'd better, since he is holding Hodgson now, who is surely trying to bribe him."

Ambury pulled out his pocket watch. "We leave in three hours. The others should be here soon. Have you heard from London? Has the post arrived?"

"Not yet."

"And if no letter comes?"

Darius assumed one would.

"We go anyway," Kendale said. "The weather is fair. The channel is calm enough. Hopefully this finishes tonight and we aren't at it a fortnight from now. Mistakes get made if there is too much waiting. That Fairbourne woman may conclude she is on a fool's errand if she signals night after night and no one comes."

Ambury set down the musket, then gave Darius a meaningful look. "You had better tell him."

"Tell me what?" Kendale eyed them both.

"Miss Fairbourne will not be signaling. She is not at the cottage," Darius said.

Kendale was not nearly as angry as Darius had expected, but then, he did not know all of it yet. True, he cursed loudly, but then he turned philosophical. "I suppose she could not face doing such a thing. That speaks well of her, but it means we are wasting our time here."

"She is not needed. We know a boat is coming. We will have Hodgson meet it, and we can—"

"Do you intend to wear a dress and go up on that cliff walk? Because we do not know if Hodgson is the only one who will be meeting that boat. Hell, for all we know someone else will be watching everything that happens."

"Neither place is easily watched. The hill with the cliff

walk is barren and open, and the road behind it very visible," Darius said.

Kendale shook his head. "We can wait on the shore, and near the house, to see what can be done, but at best you will grab another courier tonight."

"What if the puppet dances as commanded? What if I make the signal, and wait at the cottage the way I was told to?"

Darius pivoted at the sound of Emma's questions. She stood in the doorway in that old dress with the half boots sticking out below the hem. The garments were ridiculous, he had to admit, but she appeared quite regal anyway.

Silence fell in the library as all of them looked at her. Kendale's surprise gave way to a steely, knowing gaze that he turned on Darius. "When you explained she was not at the cottage, you did not mention that she was here instead."

"A mere oversight," Ambury soothed.

"Miss Fairbourne is my guest," Darius said.

"Hell," Kendale hissed under his breath.

"It would be better if you leave this to us and retire to your chamber, Miss Fairbourne," Darius said brusquely.

"I do not think it would be better at all. It sounds to me as if you have planned an intervention, but my absence will make your success unlikely. If so, I need to do my part."

"It is too dangerous," Darius said. "Please leave us now."

She flushed at his tone. She refused to budge.

Damnation, of all times for her to get stubborn. He wanted to throw her over his shoulder and carry her away from this library. He strode over to her and trusted she saw how close he was to doing just that.

"Go now, Emma." He kept his voice low and private but did not stint on the force of will behind his words.

"I want to do it. I need to."

"No. You are out of this."

A rebellious, resentful expression tightened her face. He half expected her to start a row right here in front of Kendale and Ambury. Instead she turned on her heel and walked out. He shut the door behind her.

As he rejoined them, Kendale made much of looking out the window. Ambury occupied himself with the ritual of pouring some brandy.

"What she says is true, Southwaite," Ambury said, finally. "You know it is."

"No."

"I will stay with her," Kendale said. "At the first sign of danger to her I will act. I'll kill anyone who tries to harm her."

"You can't stay with her on that damned cliff walk," Darius snapped.

"I can stay close enough to stop a man with a musket ball."

"Not once they are in the cottage. We have no guarantee they will even leave come morning. It could be days that she is alone with them. I will not allow that."

Kendale understood the danger. He would no more leave a woman that vulnerable than Darius would, and he no longer pressed the matter.

"Suppose we put someone in that cottage with her. You, for example. Up above, in one of the bedchambers," Ambury said. "You could keep an ear on her, if not an eye, Southwaite. As for their hiding there for days, we will find a means to discourage their even remaining one night."

"What you propose hardly ensures her safety. She will remain *here*. I will not discuss it further."

Kendale strode to the door.

"Damn, where are you going?" Darius said.

"To learn the lady's mind on it. You are not her father or brother or any relative. Unless there has been a wedding I don't know of, she is not under your authority. She has the right to make her own choice, seems to me."

Darius saw red. He started after Kendale, to stop him. A tight grasp on his upper arm interfered.

He turned on Ambury. "I was going to thrash Kendale but you will do if you insist."

"Thrash if you want. Better that than you forget who you are and why we are even here." Ambury's voice urged calm, but he did not release his hold. "She came within a feather of treason, Southwaite. Would you deny her the chance to right that in her mind? There can be nothing between you until she does."

He wanted to punch Ambury for that. He pictured Emma telling Kendale she was willing and his head almost split. He wanted to lock her away, and cursed himself for keeping her with him instead of sending her to the ends of the earth to protect her.

His fury gathered, darkened, and broke like a storm's wave. But it ebbed after that, and sense began giving shape to more rational thoughts. All that was left then was cold determination.

Chapter 30

"You are sure that you know what to do and say?" Southwaite asked the question yet again. Emma nodded. She tried to reassure him with her eyes and her touch, but he was not a man to be appeased this evening.

"Tell me," he said. "Repeat it all back to me so I know there is no misunderstanding."

"I am to take the lanterns and go to the cliff walk, as planned. No matter what I see on the coast, I am to make the signal."

"Kendale will be where he can see you. No one should approach you, Emma. If you see anyone around, anyone at all—"

"I know. You have told me. I will be fine, Darius. I will not get myself hurt."

"The rest. Tell me the rest."

"I then go back to the cottage, and put a lantern in the window, and wait."

"It could be a long wait. They will be out to sea, close enough to see the light on the cliff, but far enough to run if they must."

"Yes, I know. You have explained this many times, Darius. When the man from the boat is brought to me, I will say that I am sure someone was following me back. I will make sure they conclude it is not safe to stay with me and that they must change their plans."

"I will be up above. If there is any threat to you, if one of these blackguards even looks at you oddly, you are to—"

"I will cry out, so you know you are needed." She raised her head and kissed him. "I will feel perfectly safe, knowing you are there."

He slid his arm around her and embraced her. His hold proved a balm to her nerves, which were more unsettled than she revealed.

It had been kind of Ambury and Kendale to allow her this brief time alone with Darius. She heard the horse hooves hitting the ground alongside. Not only two horses made the sounds. Three others had come while Viscount Kendale spoke to her. Gentlemen all, she assumed they had been called from properties nearby.

"I told Kendale about my brother," she said. "I gave him a description of Robert, so if anyone on this boat claimed that identity, he might know if it were true. He said he would be there with Tarrington, to take the boat after the spy left the coastline."

Darius said nothing to that. She knew he did not think Robert would ever be released. He still thought Robert was dead, and Stupid Man and his master had taken advantage of hers and Papa's refusal to accept the truth.

"When they leave the cottage, what then?" She had been told her role, but little else. She doubted Lord Kendale trusted her enough for that. He probably had guessed that Darius had physically prevented her from becoming a traitor.

"You will be out of this, finally," he muttered.

"I mean what will happen with them?"

"They will be followed. The hope is to have the new man lead us to the ones who have the information. It is why he is here. Hodgson—the man whom you met and know—will be taken when they separate. He expects it. He agreed to betray his mission, and *you*, to save his neck, but he will not go free."

"Maybe he also has a relative that he sought to redeem."

"He did it for money, Emma. Most do."

The curtains were closed on the carriage, but she knew they were approaching the cottage even without being able to see the passing land. Darius must have too. His embrace became all-encompassing and he gave her a kiss so sweet that her love tore at her heart.

"When this is over, you and I need to come to a right understanding about some things, Miss Fairbourne."

"I expect we do." She wished she could think he was being flirtatious or teasing. Only he did not speak lightly, but most seriously.

She did not expect that right understanding to be pleasant. When this was over, he would calculate the costs to his honor of loving her. She did not expect to fare well in that judgment.

The horse slowed. The carriage came to a stop. She turned in his arms and kissed him. She put the future out of her mind while she did, and filled her head and heart with memories of the last two days together, and the beauty she had known sharing passion with a man she loved.

Then the carriage door opened and they were awash in the waning light of the evening. She and Darius walked to her father's cottage while the carriage and five gentlemen on horseback peeled away.

Emma waited in the small library of the cottage. She kept candles burning, and remained in a chair where she could be seen from the window should anyone peer inside. She sat in that chair for three hours with no sign of Stupid Man Hodgson or a spy or anyone else.

The part she had played on the cliff path had been easy compared to this. Not a soul had been in sight. While waiting for night to fall, she had tried to determine where Lord Kendale lurked. He had been so invisible that she would

have doubted he was there, except he was the sort of man
one did not dare doubt in any way.

She could move about down here, she supposed. She did
not have to remain immobile like this. Darius was not making a sound up above, though, so she would not either. Perhaps he listened at the window, so he would know when
someone approached.

It had been a hard parting before he walked up those
stairs, loaded pistols in hand. He did not like that she was
here, and a scowl never left his face. Except at the very end
when, halfway up, he turned and glanced at her. Her breath
had caught at his expression of love and worry and anger.

What if they did not come? The sea was calm, but there
were other reasons why they might not. She might have to
do all of this again tomorrow night, and the night after. She
wondered whether Darius would permit that.

The candle in the lantern began to fade. She looked to
the window where it sat, to see if it was going to go out. Two
eyes moved behind the wavy glass panes, startling her badly.
Her heart jumped and began beating fast. She had to force
herself not to look up at the ceiling, to where Darius waited.

The door opened. Boot steps and murmurs approached.
Hodgson entered and looked around, then gestured. A tall,
thin man with dark hair and a military bearing appeared.

She waited to hear yet one more pair of boots, her heart
in her throat. No one else came in. These two were alone.

Disappointment drenched her as if a wave of it had broken inside her head. She wanted to both weep and scream.
What a fool she had been. She glared at Hodgson, and forced
herself to swallow the words of fury and betrayal shouting
in her head.

"This here is my friend," Hodgson said. "He'll be needing that chamber I talked to you about. This is Miss Fairbourne, Jacques."

"Joseph," he said with a scowl. "My name is Joseph."

Joseph spoke with distressingly good English. He would
leave here and just disappear, with English that natural
sounding.

"The chamber is ready, as required," Emma said. "However, I fear that you use it at your peril."

"How so?" Joseph asked sharply.

"I was not alone the whole time I was making the signal. If you noticed the light not move for a spell, that is why. A man walked by, and took interest in my movements. It might be nothing, of course, but—" Her chaotic emotions caused the words to come out in fits and starts. She hoped they would attribute that to fear.

"Merde."

Hodgson looked dismayed. "I am sure it is nothing."

"How can you be sure?" Joseph snapped.

Hodgson's eyes widened. Emma thought he appeared guilty, obviously so. He heard a challenge that was not there because of his intended betrayal.

"I do not want you found here. I was promised secrecy and safety," she said.

"I promised you nothing," Joseph said. He went to the window, gutted the lantern's candle, and peered into the night.

Hodgson became nervous and agitated. Worry marked his expression. He kept turning to her with questioning eyes, as if he hoped she knew why this change in plans had happened.

She hoped he worried a lot. She was glad he would not go free. He had lied to her, and she had come close to doing something so terrible and dishonorable that even the thought would be considered unforgivable by many people.

"Where is my brother?" she demanded. "You said he would be with you."

"He, uh—I sent him to that village a bit inland. He didn't know you would be here—I thought you might like to explain that yourself—and he didn't see no point in staying with us, once that boat hit English sand. You go to the village in the morning and you'll find him there."

Her heart ached to believe him. She sought every excuse to do so. "You are lying. He did not come. I think it was all lies, and even that letter was a forgery.

Joseph looked over his shoulder. "It was no forgery. He wrote it. I saw him do it."

"Then why is he not here?" she cried. "If you think that I will do this over and over on the vain hope that one day he will walk in that door too, I will not."

Joseph looked at her calmly. Blankly. "Yes, you will." He then addressed Hodgson. "We will go now."

"Now? 'Tis dark. If anyone is lying in wait, we won't see them until—"

"If we do not see them, they do not see us."

"You go if you want. I'm thinking to stay right here."

"You are coming. You were paid to get me to London, and you will do it."

Hodgson sweated. Emma guessed that having been surprised by the change in plans, he now worried about a much bigger change waiting out there.

When he took too long to agree, Joseph touched the hilt of a knife strapped and sheathed at his waist. Emma held her breath while the threat filled the library.

With a sick expression, Hodgson nodded. He gave Emma a suspicious glare as he passed her. Emma counted their boot steps as they retreated to the front door, and exhaled only when the door closed behind them.

She sat down, to wait some more, until her guests were well on their way. And while she waited she finally succumbed to fear, humiliation, and sorrow. She wept with sobs that pained her, and buried her face in her hands to muffle the sound. She mourned the death of her hope and accepted that Darius had been right. Robert would never come home.

"Emma." Darius called her name softly down the stairwell a half hour after Hodgson had left.

She came to the stairs and looked up at him.

"Snuff the candles and come up here. It will be hours before anyone arrives to tell us how it all ends."

She put out the candles, then mounted the stairs. He pulled her into an embrace and pressed his lips to her head while he held her. He had prayed during the last ten hours and he did now once again.

She sank into him, as if standing were too much effort. "I feel as though I have been walking on top of a fence for days, all tight as I managed my balance."

"Come and get some sleep. You have had little enough of that recently."

She resisted his attempt to guide her away from the stairs. She sniffed, and he knew then that she had been weeping and still was distraught.

"As you predicted, my brother was not brought home to me." She buried her face in his coat and began weeping, hard. "I am so ashamed," she muttered with harsh fury between swells of crying.

He held her while deep, angry sobs wracked her. He caressed her shoulder and arm, hoping to reassure her. "Emma, you saw a duty to your family. Your decision was one that everyone could understand."

"You are just being kind." Her voice sounded muffled, broken, and tight. "You would never have considered such a thing, no matter what the coercion."

"I am glad you are so certain. I am not. There are those for whom I might make the same decision. My sister. You."

She looked up at him. She appeared touched that he included her. "You might contemplate it, but in the end you would not do it. You would refuse to buy us with treason. You would never agree to be a pawn, nor would you depend on the honesty of criminals either. You would do something noble and brave instead. You would execute a daring rescue of us, like men are wont to do."

But which women are not wont to do, because the skill and strength are not available to them.

"Come to sleep, Emma. It is finished now."

It was finished now. No, not quite yet, but it would be very soon.

He did not speak of their passion and love, but that was

all she thought about at that moment. How this embrace would not be there for her in the days ahead. How the comfort of his warmth would disappear. She had never been suitable, not even as a mistress, and after what she had done that was even more true.

His friends knew she had agreed to help Hodgson. Soon others in the government would know too. How else would they all explain tonight's adventure? Miss Fairbourne may have redeemed herself in the end, but that did not cleanse the stain of the sin.

"I am not sleepy," she said.

"Then just rest in my arms. This will be a long night still."

"That would be very nice, but it would be a waste to spend the time just resting, don't you think?"

His kiss said that he understood her well enough. He was a man, after all. She was grateful that he did not act as if she were too fragile right now for such a thing.

"I so love it when you are forthright, Miss Fairbourne. I would have played the chaste knight with you if necessary, but that is not where my blood is."

She giggled softly into his coat. The sound instantly lightened the mood, and put the day's dangerous events off to one side, so its shadow touched her only a little instead of owning her completely.

She squirmed out of his embrace and strolled to her bedchamber. A lone candle burned there. She used it to light another near the looking glass. The way the glass reflected the dancing flame reminded her of a ballroom and a candelabra and a magnificent chandelier.

He had his coats off by the time he was across the threshold. He went to work on her dress. "Ambury scolded me for forcing you to make do with this old dress and those boots today."

"Did you explain they were the first clothes I had worn in more than a day, and that you had most rudely torn my one dress in a fit of impatience?"

"A fit of passion, not impatience. I think of myself as a citadel of patience when it is warranted."

She insisted on carefully folding and stacking each of the garments. They might be poor but they were not hers. As soon as she was finished, he pulled her to him and laid her down.

She made herself comfortable. She looked around the chamber. "If Papa's ghost is here, it does not seem to mind."

"That is not a thought to encourage passion, Emma." He looked around too. "Do you sense it here? Not that I believe in such nonsense, of course."

"No. I did before you abducted me—"

"It was not really an abduction, Emma."

"*Before you abducted me*, the night before, it was like it had been on my last visit. But today when we arrived, no longer." She pushed down the shoulders of her chemise and bared her breasts. She joined her hands behind her head so her breasts rose high. "Now, do your worst."

He caressed and teased her breasts. The most delicious titillation made her sighs deepen. He aroused with his teeth and tongue in the delicate manner that always drove her mad. Pleasure lapped through her and she abandoned herself to its wonderful sensations, concentrating on his scent and touch and warmth, surrendering every part of herself so she might always own this memory.

Soon impatience claimed her as her arousal intensified. She begged him to take her so she might have all of him too.

"Soon," he said, kissing her stomach and shoving up the chemise. "Not yet."

She did not wait for his lead when he moved down on her. Instead she bent her knees, spread her thighs, and lifted her hips. He knelt and cupped her bottom and lowered his head in order to take her to paradise.

Darius awoke at first light. He became instantly alert as his instincts warned of nearby danger. He stretched to reach the pistol he had laid on a table near the bed.

As his senses righted he heard the sound that had woken him. Down below, boot steps paced across the floor.

He rose out of bed and silently dressed, then descended the stairs. Sounds drew him to the back of the cottage, and the kitchen. Halfway there he lowered his pistol and ceased trying to walk quietly. He knew the voices talking back there.

"You are not going to steal that food, are you?" Ambury said.

"I am sure the lady will not mind my eating a bit of bread when she hears how close to starvation I was. I was on the sea half the night." Crockery clattered. "There is some ham here too. Do you want some?"

"Of course not."

"As you like."

Darius entered just as Tarrington carved off a thick slice of the ham. From the chair where he lounged, Ambury watched with hungry eyes.

Darius took the platter with the ham from Tarrington, placed it down near Ambury, and proceeded to carve. "Share the bread, Tarrington," he said over his shoulder.

Half a loaf came flying at Ambury.

"We brought you a horse," Tarrington said as he ate and looked around. "So, where is our hostess?"

"I believe she is still asleep," Darius said. Beside him Ambury's jaw twitched, but to his credit he did not smile. "If you are here, Ambury, I assume you handed off our friends."

"Hodgson and his guest took the road to London as expected, so it went smoothly. They are now the responsibility of the Home Office agent waiting at the crossroad Penthurst indicated in the letter you received. If their trail runs cold, I will kill whoever is responsible, after all the trouble we went through."

"I trust Penthurst threatened something similar, so diligence would be employed."

Ambury stuffed a hunk of bread with ham and feasted. "You do know that it will not take the French more than a few months to replace every spy that is caught."

"Probably. One can only do one's best." He watched

Tarrington opening cupboards. "Tarrington, did you stop the boat after it left the shore?"

"Of course. This will shock you, but it was being used for free trade in addition to transporting that spy."

"So was the last one. It is the cover they have used all along."

"The last one held a few paltry items. This one was really used for smuggling. Lots of goods on it." He popped another chunk of bread in his mouth. "I am ashamed to say the lads were ours, not French. It was a galley out of Diehl, no less."

"They have been using galleys?" Ambury said. "No wonder they have not been caught. Twenty-four men at oars can escape any sloop or cutter. How long is the crossing in a galley?"

Tarrington studied the bread he ate. He shrugged. "I have heard—not that I know myself, now, being a peaceable, lawful sort—that in good weather a galley can make the run in five hours. As for this galley's crew, they got friendly with the French they deal with in Boulogne, and ended up with this bit of work every now and then too. Hodgson passed the goods for them. It was all very neat."

It *had* been neat, Darius thought. A galley rows over to France, loads wine and whatever, accepts letters or special passengers, rows back, and is met by a man willing to arrange the sale of the better goods at an auction house for full price.

"Where are those goods now?" he asked.

"Fell in the sea, they did. 'Twas a pitiful thing to see. I've the boat in a nice little cove, in case you want to check."

Darius was very sure there would be no smuggled goods on that boat now. "And the crew? Were they all English smugglers?"

"Most of them. One seemed not to belong with the others. He tried not to talk, but finally he did. He was an escort, if you will. Of that special passenger." He continued poking into drawers. "Do you know if she has any tea here? I would not mind a cup."

"He just offered that information, did he?" Ambury asked. "That was generous of him."

"Nah. He was persuaded." Tarrington still concentrated on searching the kitchen.

"A pistol to the temple, no doubt," Darius said, dryly.

"That was how I was going to do it," Tarrington said. "But Lord Kendale interfered."

"I am impressed," Ambury said. "I would not have thought Kendale would intervene."

"Most helpful, he was. He showed as how a man who is willing to die is not prepared for less than death. Said in the army they got what they wanted fastest with a very sharp knife threatening the privates of a man. Damned if he wasn't right. That fat Frenchman saw that knife down there and couldn't talk fast enough." He came to the table to attack the ham again.

Ambury closed his eyes in forbearance.

"Where is he now? The fat one?" Darius asked.

"With the others, in that cave I have, waiting for your lordships to tell me what to do with them. A few of my lads are keeping watch. Lord Kendale is with them."

"So we still have the boat, and the smugglers, and the fat man who made sure the special passenger got here safely and met his contact. Only the illegal goods are lost."

"Right. Bottom of the sea, they are."

"Ambury, I think we should have a talk with the fat man. The smugglers know from where they put to sea, and this fellow probably knows how to get from there to the lair of those who send the spies in the first place."

Ambury's eyes lit. "If you are thinking what I suspect, Kendale will be overjoyed. The admiralty will not like it, however."

"They cannot stop smugglers from crossing to France, so it is doubtful they can stop us."

Tarrington's gaze shifted back and forth between them, following the conversation. "You think to go over? It isn't as easy as you may think. They have a navy too, and soldiers crowding the coast these days. In the least, you had better bring an army with you."

"I was thinking more in terms of bringing you and your lads with us," Darius said. "I am certainly not going to rely on the traitorous smugglers in that cave of yours."

"No, no, no." Tarrington waved both of his hands. "I agreed to one night along the coast. *Our* coast. Not some foolhardy, noble, stupid—"

"Ambury, remind me to ask Kendale what happened to the goods that were on that boat he and Tarrington's lads stopped last night. Kendale might turn a blind eye, and see it as the spoils of war, but he will never lie outright if the question is put to him."

Tarrington glared with resentment. Ambury laughed. Tarrington folded his arms and shook his head with resignation. "Hell, you are a hard man, Southwaite."

"We may pay dearly for this, Southwaite, and I am not talking about the obvious risks to our persons," Ambury said. "The government does not like its citizens making unauthorized military invasions."

"If we are found out, there will be hell to pay; that is certain," Darius said. "We will explain that in truth this was not a military mission. It was a rescue mission."

Darius explained what he meant, and whom they would rescue. If Ambury was skeptical, he did not show it. Tarrington only wanted assurance that his lads could take what they could carry. Kendale, Darius knew, would be glad for the action no matter what it was called.

He sent them off to make plans, then went up the stairs. Emma was awake, lying amid the sheets in the early-morning light.

She appeared so lovely. Her hair fanned over the pillows, silken and bright. Her gaze, as she looked over at him, contained memories of last night and a warmth born of the intimacy they now shared.

She believed her brother was still alive. She felt it, she said. She insisted the letter sent to her had not been a forgery. She knew Robert Fairbourne was alive more surely than he knew most things in his life, except his love for her. Who was he to question what her heart could and could not know?

He sat on the bed and bent low to kiss her, thinking, as he always did now, that she was extraordinary in every way. She may have surrendered to him, but in doing so she had captured him, totally.

"My carriage will come for you in a couple of hours," he said. "It will take you back to London."

"Are you coming too?"

"Not yet. There are a few things still to resolve, although the plan worked perfectly."

"When will you be in London again?"

"A week, perhaps."

Her arms encircled his neck and she kissed him hard and long. He felt emotion rise in her. She bared her heart in that kiss. Amid her love was sorrow, and even some fear.

He gently released her hold, and brought her hands together where he could kiss them. He stood to go.

"Do not forget that I love you, Emma. Never doubt that."

Chapter 31

"Lord Ambury still has not reclaimed his ring and taken the earrings," Cassandra said.

"I believe he has been preoccupied of late," Emma said. "Is he even in town?"

"I have not seen him about. Perhaps he is not. However, the goal was to turn jewelry into money, not end up with more jewelry, so I hope he settles this soon."

They sat in the garden behind Fairbourne's auction house. Emma and Cassandra had stopped by here in order for Emma to meet with Marielle, who had just arrived. Marielle was busy untying the cord that closed a little sack that she had brought.

"Stupid Man is gone," Marielle mentioned as her long, slender fingers worked at the knot. "Ten days now he has not been visible."

"Who is Stupid Man?" Cassandra asked.

Marielle looked up, surprised, then turned apologetic eyes on Emma. She returned to the knot.

"A man who was bothering Marielle," Emma said. She

would like to tell Marielle that Stupid Man would never be visible again, but discretion forbade it.

"Oh. I thought she was talking about my brother."

Emma burst out laughing. Cassandra smiled with naughty pride. Marielle clawed at the string.

Emma wiped her eyes. It felt wonderful to laugh. She had not been in good spirits the last ten days. Southwaite's absence from her life had left a void. She had not anticipated that, or the way her heart had so quickly resigned itself to living with that void forever.

"Do not forget that I love you. Do not doubt that." She did not doubt it. Nor did she expect it to make enough difference. There probably would not be a public scandal, but people who mattered to Southwaite already knew what she had agreed to do for Hodgson, and more would learn of it. If his alliance with her continued, his name would be forever compromised.

A week, he had said. It had already been ten days. She had reconciled to it being much longer. At some point a letter would come, and he would explain it all to her, with sincere regrets. She waited for it the way one waited for any bad news, with a sick worry that almost wished it would just happen and be over.

"Ah. *Bon.*" Marielle finally opened the neck of the sack. She carefully poured the contents on the table.

"Cameos," Cassandra exclaimed. She lifted one. "They are exquisite. They look very old."

Emma held up one of the gems. Its tiny relief depicted Dionysus and his entourage. The agate stone from which it had been carved was so thin as to be translucent. "The carving appears antique, but the setting is later. A Renaissance work, perhaps."

"That is what I was told. The woman who owns it says it was once owned by the king and is very valuable. She will give it to your auction if you have other fine things."

Cassandra looked up from her cameo through her long black lashes. She gave Emma a quizzical look. "Are you starting to plan for the next auction already? Town is so quiet in the summer. I would have expected you to wait until autumn."

Emma rubbed her thumb over the carving. "I do not know if I will have another one at any time."

Southwaite had always wanted to sell Fairbourne's. She would no longer resist that decision. If by some miracle Robert survived and returned, the proceeds from the sale would be waiting for him.

"Eh, it is always so for me," Marielle said after a long sigh. "I find a means to eat, and something goes wrong." She took the cameos out of Emma's and Cassandra's hands. "Perhaps that other one, Mr. Christie, will give me the twenty percent."

Cassandra's eyelids lowered. She crossed her arms and looked at Emma. "*Twenty* percent?"

For the second time Marielle realized she had misspoken. She busily stuffed the cameos away. When she was finished, she stood to take her leave. Her attention became distracted however, and she did not move.

"Why is he here?" she asked accusingly. "Like Stupid Man, I thought I was free of him."

Perplexed, Emma turned and looked at the building. Lord Kendale stood at the building's garden door. He looked at them, not moving.

Her heart sank. If Kendale was in London, whatever had to be resolved on the coast had been finished. Yet Darius had not called on her. He had not even written since that parting in the cottage.

The sick worry worsened. She knew, just knew, that she would be mourning the end of her first and only love affair soon.

She returned her attention to Marielle. "Do you know him?"

"It is the one who follows me. I told you about him. Handsome Stupid Man."

"That is a very unkind name for him," Cassandra scolded.

"The alternative was Very Stupid Man," Emma said.

"He thinks to frighten me now, the way he stares at me." Marielle composed herself, assumed her most bored expression, and looked right back at Kendale. Emma kept shifting her attention from one to the other and back again. Marielle kept glaring and Kendale glared back.

Then Marielle's expression cracked, and the sweetest expression molded her face. A slow smile transformed her even more. Fascinated, Emma looked to see Kendale's reaction.

His own severity cracked too. He flushed so deeply that Emma could see the tint from this distance. He turned and reentered the building.

Marielle gave her sack's strings a final pull. "I win." She pointed to the back of the garden. "There is a gate there? I will go out that way, so Handsome Stupid Man does not follow me."

"I will walk with you," Cassandra said. "My carriage is on Piccadilly." She bent to give Emma a kiss. "I am trying to decide if I should let Kendale know his other name. I think I will save it, in case he ever looks at me with that disapproving scowl."

As her two friends let themselves out the back gate, Emma considered that she should share with Cassandra that Lord Kendale had his nicer moments. She thought about them, and the gratitude she felt for his help.

He had probably come here today to bring her some message, perhaps word that the adventure was truly over. Maybe Darius sent him, so that Darius would be spared the meeting himself.

She stood to go and greet Lord Kendale. She turned to the building. What she saw made her gasp.

A brown-haired man stood at the garden door now. He broke into a smile and walked toward her, his strides lengthening with his impatience. She watched him come, immobile from shock.

"Robert!"

E mma broke her long embrace and caught her breath. She examined her brother through tear-filled eyes.

He took her hand and urged her to sit. He appeared so

happy, and quite fit. She was relieved that he had not been starved while in his prison.

"How—" she began asking, but emotion choked the words.

He held her hand between his two. "I was rescued. By two lords, no less! They had at least twenty men with them, all armed, and Colonel Leplage was so surprised that not even one shot was fired."

"Who is Leplage?"

"He is the man who held me. He has taken residence in the manor of some French count not far from Boulogne." Robert shrugged. "I am not sure what he does there, but people come and go and even sat to dinner with us at times. Army officers and I suspect members of the government. They never spoke of any of that while I was there, though."

Emma dabbed her eyes with her handkerchief. It was startling to discover that Robert had not only not been starving in a dungeon the way she had pictured, but instead had been enjoying fine meals with his captor's guests in the dining room.

She eyed him again. "I like your hair. That is new."

He touched the fashionably short brown curls. "Do you? Leplage's valet did it for me. Everyone else had rid themselves of their queues in France years ago."

"That is a nice coat too. It becomes you."

He looked down on it and smiled. "I like it. Leplage has excellent tailors."

She pictured Southwaite and his friends rushing into that manor house, pistols drawn, and finding Robert in a fine dining room with his expertly tailored coat and finely dressed hair.

"I am relieved that you did not suffer, Robert. And I am touched that those lords risked their lives to rescue you. I will never be able to repay them, nor will you." Her eyes felt very dry now. "Perhaps, before we are interrupted, you will explain how you came to be a guest of Mr. Leplage to begin with."

Robert made a face and flushed. "I will explain to you,

and I did to Lord Southwaite, but it is too embarrassing to tell the tale to anyone else."

Somehow, she knew that already. "I promise to be discreet."

He sighed. "I heard a story that there was this estate not far from Boulogne that had been abandoned by a fleeing count and that it held a lot of paintings. Very fine ones. I suggested to Father that I go and try to get them. He refused. I mourned news of his passing, Emma, but he could be very stubborn and old-fashioned."

"If objecting to theft is old-fashioned—"

"They were just sitting there, left to rot. We are at war with the French. Is it even possible to steal from the enemy? Well, he would not hear of it. But I am no longer a boy, Emma, and I decided to do it. It would be my first auction, the consignments all brought in by me alone, too. So I found some men to take me over and help me bring those paintings back."

"Smugglers?"

"I did not ask. I only knew they were men with a large galley, and they promised we could do it all in a day. In return I offered them twenty-five percent of the money made when the paintings were sold."

"I don't suppose these men told you the story about the paintings to begin with?"

"Yes! How did you know?"

Emma listened to her brother describe this mad scheme. He had always had a reckless side, now that she thought about it. Just as he had never attended to their father's lessons as carefully as she had. She had not dwelled on his less-than-stellar qualities while she worried about him for two years and prayed for his return.

"What went wrong?"

Robert took a deep breath. "Those men sold me out. Can you believe it? We arrived at that estate, and it was not deserted. I called those men to help me fight our way out once we were seen, only instead they offered their services to Leplage. I ended up an involuntary guest, and they ended up going back without me. Leplage was decent about it, at least. He said if I pledged my parole, I could move about the grounds freely."

"At least that made it easier for Lord Southwaite to find you."

"I suppose so. Although it was raining when he came and he insisted I go with them at once. And he refused to take any of those paintings. Oh, yes, they were there, and very fine indeed. The weather did not let up and we were stuck on the coast, dodging army units, for days. It was terrible."

"But better than being a prisoner, surely."

"Oh, yes. Surely." He did not appear sure at all.

She looked at the building. "Did Lord Kendale bring you here?"

"No. He rode beside us. Lord Southwaite brought me in his carriage. We went to the house first, and Maitland told him where you were."

Southwaite. "We must go in, so that I can thank them."

She began to rise, but Robert caught her hand, and bid her sit again. "There is something that I need to explain before you go in there, Emma."

She did not miss the way he flushed when he said that. She sat and waited.

"I did not come back alone," Robert said. "While I was in France, I married."

Fairbourne's hosted one of its happiest parties that afternoon. No paintings covered the walls, and no music played. The guests enjoyed the last bottles of the smuggled claret, however. If anyone guessed their provenance, nothing was said.

Emma had returned to the hall with her brother as soon as she recovered from hearing about his marriage. As they walked through the garden, Robert had finally expressed some self-recrimination.

"I was young and stupid and a pigeon waiting to be

plucked, Emma. I was lured into that scheme to sail to France, I think. I know all about how Father was coerced, and later you too. Southwaite told me about it while we waited for the storms to clear."

Now Robert strolled through the auction house while Emma watched. He pointed and explained things to a young woman by his side. *A wife.* That had been almost as much of a shock to her as seeing him walk toward her through the garden.

Southwaite sidled close to Emma, and joined her in observing the young couple. "He married her at the point of a sword, he said. She was a maid in the household of the colonel who held him, and they were found in a compromising situation."

"I am of course relieved to know my brother did not suffer overmuch during his captivity. He experienced no deprivations at all, it appears." She sipped some wine. "She seems a pleasant girl. I think that we will get on well."

Southwaite's arm swept in an all-inclusive gesture. "You did it, Emma. You preserved it for him, as you wanted."

"I did, didn't I? So why am I little sad about that part?"

He looked at her with humor and warmth in his eyes. "Perhaps because you know that you can do it better than he ever will. Do not look indignant at the suggestion. Your brother and I had some long talks about art while we waited for the sea to settle and prayed no French troops found us first. I think you paid more attention to your father's lessons than he did."

Probably so. She doubted Robert would ever agree with that, however. Still, there might be a role for her at Fairbourne's in the future. In the least Robert might let her catalogue the silver.

She stiffened her spine and her composure. "I admit that I will be nostalgic. I will think fondly of my not-so-final final auction, and of the grand success of the last one. However, it is his legacy, and I must step aside and allow him his due."

"Actually, Emma, only part of it is his. You have a talent

for ignoring that I am half owner." He set aside his wine-glass, and took hers away too. "Now come with me. It is too crowded here."

It was not crowded at all, but she did not object when he sped her out the garden door and guided her deep into the plantings near the rear wall. He swept her into an embrace and kissed her soundly. "It has been forever, Emma," he muttered, then kissed her again.

Love poured through her, as fresh and vibrant as ever, making the arousal that stirred her sparkle with joy. "Thank you for bringing him back to me. Thank you for coming back safely too. If you had not—"

The very thought horrified her whenever she thought of it. After telling her about his bride, Robert had blurted all of the danger they had faced. Her stark realization of what she might have lost had dimmed her excitement until she dragged Robert inside so she could see Southwaite hale and fit with her own eyes.

"There was little danger," Southwaite said. "We let Kendale lead. He is actually very good at this sort of thing."

She had thanked Lord Kendale and Lord Ambury with all her heart. There had been others, who had not accompanied Robert to London. She needed to thank them too, when she could.

He kissed her again. And again. His possessive caresses thrilled every part of her.

"Southwaite." The voice spoke calmly, not far away at all.

Darius looked up but did not release her. "What is it, Ambury?"

"We are leaving. Mr. Fairbourne and his wife just departed for home. They took Miss Fairbourne's carriage."

"I will see you at Brooks's tomorrow."

As Ambury's boots crunched on the pebble path, the full meaning of the little conversation sliced into Emma's mind.

Southwaite began to kiss her again, but stopped. "What is it, Emma? You are suddenly very serious."

"I am thinking about the changes this homecoming heralds, Darius. My brother did not take my carriage. He took his own carriage. He is bringing his wife to *his* house, not mine. When he seeks a respite from town, he will journey with her to *his* cottage near the sea. I have no house or carriage now. In fact, I have nothing."

He smiled down at her while she described her pending poverty. He did not appear nearly as concerned as she thought a friend should.

"That is true, Emma. It is very unfair too. However, as it happens, I have a very nice house here in London, and much more than a cottage by the sea. And I have a lot of carriages, and one of them can be yours."

"Are you offering me an arrangement, Darius?" It touched her deeply that he still wanted her in any way, and that she might not lose him too soon. Eventually, but not yet. Even the liaison he implied would be ruinous for him, however. Perhaps he counted on his famous discretion to keep her a secret.

"I am suggesting a very special arrangement, Emma." He glanced over her head to the building. "I have half an auction house. I think I need someone to watch over that investment for me in the years to come. I am not inclined to leave it totally in the hands of my partner. Not that I do not trust your brother's expertise or honesty, of course."

"Of course." He did not seek a romantic liaison, then. He was not proposing she even be his mistress. It would primarily be a business arrangement of a different kind, it seemed. She pretended that sorrow did not already sicken her heart. "I would be proud to be your representative at Fairbourne's. I promise you that nothing will ever be done there in the future that might bring discredit to your name, Darius. That will never happen again if you allow me to watch over your interests there." She realized that he might doubt her, considering the past. "I give my word on this."

He caressed her face and looked deeply into her eyes. "I do not need your promises. Your character speaks for itself, and I know it very well now."

She tried to smile, but felt her mouth tremble. "You can

be sure of discretion too. I will see to that as well. No one will ever know you invested."

He kissed her sweetly. The emotions that his tenderness evoked pained her. She knew then that she could not bear what his caresses seemed to imply.

She broke the kiss, but remained within his embrace. She savored how his arms encompassed her for a few final moments before she spoke. "I am grateful that your trust and friendship will keep me from being dependent on my brother, Darius. However, I do not think that I can agree to being an employee with whom you might occasionally share passion. It is not for lack of desire, as I think you know. Rather, I love you too much, and an arrangement like that would break my heart over and over, I fear."

He gave her an odd, quizzical look. "I think that we have had another Outrageous Misconception, Miss Fairbourne."

"Have we?"

"Yes. I do not want to share occasional passion with you."

"Oh."

"Nor am I offering you employment at Fairbourne's. Not in the normal sense, at least. Since you misunderstood, I can see that I should have spoken plainly."

"That is often wise, if not always welcomed."

"I pray that it will be welcomed now, Emma. There is only one arrangement that will make me happy, and only one that you deserve. I am speaking of marriage, Emma, and nothing less."

He astonished her. She had certainly not expected another proposal. Not now, and not ever. Not after what had happened.

It was different this time too. He was under no obligation. She had compromised his good name, and not him hers. He should be repudiating her completely, if he cared about his reputation at all.

Her heart ached from happiness wanting to break free, but she dared not believe this was real.

"Are you very sure you want to do this, Darius? It is not

sensible at all. I can think of four reasons why this proposal is most unwise on your part."

"Can you, now?"

"Yes. First of all, your—"

His finger touched her lips. "Your honesty and forthrightness are among your more charming qualities, Emma. However, I do not need you to explain. I know every reason why I should not propose. They do not matter."

"They don't?"

"No."

"But others know what I did, Darius."

"They will know that you aided us in trapping a courier into exposing a network of spies. You will be seen as a heroine by the time Ambury and I are done describing it. However, even if anyone suspects the whole truth— When a man thinks of a woman the way I think of you, when he loves a woman the way I love you, he marries her. The only question is whether you feel the same way, and will marry me. Will you?"

He gazed in her eyes, waiting. She realized with amazement that he was not sure of her. He did not know that she hesitated only for his sake.

"I will. Of course I will, if you want me that way."

He smiled. It was a wonderful smile. The joy in it astonished her. "I want you in every way, Emma, but especially that one."

He kissed her, and his passion contained all the ways he wanted her. She gladly surrendered to the spell he cast, and accepted with gratitude the love that made her extraordinary.

Keep reading for a special look at the first novel in
Madeline Hunter's stunning Regency quartet

Ravishing in Red

Now available from Jove Books

An independent woman is a woman unprotected. Audri- anna had never understood her cousin Daphne's first lesson to her as well as she did today.

An independent woman was also a woman of dubious respectability.

Her entry into the Two Swords Coaching Inn outside Brighton garnered more attention than any proper young woman would like. Eyes examined her from head to toe. Several men watched her solitary path across the public room with bold interest, the likes of which she had never been subjected to before.

The assumptions implied by all those stares darkened her mood even more. She had embarked on this journey full of righteous determination. The shining sun and unseason- ably mild temperature for late January seemed designed by Providence to favor her great mission.

Providence had proven fickle. An hour out of London the wind, rain, and increasing cold had begun, making her deeply regret taking a seat on the coach's roof. Now she was drenched from hours of frigid rain, and more than a little vexed.

She gathered her poise and sought out the innkeeper. She asked for a chamber for the night. He eyed her long and hard, then looked around for the man who had lost her.

"Is your husband dealing with the stable?"

"No. I am alone."

The white, crepe skin of his aging face creased into a scowl. His mouth pursed in five different ways while he examined her again.

"I've a small chamber that you can have, but it overlooks the stable yard." His reluctant tone made it clear that he accommodated her against his better judgment.

An independent woman also gets the worst room at the inn, it seemed. "It will do, if it is dry and warm."

"Come with me, then."

He brought her to a room at the back of the second level. He built up the fire a little, but not much. She noted that there was not enough fuel to make it much warmer and also last through the night.

"I'll be needing the first night's fee in advance."

Audrianna swallowed her sense of insult. She dug into her reticule for three shillings. It would more than cover the chamber for one night, but she pressed it all into the man's hand.

"If someone arrives asking questions about Mr. Kelmsley, send that person up here but say nothing of my presence or anything else about me."

Her request made him frown more, but the coins in his hand kept him mute. He left with the shillings and she assumed she had struck a bargain. She only hoped that the fruits of this mission would be worth the cost to her reputation.

She noted the money left in her reticule. By morning she expected most of it to be spent. She would be gone from London only two days, but this journey would deplete the savings that she had accumulated from all those music lessons. She would endure months of clumsy scales and whining girls to replace it.

She plucked a scrap of paper from her reticule. She held the paper to the light of the fire even though she knew its words by heart. *The domino requests that Mr. Kelmsley meet him at the two swords in Brighton two nights hence, to discuss a matter of mutual benefit.*

It had been sheer luck that she even knew this advertisement had been placed in *The Times*. If her friend Lizzie did not comb through all such notices, in every paper and scandal sheet available, it might have escaped Audrianna's attention.

The surname was not spelled correctly, but she was sure the Mr. Kelmsley mentioned here was her father, Horatio Kelmsleigh. Clearly, whoever wanted to meet him did not know he was dead.

Images of her father invaded her mind. Her heart thickened and her eyes burned the way they always did whenever the memories overwhelmed her.

She saw him playing with her in the garden, and taking the blame when Mama scolded about her dirty shoes. She called up a distant, hazy memory of him, probably her oldest one. He was in his army uniform, so it was from before he sold his commission when Sarah was born, and took a position in the office of the Board of Ordnance, which oversaw the production of munitions during the war.

Mostly, however, she kept seeing his sad, troubled face during those last months, when he became the object of so much scorn.

She tucked the notice away. It had reminded her why she was here. Nothing else, not the rain or the stares or the rudeness, really mattered. Hopefully she was right in thinking this Domino possessed information that would have helped Papa clear his name.

She removed her blue mantle and the gray pelisse underneath and hung them on wall pegs to dry. She took off her bonnet and shook off the rain. Then she moved the chamber's one lamp to a table beside the door, and the one wooden chair to the shadows in the facing corner, beyond the hearth. If she sat there, she would immediately be able to see whoever entered, but that person would not see her very well at all at first.

She set her valise on the chair and opened it. The rest of Daphne's first lesson recited in her mind. *An independent woman is a woman unprotected, so she must learn to protect herself.*

Reaching in, she removed the pistol that she had buried beneath her spare garments.

Read on for a special preview of Madeline Hunter's

"An Interrupted Tapestry:
An Exquisite Love Story
of Medieval London"

A Penguin Group eSpecial from Jove
Available now!

G iselle had ample time to practice swallowing her pride. She spent most of the afternoon doing so, while she paced Andreas von Bremen's luxurious hall. She came to know his carved furniture very well and memorized every image in the four tapestries adorning his walls.

Occasionally, she paused to gaze through the unshuttered windows at the yard surrounded by stables and storage buildings. Wagons kept arriving from the docks, carrying the products that secured Andreas's wealth. As a member of the Hanseatic League, the network of Germanic traders whose famous cogs plied the northern seas, Andreas von Bremen was no ordinary merchant.

Which was why she had come.

She strove to quell not only her pride but her growing resentment. In a way, it was Andreas's fault that she was here at all. For that reason alone, he might be more gracious and not keep her waiting so long. They had an old friendship, too. That should count for something, even if they had not spoken in four years.

Irritation spiked again, colored by disappointment and hurt. She itched to stride right out of this house.

She didn't. A deeper emotion kept her waiting.

Fear.

She had to see this through. Andreas was her only hope. If he refused her, she had nowhere else to turn, and her brother would be lost to her.

Boot steps on the stairs and voices speaking lowly penetrated the noise rolling in from the yard.

She swung around. Two men's bodies lowered into view as they descended from the upper level of the house.

The short one of middle years, the one wearing a richly tucked and embroidered robe and a hat festooned with drapery, did not interest her. The other one, the young one of commanding height and lean strength, with thick dark hair and beautiful blue eyes, riveted her attention.

Other than distant glimpses in the city, she had not seen him in a long time. She had forgotten how easy it was to smile whenever he arrived. Even now, despite her worries and pique, the old joy sparkled through her.

As he escorted his guest through the hall, Andreas became aware of her. He glanced over and the light of recognition flared.

Snatches of the men's low conversation reached her ears. They did not speak in English, or French, or even Andreas's language.

She suddenly realized who the other man was. The Venetian galleys had arrived in London a few days ago, and he must be one of the powerful traders from that city.

The Venetian took his leave. Andreas stood at the threshold, watching until the horse trotted through the gate.

He turned his attention to her.

"Giselle."

He did not say anything else, but just looked at her with those blue eyes. The lights of his youth still sparked in them, but other, deeper ones did, too. At twenty Andreas had possessed good humor despite his natural reserve. Now, ten years later, his silence had grown more complex.

And dangerous. It made no sense, but she could not escape the sensation. As the pause stretched, she grew increasingly unsettled.

"My apologies, Giselle. My man said that a woman was here. He did not explain that it was you."

"You are very busy when you visit London. You could hardly ask your guest to wait while you spoke to me."

"That would have been difficult to explain, I will admit."

He smiled with wry amusement as he said it. Giselle realized that she had arrived during some very special trading.

It was rumored that Andreas had come to London to negotiate a new marriage. Not with an English family, it appeared. He was looking for a more ambitious match than that and had timed his visit to coincide with the galleys from Venice.

Years ago he had confided to her a mad dream of linking his family's network to that of a Venetian's. It appeared he was about to make the dream a reality.

Small wonder he had kept her waiting.

He moved two chairs to the windows on the side of the hall that faced the garden. He came back to her. "Please sit. I am happy to see you. It has been too long."

She hesitated. Something in his manner made her want to make a quick retreat. This was the Andreas she had known so well, but also an Andreas she had never met.

His hand almost touched her back as the other gestured to the chairs. With a phantom embrace, he guided her to the window.

A prickle of excitement and caution scurried up her spine.

They sat facing each other, their knees separated by an arm's span. Soft northern light gently illuminated the face that she knew well. Many times she had admired at close range the square jaw and straight, feathering eyebrows. None of the details had changed, but the countenance had. Youthful softness used to mute its chiselled severity but no longer did. Mature precision revealed the intelligent, shrewd mind of the man who owned it.

Despite the change, for an instant it was like old times. They might have been sitting together in her own home, by her windows, during one of his visits to the city. When he was younger and his trading brought him to London, he did not live in this grand house, but in hers, as a guest and friend of her brother, Reginald.

The joy sparkled again, reminding her of how much she had enjoyed his company back then.

It had been thus from the first time Reginald brought him home and announced that he would use the tiny, spare chamber that jutted out over the street. She had looked at Andreas's astonishingly handsome face that day and immediately seen warmth in his eyes despite his cool manner. They had formed a quick bond during that first visit. Over the years the connection had grown deep and steady and full of unspoken understanding.

And then, abruptly, four years ago, Andreas had severed the link to Reginald, the house, and her.

Remembering that insult made the joy disappear.

"You are looking well, Giselle. You are as beautiful as ever."

The Andreas she had known had never flattered her. It appeared that with his success and wealth he had assumed courtly airs.

It did not help that at twenty-eight she was no longer as beautiful as ever. The first bloom of youth had passed, and she knew it.

"It is kind of you to say so. You also appear well, and happy in your success. I always knew that you would rise high in the Hanse." She could not keep her gaze from drifting over the deep green garment he wore. Its cut and fabric spoke of his ascending status, just as her worn, mended blue gown revealed how debased her own had become.

Her gaze moved back up and met his. Her breath caught as the years fell away. She might have been seeing him at her threshold, so familiar was what passed between them. The instant bond, the promise of a quiet intimacy—it flashed through her with an intense, vital reality, just as it had when they had been friends.

No, it was not quite the same. Those reunions had never made her uncomfortable, and this one did. Something new simmered in the familiarity. As if a gauzy veil had been lifted, certain aspects of her reaction sharpened and demanded her attention. A sly, alluring disturbance wound its way around her other emotions.

She had intended to beg for his help, but his manner provoked her, and she decided to change her approach. There was no point in pleading in the name of a dead friendship. She would speak in a language he would understand and respect.

"I have not only come to visit, Andreas."

"No, I expect that you have not."

He sounded resigned. She thought that took some gall. After all, *she* had not dropped *his* friendship.

"I am in need of money. I will repay it," she said.

His gaze shifted to the garden out the window. The old Andreas completely disappeared. Suddenly she was speaking with a stranger who had heard petitions like hers before. Too often.

The humiliation of what she was doing overwhelmed her. She gritted her teeth and forged on.

"I need one hundred pounds."

He kept looking at the garden. "Your brother sent you, didn't he? It was cowardly of him not to come himself and to use you in this way."

"He did not send me. This was my decision."

"The hell it was." His gaze snapped back to her. "Since this is about trade, I must respond as a trader. I regret to say that I must refuse you. There is no way that this loan will be repaid, and I would be a fool to make it."

His abrupt denial astonished her. Her heart wanted to sink down to her toes.

"It will be repaid. If you doubt my word—"

"One hundred pounds is a great sum. You have not seen

that much in the last five years combined. You may promise to repay it with an honest heart, but your brother never will."

"It is my promise, not my brother's. I will pledge property as surety. Our house is not worth that much, but there is also a small farm in Sussex, and together they should secure this debt."

A bit of curiosity passed in the gaze piercing her. "Are you saying that the farm and the house are chartered to you?"

"No, but—"

"Then they are not yours to pledge and of no value to this discussion."

She could not believe his cold indifference. Panic began beating in her heart. She was going to fail. She would not be able to save Reginald.

Andreas appeared angry with her. That made her own ire spike. He had probably agreed to such things often before and with people he knew less well. And if not for him, she would not be in this situation.

"Since you are convinced that my word will not do and that my brother will not honor my pledge of the property, let us make this an outright sale. I see that your love of tapestries has not abated." She gestured to the rich hangings adorning the hall's walls. "I still have mine. You often admired it and told me yourself that it was worth at least a hundred pounds. I will sell it to you now."

It sickened her to say it. That tapestry, woven of silk and brought back from a crusade by an ancestor, was the only thing of value that she owned.

It would break her heart to give it up. Losing it would finally obliterate her small hold on a life she had once led. She would never let go of it to save herself, but now, faced with the need to save her brother, she had no choice.

She thought that she saw Andreas's expression soften. She was sure that he would agree. Instead, he turned his attention once more to the garden.

"I cannot buy it, Giselle."

"My attachment to it is long over, if that is your concern."

"A man does not buy what he already owns. Reginald pledged that tapestry as surety against a loan years ago. The loan was not repaid."

Shock numbed her for a ten count. Then fury crashed into her stunned mind—fury at Reginald and fury at this man sitting here in his damnable self-possession.

How dare her brother pledge her property. Bad enough that Reginald had depleted their meager wealth with ventures always ruined by unforseen misfortune. Bad enough that he had left tallies all over London to pay for garments he could not afford and wine long ago drunk. To have procured coin by using the tapestry was an inexcusable betrayal of their heritage.

Andreas knew what that weaving meant. He should have never agreed to such a thing. He only had because he coveted the tapestry.

She rose, barely controlling the anger trembling through her. "I can see that I have wasted my time and yours. I have nothing else to sell except my virtue, and I am sure that a great man like you will not consider that worth one hundred pounds." She almost spit the words and did not care that her tone sounded bitter and sarcastic and imperious.

His gaze, full of sharp alertness, swung to her. The old warmth and connection entered it, along with that other, frightening intensity that had so unsettled her today.

She had intended to make a grand retreat, but suddenly she could not move.

"Actually, Giselle, the pledge of your virtue is the only one that I might consider."

"You insult me, Andreas."

"You raised the possibility, my lady. Not I."

She dragged the remnants of her dignity around her like a shredded cloak. "I apologize for intruding on your household. It was a mistake. I knew that my brother and I were no longer of use to you, but I had not realized just how proud and arrogant you had become. I see now that you despise us. Good day to you."

Somehow she tore herself away from his blue eyes and his irritating, compelling presence and retreated with all of the nobility that she could muster.